D1270135

KINGDOM of TWILIGHT

AVATARS
BOOK THREE

Also by Tui T. Sutherland

AVATARS, BOOK ONE:
SO THIS IS HOW IT ENDS

AVATARS, BOOK TWO:
SHADOW FALLING

THIS MUST BE LOVE

Tui T. Sutherland

Kingdom of Twilight

Avatars
Book Three

An Imprint of HarperCollins*Publishers*

Eos is an imprint of HarperCollins Publishers.

Avatars, Book Three: Kingdom of Twilight

 For information address HarperCollins Children's Books, a division of HarperCollins Publishers, 1350 Avenue of the Americas, New York, NY 10019.

www.harperteen.com

Library of Congress Cataloging-in-Publication Data is available.

ISBN 978-0-06-085149-1 (trade bdg.)

ISBN 978-0-06-085150-7 (lib. bdg.)

Typography by Christopher Stengel

1 2 3 4 5 6 7 8 9 10

First Edition

For Adam, Bryan, Cyd, Erica, and Mitch

TWENTY YEARS AGO . . .

Mist drifted around Odin, swathing him in smoky tendrils as he walked across the roots toward the stag. Above him the World Tree stretched into the sky, so high it was *the sky, the canopy of whispering leaves reaching from horizon to horizon, the trunk so wide around he couldn't even see the curve of it ahead of him—nothing but a long wall of scalloped brown bark.*

The king of the Norse gods stopped beside one of the tree's thickest roots, twice as tall as he was. Water bubbled from below the root, and a golden stag was sniffing at the stream. When it noticed that Odin was there, it carefully took a leaf from one of the lowest branches and stood chewing, staring innocently off at the horizon as if it had no idea who he was and, in fact, had not a single brain cell in its head.

Well, that's not far from the truth, Odin thought. He leaned against the root and crossed his arms.

"Why are you here, Zeus?" he said.

The stag stared at the horizon, chewing slowly, eyes wide. After a long moment, it blew out a loud snort through its nostrils, took another leaf, and started chewing again.

Odin chuckled. "Zeus, you blithering idiot, did you do any research at all?" he asked. "I know all four of my stags, and what's more, they have normal conversations with me all the time. Unless one of them traded his head for one stuffed with lint, you're not my stag, and you're not supposed to be here at Yggdrasil."

The stag's eyes wandered to the branches above as if searching for a chariot to whisk it away. Finally, with a grumbling noise, it lowered its horns to the ground and shook itself briskly. Its fur fell away, vanishing into the air, as Zeus, king of the Greco-Roman gods, stood up, shaking back his long, storm-gray hair and smoothing his beard.

"Hello, Odin," he said with dignity. The Norse god inclined his head, a small smile playing across his features.

"To what do we owe the honor of this . . . unusual visit?" Odin asked.

Zeus flicked a leaf off his shoulder, avoiding Odin's eyes. He's not much more useful as a god than as a stag, *Odin thought.*

"Just wandering around," Zeus said. "Rather boring on Mount Olympus, you know."

"I can believe that," Odin said. Zeus bridled.

"Oh, and I suppose Valhalla is still fascinating after thousands of years."

"Well, the warriors' souls don't mind," Odin said, stabbing at the ground with his staff. "Wake up, feast, get drunk, sing battle songs, pass out. Day in and day out. They're like goldfish; every day is a new day."

"But we're not goldfish," Zeus growled. "We're gods. Our minds encompass everything; our powers should command the world. Instead we've been trapped for thousands of years with the same confounded immortals, living in circles, watching the mor-

tals drift farther and farther away from us." He sat down on a boulder by the spring, hitching his robes above his ankles. "It's unfair. And boring."

"I remember that Loki predicted they'd come back to us," Odin said. "As the rites grew shorter and more hurried and the gifts became ever more measly and the prayers weakened and faded, Loki said, 'Don't worry, it won't last. Humans need us. They'll come crawling back soon enough.' Ha."

"Where is Loki now?" Zeus asked.

"He is being punished for a few things . . . until Ragnarok comes," Odin answered.

"Ragnarok." Zeus narrowed his murky green eyes. "Your big apocalypse. Why could you foresee that, and not this long, slow death we're all suffering through?"

"My visions are not like those loud mortal picture boxes, where the story is laid out in one straight line," Odin said. "They are flashes of insight, and clearest of all is the cataclysm that will come with the Twilight of the Gods. Evidently my powers of prophecy did not find these intervening years interesting enough to warn me about. I certainly don't find them interesting either." He looked down at the water, the corners of his mouth twitching. "Ah. You came to drink from the spring, didn't you? You were hoping for the power of wisdom because you think it'll help you see the future."

Zeus's shoulders slumped. He rubbed his eyebrows. "We just want to know how long this will go on. We're all going mad up there."

"I don't deny that you could use a dose of wisdom," Odin said, "but drinking from this spring won't get it for you. I had to sacrifice an eye for my taste of wisdom, remember. It's a little more complicated, getting to the truth of things. Otherwise we'd

have some awfully clever stags around here, wouldn't we?"

"All right, no need to be snide," Zeus muttered, picking up a rock and tossing it into the water with a small plop. "But we can't keep on like this for the rest of our dreary immortal lives. It almost makes one wish we could *die. Er, not really," he added quickly.*

Odin studied Zeus for a long moment. The Greek god looked old and tired, as if he ought to be snoozing on a mortal couch in front of a picture box. Odin wondered if he himself looked that way.

His empty eye socket twitched, and he reached up to cover it. It had been doing that a lot lately, reacting as if his eye were still there. As he pressed his hand to the withered skin, something flashed through his mind—an image, a glimpse of a big red-haired boy fighting a dark girl with a tattoo on her arm. In the scene, gods he knew too well were gathered around them, cheering and whistling, more alive than he'd seen them in centuries. A stone exploded in the air, and the vision disappeared. He stepped back into the embrace of the tree's roots, momentarily thrown by the shift in scenery.

"What?" Zeus demanded. "What was that? Too much mead, old man?"

Slowly Odin smiled with a razor-thin twist of his pale lips. He raised his hands, letting his hood fall back, and called silently to his ravens. They were his spies; today they would also be his messengers.

"You know what we should do, Zeus?" Odin said, sensing the flapping of black wings at the edge of his hearing. "We should work with the other pantheons. With all our power combined . . . I think we can find a way to end our boredom permanently.

"We're going to play a little game."

Cavern of Bones

Tigre was up to his elbows in blood, trying not to pass out. The ship surged beneath his feet, making him dizzy. As the waves tossed *Skidbladnir* violently from side to side, Viking weapons clanked ominously inside a huge chest shoved against the curving far wall. He clutched the carved wooden post of the bed with his free hand, feeling the raised shapes of ships, and boars, and dragons, and giants beneath his fingers.

The expensive-looking sheets on the bed, once crisp and white, were soaked through and dripping, and all the pillowcases he'd pressed to Diana's wound were wet red blotches on the floor. It looked like a battlefield after vultures had gone around ripping out everyone's organs.

He dropped the last pillowcase on the bearskin rug, pulled off his shirt, and pressed that to the deep slash in Diana's stomach. He couldn't think of anything else to do. Kali insisted that his experience working in a vet's office should help, but the truth was that Tigre's mind had gone blank. He couldn't remember a thing about helping

Dr. Harris. The only memory that kept coming back to him from that time was Dr. Harris's daughter Vicky—Tigre's ex-girlfriend—mocking him for being such a useless waste of humanity.

If she were here, Vicky wouldn't be at all surprised that Anna had betrayed him, that the Sumerian avatar had never really liked him, and that he'd been dumb enough to fall for her love goddess tricks.

Panic flared up inside him again. This was his fault. He'd been the closest to Anna; he should have noticed her dark side. Or he should have done some research on her goddess, Inanna, before trusting her. It wasn't often you could look up your potential girlfriend in a library book and spot warning signs like "also a war goddess" and "has no problem with killing people."

If Diana died, Kali and Gus would blame him. But all this blood—the smell, the sticky warmth—took him back to the bus shelter where he'd found the body of the old man, and then he felt even more guilty.

Plus, it did not help that the ship kept pitching violently from side to side. He ducked as an unlit lantern flew across the cabin and crashed into the opposite wall.

Diana made a soft sound of pain. She lifted one hand slightly, then let it drop and subsided into silence again.

If only he could open a window, let in some fresh air. But the portholes high in the wall wouldn't budge, and the rain was pouring down so furiously outside that the cabin would probably fill with water instantly, flooding the ship and drowning them all.

"That would be typical," Tigre muttered. "I mean, if anyone's going to accidentally kill us all, it'll definitely be me."

"Well, if anyone's going to *intentionally* kill us all, it'll probably be me," Kali said, coming into the room. "You know, being a goddess of death and destruction and stuff. And also considering how annoying you all are. If that makes you feel any better."

"Not really," Tigre said.

The ship shuddered convulsively and then seemed to leap into the air, where it paused for a moment before smashing down again. Tigre clutched the bedposts to stay in place, while Kali hung on to the door frame.

"Our fearless navigator isn't doing so well, in case you hadn't noticed," Kali said, jerking her thumb at the deck above them.

"Gus is probably doing better than I am," Tigre pointed out.

"I'm sure he'd love to trade places too," Kali said, "but remember, he's soaking wet out there. Trying to drive a ship in a god-crazy thunderstorm isn't much more fun than what you're doing." Kali herself looked like she'd been swimming alongside the ship instead of standing on it. Her long dark hair was loose and dripping around her shoulders and water streamed off her into a small lake around her feet.

"Here." She stepped forward and set a leather case on the bed beside Diana. "I've been searching the cabins and I found this. We're on a freaky boat, let me tell you. The food in the kitchen replenishes itself as soon as you eat it, and the whole place is a weird mix of ancient-Viking-longboat-meets-luxury-cruise-liner-for-the-gods. I guess

Frey and his friends are pretty keen on creature comforts. No TVs though, sadly. Or casinos."

"Wait," Tigre said. "You ate?"

An expression of guilt briefly flitted across Kali's face. "No?" she tried. He frowned at her. "Oh, fine, stop whining, I'll bring you food in a little while," she said. "I thought this was more important."

She took over applying pressure to Diana's injury while Tigre untied the leather ribbon and opened the case. Inside there was gauze, needles made of reindeer horn or something like it, thread, and strange bundles of herbs. He picked up a packet of long dark leaves.

"What am I supposed to do with this?"

Kali shrugged. "Hey, I found you a first aid kit, didn't I?"

"I guess," Tigre said, sniffing the leaves. They smelled sharp and totally unfamiliar. "Either that or a spice rack."

"Well, this ship belonged to Norse gods," Kali said. She peeked under the shirt at the long slash in Diana's stomach. "They're gods, but they're still Vikings, and that means battle—lots of battle. I assume even gods need sewing up now and then, when other gods stick giant axes in their arms and stuff."

Tigre looked down at Diana, feeling ill. "You want me to sew her up?"

"Come on, Tigre," Kali said sharply. "Snap to. You've been down here with her for hours; surely you remember something. You like animals, right? Just imagine she's a wounded pet or whatever you have to do."

Tigre rubbed his face. "I wish we hadn't lost Quetzie."

"She's staying clear of the storm," Kali said. When the

clouds had rolled in and the winds increased to hurricane force, the giant bird that had been helping them had whistled a cheery good-bye and vanished higher into the sky. "I wouldn't want to fly in this weather, either. She'll find us again when it dies down."

"If it ever does," Tigre said. He already felt like they were going to be trapped in this nightmare forever. All he wanted to do was sleep for the rest of his life.

"Okay," Kali said, grabbing one of his hands and placing it back on the blood-soaked shirt. She stood up and stepped back, pulling her hair into one long rope and wringing it out. "You and Gus are seriously driving me nuts. Yes, boo hoo, we're trapped in a post-apocalyptic future, gods are trying to kill us, Diana is dying, and we're experiencing a little turbulence. Well, shut up about it already. I'm not little miss everything's-going-to-be-fine, happy happy sparkle sparkle no worries. If you want a cheerleader, you're going to have to wake up our chipper unconscious friend here.

"But if you two boys seriously need that kind of incessant encouragement to do *anything*, then maybe I should have left you both for Anna to kill and gone to Africa on my own."

"Maybe," Tigre agreed glumly.

"Do *not* tempt me," Kali snapped. She turned and stormed out of the cabin, slamming the door behind her. Answering slams echoed up and down the ship as the wind rocked it forcefully to the side, and Tigre grabbed the case to prevent it from flying away.

Even if he could figure out how to sew up the wound,

in a storm like this, it'd be like trying to perform surgery on a roller coaster. He sighed and lifted the shirt again to look at the wound. To his surprise, the blood flow had slowed to a trickle. He wasn't sure if that was good or bad.

A memory surfaced of a small white cat that had been brought into the clinic with a large shard of glass in its side. The owner had been sobbing incoherently in Spanish about a window and a tree and a bird, but Dr. Harris hadn't needed Tigre to translate to figure out what was wrong with the poor animal. What had the vet done? How had he treated it?

Tigre fingered the needles in the kit dubiously, then lifted one out.

Yeah, right, Vicky's mocking voice sounded in his head. *As if you could ever save anyone. As if you could ever do anything right. You never do anything, period. You just wait for things to happen to you. It's all been decided already, right, Tigre? Your fate is predetermined. A nobody like you isn't going to change anything.*

The other Mesoamerican gods that visited his dreams had said the same thing. *Your fate is to give up and die. That is how this cycle is written. Why fight it?*

Just do nothing, Vicky whispered. *Like you always do.*

Tigre looked down at Diana's pale face and shook his head.

"Not this time," he said.

Like most people, Diana had often wondered what would happen when she died.

When she was younger, she had liked the idea of

Heaven. She could imagine the white robes and harps and angels floating around on clouds. It sounded pretty and peaceful. Loud screaming fights like the ones her parents had probably weren't allowed in Heaven.

As she got older, she tried not to think about death or what would happen afterward. It seemed like something she wouldn't have to deal with for a long, long time.

Apparently she was wrong about that.

When she found out she was a Greek goddess—or, to be more exact, *two* Greek goddesses in one mortal body—she figured that meant she was destined for the Greek underworld after her death. She could remember that it was called Hades, and that there was a river to cross and a three-headed dog guarding the gates.

She was pretty sure she hadn't been told anything about giant snakes.

The snake's head alone was the size of a house, and its long, pale body twisted off so far into the darkness that she couldn't see its tail from where she stood. The snake stared at her with hooded pale red eyes, its dark forked tongue flickering in and out between long fangs. Its gleaming white scales shimmered in the shadows.

Diana shivered. A cold wind whipped through the cavern, slicing through her clothes as if it were made of freezing needles instead of air. She didn't know how long she'd been standing here. Or how she'd gotten into a vast underground cavern in the first place.

She could remember standing beside the ocean in downtown Manhattan. She could remember a tall ship unfolding behind her, and Gus standing next to her, and the building excitement of knowing their plan had worked and escape was moments away.

And then—sharp pain, surprise, Anna's face full of rage, a knife covered in blood.

Now she was here, wherever here was. It felt like a cavern, but so vast that she couldn't see any walls from where she stood. All she could see was the white snake draped over the rocks, the length of a small auditorium away from her, watching her grimly. Its pale scales seemed to give off a glowing light; otherwise, everything was darkness.

She squinted. There was a dark red glow in the distance, beyond the snake, lighting up what seemed to be mountains at the far, far distant end of the cave. But she couldn't tell how big they were, or how far away; there wasn't enough light to give her any context.

Diana held out her hands, clenching them into fists and then unclenching them again.

"I don't *feel* dead," she muttered.

Was this Hades? Could she go back to her life if she just refused to go any farther? She looked over her shoulder, but the thick darkness behind her felt like a curtain, pressing against her back.

Maybe she hadn't died. Maybe Gus had saved her and brought her . . . here? It didn't look like Africa either. And where was he?

Her hand moved to her stomach. Taking a deep breath, she lifted her shirt a few inches and touched the smooth skin underneath. No knife wound. No scar.

So maybe I am dead. The wind chose that moment to

make a low moaning sound, and Diana shuddered.

At the very least, she would have expected death to be less . . . ambiguous.

Also scarier. She wasn't terrified, which surprised her. There was a giant snake lying not that far away, after all. But if she was already dead, what could it do to her?

"Tsk."

The sound was so subtle that at first Diana mistook it for another twist of the wind. But then it came again. . . .

"Tsk."

And then she realized that it was a noise of disapproval, and it was coming from someone standing on a ledge of rock ahead and to the left of her and the snake.

Diana froze. The stranger—a tall, forbidding figure, now silent—stayed hidden in the shadows. Moments passed, and nothing happened. Was he staring at her? Preparing to attack? Sizing her up? The chilly stillness seemed to creep along Diana's skin, until she felt as if she'd been standing frozen in place for eternity.

All right, *now* she was scared.

With a hiss that sounded exasperated, the snake twitched, adjusting its coils. In the glow from its scales, Diana caught a glimpse of the stranger's bare feet. They were facing away from her, toward the rocky valley beyond.

So perhaps he hadn't seen her yet. Perhaps his disapproval—and his dark attention—were directed at something in the other direction.

Diana relaxed, taking a deep breath.

"No, this is quite wrong," a voice said suddenly. To

Diana's horror, the stranger started toward her, stepping carefully down the pile of rocks even though his feet were still facing the other way. She covered her mouth with one hand and took a step back.

Something crunched beneath her shoes. Diana glanced down and saw that it was something white and thin. It looked horribly like the bones of a human hand.

"In the first place," the voice continued implacably, "you're certainly not an Aztec."

A torch flared in the stranger's hand, casting flickering light across sharp teeth and torn, flapping ears. It took Diana a moment to realize that he had the head of a dog on top of a man's body, and that his feet were definitely pointing in the wrong direction. She shuddered.

"Secondly," the dog-headed man went on, looking her up and down, "you are a warrior, although it's debatable whether you died in battle."

"What would that have to do with anything?" Diana asked.

"Well, obviously in that case your soul would go to Tonatiuhichan instead of Mictlan," he said.

"Oh," Diana said. "Obviously."

"The House of the Sun," he said. It was odd to hear such a matter-of-fact voice coming from a dog's mouth. "For warriors who die in battle or women who die in childbirth."

"Battle or childbirth? Because they're equally hard?" Diana guessed.

"Equally honorable," said the god. "But you . . . I suppose it could be called murder instead." He tugged on his ears and his tongue lolled out as he thought for a moment. "You didn't exactly fight back."

"I didn't have a chance," Diana pointed out indignantly.

"So perhaps you do belong here," he mused.

"Where is here?" Diana asked. "And who are you?"

"I am Xolotl," he said, shaking his head so his ears flapped loudly against his skin. "The god of lightning." He held out his free hand and a spark of lightning burst up from it, disappearing with a small boom. "And this is Mictlan, the underworld. I am here to guide spirits on their journey through death."

"So I am dead," Diana whispered. "And the Aztecs were right? This is what happens when people die?"

"Not all people," Xolotl said. "It is rare that we get anyone who's not an Aztec or of Aztec descent. Your murder being so violent, and with so many different god-forces present, it must have jarred you into this underworld by accident instead of taking you wherever you should be." He looked her up and down. "Of course, it's even rarer to get someone who's not completely dead yet. Maybe your spirit requires a journey before it rests."

Diana's heart leaped. "You mean me?" she said. "I'm not dead?"

"You're mostly dead," Xolotl said. "I'm sure you will be by the time we reach the other side of the underworld."

"But wait," Diana said, stepping back as Xolotl reached for her hand. She winced as she heard another crunch under her feet. "What if I want to go back to my life? You said yourself, I'm not supposed to be here."

Xolotl shrugged. "But you are here. I don't decide these things. Perhaps the lord of Mictlan can be talked into letting you go."

"Who's that?" Diana asked.

This produced an offended expression, which Diana had never seen on a dog's face before. "Mictlantecuhtli is our king," Xolotl said. He waved the torch before her eyes, and in the dancing flames Diana could see images, like an old movie flickering on a screen. She saw a skeleton flecked with blood, wearing a tall, bony crown and a necklace of eyeballs. Beside him sat an emaciated woman, also in a crown. Their thrones seemed to be writhing with movement, and Diana managed to make out a seething pile of spiders and several fluttering bats before Xolotl pulled the torch away again.

"Well, he looks cheerful," Diana said. "I'm sure he can be reasoned with."

"You have to get there first," Xolotl said, snorting. "He and his wife, Mictecacihuatl, live in a windowless house on a hill of bones, a long, dangerous journey from here."

"I'm not afraid," Diana said. "I'll do whatever I have to do to get out of here."

"Are you sure?" Xolotl said. "You must travel through the mountains, past the great snake, crossing eight deserts and a mighty river, and braving a wind of obsidian knives. And I don't suppose you brought a piece of jade to feed the jaguar at the gates."

"Um," Diana said. "No?"

"Then he'll probably eat your heart," Xolotl said.

"Nice," Diana said. "But if I make it through all that,

Mr. Mictlantiwhatsit might let me go back to life?"

"Or he'll declare you dead and keep you down here forever. Or he'll send you to the House of the Sun. One of those three, I'm sure."

"Hmm," Diana said. "Well, if I have to do it . . . where do I go?"

"This way." Xolotl headed toward the giant snake, and Diana started to follow him. "The journey only takes about four years."

Diana stopped abruptly. "Four *years*?" she repeated. "In real time? Like, Earth time?"

"What other kind of time is there?" Xolotl asked. The snake lifted its head and hissed at them.

"I don't have four years," Diana said. "My friends need my help now."

"Perhaps you should have thought of that before you let yourself get murdered," Xolotl said sternly.

"There must be something else I can do," she said, turning to look around again. In the torch's light she could see more bones littering the ground in every direction, except behind her, where there was just the still, oppressive darkness.

Xolotl sighed. "Well, Mictlantecuhtli won't be pleased with me for telling you this," the dog-headed god said, "but there are other underworlds. You could try getting out through one of them instead."

"I can't just walk back that way and return to my life?" Diana asked, pointing into the darkness behind her.

"No. That way leads to the other underworlds, if they're still out there. The only way to return to life from here is to get the lord's permission, and for that you have to take the four-year journey to the other side and find him."

"And then he might not even let me go," Diana murmured. She looked up at the mountains in the far distance. Should she try fighting through what was in front of her, or risk looking for a better option in the even-more-unknown?

Four years for a slim chance was too long. Surely even Gus would have given up on her by then. The whole world could be different by the time she returned. Everyone else might be dead, especially without her there to help keep them alive.

"Sorry, Xolotl," Diana said, stepping back. "I appreciate your offer to help guide me, but I'm going to try my luck out there."

Xolotl shook his head and his ears flapped noisily again. "Mictlan may not be the most beautiful underworld," he said, "but our lord is fair, and if you behave and are lucky, you could return to Earth eventually as a butterfly or a hummingbird."

"That sounds pretty," Diana said, "but I want to go back as me. As soon as possible."

The lightning god bowed, his ears and tongue dangling. "Then I wish you luck, young warrior."

"Thanks." Diana wanted to pat his head or scratch him behind his ears or something, but she had a feeling that would be disrespectful. Instead, she bowed to him, and then turned to step into the suffocating darkness.

Immediately she was surrounded by black, unable to

see even a glimmer from the torch or the snake anymore. She rubbed her arms, trying to work up her courage, and took another step forward. She felt blind—not only blind, but as if all of her senses had been shut off. There was nothing around her but the dark.

She did hear one last thing as she walked off into the shadows. Faintly, just at the edge of sound, she thought she heard Xolotl whisper:

"Poor girl. You have no idea what's out there."

Half an ocean away, Kali's husband and soul mate was probably still standing on the Manhattan shoreline, staring at the horizon where his true love had disappeared, wishing she would come back and be with him.

And where was she? Clinging to a mast in the pouring rain, watching lightning crackle around the sails, and seriously considering throwing Gus overboard.

Kali had gone belowdecks to get away from Gus, but upon discovering that Tigre wasn't any better company, she'd returned to the gale outside. Here it was wet, but at least there wasn't any moping.

There was, however, enormous incompetence.

"What are you doing?" she yelled in Gus's ear. He jumped, then slipped and fell on the wet floorboards and nearly went sliding overboard. Kali grabbed his shirt as he skidded toward the edge and hauled him back to the steering oar, an enormously long rudder attached to the stern of the ship.

"I don't think this is a normal Viking ship," he hollered over the wind.

"What tipped you off?" Kali retorted. "The fact that it unfolded from something the size of a Post-it note, or the fact that it's magically taking us to Africa despite your unimpressive navigational skills?"

"What?" he called, cupping one hand around his ear. Kali sighed. It wasn't much fun insulting someone when they couldn't hear half of what you said.

Gus pointed at the two masts. "I think there's only supposed to be one sail," he shouted. "And there's no belowdecks and bedrooms and stuff on a Viking ship. Just oars and places for people to sit while they row."

"Who cares?" she bellowed. "They're gods! They can make their ship look like anything they want! Just try to stop it from banging around so much."

"I'm just saying, it'd be easier if it were more like a Polynesian ship," he said. "How's Diana?"

"What?" Kali shouted, feigning deafness.

"Diana!" Gus yelled. "Is she okay?"

Kali tapped her ear and lifted her hands in an *oh, well, can't hear you* gesture.

A huge wave of salt water slammed into the side of the ship and washed over the two of them. Sputtering, Kali shoved her hair out of her eyes and made her way to the edge of the ship, where she could look down into the murky, churning ocean below them.

Of the attackers surrounding them, the only god she was pretty sure she'd identified was Poseidon. He had the same flowing beard and arrogant expression as Zeus—plus, the trident was a big clue. He was riding a chariot in the ocean alongside *Skidbladnir*, pulled by four large golden sea horses that looked like something off an elaborate Italian fountain—literally half horse, half fish. Every time Kali came to the rail, he brandished his trident at her and bellowed curses she was happy she couldn't hear.

But there were other deities down there too. In particular there were lots of angry-looking women, including one extremely pale, coldly beautiful, vicious-looking one dragging a huge net behind her, as if she were waiting for someone to fall overboard so she could snatch them up.

Kali could see gods flickering among the storm clouds, too, carrying axes, riding chariots, throwing thunderbolts, and ducking behind clouds whenever she looked up at them. As if they thought she could do anything from the ship.

She drummed her fingers on the wooden rail, fighting her queasiness. She would never admit it to Gus or Tigre, but she wasn't a big fan of boats, or oceans, or the imminent possibility of drowning. Since she couldn't swim, she'd be in big trouble if anything happened to *Skidbladnir.*

Kali cupped her hands around her mouth.

"Hey, POSEIDON!" she yelled at the top of her lungs. "Is this all you got?"

The Greek sea god waved his trident angrily.

"No wonder your brother got to be king of Olympus instead of you!"

"Tell me you aren't taunting the gods right now," Gus shouted from the rudder. "As in, the literal gods who are literally attacking us?"

"I'm making a point," Kali explained. "As far as I

know, they can't attack the ship directly, because *Skidbladnir* is magically protected, and also they're not technically supposed to kill us themselves. So they're just making our lives miserable, and I figured I'd return the favor.

"Come on, Poseidon! The ship is right here!" she hollered at the ocean. "Why don't you just hit us with your trident or something? I mean, where's the excitement? Oooh, you'll make us seasick, whatever shall we do?"

"Could we not actually make it worse?" Gus pleaded.

Poseidon lashed his sea horses into a foaming frenzy until they brought him up alongside *Skidbladnir.* Kali leaned on the rail and looked down at the sea god with a yawn, trying to look as if she sailed through hurricanes every day.

"Listen, death goddess," Poseidon boomed. "If I hit your little ship with my trident, do you know what would happen?"

"It would bounce off," Kali guessed. "And you'd be in some serious recoil pain. Magically protected, remember? Ship of the gods?" Her hair whipped wildly around her face and she made a mental note to clip it back before her next I'm-tougher-than-you-are conversation with a god.

"Ha ha ha!" Poseidon guffawed theatrically. "That is where you are wrong, tiny avatar!"

"You think *I'm* tiny—you should see your own avatar," Kali said, jerking her thumb at the trapdoor to the cabins behind her.

"This is an INVINCIBLE TRIDENT!" Poseidon bellowed. "It makes the Earth tremble! It brings the storms!

This was the instrument of destruction for the Polynesian islands!"

"You might not want to brag about that in front of one of their gods," Kali said with a nod at Gus. "I'm pretty sure Miss Manners wouldn't approve."

"This trident can shatter any object," the sea god said menacingly. "Including your precious ship. It is the most powerful weapon in all the pantheons."

"I bet Thor and his hammer might disagree with you there," Kali said, but she filed that detail away for future reference. If that was true . . . well, it certainly wouldn't hurt to have the most powerful divine weapon, especially once they got to Africa. Kali hadn't mentioned this to Gus and Tigre, but she hadn't forgotten that there were gods over there, too . . . and she wasn't at all sure they'd be happy to see the avatars.

TWENTY YEARS AGO . . .

Moonlight turned the pale sand to ashes and slipped like silk between the stone arches, making everything look black and white like the artistic postcards in the stalls outside. But most of the gods present could still smell the blood pounded deep into the earth. The seats beneath them still prickled with the life force of thousands of spectators. Great sacrifices had been offered to the gods here; the echo of that power rang with the centuries-old sound of swords clashing and men shouting and lions roaring. Hundreds of years had passed, but this place still tasted of death and worship.

It made them hungry.

Behind Isis in the stands, the Egyptian cat goddess Bastet licked her hands and cleaned her whiskers, her feline tongue rasping along her pink human fingers. Her wide yellow eyes darted from Zeus to the other bearded man in the center of the amphitheater. Bastet had never met Odin, but everyone knew who he was. He leaned on his staff calmly, radiating authority, whereas Zeus only gave off a whiff of desperation and arrogance.

"This is stupid," Maat hissed in Bastet's ear. The dark-eyed goddess grabbed her husband's beak and turned his long ibis head to look at her. "Thoth, I want to go home. I don't want to be lectured by a pair of feeble old gods."

Thoth gently removed her hands from his beak and ran his fingertips along it as if making sure she hadn't dented it. Maat hated the fact that having the face of a bird made him extra-inscrutable, and he knew it. Bastet liked the way his beady eyes blinked mysteriously, although she wished he could smile. At least she *could purr to let people know she was happy, which was most of the time—although she wished cats were still worshipped, as they deserved to be, instead of petted and trivialized and made to wear silly outfits on the front of greeting cards.*

"We should hear them out," Thoth said in his gentle, wise voice. "Amon thinks they have an interesting idea."

Maat rolled her eyes. "If it involves some of these *gods, I don't want anything to do with it." She nudged Bastet, tilting her head pointedly at the Mesoamerican contingent. "I mean,* what *is going on there?" Bastet followed her sidelong glance to a god with pitch-black skin whose face was a black skull with yellow lines emblazoned across it. His eyes looked as dark as the rest of him, but when he moved, light reflected off them like flashes in a mirror.*

Thoth clacked his beak lightly, a sound Bastet guessed was as close as he came to laughing. "I hardly think we're in a position to point fingers, my dear," he said. "Or claws, or feathers, as the case may be."

"But we're beautiful," Maat protested. "That is just grotesque."

Bastet wondered if the other pantheons were studying the

Egyptian contingent with the same contempt. The Norse gods and the Greco-Romans were all so human-looking, no more exciting than mere mortals, except perhaps a little taller, a little shinier, a little more perfect-looking. The Sumerians too were on the whole very ordinary, although the two women standing on the bottom step and leaning on the stone wall below them were striking extremes of beauty and ugliness.

The Native American gods were a mix of people and animals. Men and women with long dark hair, wearing bright colors and buffalo skins, sat alongside a giant, fierce-looking bird and a coyote whose tongue lolled out of an enormous grin as he panted. Bastet shivered; she didn't like being near anything that chased cats, and he had a particularly wicked look in his sharp eyes.

Odin stepped onto a dais, facing the seats where the gods had gathered at one end of the stadium. Once we could have filled this place, *he thought.* Once there were many more thousands of gods, all powerful enough to manifest, and we could have held our own magnificent war games here. How many of us have we lost without even noticing it? Gods unremembered by a single mortal left on the planet . . .

He touched the socket where his eye used to be. We will have that time again. We will have our war games . . . and that is how we will return to glory.

"Greetings, fellow immortals," he announced, then paused, waiting for them to adjust their hearing to his language and volume level.

A movement by one of the entrances caught his eye, and he gestured to the two young men who had appeared there, hovering warily as if they planned to bolt at any moment. One had four arms and a third eye in the middle of his forehead; the other was dark blue and wore a lotus blossom in his smooth dark hair.

"Ah, the gods of India have arrived," Odin said. "Nice of you to join us at last." He stroked his beard, wondering why there weren't more of them. He knew they were a long shot, but he hoped they'd be tempted by the possibility of even more power, more strength, more worshippers. If they joined in, he'd be able to enact his entire elaborate plan, which would be beautiful.

"Get on with it, Odin!" Mars bellowed from the Greek section. Zeus chuckled, and Odin resisted the urge to throw his javelin at them. That would not be the best way to begin all this. Remember, if things go as you want, you'll be ruling them all someday soon.

"I don't need to tell you why you agreed to come here," Odin began. "We all feel frustrated and powerless. We all remember how it used to be; we all miss it. We know that it will be like this for eternity, or until we're forgotten, and then what? Nothingness? Is that all we have to look forward to?"

"Not anymore!" Zeus bellowed beside him, and Odin sighed. It could not possibly be helping his credibility to have this oaf at his side, but unfortunately Zeus's pantheon was too necessary to alienate.

Odin spread his arms to the assembled gods. "We propose a contest. True, it is not in our natures to work together. I would almost rather lose another eye than spend another moment with Zeus." He clapped the Greek thunder god on the shoulder and everyone chuckled, including Zeus, but the smart ones (who did not include Zeus) knew he meant it. "But what if we used all our powers for one great, final effort—one that, in the end, would restore the greatest power of all to one of us?"

He pointed to the Egyptians. "Imagine if the entire world returned to the age of the pharaohs." His gaze swept over the

Native Americans. "Imagine if the plains were yours again—and not just the plains, but the mountains, the oceans, the ice caps, the whole planet." He looked up to meet the gaze of the blue-skinned man, Vishnu. He poured his powers of persuasion into his voice. "Imagine that your millions are hundreds of millions—that you could lift your people from their crowded cities and spread them across all the Earth."

"Well, don't get too excited about any of that," Zeus boomed. "Because we are going to win, and then it'll be bacchanalia and wine and grape leaves every night!"

Odin rubbed his forehead. He could see Isis raising her eyebrows eloquently.

"Now imagine that you have the power to shut Zeus in a tree and leave him there for the rest of our immortal lives," he said, forcing a smile. Most of the gods laughed. "Tempting, isn't it?"

"Ha ha ha!" Zeus chortled. "We shall see!"

"So how would it work?" Thunderbird asked from the Native American side. "How would we decide which pantheon got all the power?"

"A battle," Odin said. "Each of us picks a representative to fight to the death."

Mars snorted. "Fat lot of good that would do. We'd just keep resurrecting. It'd go on forever. There'd be nice blood and guts, though. I'd be in favor of that."

There's a shock, Odin thought. "That's the beauty—and the danger—of this plan," he said. "We send the warriors we choose into the world, to be reborn . . . as humans."

"Gods in human form?" one of the Mesopotamian goddesses said. "You mean avatars?"

"Ooooh, it sounds horrible," Maat interjected, shuddering. "Stuck as a horrible, tiny, flailing mortal. No, thank you!"

"It's not so bad," Vishnu said quietly. "It's very . . . instructive, being human for a while."

"You've done it?" Bastet asked, wide-eyed.

"Now and then," he said with a small smile.

"Yes, but," Odin said, drawing their attention back to him, "the difference is that Vishnu could return to his divine form after his sojourn in the human world. These avatars would be truly human—so when they die, they will stay dead."

A hush fell over the stadium. Even the gods of death did not truly know death. None of them could imagine it. None of them wanted to.

"The battle must have high stakes in order for it to matter," Odin went on. "The power of the winning avatar—and the winning pantheon—must be consecrated in the blood sacrifice of the others. That is how we will all know who deserves to be the strongest . . . who deserves to rule this next age of the world." He could see most of the gods nodding. Already their minds were jumping ahead, to the power and the glory and the moment of triumph. Not a god in that stadium truly believed that his pantheon could lose. They were too used to victory, even now.

Perhaps not the Mesoamericans, though. They were exchanging nervous glances. He might have to sweeten the pot for them. Didn't they have an apocalyptic date coming around soon? Perhaps he could use that to lure them in, selling this as a part of one of their "cycles." He wanted them in the contest. As useless as they were on the whole, they had one particular object of great power that he needed for his plan to work.

"But Odin," said a voice from the Native American gods, "why should we trust you?" The speaker was a woman, her hair hanging in a long braid over one shoulder, dark against the soft white of her shirt. She was beautiful in much the same way as

Odin's own wife, Frigg, with a warm aura that crinkled and spun around her almost palpably. If Odin squinted, he could see the faint shimmering outline of cobwebs woven between her fingers and through her hair. He could almost see the eight misty legs of her other form.

"After all," Spider Woman went on, "you are blessed with the gift of prophecy, aren't you? How do we know you haven't foreseen all that is to come—including the victory of the Viking gods? How do we know you're not setting a trap for the rest of us?"

"Well, first of all, that would be unsportsmanlike," Odin said, but the gods were in no mood for humor now. "More seriously, my visions don't work like that. To know all that is to come, in my pantheon we would have to ask the Norns, and they are far from forthcoming." Of course, that hadn't stopped him from trying. He had visited the three sisters of fate at the well they guarded, hoping they could give him some guarantee. But in their usual way, the giantesses had stared blankly at him, stirring the waters and waving their fingers, too busy making fates for the current-born to stop and hand out hints about the future. Besides, they gave him the creeps.

"Listen, I'm not the only god in the world with prophetic powers," Odin said, pressing his hands to his chest like a human politician. "Look within your own pantheons for clues about the outcome. I'm sure you'll find them as ambiguous as I did."

"That's because fate is changeable," Athena spoke up at last, from the Greek side. Odin knew if he could sway her, he'd win over many others, too; she was one of the more respected goddesses across all the pantheons. The goddess of wisdom lifted her owl from her shoulder to her knee, its contemplative expression a mirror image of hers. "Mortals always muddy fate. We may think things will go one way, and in a clear, orderly world, they would. But

mortals get in the way. As soon as they're involved, anything could happen. That's why none of us knew this was going to happen to us. Mortals are really much more unfathomable than we are."

What a perfect segue. *Zeus was fairly bouncing in place, he was so eager to announce the master stroke of their plan. Odin had to talk fast to get in ahead of him.*

"Yes, thank you, Athena," he said politely. "You are exactly right—mortals complicate things and wander off the prescribed paths of fate. And so, for this contest, we have a plan . . . to get rid of them."

Most of the gods let out shocked gasps, and there was an instant murmur as they leaned into one another to confirm they'd heard him right. Up in the stands, several gods were smiling—Hera, Mars, Ereshkigal, a few other Mesopotamian gods, and a couple of gruesome Aztec gods whose names Odin couldn't pronounce. But Athena's expression was concerned, and Spider Woman looked heartsick. Shiva and Vishnu didn't look very pleased either.

"Hear me out," Odin said, lifting his hands to quiet the gods. "There is a plan, and if Tezcatlipoca will see me afterward, I can work out the details. But the important thing to remember is that we need a world cleansed of mortals in order to make this work. Only with all of them gone can we be sure to avoid any funny unexpected twists."

But Spider Woman was on her feet, shaking her head, and the other Native American gods were standing up behind her. "I will have no part in this," she said. "It is foolish and risky, and it goes against everything we are. Those little humans believed in us; they made us real. They trusted us to protect them, not destroy them in a desperate grab for power. What good is it to rule the world if the very people we love are not a part of it?" Thunderbird flapped his wings angrily, and even Coyote slowly rose to his paws, although Odin saw reluctance and curiosity in his eyes.

"But—" Zeus sputtered. "It won't be—"

"Shhh," Odin interrupted him, touching the Greek god's shoulder. No need to reveal everything, especially if the Native Americans weren't going to participate. "If that's how they feel, they can go." He bowed to Spider Woman. "Your powers are not significant enough to make much of a difference." Anger flared in her eyes, and Coyote bared his teeth, but Odin went on, his voice cold and cruel. "We only invited you out of courtesy, since we plan to use your vast, marvelous territory as the battleground. But we know there's nothing you can do to stop us. It doesn't matter if you join us—you will serve us in the end, whether you do it by losing the game or by not playing at all."

Spider Woman stepped over the wall between them, covering the distance in long strides that brought her up to the platform much faster than Odin would have expected. He managed not to step back as she poked him in the chest, but he hoped she couldn't see that he was rattled. She was so close he could smell her breath, like warm corn bread, much sweeter than her words.

"You think you're very clever, Viking," she said softly. Over her shoulder, Odin could see all the gods leaning forward, straining to hear her. "You believe you've thought of everything; you scoff at the other pantheons who think they will win because you yourself can't imagine losing either. You think you can create a world where things are predictable, where events proceed exactly as you wish them to." She poked him in the chest again, and he felt as if spiderwebs were wrapping around his heart, squeezing. He narrowed his eye at her.

"You have your clever, clever plan so no mortals can muck

things up." She leaned even closer to him. "But you forget one thing. Your avatars—they'll be human. They'll have been human for years. They'll have all the frailties of mortals . . . and all the power mortals have to rewrite fate in any way they want." Spider Woman stepped back, her dark eyes fixed on Odin. "No matter what you do, I promise you, something unexpected will happen, and your funny game will end in a way that I predict you will not like at all. I don't need the gift of prophecy to know this—I just need to know mortals. Think on that."

She vanished into the air, and one by one, the other Native American gods did as well. Odin glanced down and saw a spider scuttling off the edge of the platform. He was strongly tempted to step on it, but he didn't, just in case it was her. He didn't need her coming back to lecture him some more.

"All right," he said smoothly. "Now that we've gotten rid of the gods we don't need, let's figure out the details of how this will work." He paused as a late-arriving Sumerian god hurried in and took a seat—Enki, if he remembered correctly. Shiva and Vishnu were murmuring to each other, but most of the other gods were watching Odin with rapt expressions. The temptation of having their power restored was enough to outweigh any risk. He'd been counting on that.

She can't be right, *he thought, glancing down to where the spider had been.* We'll shove our gods into human form, yes, but that won't make the avatars as troublesome as regular mortals. They'll still be gods, deep inside, won't they?

How much harm can a little humanity do?

CHAMBER OF JUDGMENT

Honestly, if she'd had a choice, Diana probably would not have walked *toward* the screaming.

The first time she heard it—a bone-chilling howl of agony in the distance—she stopped, listened, and tried to go in the other direction. But it seemed that no matter which way she turned her feet, the screaming lay ahead of her. Soon the sound was all around her and she gave up trying to move away from it.

Slowly, like the beginning of dawn, a red light began to glimmer above her. Diana squinted up at it, but she couldn't see a sun or stars or anything recognizable. There was just the glow, as if she were deep inside the Earth.

With her face tilted up, Diana didn't notice the door until she almost walked right into it.

She jumped back in surprise.

A door. In a very, very long wall blocking the way forward.

The door was made of wood, the wall of stone.

And the screaming was coming from the other side.

Diana took a step back, and then another, and backed directly into another wall.

That had definitely not been there before.

There was a door in this wall, too, and as far as she could tell, still more screaming was coming from behind it. Diana glanced off in either direction along the parallel walls. She had a feeling that if she tried to walk along them, another wall would appear.

She had to go forward, into whatever this was.

Diana stepped up to the first wall and pushed the door open gently. She found herself in a long, serene corridor of dark red walls, lit with flickering candlelight from sconces hanging at even intervals. Serene apart from the screaming, of course. A chorus of wails was coming from the passageway to her left; one endless, high-pitched shriek of pain echoed from a hall farther down to her right.

Diana took one of the candles from its sconce, blew out the flame, and stuck it in the door behind her to keep it ajar, just in case. This seemed like the kind of place where doors would disappear, or end up leading somewhere different when you opened them again.

She brushed her hand along the right-hand wall and walked to the first branch, where more identical corridors went off in either direction. Along these she could see an occasional door, each hung with a small painted scroll. She also spotted polished wooden stairs leading down to lower levels.

Curious, she walked up to one of the doors and studied its scroll. The symbols painted on it looked like

Chinese or Japanese characters.

"You were right!" a voice exclaimed behind her. Diana whipped around and gasped with surprise. There were two people standing in the corridor behind her. Well . . . sort of people.

"Of course I was," said the one with the head of an ox, in a deeper voice than the first.

The one with a horse's head snorted in a rubbery way, spraying spittle. "Well, can you blame me?" he said. "We weren't expecting anyone. I've been keeping an eye on that eighty-year-old in Beijing, but the scrolls say she won't be joining us for another two years, poor lonely thing."

"The scrolls didn't mention this one, it's true," said the ox-headed man. "But you heard the boundary alarm as well as I did."

The horse head's ears swiveled toward Diana. "She's suspiciously young," he said.

"And suspiciously divine," the ox head said, his nostrils flaring as he sniffed her. "This might be one of those toys the gods were playing with on the far side of the world."

"Oooohhhhhhhh," the horsey one declared in delight. "Then I'm sure she's done lots of fabulous horrible things we can punish her for."

This seemed like a good time for Diana to interrupt. "Hey, don't you want to introduce yourselves before punishing me?" she asked. "Can I ask, what's with the animal heads? Is that an after-death thing? Are there not enough human heads to go around in the underworld?"

The two of them glared at her. Whoops.

"Ha ha?" Diana tried. "No? Touchy subject?"

"Taunting the gods," the ox-headed one said frostily. "Hmmm. Perhaps the Chamber of Tongue-Ripping for this one."

"Or the Chamber of Ice," said the other with relish. "Disrespecting her elders."

Diana didn't like the sound of that. "I'm sorry," she said. "I'm kind of tired, and possibly mostly dead, which apparently does funny things to my sense of humor. Or, I guess, *un*funny things."

"Insincerity," snapped the ox. "Perhaps the Chamber of Disembowelment, then."

"Can we start over?" Diana said. "I'm Diana."

"Oh," said the horse. "Greco-Roman," he explained dismissively to his partner.

"Who are you?" Diana asked. "Where am I?"

"I am Ox-Head, and this is Horse-Face," the ox-headed man said with immense dignity.

Diana stared at them for a minute, trying really hard not to laugh. She felt a strong pang of wishing Gus were there—he'd find this all completely hilarious. Except maybe the Chamber of Disembowelment.

"Is this the Japanese underworld?" she asked once she could compose herself to speak normally. She touched the scroll beside her.

"Chinese," declared Horse-Face. "This is Diyu, where Yanluo Wang rules."

"Oh," Diana said. She'd never heard of it. She couldn't think of a single bit of information about Chinese mythology. *Man, they never teach you the useful stuff in school, do they?* "What's through here?" she asked, stalling.

Horse-Face in particular looked ready to fling her into a Chamber of Horrible Torture as fast as he could.

"That is the Chamber of Torso-Severing," Ox-Head said, pointing to the scroll. "As it *clearly* says *right here.*"

"Do you want to see?" Horse-Face offered eagerly.

"Um, no thanks," Diana said, but he was already leaning around her and opening the door. His dark green silken robes swung close to her, smelling of stables and decaying hay, and she stepped away, pressing her back into the wall of the corridor. She didn't trust him not to grab her and throw her into the Chamber of Torso-Severing, which, whether she was already dead or not, sounded really unpleasant.

A prolonged shriek blasted out through the doorway as Horse-Face pushed it open, and Diana caught a glimpse of enormous bloody blades whirring through the air inside. Quickly she covered her face and looked away.

"We should take her to Yanluo for judgment," Ox-Head said as Horse-Face closed the door again, grinning.

"I have a better idea," Horse-Face said. "He doesn't know she's here, right? She's not on his list. So why shouldn't we get to pick the punishment for once? We know the chambers better than anyone. Maybe we can cycle her through all of them! Come on, Ox-Head, it'll be fun. Don't you miss the Chamber of Maggots?"

"That's true," Ox-Head said wistfully. "And we haven't taken anyone to the Chamber of Dismemberment by Sawing in such a long time."

"We can make her climb the Mountain of Knives!" Horse-Face cried ecstatically.

"But first the Eye-Gouging!" Ox-Head suggested. "Or the Heart-Digging!"

"Eye-Gouging!" Horse-Face yelled with great enthusiasm.

They both paused and looked around.

"Where'd she go?" Ox-Head asked.

Diana hadn't stuck around past "Chamber of Maggots," although she could hear their horrible discussion all too clearly as she snuck along the corridor. As soon as she reached the first set of stairs, she fled down them as fast and silently as she could.

She couldn't get back to the door she'd come in by because the animal-headed gods were blocking the way. And at this point she cared less about escaping the corridors than about getting away from those two. Surely if she ran far enough she'd get out of this world eventually.

She raced through the maze of passages on the next floor down, taking frequent turns to make it harder to spot her if she was followed. She came to a door that she thought might be directly below the door she'd come in through. The Chinese writing on the scroll gave her no clues, so she tentatively pushed the door open and peeked in.

The room beyond was full of flames and screaming, burning people. The blistering heat instantly drove her back into the corridor, and she slammed the door behind her, gasping for air.

Maybe Xolotl was right. Maybe she should have stayed in Mictlan and tried her luck with the bloody skeleton king.

Well, there was nothing she could do about it now.

She turned down the next passage and kept running.

It's not that I'd rather be lying on the brink of death, Gus thought as another wave of salt water crashed over him and the deck, *but Diana sure is lucky to be missing this.* Unconsciousness had to be better than this never-ending storm. He wished he could sleep all the way to Africa. He wished he could sleep at all. Even ten minutes sounded like heaven after the hours he'd spent wrestling with the rudder, soaked to the bone, shivering, and accomplishing nothing.

Kali kept going below and coming back out, pacing restlessly around the ship and glaring at the lightning, but she wouldn't tell him anything about Diana. Now she was leaning on the railing, watching Poseidon again.

The last time Gus had slept was in the Metropolitan Museum of Art after Diana's battle with Amon. Since then he'd run around Central Park trying not to be killed by Kali; been caught and hung from a tree branch by Ereshkigal, Anna's creepy sister; gotten rescued by Quetzie; helped the two robot boys from the museum defeat the crystal hunters and become human; pulled Kali out of the ocean; seen Diana get stabbed by Anna; and escaped onto the ship with a horde of angry gods behind them.

That probably explained why he was so exhausted.

His clothes clung wetly to his skin, where his eerie Polynesian tattoo had spread even further. It was starting to ache sometimes, as if the ridged green designs had been recently carved there instead of appearing magically. The war god inside him was more restless too, almost as if he were literally pounding on Gus's skin to get out.

He pushed his wet hair out of his eyes and tried shoving the heavy rudder once more, but as usual, it wouldn't budge. He could keep it still for a few moments if he put all his weight into it, but for the most part it thrashed around however it wanted to, dragging him back and forth across the deck. Being from the seafaring Polynesian pantheon didn't do him much good when he was still just a mortal teenager trying to steer a ship designed for enormous, mythically strong Viking gods.

He needed to check on Diana. And he needed to sleep and eat. Kali had tried to bring him a loaf of bread and a hunk of cheese, but as soon as she stepped out into the storm with them, they'd crumbled into a soggy mess.

Kali was at the far end of the deck, examining the busty figurehead that looked disturbingly like Frey's sister, Freya, the Norse goddess of love and beauty. Gus let go of the rudder and took a step back. Nothing changed; the steering oar stayed exactly where it was, as if amused that Gus had thought he'd had any effect on it.

"Steer yourself then," Gus said to it. "See if I care." He slipped and slid across the wet planks to the covered opening that led to the cabins below the deck. He kept an eye on Kali as he went, but she didn't notice that he'd left his post.

Gus tugged open the trapdoor, climbed quickly onto the slanted wooden steps, and pulled the door shut behind him, struggling for a moment as the wind tried to wrench it out of his grasp. Finally it slammed down and he was left standing on the steps, breathing in the first dry air he'd felt in half a day.

He started shaking almost immediately, an uncontrollable shiver that made him realize how cold and wet he was. Carefully he felt his way down the steps, which were slick with the rain he and Kali had tracked in.

The steps led to a long passageway that ran from one end of the ship to the other. At either end there were opulent cabins furnished like honeymoon suites with Viking flair—silk sheets on king-sized beds, large private bathrooms, bearskin rugs, and the occasional axe or sword hanging on the wall. Kali had taken most of those down in the early stages of the storm so they wouldn't "fly about and behead somebody," as she put it.

The other doors in the hall led to kitchens, suspiciously large eating halls, and more cabins—so many of them that Gus was sure this ship was bigger on the inside than the outside. It was supposed to be large enough to hold the entire Norse pantheon, after all, and presumably the only way to do that was with magic.

He wanted to go straight to Diana, who was in the big cabin at the front of the ship, but water was flying off him, and he was afraid he'd be bringing the storm to her if he tried to see her like this. He tried the door closest to the stairs and found a room decorated in shades of green, from the pale sea-foam curtains to dark forest blankets on the bed. Just inside the door was a bathroom with an actual bathtub in it. Gus pulled off his shirt, wrung it out, and hung it over the tub. The towels were fluffy and huge—three times the size of normal towels. The whole ship made Gus feel like a hobbit, surrounded by things just a bit too big for him.

He wrapped the towel around his shoulders and went back into the cabin, where he found a deep wooden chest at the foot of the bed. Inside were strange clothes—all too big, of course—but he pulled out a thick woolen tunic and put it on. It hung to his knees, but he felt instantly warmer.

Gus dug through the chest until he found leggings that weren't too embarrassing, a corded belt to keep them on, and a pair of gigantic socks. He toweled off his hair, left the towel on the bed, and went back into the hallway.

Kali was standing outside the door, her hands on her hips, frowning.

"I was wet!" Gus protested before she could say anything. "And tired, and hungry, and it's not even like I was doing anything that useful up there, and I want to see Diana, so don't yell at me."

Kali looked amused. "I wasn't going to yell at you," she said. "I've been waiting for you to take a break for ages. I'm just watching this door try to figure out who you are."

"You've been waiting for me to take a break? Why didn't you say so?"

"You are your own person, Gus," Kali said. "It's not like I'm the captain and you're following my orders or something."

He realized that was exactly how he'd been thinking of it.

"My door is trying to figure out who I am?" he said, deciding to choose the safer topic.

"Check it out," Kali said, pointing at a sign on his door which he hadn't noticed before. It said NJORD in carved wooden letters, but as they watched, the *O* and the *R* were getting longer and taller, while the *N* and the *J* slowly shrank back into the grain of the wood.

"I think it's trying to spell 'Oro,'" Kali said, cocking her head. "Weird."

It was weird. Gus didn't want to think about magical ships thinking about him. "All right," he said. "I'm going to see Diana." Kali was staring up at the trapdoor, looking thoughtful again. He took a few steps, then turned back to her. "You might want to try changing into something dry too," he suggested. "You wouldn't want to get sick in the middle of saving the world and all."

Kali shrugged. "I don't get sick. Besides, I'll be going outside again soon, so there's not much point."

Gus nodded and turned around again. Being the strongest avatar apparently came with perks like ridiculous stamina and invulnerability to germs. On the other hand, she seemed less human than the rest of them, and Gus would rather have his humanity. He'd seen enough superhero movies and read enough comic books to know that superpowers were great, but not very good for your soul—or for your friendships, or for falling in love. Maybe he'd wanted them when he was younger, but after losing his parents, he'd thought about things a little differently. After that, all he really wanted was the chance to have them back again.

He opened the door at the end of the hall and slipped inside Diana's cabin. For a moment his senses were confused. The smell of the blood and the sight of the sopping red sheets was more of a shock than he'd been prepared for.

His eyes adjusted to the dim light as Tigre's head popped up from the far side of the bed.

"I'm awake!" Tigre said with a note of panic in his voice. "I am, I swear, I'm watching—oh. You're not Kali." He slumped back down to the floor.

"What's happening?" Gus asked, making his way over to Diana as the ship slammed up and down with the waves. "Is she all right? Is all this blood hers?"

"She's stable, I think," Tigre mumbled. He was lying on the floor on top of a blanket that was still partly folded, as if he hadn't had the energy to unfold it or get to a real bed in another room. His arms were crossed over his face. "But I'm only saying that because it's the kind of thing you hear on TV. I actually have no idea, except that blood isn't pouring out of her anymore, she has a pulse, and her breathing is slow but regular."

"Has she woken up?" Gus said anxiously. He picked up one of Diana's hands, which felt terribly cold and small.

"No." Tigre paused, then sat up to look straight at Gus. "I'm sorry, Gus."

"Don't be sorry," Gus said. "I know you've done everything you can to help her."

"Yeah, but—this shouldn't have happened. I should have known. I should have been able to stop Anna."

Gus had had plenty of time to think about Anna while the storm had been lashing him outside. "None of us knew," he said. "Anna seemed normal, like us. We're not cut out for deception and betrayal and ancient wars between gods. That's the mistake the pantheons made—by making us live regular mortal lives for sixteen, eighteen years, they left us thinking like regular human teenagers. We don't want to fight and kill and rule the world from a cloud in the sky. We just want to watch TV and fall in love and maybe see the Taj Mahal one day, or beat our brothers at *Mortal Kombat*, or get into a good college, or start a band." He shook his head. "It's just . . . different. I don't know if gods can understand all that."

"But Kali and Amon and Anna—they picked it up pretty quickly," Tigre pointed out.

"Kali has most of her goddess memories from Shiva," Gus said, "and she's still more complex than most of the gods we've met. I don't think Amon and Anna were purely evil, either. They just had different goals from us, and their own way of getting to them."

Tigre blinked, looking even more tired. "You sound all wise and serene like your girlfriend."

"I wish," Gus said. "Sometimes I think it would be easier to let go and let my war god take over. He knows how to survive and how to take care of himself, and how not to get hurt. It would certainly be a less complicated way to live." *But I won't do that—not as long as there's still hope for me and Diana and for us getting home again.*

He stroked Diana's hair and for a moment he thought he saw her eyelids flutter. But when he stopped and watched her more closely, she seemed as still as a mannequin or a prop dead person in an opera.

"If she's stopped bleeding," Gus said, "can I take her to a different room?" He didn't like the dark carnage of this cabin, the battlefield-hospital aura. Wherever Diana was, this couldn't be giving her very pleasant dreams.

"I guess," Tigre said. "But be very careful—we don't want to split her stitches."

Gus slid his arms under Diana, trying not to shudder at the clammy stickiness of the blood-soaked sheets. Gently he lifted her up, adjusting her head to lean against his shoulder.

Tigre dragged himself to the door and opened it so Gus could slip through sideways, holding Diana close to him. He went straight down the ship to the cabin at the far end with Tigre close behind him.

Gus was a little surprised that Kali hadn't claimed this room already, but she probably hadn't stopped pacing long enough to think about where she was going to sleep. He knelt down and slid Diana onto the clean white sheets. She shifted as he moved his arms, letting out a small sigh, and Gus felt better. This room was better for her; it was not only cleaner, but calmer as well, since the waves were mostly crashing against the front of the boat.

"You guys should get some sleep," Kali said from the doorway. "We won't get to Africa until late tomorrow at the earliest."

"That soon?" Tigre said. "I thought crossing the ocean would take a lot longer than that."

"Magical ship, remember?" Kali said, pointing up. "And you'll need your rest. Who knows what we'll find when we get there?" She winked and left the room.

Well, that sounds ominous, Gus thought. But he wasn't about to argue with the idea of sleeping.

"I could stay here with Diana," Tigre offered doubtfully.

"That's okay—I'll sleep here in case she wakes up," Gus said. Looking relieved, Tigre nodded and made his way to the door, stumbling as the storm slammed the timbers of the ship.

Gus went around the bed and cautiously climbed onto the far side, watching Diana for any movement. The bed was vast enough that he could sleep without disturbing her, but if she woke up, he should notice. He lay down on his side, facing her, and as his exhaustion rose, he felt all the worries he'd pushed to the back of his mind come flooding forward.

She didn't look peaceful. She looked more . . . concerned, as if she knew she was missing something and she wanted to come back to life as much as he wanted her to. It was unsettling to see her without the hope and energy that usually carried her—and everyone around her—through the hard stuff.

"Don't die," Gus whispered. He reached out and touched her hand. Were there superpowers that could bring her back? Would there be gods in Africa that could help them save her?

"I stayed alive when you ordered me to. Now you return the favor, okay? Just . . . whatever you do, don't die."

Being dead was a lot tougher than Diana had expected. Or at least, being *almost* dead (which she hoped was still the case). She didn't think it normally involved being chased through a labyrinth by torture-happy animal-headed gods.

She had run down at least three flights of stairs, and she kept finding more stairs leading down and more doors and more corridors. She leaped down the last set of stairs three at a time and discovered a corridor that looked different from the others. There was only one double door, at the far end of the hall from the stairs, and it was much larger than the others.

Diana ran down the hall and pulled open one side of the enormous door. It creaked and groaned loudly as she dragged it back, and she was sure that every demon in the Chinese underworld now knew where she was.

The other side was dark and vast, with flickering candles faintly illuminating huge columns that stretched to a shadowy ceiling high above.

The Chamber of Things That Go Bump in the Dark? Diana wondered. *Or the Chamber of Making You Feel Tiny?* At least it didn't sound like the Chamber of Dismemberment by Sawing.

She left the door partly open and walked between the columns, trying to make as little noise as possible. After a few steps, she started to feel like there were other people in the room with her, somewhere far back in the shadows, but if they were there, they kept silent. It was like the feeling she had often had walking through airports when she was on tour—that millions of eyes were on her, people who would never speak to her but were just watching and waiting for her to do something wrong or embarrassing or newsworthy that they could post all over the Internet. It made her feel claustrophobic despite the size of the room, and she started walking faster, hoping that the glow she could see in the distance was some sort of end and not just more candles.

It was the end, but once she got there, she wasn't sure whether she should be happy about that or not. Seated at a high table were ten forbidding-looking figures. Nine of them wore black robes, and the tenth, seated in the middle, wore long red robes. It was hard to tell in the flickering light, but his skin seemed to be dark green, like polished jade, and he had a long thin mustache and a pointy beard.

In front of the high table was a parallel row of ten desks, only one of them occupied. Most of the desks had scrolls neatly piled on top of them, but the one desk with a person at it was covered in a wild mess of unrolled scrolls and dripping ink bottles. The man standing behind the desk looked harried and upset; he kept running his finger down the writing on the scrolls, looking up at Diana, shaking his head, and then flapping the scrolls around to examine another section.

The red-robed man frowned as Diana stopped.

"Have you found her yet?" he grumbled.

Found me? I'm right here.

"N-n-no," stammered the man with the scrolls. "I'm sorry, Your Excellency, I'm sure she's in here somewhere."

"Evidently she is not," said His Excellency. "Our records are impeccable, and we have innumerable administrative cross-checks in place. So there is only one answer: she should not be here."

"I agree," Diana called up to him. "Can I please go?"

"Wait!"

"Wait!"

A flurry of footsteps announced the panting, flustered arrival of Ox-Head and Horse-Face from a far corner of the vast hall. They hurried toward Diana with their robes flapping, and she stepped back, prepared to run if they got too close.

"You are terrible guardians," the red-robed man said to them sternly. Diana guessed that this was the Yanluo king guy that they'd mentioned earlier. "How did this soul get past you?"

"She didn't, my lord," Ox-Head said breathlessly.

"She escaped," Horse-Face added. "She ran away!"

"Yeah, when they wanted to throw me in the Chamber of Maggots!" Diana protested.

Yanluo frowned even more. "I do not smell that kind of wrongdoing on her," he said. "Why the Chamber of Maggots?"

Ox-Head and Horse-Face exchanged sheepish glances. "It was just an idea," Horse-Face said with a shrug.

Yanluo steepled his fingers together, glancing sideways at the silent figures on either side of him. "She should be judged by each of the courts," he said. "We must determine her sins so we may decide on the fairest punishment."

"Um . . . must we?" Diana said. "If I'm in the wrong place, shouldn't I just be going?"

"And we have no information on her," said the flustered man at the desk. "None of the details of her life are in these scrolls. How will we know what she's done?"

Well, that's lucky, Diana thought. She didn't love the idea of these guys having her whole biography laid out in front of them. *They could just check the nearest newsstand for another magazine full of made-up lies about me.*

"There is another way," Yanluo said, gesturing to his left. "Bring us the Mirror of Retribution."

There was a rumble from the shadows, and soon two women in blue silk robes emerged, pushing an enormous rectangular mirror on wheels. It was twice as tall as Diana and set in a dark stone frame, but instead of her reflection, the glass only showed billowing clouds of smoke.

"Mirror of Retribution?" Diana echoed nervously. "Is it going to shoot flames at me if it doesn't like me?"

"It will merely help us see," said Yanluo, leaning forward to study the mirror. Diana realized that more people in blue robes had appeared behind her; one of them took her arm and steered her to stand directly in front of the mirror. Diana wondered if she should try to run, but at least this seemed better than being thrown into the Chamber of Eye-Gouging by Horse-Face. She tried to calm her racing heart by breathing deeply and staring into the mirror smoke.

There *was* a face in there, she realized suddenly. But as it came forward, it looked less and less like her and more like a total stranger. It was a girl, maybe a year or two younger than Diana, with an eager expression.

Then Diana saw herself, and the scene behind them

began to solidify. She took a sharp breath as she recognized it—one of her favorite restaurants in LA, although she had had to stop going there after the tabloids began to stake out the place. In this moment she was leaving the restaurant with her mother, and there were cameras flashing all around her.

She remembered this now. She had just finished her first major national tour, and although she was exhausted, her mother had dragged her out to celebrate. Mom had always liked being photographed with her famous daughter, and after "Venus" had been on the road for several weeks, Mom wanted to take the first opportunity to get back in the limelight again.

Diana also remembered what came next. It must have been hard for the girl to work up the courage to approach her, but somehow she got through the photographers and close enough to push her notepad at Diana. In the mirror, it all played out again.

"Please, Venus," she chirped. "Can I please have your autograph?"

But "Venus" barely even glanced at her. "Please leave me alone," she snapped at the air over the girl's shoulder, and then dove into the waiting limousine with her mom right behind her.

Diana felt the guilt like an ache in her chest. Even at the time, she'd felt awful, and now, watching it again, she could see the girl's face crumple, almost in slow motion. She didn't know why they'd picked this particular interaction to watch. There were hundreds of other fans like that whom she had been equally terrible to when they caught her at a bad time. Hence her mixed online reputation: "I don't know why I love her so much, because she's SO MEAN, but I love her anyway—what's that about?" And so forth. Her Venus power made people love her despite the private snappishness of her Diana instincts.

"Cruel," Yanluo commented.

"Impressively cruel," Horse-Face agreed.

The scene in the mirror blurred and faded into a dressing room, backstage at a concert hall. Diana was sitting in the makeup chair while her stylist, Leila, fussed with her hair and her costume designer, Bruce, perched on the counter, sewing a rip in one long silver glove. They were all giggling.

"And *then*," Diana said, "he called me *again*! As if me not answering the phone the first six times wasn't clear enough!"

"Well, he wasn't cast on that show for his brains, if you know what I mean," Leila said, rolling Diana's hair around a large brush and spraying it.

"*I* know what you mean," said Bruce. "He's yummy. Darling, if you don't want him, I'll take him in a heartbeat."

"Surely you can do better, Bruce," Diana said, rolling her eyes. "I mean, Kenneth? He's got about as much soul as this bottle of nail polish, and trust me, 'Ravishing Red' would be a better conversationalist. Wow, Leila, really? Ravishing Red?" She shook the nail polish and studied the bright color.

Bruce cackled. "You're so much fun when you're tired and cranky."

"I'm being mean, aren't I?" Diana wrinkled her nose at the mirror. "He's never been anything but nice to me. I'm sure he means well, but it's hard to like someone who Mom keeps throwing at me. She has *awful* taste, plus she's crazy-unsubtle. Like, Mom, the part where you sat me next to him on the flight to that awards show? Oooobvious! I wish she'd cut it out."

"You and Kenneth would make a cute couple," Leila pointed out. "All your fan sites agree."

"Blech." Diana tilted her head back so Leila could comb out her curls. "Besides being boring, I've heard he's really into older women, actually. Like, *super*-old, like in their *sixties*. I mean, gross."

"Gross!" Leila agreed.

"Well, even if he's not, we should start the rumor that he is," Bruce suggested. "I bet *that* would convince your fans he's not good enough for you. Of course, it might ruin his movie career, but I mean, your love life is at stake here, sugar. Drastic measures must be taken."

"And then maybe they'll set their sights on Ben instead, the cute guy on that new ABC show," Leila said. "Isn't he adorable?"

"Too totally," the Diana in the mirror said as the smoke rose up to cloud the scene again.

"Gossiping," Yanluo noted.

"Malicious gossiping," Ox-Head agreed.

"But everyone does that," Diana protested. "I mean, it's Hollywood. You have to, or everyone hates you and assumes you're hiding something really terrible. What am I supposed to do when Leila and Bruce start talking like that? Pretend I can't hear them?"

Ox-Head and Horse-Face exchanged significant glances, and Diana felt a knot of worry start to form in her stomach.

Now "Venus" in the mirror was on a couch at a late-night talk show, laughing with the host. "Oh, Hollywood is awful," she said cheerfully. "All the whispers and rumors . . . I try to stay out of it. I'm really a pretty private person. And I like everyone! I swear! I have nothing bad to say about anyone, and you can't make me." She winked at the host, and the studio audience applauded.

"Hypocrisy. Are you writing these down?" Yanluo asked the desk official.

"Yes, Your Excellency," the man said, nodding and scribbling.

"Do you have to?" Diana asked. "I mean . . . is this really so bad?"

Nobody answered her. They were all staring at the mirror again, where Diana was lying on a bed in her Los Angeles hotel room, watching TV. On-screen, the entertainment news was reporting on an actress who'd spent her summer building houses for tsunami victims.

"Man," the mirror Diana scoffed. "Of course she would. She's such a poser. Hey, Mom, look at this!" As her mom came into the room, Diana pointed at the TV. "I need to found an orphanage or something. I'm totally losing out on the humanitarian stuff. Did we give any money to charity last year? Didn't I want to save some pandas or something?"

"You've been busy, sweetheart," her mother said, patting her head. "And we have financial advisors keeping track of all that. There will be plenty of time to save pandas and orphans when you're an even bigger star, don't worry."

"Are you sure? Shouldn't I start now?"

"Giving to charity is what established stars do to save their reputations," her mother said knowingly. "The press wants young newcomers like you to be out having fun and dating other celebrities. Trust your image consultants on this one."

"I guess," Diana said, lying back on the bed again. "But let's not forget. When I'm super-famous, let's use some of it to save the world. Promise?"

"Sure, dear," her mother said, leaving the room again.

There was a short silence as the smoke covered the mirror again.

"But you never did, did you?" Yanluo asked.

Diana shook her head, feeling sick to her stomach. It was painful to watch her worst qualities highlighted. She knew she'd done things that she wasn't proud of, but she tried not to dwell on them, hoping the good things would outweigh the bad in the end. But after seeing this, she felt like maybe they didn't. She'd let her lifestyle, her mother, and that world affect her more than she'd realized.

Is this what all goddesses are like? Or is that the human side of me? She thought about Hera and Zeus squabbling, Mars acting like an entitled jerk, and the other Greek gods whispering and gossiping in the museum. Maybe there wasn't much difference between them and humans, after all.

If their plan succeeds, someone like me is going to rule the gods and be in charge of this world. Someone with all these flaws and petty thoughts and selfish impulses. What could possibly give us that right? How can I take care of the whole world when I couldn't even be a good person in my normal life?

Finally the mirror cleared to reveal the moonlit interior of the Metropolitan Museum of Art. The Egyptian avatar, Amon, was standing in front of Diana, looking furious. He'd expected a romantic rendezvous, but instead she had challenged him to battle.

All the Chinese gods leaned forward expectantly, looking fascinated. Diana covered her eyes and turned away. She couldn't watch this again.

"Betrayal," Yanluo murmured. "Deception. He trusted you."

"He was using me," Diana whispered, but she didn't know if they heard her.

The fight was eerily silent, much quieter than she remembered it. She could hear their footfalls on the marble floor, and the crash of statues falling around them. Amon taunting her, Diana striking back. She could tell when they reached the Temple of Dendur because the ghosts and gods around her all murmured in surprise.

And then it ended, and there was a long pause. Diana uncovered her eyes and saw that the mirror had frozen on her and the stag that had once been Amon. In the mirror, she was touching the stag's soft nose, and her eyes were sad.

"Compassion," Yanluo said finally.

"A surprising lack of ambition," Ox-Head added.

They were quiet again for a moment.

"I think we shall let you go," said Yanluo at long last. Horse-Face snorted, but didn't say anything.

"Really?" Diana said. "But—the mirror—all those awful things. . . . "

"You should reflect on them," Yanluo said, "but much as I would love to make use of the Chamber of Grinding or the Chamber of Tongue-Ripping again, I do not think you are right for this place."

The official at the desk sighed with relief. "A wise decision, Your Honor. She isn't in our system, and we'd have to adjust all of our charts and scrolls and timetables and personnel requirements, and I'm afraid the paperwork could take centuries."

"Anything to avoid more paperwork," Yanluo said with a hint of a smile. "Before you go, child, please accept our offer of tea." He clapped his hands. "Meng Po!" he commanded.

An old woman trundled out from behind the high table, pushing a cart laden with teacups and a plain earthenware teapot in the center, steam rising from its spout. As she came closer, Diana could smell a strong, intoxicating herbal scent that made her want to curl up and go to sleep for a long time. The old woman nodded at her, smiling. She poured a cup of tea and held it out to Diana.

Diana nearly took it. She was tired and hungry, and tea sounded so appealing, and the woman had a sweet face; Diana didn't want to disappoint her. But as she reached for the cup, a memory flitted across her mind—something about Persephone in the Greek underworld. She stopped and pulled back her hand.

In the myths she remembered, it was a bad idea to eat when you were in the underworld. It meant that you would be trapped there forever. At least, that was true in Hades, and she didn't want to risk it in one of these peculiar underworlds either.

"I'm sorry," she said, bowing politely to the old woman. "I'm afraid I cannot take refreshment until I return home."

Meng Po grinned toothlessly. "Clever," she whispered.

"Indeed," Yanluo chimed in. "That is the tea of forgetfulness. We give it to those who are about to be reincarnated so they'll forget their former lives. If you had taken it, we would have sent your soul back in another form—a songbird, I think, would be suitable."

"Can't you send me back to my own body?" Diana pleaded. "I'm not completely dead, right? Can you bring me back to life?"

Yanluo consulted a scroll in front of him for a moment, then shook his head. "We cannot do that. We have little power within the real world anymore. But we can send you on to the next underworld. Perhaps they can help you." He stood and pointed to the darkness behind the high table. "Keep walking that way. You will find your way out soon."

Diana knew she should just be thankful that she wasn't having her tongue ripped out by winged monkeys or something. She bowed to Yanluo and the panel of silent judges, took the long way around Ox-Head and Horse-Face, and set off into the void beyond Yanluo's table.

When she glanced back, all she could see was the silhouette of their tall chairs outlined against the candlelight.

And when she looked forward . . . all she could see was more darkness.

"OUT! GET OUT!"

Kali started awake and sat up in bed, her heart pounding. Had she dreamed the loud, bellowing voice? Outside, the thunder was booming louder than ever, and the ship was being slammed around so hard she was surprised she'd been able to sleep at all. The cabin was dark, with no light coming through the portholes.

She stumbled across the room to the bathroom, retrieved her drying clothes from the towel racks, and put them on. They were still damp, but she preferred that to the enormous, silly-looking furs and robes she'd found in the trunk at the foot of the bed.

"OUT!" the voice thundered again. *So . . . not imaginary*. It seemed to come from beyond the portholes, from somewhere overhead. "YOU ARE NOT WELCOME HERE!"

The ship pitched sideways, knocking her into the wall, and then suddenly gave a little jump and fell still. Kali scrambled to the door and ran to the stairs. Gus and Tigre emerged from their cabins, rubbing their faces sleepily.

"What's happening?" Tigre asked.

"Why did the storm stop?" Gus asked.

"Let's find out," Kali suggested, climbing the stairs two at a time. She swung open the trapdoor and stepped out onto the deck. The rain had stopped, although the sky was still full of dark storm clouds. Kali squinted at them until she spotted a god she recognized: Tlaloc, Tigre's Aztec storm-god guide who had mostly spent his time yelling at Tigre. He peered out from behind a storm cloud, saw her watching, and ducked back into hiding.

Most of the gods who had been following them had vanished. The woman with the net was still lingering in the wake of the ship, gnashing her teeth angrily. Even Poseidon had dropped back to the rear of the ship, his sea horses bobbing halfheartedly in the waves.

Kali leaned on the stern and looked down at the Greek sea god. "Hey there," she said. "What's the matter? You guys get bored? Because we were just starting to enjoy that."

"You will regret this, little death goddess," Poseidon growled, twisting his trident. "We would have kept things fair and civilized. Now we can't predict what will happen to you. It's in their hands."

"YOU'VE COME TOO FAR ALREADY, TRIDENT BEARER," boomed the voice in the sky. "THE LINES WERE CLEARLY MARKED, AND THIS IS OUR TERRITORY NOW, AS WE ALL AGREED."

Kali turned and shaded her eyes, looking up at the sky again. The clouds ahead of the ship were different from the ones behind it; they were redder in color, with flashes of white lightning in them, and clumped in a strange way, like stacks of stone slabs piled on top of one another.

Her gaze traveled up the pile to the top, where she finally saw the owner of the booming voice standing on the topmost cloud with his arms crossed. His skin was dark like polished mahogany. He had ram's horns and a double-bladed axe protruding from his head like a headdress, and he had six eyes.

"I-is that a god?" Tigre asked, coming up beside her.

"Gee, I don't know," Kali said. "What do you think?"

"There's no need to be snippy," he said.

She glanced over the railing again and saw that the other gods had stopped in the water, so *Skidbladnir* was now sailing away from them. She waved good-bye to Poseidon with a cheerful smile, which he did not return.

"Guys, look," Gus called from the bow of the ship. Kali and Tigre stepped carefully around the shining puddles on the deck to join him. Ahead of them, on the horizon but closer than she would have expected, Kali could see the dark outline of land.

"Africa," she said quietly.

All six eyes of the god in the sky seemed to be glaring at them sternly as they sailed closer to the African shoreline. Kali tried waving at him, but he just frowned.

"Hello?" she called. "Who are you?"

"I AM SHANGO. YOU WERE NOT INVITED HERE EITHER," the god boomed. Tigre gave Kali a nervous look.

"Do you want us to leave?" Kali asked. "I'm not sure we can stop this ship once it has a destination in mind."

"I WILL LET OBATALA DEAL WITH YOU," he answered, and then refused to speak anymore, although Kali tried calling to him a few more times.

The sight of the land made it clear how fast they were going; it seemed to be coming at them shockingly quickly. Gus climbed up on the railing and shaded his eyes, squinting.

"There's something weird about it," he said. "Does Africa have cliffs? I thought it was all deserts and jungles."

"I don't know," Kali said. "Everything I know about Africa I learned from watching *Meerkat Manor*. So, watch out for birds of prey, and no fooling around with boy meerkats from other tribes."

"Thanks," Gus said, cracking his first smile since Diana was stabbed. "I'll keep that in mind."

Kali could see what Gus meant about the African shoreline. It rose up sharply ahead of them, looking more like a cliff than a jungle beach.

"It's some kind of wall," Tigre said.

"Kind of," Kali said. "More like a fence, I think." There was a barrier running all along the coastline, as far as they could see in each direction. It wasn't straight and flat like a wall; it was bumpy and pointy around the edges, and the top wavered up and down. As the ship approached, Kali realized that the whole barrier was made of vines and tree trunks, knitted together so closely and packed so deep that there was no way to see through it. The branches were in shades of shimmering gold and deep velvety brown, like a dance of lions and panthers. It looked almost beautiful, like a bronze and wood sculpture, until you saw the enormous, wicked-looking thorns. Some of them were as tall as Kali.

"It's like the hedge around Sleeping Beauty's castle," Gus pointed out. "The one the prince had to get through to kiss her and wake her up." He paused, and Kali guessed what he was thinking.

"You don't have to get through the hedge to do that," Kali said. "You can run down there and kiss her right now. Hey, it might work. We won't judge you."

"I wasn't going to do that," Gus said, blushing.

"Well, I feel sorry for the prince that tackles that hedge," Tigre offered. "You'd impale yourself on one of those thorns before you got within sword's reach of it."

"There's got to be a way in," Kali said. "*Skidbladnir* will find it."

"Hopefully," Gus said.

"Or," Tigre said, "we'll sail right into it and die, and someday Thor, new king of the gods, will find vultures picking at our skewered, rotting corpses."

Kali and Gus turned to stare at him.

"Sorry," Tigre muttered, pressing his head between his hands. "Um, creepy dreams. Too much death imagery going on in here."

"All right," Kali said. "Just try not to use 'corpses' and 'skewered' in the same sentence again, if that's okay."

"He's got a point, though," Gus said. "I mean, it's a ship. How advanced can its thinking be?"

"You guys have no faith," Kali said. "Frey's been using it for centuries, and he's survived."

"He's immortal," Gus pointed out, "and he probably usually gives more specific directions than *that big continent over there, please.*"

"Oh, shut up," Kali said. The wall of thorns *was* coming up on them awfully quickly. "We are not going to survive Thor and Amon and Inanna and freaking Ereshkigal and then get killed by a big hedge." She pulled back her hair and tied it with a piece of rope from the ship.

"Go get Diana," she said. "I'll get some weapons."

Soon they were all back on deck. Tigre and Gus had both changed back into their own clothes, and Gus was carrying Diana, who was pale and limp in his arms. Kali touched her wrist and felt barely a flutter of a pulse. The wind lifted Diana's red-gold curls and brushed them against her stone-white face like lost butterflies.

"She'll be all right," Gus said stubbornly, his arms tightening around her. Kali knelt and tied a small axe to his belt with a loop of leather. "She's still alive, and we'll find a god in Africa who can heal her."

Can, perhaps . . . but who knows if they'll be willing to help us? Kali hoped she had done the right thing, grabbing Diana and taking her onto *Skidbladnir* with them. At least this way there was a ghost of a chance for her—otherwise Anna would have made sure she was dead and taken her goddess powers.

She remembered Anna's last cry of rage and frustration. *"Kali, don't you dare steal her and her powers from me!"* To be honest, part of Kali was tempted. It would be useful to have Diana's natural talent for navigating the forest and battling with her wits. And the other goddess, Venus—with her power Kali could make anyone love her. Wouldn't that be odd, everyone loving a goddess of death and destruction?

Back in the real world, Kali had often seen doubt in her mother's eyes. If she had had Venus's powers, Kali would not have been the first person her mother looked at whenever she saw an explosion on the TV. She wouldn't have faced the months of quiet suspicion when her stepfather was ill. If she were powerful like Venus, her mother would love her no matter what.

Kali shook her head, blinking. This was crazy. She didn't need that kind of love, and she certainly didn't want to get it through supernatural powers. Also, Diana was still alive, and they'd made a promise to stick together. *I may not be lovable, but I keep my promises.*

So . . . maybe only if it looks like she's definitely *going to die. I mean, she wouldn't want them to go to waste, right?*

She looked up and saw Gus watching her with a concerned expression. "You're right. We'll find someone to fix her," Kali said, turning back to the rail. She realized that the tall thorn barrier was now to their left, and they were humming along parallel to the coast of Africa.

"Where do you think we're going?" Tigre asked.

"Not sure," Kali said. "Wherever there's a way in." She glanced up; Shango, the six-eyed god, was still floating above them. What was Africa like behind the wall? What was waiting for them?

"We're still going east," Gus said, "so my guess is that we're off the south coast of that part of Africa that looks like the top half of a *P*. Only, um, backward. You know?" The other two nodded. "So maybe we're heading for the part where it curves down. But I don't know anything about which countries are in this part, and even less about what their mythology is like."

Kali sighed. "Same here."

"Ghana?" Tigre guessed. "Benin? Nigeria? Something

about the Ivory Coast? Is that a country?"

The ship was starting to slow down. Soon they could see that the coast took a turn ahead of them, heading south, but the ship didn't turn with it. Instead it slowed down even more, aiming for a long white sandbar offshore from the hedge wall.

Skidbladnir pulled up alongside the sandbar and stopped. The sails flapped softly in the breeze and the ship bobbed a little from side to side, like a dog pleased with itself for doing a trick. Without the wind rushing past, it suddenly seemed very quiet. Kali had the creepy feeling that the thorn hedge was full of eyes, watching them. It looked no thinner here than anywhere else; there was no big open gate like she'd been hoping for.

"Well, we're here," Kali said. "The question is how to get down there." She nodded at the water far below them. "Since certain people threw our ramp overboard when the ship left New York."

"Um, hey, being chased by homicidal gods, remember?" Gus said. "Sorry we didn't measure up to your nautical standards."

"I don't see Quetzie," Tigre said, scanning the sky for the neoquetzal. Kali hadn't seen the giant bird since the beginning of the storm had frightened her away. "Do you think she'll find us again?"

"I'm sure she'll try," Kali said.

Suddenly there was a light snapping sound, and they all looked up to see the sails smoothly rolling themselves up to the masts. As soon as the sails were neatly tied back, the masts began to fold down, piece by piece.

"Uh-oh,"Tigre said.

"The ship's going back to Post-it size," Kali said. "Which means we should probably get off. You know, quickly."

"I think I saw a ladder that way," Gus said, jerking his head to the long side of the ship facing the shore. Kali and Tigre followed him over and found a rope ladder tied to the railing. She threw it over the edge, and the far end splashed down into the water below. Gus shifted Diana's weight in his arms, looking nervous.

"I can probably carry her down," Kali offered, "if I balance her over my shoulder."

"I'm worried about her wound, though," Gus said. "I don't want it to start bleeding again."

"I WILL TAKE HER."

They all jumped and spun around. Shango, the six-eyed god from the sky, was standing on the deck behind them, staring at the rapidly collapsing masts. Kali had nearly forgotten he was following them.

"But—" Gus started.

"I CAN CARRY HER DOWN WHILE YOU CLIMB," the god insisted. Kali winced, touching her ears.

"You're always that loud, huh?" she said. "I guess we shoud just count ourselves lucky you speak English."

"PERHAPS YOU SHOULD SAVE THE WITTY BANTER UNTIL AFTER YOU ARE OFF YOUR CURIOUS FOLDING SHIP." The god stepped forward and neatly lifted Diana out of Gus's arms in a smooth, strong movement, as if he were just sliding her through clouds. Then he stepped back, up, and over the railing before any of them had time to react.

Gus sprang over to the rope ladder and swarmed down with impressive speed. Kali wished he had that kind of energy when *she* told him to do things. She swung her legs over and followed him. The rungs were stiff and scratchy under her palms. At the bottom, she hesitated, then dropped into the ocean with a grimace. To her surprise, the water was shallow and warm here, reaching just above her waist, so she could stand. The waves were calm and small, but she still felt a little nervous as they tugged playfully at her pants. She glanced down at the axe she'd tied to her belt, hoping it had some magical protection against rust.

Gus was already floundering away toward the shoreline and the hedge, following the god as he drifted through the air far above them with Diana in his arms. *Lucky girl gets to stay dry*, Kali thought, turning back as Tigre jumped off the ladder and splashed down beside her.

The ship was folding up more quickly now, the bow and stern caving inward as it shrank toward the water. Kali saw a spider scuttle over the railing and leap into the sea. *Poor thing probably figures the ocean can't be any scarier than a magical shrinking ship.*

"Go ahead and catch up with Gus," Kali told Tigre. "I'll stay and wait for it to finish." She pulled Frey's ice-blue pouch out of her pocket. Tigre should at least be able to keep Gus from throwing himself on the thorns until she got there.

After that . . . I have no idea what will happen.

• • ● • •

"Wait!" Gus yelled. The water tugged heavily at him, slowing him down. The god made it to the thorny wall long before Gus and sailed right over it, carrying Diana. By the time Gus was close enough to touch the vines, the god—and Diana—had vanished.

"HEY!" Gus shouted. "Open up! Let us in! Where are you taking her? Hey!"

He wanted to pound his fists against something, but there was no door here; only twisting branches, gold leaves, and thorns of every shape and size, from clusters of deadly points as tiny as acupuncture needles to jagged spikes as long as a car to hooked claws like a hawk's talons. There was nothing he could safely punch.

"Where'd he go?" Tigre waded up beside him, and Gus felt a violent impulse to turn and bash the other avatar in the face. The desire was so strong that he had to kneel and bury his hands in the sand below the water to control himself.

"Gus, are you okay?" Tigre asked. Gus realized that he was shaking, and he rubbed his wet hands along the ridges of the tattoos on his arms to try and stop.

"Yeah," he said in a strangled voice. This was no time to suddenly become the crazy homicidal avatar. *That's Kali's job.* "He took Diana. We have to get in there."

"We will," Tigre said.

The water went all the way up to the fence, and as far as Gus could tell, the hedge extended down into the sand, as if it was growing from the ocean floor itself. He pulled out the axe Kali had given him. Cautiously he slid forward and swung the axe at the longest thorn, a black needle as thick as a fist with a sharp tip directly at the level of his heart.

The axe sliced smoothly through the thorn, lopping off the last foot of it. A wild shriek pierced the air, and Gus stumbled back. The hedge seemed to contract, squeezing in around the injured thorn, and then sprang back into position. A long golden vine swarmed down a branch and along the thorn to the missing end, wrapping itself around the tip. Gus saw three drops of dark purple . . . what? sap? blood? . . . fall into the ocean. Then the thorn sighed softly, and a new point sprouted from the end, longer and sharper than before.

"Tell me you saw that too," Gus said to Tigre.

"Oh yeah," Tigre said from farther out in the water. "I'm not going anywhere near that thing."

"What did you do?" Kali shouted, splashing through the water toward them.

"I tried to get through the hedge," Gus said defensively. "Isn't that what we're here to do?"

"Not if it's going to scream about it," Kali said.

"And bleed," Tigre added helpfully.

"Please," Gus said. "You would have done the exact same thing, admit it. I mean, *you* gave me the axe."

"Yeah, but I didn't tell you to go slashing at strange things with it," Kali snapped. "You couldn't try knocking or something first?"

"On what?" Gus said, waving the axe at the hedge. Was it his imagination, or did the hedge bristle at him? "That god took Diana over there!"

"So presumably he's expecting us to follow him," Kali said. "It's not like they have any particular reason to be kidnapping Greek goddesses."

A whole host of reasons popped into Gus's head, all of them nefarious and sinister and most of them involving African gods stealing Diana's powers and killing her.

"LET US IN!" he bellowed angrily.

Kali grabbed his arm before he could attack the hedge again. "Stop being an idiot," she said. "There must be a way in, or *Skidbladnir* wouldn't have stopped here."

"It didn't stop here," Tigre said. "It stopped over there." He pointed to the sandbar.

Kali paused, then snapped her fingers. "Tigre, you're a genius," she said. She let go of Gus and began wading out to the sandbar. Tigre followed her, looking bashfully pleased.

Gus didn't know what was happening to him. The raised edges of his tattoos were prickling, as if fire ants were running along them. He just wanted to find the six-eyed god and *murder* him.

"Stop it," he whispered to himself, opening and closing his fists. He paused and glanced up to see that Kali and Tigre were out of earshot. "Oro, if that's you, *back down*."

A strange, dark laughter bubbled up from inside him and he found himself chuckling in a malevolent way that didn't sound anything like Gus.

Terrified, Gus clutched his throat. A moment passed, and nothing else followed the laughter. He looked at his hands again and realized that now he felt more scared than angry. Whatever that was, Oro had apparently subsided.

God, I hope he stays that way.

Gus caught up to Kali and Tigre on the sandbar. They were standing at one end of it, where there was an oval depression, like an eye in a needle. Sand was pouring into it, disappearing in a cloud of tiny sparkling particles. Tigre no longer looked pleased.

"Please tell me you're not thinking what you're thinking," he said to Kali.

"We're going in!" she said with a grin.

"What if it's just ordinary quicksand?" Tigre pleaded. "What if we jump into it and die and—"

Kali clamped a hand over his mouth. "I don't want to hear about Thor finding our shiny white bones," she said sternly. "This is obviously magical—look at how the whole sandbar is shrinking as it collapses into it. That's not normal. I don't think."

"How about one of us goes through and then signals the others that it's okay?" Gus suggested.

"All right," Kali said. "Someone hold my hand and I'll go in. I'll give it two squeezes if I think it's okay, one if I want you to pull me back out."

Gus stepped forward and took her hand. Kali gave him a nod and stepped slowly down the edge of the depression, through the sliding sands. At the center of the oval, she took a deep breath and sank below the sand. Gus lay down along the edge and leaned out, giving her as much distance as possible. The sand was warm and impossibly white, even from up close. He felt it close around his hand, tickling his wrist like a rising wave of tiny spiders. Then he felt Kali give two quick squeezes and let go. He released her and pulled his hand back, rolling clear of the hole.

"What happened?" Tigre demanded anxiously. "Did you drop her? Did the sand suck her under?"

"She squeezed twice," Gus said. "I guess that means it's okay." He stood up, brushed off his clothes, and walked forward into the depression.

"Really?" he heard Tigre say. "Should one of us wait here? What if it isn't—"

Then there was a *swoomp* sound and Gus fell through sand—sand going up his nose, sand filling his ears, sand catching in his hair. It was like shooting down a water-slide filled with sand. He couldn't breathe, and even though they were closed, his eyes stung with pain as grains of sand tried to force their way under the lids.

Gus shot into open air in a spray of white sand and landed with a thud, rolling head over heels down a long hill of sand. He threw out his arms and legs to try and stop his slide, but the slope was too steep, and he kept rolling until he hit something tall and hard with a bone-jarring crash.

"Yikes," Kali said.

"OW." Gus pushed himself to sitting, his whole body aching, and brushed the sand out of his eyes until he could see the blurry outline of Kali standing over him. She had let her hair down and was shaking her head, trying to get all the sand out of it.

"That was graceful," Kali said. "Glad I didn't hit one of

those." She jerked her head at the pillar that had stopped Gus's headlong tumble. He squinted at it, then around at the rest of the room, then shook his head again. There must be more sand in his eyes than he'd realized.

"No, you're seeing what you're seeing," Kali said. "I've been doing the same thing."

The room they were in was less of a room and more of a hotel lobby, except instead of gleaming marble staircases and potted ferns, it had a large ship in the middle of the room and tall Doric columns all around the walls. Gus remembered enough of Greek history to recognize the shape of the columns.

"But those are Greek," he said. "We're in Africa. Not even the side of Africa close to Greece."

"Well, we're nowhere near any icebergs, either," Kali said, "and yet somehow *that* is there." She pointed.

Gus finally read the name on the side of the ship. He climbed to his feet, shaking his head.

"That's impossible," he said. "James Cameron went down and explored the whole thing. I saw it on TV. And it's broken in half, not whole like that."

Kali shrugged. "We are talking about gods here," she said. "They can probably do anything they want. Especially without people around to stop them."

Gus turned, looking back at the giant mound of sand covering their end of the room. It stretched almost all the way up the wall to a hole at the top, where sand was flying out in a continuous spray.

"YAAAAAAAAAAAAAAAAAAAAAAAAAAAAA!!!! !!!!"

Tigre shot out of the wall, bouncing and sliding down the slope the way Gus had. But instead of crashing into a column, he made it to the part where the sand leveled out and slid to a sprawling stop near their feet on the mottled green marble floor.

"Nice work, Tigre," Kali said, seizing his hand and hauling him up.

"You lied!" he gasped when he could breathe again. "You couldn't have known this was here from how far down Gus lowered you."

Gus realized that was true; she would still have been in the sand tunnel when she squeezed his hand.

Kali shrugged. "Well, lucky that it is here, then, right?"

Tigre huffed in outrage, showering sand in all directions. "But—but—wait . . . is that—?" He pointed at the *Titanic* in disbelief.

"Yup. And I think that might be a Gauguin painting," Kali said, pointing at the side wall, where a Polynesian-looking woman lounged among bright red flowers.

"If they were going to steal famous artwork," Gus mused, "I wonder why they wouldn't go with, like, the *Mona Lisa*."

"BAH!" shouted a voice from above them. "Da Vinci, bah! Gauguin is the only Western artist worth owning! And it isn't stealing—the riches of the world are mine by right!" They all whirled around, and Gus spotted the speaker standing on a balcony that overlooked the great ship, facing the wall with the Gauguin painting. It looked like a woman, with dark green skin and wild green hair and strange fishy legs. She pointed to the far end of the hall.

"Now go! I don't want you here and I'm only letting you through because Obatala promised me a weaving I want, but I'm tempted to change my mind, so get out!" Her hair rose up around her face like waves crashing against rocks.

"Wait, who—" Tigre started to say, but Kali gave him a shove toward the giant green doors at the other end of the hall.

"Don't argue with the angry sea goddess," she said. "Come on, run." She raced down the hall and Gus followed, staring around him as they ran. Strange treasures were piled everywhere—chests overflowing with gold coins, giant iron anchors the size of two men, elegant silk ball gowns, some with the skeletons of the drowned still in them. He shuddered and ran faster.

A smaller door was set in the large doors, and Kali grabbed the iron ring on it and yanked it open as Gus and Tigre caught up to her. On the other side was a winding wooden staircase, encased in more wood, as if it went up through the trunk of a tree. *Perhaps it does*, Gus thought. He jumped ahead of Kali, taking the stairs two at a time. He could feel the footsteps of the other two shaking the stairs as they pounded up, around and around until he felt dizzy and winded.

"More stairs," he heard Tigre whimper.

"Chin up, storm god," Kali said. "It's shorter than the Empire State Building. Look, you can see the light at the top already. Plus, bonus, no big glass pterodactyl waiting for us."

True, but who knows what else there might be, Gus

thought. The light had a juicy orange quality, as if they were climbing into a mango. He could also feel heat pouring down from above, chasing away any chills from the underwater palace. He was sweating by the time he reached the top and climbed out of what appeared to be, when he turned around to help Kali out, the stump of a tree trunk.

In the center of a plaza. In the middle of a giant, sprawling, beautiful city unlike anything Gus had ever imagined.

Kali's eyes were wide with surprise as she emerged. Gus gave Tigre a hand out and they stood together, facing the crowd.

The city was full of people.

EIGHTEEN YEARS AGO . . .

"The hounds are going to miss you."

The bright, constant light of Mount Olympus shone around them, creeping through the walls of the stable, catching the gold in Apollo's hair, and the red in hers. Diana tugged on Manslayer's ears and he scrambled up to lick her face, knocking her back into the straw.

"They'll be all right," she said, wrestling with the large gray dog until she had him pinned. His tail thumped on the wooden floor, and the other two hounds nosed at her shoulder, wanting to play as well. "Once I'm gone, they'll forget all about me."

Apollo rubbed his head, looking worried. "I'm going to miss you too, Diana. And I'm not going to forget about you."

"Please," Diana said. "You'll get to see me all the time. And then you'll come down and be my guide and we'll get to hang out on Earth just like we used to. Too bad there won't be any mortals to hunt. I mean, except the old kind, which are boring because they don't run fast enough."

Apollo winced. "We're supposed to be helping them, not hunting them."

"Why?" Diana said. "It's not like they've ever done anything for us. Not lately. Not since the sacrifices stopped." She sat up, and all three hounds curled themselves around her, as if they knew what was happening and were trying to keep her there, with them, where she'd always be safe and never have to die. "I miss the sacrifices," she said wistfully. "Ripe olives and splashing wine and golden bulls and sometimes a wayward man, if he bothered my priestesses at the wrong time."

"I hope you don't talk like that when you're human," Apollo said. "They'll lock you up in one of their boxes for prophets and lunatics."

"Well, I won't remember any of this, will I?" Diana said. "That'll be peculiar. I'll have to spend a lot of time with mortals." She shuddered. "Mortal boys, *yuck. I hope I'll at least remember that I don't like them."*

"Maybe you'll find out that you actually do," Apollo suggested. She climbed to her feet, dislodging the dogs, and brushed gold strands of straw off her robe.

"No, Apollo," Diana said. "This is not a humanitarian mission of understanding and becoming one with our worshippers, all right? This is about punishing them and regaining power. That's it. I will never never be like those goddesses who fall in love with mere mortals and get all swoony and stupid around them."

"Well, except there was that one guy—" Apollo started, and she kicked him in the shins.

"Shut up with the ancient history," Diana ordered. "Anyway, I was never swoony about Orion. Not like featherbrained Venus is about her men. This morning at breakfast she tried to convince me that affairs with mortals are more exciting

than you'd think. And then Mars winked at her from the doorway, and she skipped away blithely as if Vulcan and all the rest of us don't know exactly what they're up to. After all these centuries. Gross." She pulled the leather tie from her hair and shook it loose. "Love makes you blind and irritating and empty-headed; she's the clearest proof of that." Diana tied her hair up again, scratched each of the dogs on their heads, and strode out the stable door.

Apollo followed, feeling as if his sister was slipping through his fingers like rays of sunlight. Thousands of years together, and he still lost every argument with her. And now this might be the last time he saw her. Even with divine protection, anything could happen to her in her mortal form between now and the change. How would someone like Diana fit into the human world? Wouldn't her divinity shine through her, exposing her? How could anyone look at her and not know that she was a goddess?

Diana turned and smacked him on the forehead.

"Ow!" Apollo yelped, jumping back. "What was that for?"

"Giving me moony eyes," Diana said. "I could feel you doing it. Like you're never going to see me again, blah blah, tragic face. It's not the end of the world, Apollo."

"Oh yeah?" Apollo said, putting his hands on his hips. "What if you lose? Then some other god will be in charge, we'll have to do whatever they say, and, oh yeah, you'll be dead. Dead, *Diana—can you even wrap your brain around that? How final it is?"*

"I'm not going to lose," Diana said. "Besides, no one else would do it."

"That's because they're all smart enough to be scared of mortality," Apollo grumbled.

"Stop worrying," Diana said, starting to walk across the courtyard again. "I'll be back in seventeen years, and I'll still be me, only with more power. Won't that be fun? Imagine me in charge of the universe. First I'll outlaw falling in love. Maybe I'll get rid of men altogether—Zeus could probably populate the planet by himself anyway. And we'll tear down all these city spires that poke the clouds and choke the trees. Nothing but natural wilderness as far as the gods can see. Like the old days." She spun as she walked, her red hair flying out behind her, grinning at Apollo. "Tribes hunting, procreating for children but without the nonsense of relationships, and of course deer everywhere, everywhere, dancing in the streets. You wait and see. I'll win, and everything will be wonderful."

This wasn't exactly Apollo's idea of the perfect world, but it was infinitely preferable to one without Diana in it.

He managed a smile, trusting the brightness of his sun to hide the worry in his eyes. "I know you will," he said. "It'll be perfect."

Abyss of Lost Souls

This time the first thing Diana heard in the darkness was a soft *shhh-shhhhush*ing noise. It sounded like someone brushing palm fronds across the floor, but as she walked closer, her nose picked up a wild, fresh, salty smell in the air, and she realized that she was hearing the ocean.

Something brushed against her foot, and she jumped sideways, landing with a splash in shallow water that soaked her sneakers. She crouched and trailed her hand through the warm water, feeling small waves flow around her fingers.

After a moment, she noticed that she could see indistinct outlines around her. The dim light was greenish and murky, and it seemed to emanate from the water instead of the sky, as if pods of glowing green jellyfish were skating along below the surface. It looked like she was in a flooded valley, surrounded by the large, distant shapes of mountains.

A faint trail of light through the water in front of her looked like a path, so she followed it, water squishing through her soles. Soon the path ended abruptly, and even with her careful footwork she nearly stepped right into a vast abyss that suddenly yawned in front of her, disappearing into darkness below.

She examined her surroundings in the greenish light, wondering if she could get around the abyss, but it stretched from one end of the valley to the other. *Perhaps I'm supposed to go into it?*

Next to the edge of the crater was a flat wooden board propped against a pile of rocks. A long, thick woven rope of vines was attached to the middle of it, vanishing into the rocks. She turned it around in her hands a few times, testing the strength of the vines. They felt powerful, and they didn't snap or fray when she tugged on them.

She tried sitting on the board with her legs on either side of the vine rope. It was kind of like a swing, except with one rope instead of two.

Diana had an idea. The downside was that she might end up plummeting into the abyss, and for all she knew it was the unpleasantly endless kind. But she had to keep going forward, and this could be the way dead souls got to this underworld.

She slung the rope around the largest, heaviest boulder. At the short end was the board, which she sat on with her feet braced against the wet, slippery wall of the abyss. The other loop of the rope she held in her hands so she could lower herself down a bit at a time.

To her surprise, it seemed to work. The hardest part was scooting backward over the edge, not knowing if the rock would hold or if she could keep herself balanced.

But once she got used to the strangeness of the movement, she found she could walk herself down the wall fairly smoothly.

"Nice," she whispered to herself. "Points for the dead girl." She felt a pang of guilt from the beating her self-esteem had taken at the Mirror of Retribution. *Arrogant, gossipy, cruel, selfish, thoughtless, ambitious* . . . just as self-involved and shallow as the other gods and goddesses of the Greco-Roman pantheon.

It was unfortunately easy to think of other things the mirror might have shown as well. She could have been nicer to Andrew, Gus's brother. She could have been nicer to Gus at first, too.

Her arms began to ache, and she had to stop and rest a few times because she felt so light-headed. She couldn't remember the last time she'd eaten anything.

She had been moving steadily downward for about an hour, she guessed, when suddenly the rope jerked and stopped abruptly. Her mind had wandered, letting the vines slide through her hands, so she nearly lost it and had to scramble to grab the free rope with both hands. She tugged on it, but nothing came.

Well. This is brilliant. She had no idea how much farther down she had to go. She tried yanking on the rope to move herself up, but her tired muscles didn't want to grapple with a new, more difficult exercise. She rested her arms in the loop of the rope and let herself hang for a moment with a sigh.

I can certainly see the appeal in immortality, if it means not having to go through this nonsense after you die.

Suddenly the rope jerked under her arms. She looked up at the pale green light far above her and thought she caught a glimpse of movement. Was there someone up there?

The answer came from the rope, which was suddenly yanked out of her hands. The swing started to drop, and with a panicked cry, Diana wrapped herself around the rope and closed her eyes.

The swing stopped with another jerk, banging her into the wall with a jolt of pain in her knees. After a moment, Diana opened her eyes again.

The rock wall was gliding past a few inches from her face. The swing was being lowered into the abyss by whoever was up above.

Okay, thanks, but wasn't there a way to do that without frightening me nearly to death? Her heart was still pounding, and she wondered if she could trust her mystery helper not to drop her.

Fortunately, she didn't have to worry about it for long. Soon her feet brushed against a sandy floor, and the swing halted, swaying gently against the wet rocks in a cavern full of the sound of splashing and burbling. She could see lizards darting across the floor and skittering under rocks.

Gingerly Diana climbed off the swing, her legs aching. She staggered for a moment and then sat down on the sand, rubbing her sore muscles. The light was a little brighter down here, but still green and murky, and she couldn't hear anything but the water, so it took her quite by surprise when she suddenly noticed that the cavern was full of people.

Weirdly, they seemed sort of liquid, as if when she touched them her hand would go straight through and if they fell over they'd splash out into giant puddles. They were all staring at her with expressions of mild surprise.

"That can't be right," commented a tall, brown-skinned man with dark hair. He turned to the woman sitting behind him on the ledges of rock around the cavern. "Are we seeing things again?"

She had long dark hair and an ugly, oddly masculine face with green tattoos carved into her chin. "It seems real," she said, blinking. "But it can't be."

"I mean, who would it be?" said the man. "How would it get here? What would it want from us? Would it even know of us? I thought no one knew of us anymore."

"It doesn't seem to know of us," the woman said, peering at Diana.

A man across the cavern sniffed loudly. "It doesn't smell dead, either," he offered.

"You're right!" said the first woman. "I think it's still alive."

"Almost dead, though," said the first man. "If it dies in here, I bet we could keep it."

"I'm not an it," Diana said. "I'm Diana, and I'm looking for a way back to my life."

"I think you went the wrong way," said the woman, tapping her tattooed chin. "Perhaps you don't know this, but the underworld is down and the living world is up." She jabbed her finger toward the top of the abyss. "Hence the term 'underworld.'"

"Yes—I mean, I figured that," Diana said. "But I'm

kind of stuck in the loop of underworlds, and I'm trying to find one that I can get through so I can get out, instead of going on to the next."

"I doubt this is that one," said the first man. "All we can do from here is watch."

"Where is here?" Diana asked.

A hubbub of voices rose from the crowd around her, all giving her different answers, as far as she could tell. They fell silent again, and she looked at the pair that had spoken first, confused.

"It's hard to remember," said the man. "We have no more believers, and since the last wave of so many millions of souls at once, we've had no visitors either. There are none of us left up there, and there haven't been for too many years. By all rights we should have popped out of existence completely, but instead we're just fading away."

"I think I was once called Rohe," said the woman dreamily. "Goddess of the underworld."

"I might have been Milu," said the man. "Or Elo. Or Tawhaiki. A king by many names, for many peoples."

"There used to be many different underworlds and many different gods," Rohe said, "but with so much lost and forgotten, we that remained drifted together."

"You're the Polynesians," Diana realized. "Your people were wiped out so you couldn't participate in the avatar battle."

Rohe smiled thinly. "You know about that?"

"Perhaps she's one of them," Milu said, narrowing his eyes.

"It wasn't my idea," Diana said quickly. "I think it's awful, what they did to you—what they've done to everyone, to the whole world."

"But you're an avatar?" Rohe asked, leaning forward.

Diana wondered what would happen if all these watery people jumped her at once. Would she drown? "Y-yes," she admitted.

Milu's face lit up. "Do you know Oro?" he asked.

"Oro," Diana said. "You mean Gus—yeah, I definitely know Gus."

"Come, come here into the light," Rohe insisted, standing and stepping forward to take Diana's hand. Her hand didn't melt in Diana's, but it was damp and softer than normal flesh. She led Diana to a spot where iridescent moss glowed a brighter green than elsewhere in the cavern. As she turned Diana toward the light, she let out a small gasp.

"It's her!" Rohe announced. "The one we've been watching with Oro."

"What?" Milu sprang down from his perch and came over to examine Diana's face. The other spirits crowded up behind him, their interest in Diana suddenly rising. It felt like the time her manager, Doug, had accidentally signed her up for a local news station's early morning show, where they almost never got real celebrities, and everyone was so busy staring at her in awe that they could barely come up with anything to talk to her about.

"How have you been watching us?" Diana asked, trying to deflect their attention.

"In the waterfall," Rohe said, pointing to a cascade of

water on the far side of the cavern. "That's all we can do—watch the living."

"In the old days," another woman said, her voice full of nostalgia, "we could sometimes turn the living into stone if we stared at them hard enough."

"But we hardly ever did," Milu said hurriedly, seeing Diana's expression.

"Can you still watch them?" Diana asked, hope leaping inside her. "Could we see what Gus is doing right now?"

Several of the spirits started clapping, and Rohe smiled. "Certainly. With your energy here, believing we exist, we might even be able to see more than a minute of time."

Diana followed the tattooed woman to the waterfall, which fell in a long, clear, glassy sheet to the sand, where the water disappeared in a small puff of smoke. Rohe took one of Diana's hands and Milu took the other, without asking. Diana felt a bit weird about that, especially since it felt kind of like holding hands with sponges, but she didn't want to be rude and pull free.

Silence filled the cavern, and Diana could almost feel the weight of all the spirits' eyes gazing at the waterfall. Slowly, an image began to form—blurred at first, but gradually clearing.

Diana inhaled sharply. It was Gus, in a strange jungle city, and he was kneeling beside her body. *Her body*. She had a moment of panic, and then her mind seemed to shift sideways, and what she was seeing no longer seemed real. It was like watching one of her music videos after recording it: just an image on a screen. *This would be a pretty depressing song, I'm guessing.*

Gus looked grim and tired with streaks of dirt along his face and arms. As they all watched, Kali came up beside him with a gesture. There was no sound, but Gus shook his head and tightened his grip on Diana's hand. With a shrug, Kali stepped forward and began speaking to the African man in white robes who was standing in front of them.

"So they made it to Africa?" Diana asked.

"We don't know for sure," Rohe answered. "But it looks like it."

Tigre was standing behind Gus, looking hot and uncomfortable. He swatted at a fly that was buzzing near him, and then nearly jumped into the nearest tree when the fly suddenly turned into a big-eyed person and glared at him.

"One of their earth spirits," Milu said to Diana. "They can transform back and forth as much as they like now, with no mortals to see them."

"Where are they going?" Diana wondered. "And what are they going to do with me?"

The image wavered. "Wait," Diana said, letting go of Milu's hand and reaching for the waterfall. "I want to see more."

But it was gone. "That's more than we can usually do in a day," Rohe said. "But we have seen you before. Oro could work well with you, if he knew how to be a partner and not just a leader."

"Tell us about him," said another one of the men on

the rocks behind them. "What is he like? What is his mortal like?"

"Um," Diana said. "Well, I don't know if I can tell you which part of him is Oro, but Gus is funny, and smart, and brave—really brave. Too brave, sometimes, I think."

Milu nodded. "That sounds like Oro."

"And he's warm and kind, and stubborn, and he cares a lot about his family; more than anything else, I think, even though all he has . . . *had* left is Andrew. He's kind of sad, deep down, but in a quiet way. It's not the kind of sad that wants attention or comforting. It's the kind that knows it can't be comforted and so it stays quiet."

"Oro lost his family too," Rohe said. "He is a warrior, and too strong to admit it, but he must miss us."

"Gus is a fighter too," Diana said. "I don't think he'd ever give up if he really cared about something."

"So is Oro," Milu said proudly. "Maui found him a good match."

"We were lucky," Rohe pointed out. "We had to take whatever we could get."

"You were lucky," Diana agreed. "Gus is . . . Gus is awesome."

Rohe beamed, and the rest of the spirits in the cavern seemed to be shimmering with happiness. "Maybe there is hope for us, then," Milu said. "Maybe he'll win the battle and restore us."

Diana remembered Gus in New York before his fight with Amon, arguing about how he didn't want to win any battles or become immortal or rule the world. He just wanted to survive, go home, and have his regular human life growing up with his brother and a world full of other regular human people. She knew the gods here couldn't understand that. They believed in Gus; she should let them.

"Well," said Rohe, stroking her tattooed chin again with a cheerful smile, "I was planning to keep you here for the novelty of having a new person around."

"But I think we agree that you'd be more useful to Oro alive than dead," Milu said, nodding. Diana was surprised to hear that—to win the battle, wouldn't he have to kill her eventually? But she certainly wasn't about to point that out. She did not want to stay here for the rest of eternity, watching snatches of real life in a waterfall and eating lizards.

"Can you help me get back to life?" she asked hopefully, but Milu and Rohe were already shaking their heads.

"I'm sorry," said Rohe. "That's far beyond our power right now."

"I don't even know how we'll get you out of this cavern," Milu said. "The paths all lead down to other caverns full of more dead souls."

"I can go back up on the swing," Diana suggested. "If whoever lowered me down is still there to pull me back up."

Rohe and Milu exchanged glances. "Who did that?" Rohe asked.

"I don't know," Diana said. "I couldn't see who it was."

Rohe exhaled angrily, scowling, which made her face even uglier. "It was probably my bastard husband."

"Still?" Milu grumbled.

"He won't stay dead!" Rohe said, throwing up her hands. "No matter how many times I kill him. Oh, I could just strangle him with my bare hands. Why should he get to wander around up there while we're all trapped down here?"

"He was always like that," said another woman in a fawning voice. "He could do whatever he wanted." She had a moonstruck look on her face, and Rohe glared at her with such venom, Diana was surprised the woman didn't keel over from the force of it.

"Don't you fall for his tricks," Rohe said, poking Diana's chest with her finger, which didn't hurt as much as Diana would have expected because her finger just went *squish* and left a damp spot on Diana's shirt. "He's charming, yes, and he's certainly beautiful, but do you know why? Because he *stole my face*!" She pointed at her ugly features. "This is what he should look like! This! And instead he's cavorting around the world with my beautiful face. It's unspeakable."

"And yet you speak about it quite a lot," Milu pointed out. Rohe glared at him, too.

Well, the gods certainly have more interesting domestic disputes than we do, Diana thought. *My husband stole my face . . . Jerry Springer would love it.*

"You've been warned," Rohe said to Diana, leading her back to the swing. "If it is him, run as far and as fast as you can."

"How will I know if it's him?" Diana asked, sitting on the swing and wrapping her arms and legs around the rope again. Her weight pulled the vine rope down, and with an answering tug, the swing started to ascend up the wall of the cavern.

"His name is Maui," Rohe called after her. "Don't trust him, whatever you do."

"Thank you for coming!" Milu called. "Please come again when you're completely dead!"

Diana watched the crowd of spirits, faces upturned and glowing in the green light, as they slowly vanished into the depths, until all she could see was darkness below and the faint glow of the mountains above.

Who was pulling her up? Was he friend or foe? She was putting a lot of trust in him or her already, not that she had much choice.

As the top drew closer, Diana braced herself to run if she had to. Then a strong brown hand reached down, wrapped around her wrist, and hauled her over the edge.

Diana rolled away and scrambled to her feet, brushing the damp sand from her clothes. The guy standing opposite her looked no older than she was. He was compactly built with riotous curly black hair, twinkling brown eyes, a flat nose, and the hugest grin she'd ever seen. He looked a little like a Samoan bodyguard she'd once had. His was the friendliest face she'd seen since her death—maybe the friendliest face she'd *ever* seen.

Please don't tell me you're Maui, she thought as he held out his hand and beamed at her.

"Hiya," he said with a cute New Zealand accent. "Nice to finally meet you, Diana. I'm Maui."

• • ● • •

If you cleared a swath of jungle and planted seeds of mahogany, ivory, gold, kudzu vines, mangoes, spiderwebs, lizards, bananas, crocodiles, waterfalls, baobab, and leopard fur, the city that sprouted from them might look a lot like the place where Tigre, Gus, and Kali now found themselves.

The houses seemed to have grown up out of the dark, rich earth, tree trunks twisting into walls, vines weaving into roofs, delicate strands of dewy cobwebs fluttering over windows like the ghosts of curtains. Banana trees grew between each of the houses, heavy with bright yellow fruit and alive with lizards darting behind the wide leaves. Tigre could hear the murmur of water everywhere as small rivers wound through the city, bubbling under bridges and circling around the houses.

Short-haired brown dogs, long and sleek and looking well fed, rolled playfully in the dirt yards with sharp-toothed, fluffy-faced leopard cubs. Tigre felt a twinge of sadness, missing the dogs at the veterinary clinic. He wondered if anyone had played with them after he disappeared. He saw a zebra and an antelope trot between the houses, their heads lowered toward each other as if they were gossiping about the weather and Aunt Tilly's arthritis.

Wide stone avenues spiraled off from the plaza where they stood, forming a web that connected all the tallest buildings. The closest large building, up on a small hill at one end of the plaza, was a shining white house that looked like it might have been carved out of one giant piece of ivory, which Tigre knew was impossible—no elephant's tusk was that big. But it all fit together like it had grown that way, with large windows on all sides and a small stream running right through the house. He could see other buildings towering over the trees in the distance, including one that looked like the stepped stone pyramids of the Mayans and one like a wooden needle shooting up into the clouds.

He wondered again what had happened to Quetzie and glanced up at the sky. It looked strange—bright blue, but too close, as if it had come down to be closer to the beautiful city. He reached up toward it, feeling like he could almost touch it . . . but that was silly; the sky was just air. There was nothing to touch, surely. And yet it almost felt as if his fingers brushed something soft, like an invisible carpet above them.

But in all this strangeness, there was nothing stranger than the people. There were people *everywhere*—milking goats, carrying water jugs, strolling down the avenues with baskets on their arms or balanced easily on their heads. He guessed there were probably thousands of them living in the city.

Most of them seemed to be gathered in the plaza, surrounding the tree trunk that he and Kali and Gus had climbed out of. Tigre hadn't seen so many people in one place since the change that had brought him forward in time. Even the colony of Forever Youngermen that he'd run into in Mexico had had no more than a hundred members, and when the gods had gathered to watch the battles, there had never been more than about fifty of them at once. And these people weren't ancient survivors from before the change; none of them looked particularly old.

"If the rest of the world stopped reproducing, why didn't they?" Tigre whispered.

"That's assuming those are humans," Gus whispered back.

"I'm guessing not," Kali murmured. "Check out their eyes."

Tigre had thought at first that their eyes were just strangely large, but now he could see that they had enormous dark pupils filling the whole eyeball, blocking out any white or other colors. But around their eyes they had chalk-white outlines like thick reverse-colored eyeliner. He couldn't tell if it was natural or painted on, but it had the effect of making their eyes look like they covered half of their faces.

A thin, long-limbed young woman near the front of the crowd gave a little hop and disappeared. Where she had been standing there was now a pale green frog, which bounced away toward the white house. Tigre glanced at Gus and Kali, wondering if they'd seen that too, but neither of them reacted.

"Hello?" Kali said, stepping forward. "Are you all gods?"

Some of the people in the crowd laughed. One tall man turned toward the white house, cupped one hand around his mouth, and bellowed: "OBATALA! They're here!"

"They're so flimsy," said a stout woman with a wide smile and small ears. She grinned at them with unevenly spaced teeth. "I always thought they'd be the size of trees."

"Silly," said another woman, shoving her. "Avatars are gods in human form, remember? They'd stand out a bit if they looked like trees!" Tigre thought this was kind of funny, since the woman speaking looked a bit like a tree herself. Her skin was mottled like bark, her hair was gathered into a puff at the top of her head, and she wore long vines draped over her shoulders on top of her bright green robes.

Tigre noticed a girl standing behind the arguing women. She seemed to be staring at Tigre, although when he met her eyes she looked away quickly. She looked no older than he was, with skin the color of burned copper, redder than the others'. She was small and round, with a sweet face surrounded by a fluffy halo of reddish-black hair, and a body made of globes and ovals. He was surprised to realize that he found her pretty—she was just about the opposite of skinny, sharp-edged, pale, blond Vicky, or exotically beautiful Anna.

"Where's our friend?" Gus demanded. "Where did he take her?"

"Who?" said the stout woman.

"Mister Six-Eyes," said Gus, his voice rising. "He said his name was Shango. He flew off with our friend Diana. Didn't he bring her in here?"

"I'm just teasing you," the woman said, clapping him on the shoulder. The crowd chuckled again. "She's over here."

The tree stump where they stood was in the center of

a circle of fat baobab trees, and as several of the onlookers stepped aside, Tigre saw Diana lying in the shade of one of them. Underneath her was a moss-covered mound that looked as if it had pressed its way out of the ground in exactly the right shape to fit her. A woven blue and black blanket had been spread over it for her to lie on. She was pale and still, and Shango stood beside her, his arms folded.

Gus ran over and knelt on the blanket beside her, taking her wrist to feel her pulse. Tigre saw the round-faced girl press her hands to her chest and make a sympathetic face. He followed Kali over and stood awkwardly as she crouched next to Gus.

"We need help," Gus said, looking up at the people surrounding him. "Please—she's dying."

Several of them nodded in agreement. "She sure is," said a thin, jumpy man with two twists of hair like antelope horns. "Look how stretched her spirit is; you can see right through it."

"Here comes Obatala," said the stout woman, shooing people back from Diana to clear a path for the man who was striding down from the white house. He was taller than all the rest and wore shining, clean white robes, which stood out starkly against the darkness of his skin. He also had normal, dark brown eyes. The others all stood back respectfully as he walked through and looked down at Diana and Gus.

"So, Shango," the new man said to the six-eyed god, "I see you decided to let them through."

"I SENT BACK THE MEDDLING GODS," Shango

said, "BUT THE SHIP BORE ONLY FOUR OF THEIR AVATARS. IF THEY ARE TROUBLE, I THINK WE CAN HANDLE THEM."

"Four," Obatala mused. "I see the dying girl is Greco-Roman, and the other girl-child is the Indian avatar. Is this young man Mesoamerican?" He reached out and tugged on a tuft of Tigre's hair with a curious expression. "And who is this one?" He leaned down to do the same to Gus, who ducked instinctively away.

"Um, yeah," Gus said. "That's Kali and Tigre, and this is Diana, and I'm Gus . . . um, sir."

"Gus," Obatala responded. "I don't believe I'm familiar with a god named 'Gus.'"

"Obatala," the antelope man interrupted, "look—look carefully at these two."

Obatala squinted at Diana and Gus. After a moment his face went still, and he said, "Ah, yes. I see."

"See what?" Gus asked.

Everyone, including the copper-skinned girl, was staring at Gus and Diana now with fascinated looks on their faces. Tigre felt insignificant, but he was used to that. Even in his real life, he'd never been anyone special; why should things be different now that he was allegedly a god?

"They have twin spirits inside them," the stout woman said, lightly moving her hand through the air above Gus's head. "They are both twofold, but in one."

The others nodded. It was hard to read their faces, especially with their strange eyes. Tigre couldn't tell if having twin spirits was a good thing or a bad thing.

Obatala touched his finger to Gus's chin and tilted the

avatar's face up. "In this one they struggle. It is a recent and somewhat unwilling twinship, like two birds sharing one nest—until one is large enough to push the other out. But in that one they are interwoven," he said, pointing to Diana. "They are like trees grown so close together their trunks have merged into one."

Tigre wondered if Diana saw it that way, or if she thought of Venus and Diana as being two completely separate, warring parts of her. He had never thought of Gus and Diana as having similar problems before.

"I am Obatala," the white-robed man said. "Father of the orishas." He gestured to the villagers around him.

"Orishas?" Kali asked. "What does that mean?"

"Orishas are the spirits of the world," Obatala said. "They represent all the elements of nature. I created them along with humankind."

"Oh," Gus said, sounding disappointed. "So they're not human. There aren't any humans here?"

"Not many," Obatala said. "This is our home now, as it once was. That was the bargain we made with your gods, and you were supposed to leave us alone." For the first time Tigre saw the possibility of something terrifying in the white-robed god—this was not someone you wanted to anger, and the bad news was that they probably already had.

Kali stood up. "We're sorry to trespass on your land. We had to find somewhere where our pantheons couldn't follow."

"THEY'D BETTER NOT," said Shango.

"Why are you hiding from your gods?" Obatala asked.

"Shouldn't you four be trying to kill each other instead?"

"We don't want to," Gus said. "We want to get back to our own world and our families."

"We want to know what's really going on," Kali added.

"Instead of being gods?" Obatala said. "How odd. Well, you can't do it here. Unfold your ship and go."

"Wait, please," Gus pleaded. "We'll leave if you want, but can't you please help Diana first? She—I'm afraid she'll die if we don't get help soon."

The orishas nodded again. "Remember the twin spirit," the same woman said to Obatala. "It's sacred and we must protect it."

Obatala shook his head. "She is not *our* twin spirit," he said. "We're not responsible for her. And these avatars could be dangerous."

"PFFT," said Shango, the six-eyed god from the sky. "WE CAN EASILY DEFEAT THEM. YOU, BOY," he said to Tigre, who jumped with surprise. "AREN'T YOU A THUNDER GOD?"

"Well," Tigre said hesitantly, "I guess."

"THEN LET'S DUEL!" Shango bellowed enthusiastically.

"He's a thunder god too?" Kali asked, jerking her thumb at Shango. Obatala nodded. "That explains a lot," Kali said. "Except how on earth you ended up so quiet, Tigre. You must be, like, the only non-bellowing thunder god on the planet."

Tigre sighed unhappily. His "guide" Tlaloc, the Aztec god of storms, had been a scary, loud, angry fellow too. Tigre wondered if his powers would be any stronger if he did shout all the time. It didn't sound appealing.

"I'LL EVEN LET YOU GO FIRST!" Shango boomed. "GO AHEAD, KID. GIVE US YOUR BEST STORM."

Had he really been wishing for attention? *That was foolish of me.* The last thing he wanted was to embarrass himself and his friends in front of a crowd of African gods. But he didn't have much choice.

Tigre looked up at the sky, crossed his arms, and tried as hard as he could to conjure up a storm. *Maybe if I think about the science of it. Think about rain clouds. Think about lightning. Think about, um, electricity and water and energy colliding.* He tried to remember what he'd learned about storms in school. Which mostly made him think of long, miserable, hot days trapped behind a desk while the other kids whispered about him and laughed. He remembered Vicky poking him in the back with a pencil whenever he took too long to answer a question.

"Tigre?" Kali's voice snapped him out of his gloomy reverie. He blinked hopefully, but nothing had happened. The clouds that were already gathered in the sky stayed where they were, gray and forbidding, but silent.

"WOW," Shango observed. "THAT WAS ASTONISHINGLY PATHETIC. WORSE THAN I EXPECTED."

"Yeah, thanks," Tigre muttered, pressing his hands to his temples. Vicky would have made a much better storm god than he was. She loved shouting and competing and impressing people.

"SEE, OBATALA?" Shango went on. "WE HAVE

NOTHING TO WORRY ABOUT FROM THEM."

"Hmmm," Obatala said, giving Kali a searching look, as if he knew perfectly well that she was much stronger than any of the others, and was in fact very much something to worry about.

Suddenly Diana made a sound almost like a tiny gasp, and they all whipped around to look at her. But her eyes were still closed. Gus leaned forward to brush her hair out of her face.

"Obatala!" the treelike orisha woman cried. "Look at his arm!"

Tigre glanced down and saw that Gus's sleeve had ridden up, exposing the intricate green pattern of the tattoo winding down toward his wrist. Gus hastily tugged his sleeve down again, but the orisha who'd noticed it seized his hand and yanked Gus to his feet, shoving Gus's arm in front of Obatala.

"This tattoo," said the orisha. "The markings are unfamiliar to us, but the meaning is the same. It shows his strength—he must be very brave to have undergone such pain. This is a warrior to be respected."

"It's all over him," Kali piped up, stepping over Diana to stand next to him. "Check out his back. And his legs."

"Hey," Gus objected, but orishas were already lifting his shirt and peering at his ankles.

"Ow," one of them marveled.

"This must have taken *years*," said another.

"For a mortal—what impressive pain!" said a third.

"Well, actually," Gus started to explain, but Tigre saw Kali give him a swift kick in the ankle and he shut up.

"We should help them," the round, copper-skinned orisha said beguilingly to Obatala. "They have risked so much to get here."

"Yes, let's help them," said the stout woman, and a mumble of agreement ran through the crowd. The tall god in the white robes stroked his nose thoughtfully, and then sighed.

"Very well," Obatala said. "If you all insist. But I reserve the right to throw them off the continent if and when they annoy me."

Tigre saw Kali hiding a smile. This guy sounded a bit like she did.

"Do you have a god of healing?" Gus asked. "Someone who can fix Diana's wound and bring her back?"

Obatala was already shaking his head. "That is not what she needs," he said. "It is not just her body that is hurt. We must see what is holding her soul, and where her path leads from here."

"WE NEED DIVINATION," Shango said, clapping his hands together with a sound like thunder crashing.

"Orunmila," whispered some of the orishas. Something about the awe and fear in their voices filled Gus with dread.

The god nodded and pointed at the tall needle-shaped tower in the distance.

"Yes," he said. "We must take her to see my brother."

Diana knew perfectly well that cute and charming people were not necessarily to be trusted. She'd known enough pop stars who were sweet on the outside but vicious when they wanted to be. *And of course there's Anna, who was really nice up until the point where she killed me.*

But she had a hard time not smiling back at someone who was smiling at her. Even as she let Maui clasp her hand in his, she wondered how fast she could run away through the water. Rohe was probably right that Diana couldn't trust him, but then, why should she trust Rohe, either? Rohe had let her leave the Polynesian underworld, but Maui was the one who had pulled her out.

"That was bloody brave of you," Maui said, nodding at the chasm beside them. "No worries about sea monsters? Or that it might be one of those bottomless pits?"

"Plenty of worries, believe me," Diana said. "But I had to do something. How did you know my name?" She liked that he'd called her Diana instead of Venus, but that did mean he hadn't recognized her from being a pop star. Did gods recognize pop stars? Maybe they just knew everything.

"Ah, your fame precedes you," Maui said, brushing the sand off his knees. "Everyone knows about the little twofold goddess wandering around the underworlds." Diana realized with amusement that he was wearing ordinary khaki shorts and a faded T-shirt that could have come from Old Navy, except it had a symbol on it that she hadn't seen before. It looked a bit like some of the tattoos on Gus. He also had a greenstone pendant hanging from a leather cord around his neck, carved in a shape that looked like an infinity symbol on end.

"I was told not to trust you," Diana said, watching him for a reaction.

"Oh, Rohe," Maui said with a sigh that blew his curls up and to the side. "I'm sure one day we'll be friends again, but it might be a few eons from now." He smiled. "Did she also tell you the part about killing me? She's not so reliable herself. When we were married, sometimes she would get up in the middle of the night and chow down on everything in the refrigerator so there was nothing left for breakfast the next day. I mean, *everything*. Mussels, strawberries, soy sauce—bottle and all, mind you. It was bloody rude."

"Aren't you still married?" Diana asked, trying to grapple with the mental image of Rohe and Maui living in a high-rise apartment with a fridge and a toaster.

"Till death do us part—oh wait," Maui said gleefully, wagging his ringless fingers. "But you've got nothing to worry about from me. I'm only here because I was curious to meet you, and whale riding was getting a little dull. It's not much fun being a Polynesian god these days."

"I bet," Diana said.

"So where are you off to now?" Maui asked.

Diana glanced up at the ring of mountains around the flooded valley, lit by the pale greenish glow from the water. "Well, I could go back that way." She pointed to the path that led back into the darkness, where she'd come from. "Or I guess I could try finding a way around the abyss, maybe up in the mountains."

"That sounds like more fun, doesn't it?" Maui said. "New adventures are always better than what you've done before."

"I agree, as long as they don't kill you," Diana said.

"Ah, death isn't so bad, is it?" he teased.

She gave him a skeptical look. "Have you seen the other underworlds?" she asked.

"Sure," he said. "Hades isn't too bad, by comparison. Unless you're being punished for something horribly specific."

"Really?"

"Well, it helps if you get to live in the Elysian Fields," Maui said.

Diana stretched and rubbed her face. Her pale arms glowed greenly as the reflections shimmered across her skin. The dim light and the soft shushing of the water were making her sleepy. From where she was standing, the mountains in either direction looked equally far away. But to her left the glow seemed brighter, almost as if there might be a city beyond the mountains.

"Do you know which way I should go to get to Hades?" she asked. "Maybe they're the ones I should talk to to get back to my real life."

"Well, all things are a bit fluid in these parts," Maui admitted, "but I think you could get there by wandering thataway for a while." He pointed toward the brighter mountains.

"All right, you convinced me. I'll try the mountains," Diana said. She bent over to roll up her pant legs and then waded out into the shallow water. Her sneakers sank into the white sand, and she saw a small fish dart over to nibble at her shoelaces.

"Want some company?" Maui asked, falling in beside her as she started to splash along the edge of the abyss toward the mountains.

"Sure," Diana said. She tried to remind herself that it was probably dangerous to feel so comfortable around him. "How can you go between the underworlds? Don't you have to stay with the other Polynesians?" A pebble skittered away, bouncing through the sand underwater until it plummeted over into the chasm.

"I'm not much of a rule follower," Maui said. He strolled through the ocean with his hands shoved jauntily in his pockets. He grinned at her. "Aren't gods funny? They create the world and everything in it, and then they make all these walls and rules so they can't do what they like anymore. And humans end up with all the power, until they don't even need the gods, and then where are we? Stuck, stupid, and powerless. Not me, no thanks."

"I guess lots of people must have believed in you," Diana said. "I'm sorry I've never heard of you."

"No worries," Maui said cheerfully. "Maybe you have, and you just don't know it."

Diana stopped and glanced behind her. The water lapped softly around her knees, and she could see it glowing green and smooth off to the distant horizons. But for a moment she'd been sure she'd heard something quite unlike the swishing of the waves. Something more like . . . rattling bones.

"Did you hear that?" she asked.

Maui tilted his head around and waggled his ears impressively. "Sorry, love," he said. "All I hear is the ocean and the wind and the fish giggling about what lovely white toes you have."

Diana laughed. "They can't see my toes, you big goof," she said.

"Fish have vivid imaginations," Maui said, "and terrible memories. Never play Telephone with them. By the time this rumor reaches the far side of this sea, you'll be an eight-foot mermaid walking on her hands."

Diana laughed again and kept walking, feeling better. She must have imagined the strange sound. "I suppose you're going to tell me that you've played Telephone with fish."

"They're pretty dreadful at it," he said. "And don't even get me started on Go Fish. You explain the rules for an hour, and then they're like, okay, got any fives? And you're like, nope, sorry, go fish! And they scatter like tadpoles, thinking you've just started a race."

Diana giggled.

"Sweet, but dim, is what I'm getting at," Maui said.

"So what is Hades like?" Diana asked.

"It's what you'd imagine," Maui said. "A bit gloomy. The River Styx is sort of smelly and dead—no fun-loving fish in there, trust me. Their giant three-headed dog, Cerberus, turns into a big fluffball if you bring him cheese. King Hades wasn't too pleased when he discovered that I'd figured that out. He's not particularly keen on other gods gallivanting about his kingdom."

"Do you think he'll let me go?" Diana said. "If I tell him I'm not ready to die yet?"

"Well, you can try it, love," Maui said, "but don't forget that nearly every corpse says exactly the same thing. You don't get a lot of 'yup, that was my time, thanks muchly' down there."

"But wouldn't he want me to go back? So I can keep representing our pantheon?"

"It's not up to him," Maui said, shaking his head. "But I'm sure it wouldn't hurt to ask. He's granted some funny requests in his time."

"And what's on the other side of those mountains?" Diana asked. She turned around again. Was that a hiss in the darkness? Or was it just the water sliding into the chasm?

"Depends," Maui said with a shrug. "Could be the Hindu underworld. We'll find out soon, won't we? Isn't this fun?"

Diana noticed that the water seemed shallower here, coming only halfway up her calves. She peered down and saw that it was dropping rapidly; in fact, it was being sucked away behind them, toward the distant, darker mountains.

"Maui?" she said. "What's happening?"

He glanced down, and for the first time the smile left his face. They both turned, and Diana saw that the water was rushing away, leaving her standing on a wide stretch of sand. The light went with the water, piling into an iridescent green wall as the water stacked up higher and higher. Darkness fell around Maui and Diana, and then, silhouetted against the emerald water, Diana saw a giant, monstrous shape—long, twisted, writhing, with sharp fangs jutting out of the shadowed face.

She remembered the albino snake in Mictlan, but this one looked larger, more ferocious, and much, much more active.

"Diana, run!" Maui said, shoving her. "Get out of here!"

"What about you?" she asked.

"I'll distract him." He pushed her again, standing between her and the tidal wave. "Don't worry, I've both drowned and been eaten by snakes before. Now GO!" He turned and ran toward the churning waves lashed up by the enormous serpent.

Diana didn't wait to see any more. She ran, skidding through the wet sand, dodging flopping fish and dying jellyfish, jumping over clusters of sharp-edged seashells. She ran toward the mountains, wondering what happened to semi-immortal souls when they were killed in the space between worlds, and if she would have to spend eternity in the guts of a malevolent snake.

She ran.

Tigre hoped that this new god, Obatala's brother, would be able to help them—divination sounded like prophecy, which sounded useful.

The closer they got to Orunmila's tower, the more it seemed to be writhing in the air. It wasn't just made of wood, as Tigre had first thought due to its dark brown color. Streams of water were pouring down from the top, winding around and around each other so that it looked like a maypole of shimmering silver ribbons. Trailing in the water were long green vines with enormous leaves the size of stingrays. Strange eyes blinked at the visitors as the shapes of chameleons emerged from the glossy backdrops.

They had nearly reached the foot of the tower when Tigre spotted what looked like tiny brown jewels scattered among the leaves. They shone wetly in the spray from the streams and were dark like chocolate and dusted with a constellation of white speckles. As he stared at them, he realized they were moving, very slowly, across the vines.

Snails, he finally realized. *Cowry shell snails*. They were all over the strange tower.

"Your brother lives up there?" Kali asked, tilting her head back to see the top of the tower as they came to a stop. "That's dramatic of him." The crowd that had followed them from the square stopped too, and began to whisper. Tigre noticed that the small, round girl was among them.

"He used to live in a cave overlooking a river," Obatala said, "but like most of us, once Africa was ours again, he traded up."

"How do we get up there?" Gus asked. Tigre could see the tension in Gus's shoulders as the other boy shifted Diana's weight in his arms. The heat was oppressive, even in the shade of the trees; sweat was rolling down Tigre's back under his shirt, and he knew Gus must be suffering even more. The sun was hidden behind a bank of low clouds that were clustered just above the treetops, but it seemed closer and warmer than usual.

"We call," Obatala said simply. He cupped his hands around his mouth and bellowed "ORUNMILA!" in a voice so loud it made the vines on the tower shake, spraying cold, glittering droplets all over them.

"Doesn't he just know we're here?" Gus asked. "I mean, if he's a god of prophecy?"

"Prophecy and divination are not the same things," Obatala said with a frown. "Perhaps if he had asked the universe *Will nosy trespassing intruders ride up to our shores today?* he'd have gotten the right answer, but divination is about finding the right questions first—and then the right path to follow."

Something moved at the top of the tower, and then the vines began to rustle, and soon Tigre could see someone sliding down them, swinging from one to the next in a graceful way, more like a surfer or a Cirque du Soleil acrobat than like Tarzan. When he hit the ground, the vines were still swinging, and Tigre looked up to see a second figure slide down and land alongside the first.

The first man had long ringlets of thick dark hair, a short beard, and white robes like Obatala; there was also a resemblance in the shape of their noses and chins, so Tigre guessed that this was his brother Orunmila.

The other was shorter than the first two gods and walked with a slight limp as he scooted forward beside Orunmila. He was clean-shaven, with an easy smile and bright, watchful eyes. His skin was a little lighter than the others', as if he'd been rolled in cinnamon. Tigre got a strong vibe from him of wild energy barely contained, like a hare he'd once seen at the veterinary clinic, penned in a cage but ready to bolt at a moment's notice. For no clear reason that Tigre could pinpoint, he mistrusted this new god on sight. There was something a little *too* clever about his face and the way he looked at them. Tigre had the strange impression that he not only recognized them, but was pleased to see them.

"Orunmila," Obatala said, taking his brother's hands in his. The other god hung back near the tower, fiddling with a cowry shell bracelet on his wrist but clearly listening. "I bring you mortals in need of guidance."

"Mortals!" Orunmila said in surprise.

"Well, for now," Kali said. "It's just a phase."

"Aren't you going to say you were expecting us?" Gus asked, his breath coming in short gasps. He folded to the ground, resting Diana's inert body against his legs.

Orunmila, Obatala, and Kali all frowned at him. Tigre was glad *he* wasn't on the receiving end of any of those looks.

"I'm not sure they are ready for *ifa*," Orunmila said. His hands moved constantly as he spoke, like they were dancing with each other. "Are they here for the right reasons?"

Obatala looked at them seriously.

"Oh, we so are," Kali said. "I don't know how much you know about it, but basically we're pawns in a game we don't want to play. The path our gods want us on involves murder and betrayal and death and unlimited power and charming stuff like that. But most of us only want to go home."

Tigre wondered if she included herself in that.

"We want to be with our families," Gus interjected. "We want to live normal lives."

"We want the world back the way it was," Kali said.

The god with the limp flicked a stone up in the air and

caught it like a coin, checking for heads or tails.

"That is your reason," Orunmila said to Kali. "You are a leader and a fixer; the world is out of balance, and you want to correct it."

"Ironically," Kali said. "Normally I'm all yay chaos, down with people."

"Not really," Orunmila said with a small smile. "And you," he said to Gus. "You are a caretaker. I can guess from the burden you carry, but tell me why you are really here."

"This is Diana," Gus said, gently brushing Diana's hair back from her face. "I want to know what I have to do to save her. Whatever it is—I'll do anything."

"Hmmm." Orunmila stepped forward and passed his hand through the air above Diana. "Ah, I see. Yes, this is a good reason too." Abruptly he turned to Tigre, his long hair spinning out behind him. "What about you? Why are you here?"

"Oh," Tigre stammered, caught off guard. "I—I'm with them." He glanced at the unnamed god, who was smiling—maliciously, Tigre thought.

"No wishes of your own?" Orunmila mused. "And yet you are farther from your true path than anyone. Let us see. I think you should all come inside." He made a twisting motion in the air with one hand, and one of the streams of water folded around the tower, rearranging itself into a set of stairs with the water flowing upward.

Yahoo. More stairs, Tigre thought, but then Orunmila stepped onto the lowest stair and Tigre realized to his relief that it was like an escalator, carrying them up smoothly. The stranger god hopped up next to Orunmila, and they sailed around the bend while the others were still blinking.

"We learned a few things from humans," Obatala said, smiling at their expressions. "An ingenious idea, stairs that move themselves. In the past we did a lot of rope climbing between Heaven and Earth. This is much more convenient."

Kali crossed over to Gus and picked up Diana before he could object. He pushed himself up and stumbled after her, and Tigre followed, stepping gingerly onto the clear, moving step. It looked like he should sink right through it, but it held his weight with a little splash, as if he were stepping into a bog. Obatala stepped onto the stair below him and turned with a sharp gesture to the orishas that were pressing close.

"No," he said firmly. "You all stay here."

"But—" one of them protested. Obatala shook his head, and they fell back, looking disappointed.

Tigre glanced at Obatala, whose eyes were level with Tigre's while the god was a step down.

"Who is that?" he asked, pointing to the strange god above them.

Obatala glanced up. "That is Eshu," he said in a low voice. "He is Orunmila's best friend, although it doesn't make sense to most of us."

"Really? Why?" Tigre asked. A pair of vines smacked him in the face and he flailed, disentangling himself before he was swept off the water escalator. "Is he evil?"

Obatala smiled. "No, Eshu isn't evil. He's . . . complicated."

"What is he the god of?"

"Many things," Obatala answered. "Crossroads. Travelers. Trouble."

Tigre expected the tower room at the top to be full of sunlight, but when they reached it, the water stairs sailed him through a hanging curtain of vines into sudden darkness. He was still blinking and pulling leaves out of his hair when the river dumped him off unceremoniously, and he stumbled, skidding across a sandy floor.

His eyes adjusted slowly, and he realized he was in a large cave, lit only by a crackling fire in the center. The flames were green instead of orange, but it looked like a normal fire in every other way, and it was surprisingly warm. The speckles in the stone walls that curved around them glinted in the firelight, and the vine curtain shut out the sunlight almost entirely.

Orunmila seated himself on a wide, flat boulder behind the fire and waited for Tigre, Kali, and Gus to arrange themselves on the sandy floor opposite him. The green light reflected glittering shadows in Eshu's eyes as he took a seat on a rock behind Orunmila, and when he caught Tigre looking at him, he winked. Tigre looked away quickly.

Kali laid Diana on the floor with the unconscious girl's head resting on Gus's knees. Gus took Diana's wrist, checked for a pulse again, and smoothed back her hair. Tigre crouched on Gus's other side, awkwardly bending his long limbs around into a kneeling position.

Orunmila took a handful of palm nuts from a woven basket beside him. Tigre couldn't see exactly what he was doing in the flickering firelight, but it looked like the god of divination was passing them from hand to hand, glancing at them, scattering them in front of him, and then picking them up to do it again. He did it all so quickly, Tigre could barely keep track of where the nuts were, and as he worked, the god nodded and mumbled to himself.

"Yes," Orunmila said suddenly. "Catequil, god of storms." Tigre jumped.

"Oh, you don't have to start with me," he said.

"You should be a god of thunder and prophecy," Orunmila continued implacably. "Something I know a little about. What don't you believe about that? Why are you so far astray?" He turned and gave Eshu a hard stare.

Tigre hesitated. He didn't like the way Eshu was leaning forward with a smirk.

"I just—it doesn't make sense," Tigre admitted. "I don't ever have any prophecies or prophetic dreams or whatever. And I can't call storms when I try; it only happens accidentally. And I've been wondering if I might have something to do with animals instead. I mean, I like them and I get along with them, and I thought perhaps I might . . . turn into one, maybe."

Kali gave him an incredulous look.

"Have you experienced this?" Orunmila asked.

"Not consciously," Tigre said. "I wake up after I've turned back." His confidence grew a little stronger. It felt empowering to finally say what he'd been worrying about, to put words to the weirdness.

But Orunmila was shaking his head. "You'll never find your power if you can't believe in who you are. You are like a man with a great talent for carpentry and house building who is convinced that he should be a hunter. He devotes all his energy to spear throwing and stalking, but he will never achieve the greatness he wishes for, because he is not on the right path and he won't use his true skills."

"But I have no true skills," Tigre protested. "I have no 'great talent' for storms or anything like that."

"Well, you never will with an attitude like that," Eshu chimed in, speaking for the first time. His voice had a light edge to it, as if he were on the verge of laughing.

"My friend is harsh, but he's right," Orunmila said, holding up his hand to stop Eshu from going on. "Even the man with the woodworking talent must use it, practice it, and cultivate it before his skill will truly shine through."

"What about the way I get along with animals?" Tigre said desperately. "Doesn't that mean something?"

Orunmila glanced down at the palm nuts again. "It means you have a strong streak of humanity," he said, scooping them up in one hand. "Your human side is good with animals; if you had been born an ordinary mortal, that would still be the case. But you are a god, and I'm afraid you are not a god who turns into animals. According to my reading, you never have and you never will. You must accept that in order to move on."

Tigre exhaled, feeling as if all the logic had been drained out of him. He realized he'd been clinging to that explanation—that someone must be wrong about his powers. Otherwise how had he killed the old man in the bus shelter? If he hadn't turned into some kind of ferocious animal with claws, how could he have shredded the man's chest and brought all that blood pouring out? Those weren't the kind of wounds a regular person could inflict.

It didn't make sense.

Unless . . . unless he didn't do it, after all.

His skin was prickling. If there was a chance he wasn't a killer. . . . He wanted to ask Orunmila who had really done it, but he had never told Kali or Gus about the dead man, and he wasn't sure how they'd react.

It was too late anyway; Orunmila was already shifting the nuts back and forth in his hands again. The god's eyes were on Diana now, and so were Eshu's.

"She is traveling," said Orunmila, and something sparked in the green flames, throwing them higher for a moment. "She is lost." The shadows danced across Diana's pale, still face.

"Lost?" Gus repeated in a worried voice. He stroked Diana's hair.

"She wanders the underworlds," Orunmila said.

"Wow," Eshu added. "What a wild trip that must be. They're all lunatics down there. Half of them have animal heads, and they're all desperate for company."

"Eshu," Orunmila said sternly. "You know how I feel about you interrupting my divination."

"I'm *helping*," Eshu objected, but he sat back on his boulder and crossed his arms.

Orunmila tilted his head as if he were listening, and then he nodded. "She is working her way back to the right path."

"Really?" Gus said, brightening. "She's coming back to us?"

"I did not say that," Orunmila answered. "She is moving gradually toward Hades, the Greek underworld. She has some distance to travel yet, but if she gets there before you can awaken her . . . she will die, and then it will be forever."

EIGHTEEN YEARS AGO . . .

It was easier to love her in the summertime.

When the air smelled like oranges and blue sky, when blossoms drifted from the trees, when his feet sank into green grass and rich earth and he could breathe and sleep and live, then he could still look at her and feel the old twist of heartache that he thought must be love.

Her black hair floated on the grass as she lay on her back, smiling up at him. He'd fallen in love with her here, in these fields. She had appeared through his flocks of sheep, the light in her face brighter than the white woolly animals around her.

He'd loved her so much. He was the only one who had known that she couldn't be dead when she disappeared. He'd known that if she were really dead, he'd feel it, like a knife in his gut. He knew her strength and he respected her power, and so, instead of mourning, he'd carried on as king in her absence, awaiting her return. For that, he'd been punished.

And now she was leaving him again . . . but this time, she really might die.

He wasn't sure how he felt about that. If she were dead, he would no longer have these six months a year in the summer light with her. But if she were dead, he could have the whole year in the light by himself—no more soul-sucking days in the Irkalla fortress, serving as the butt of all the jokes at Ereshkigal's court, occasionally tortured for her amusement.

It twisted his spirit. A nature god shouldn't think about death; he certainly shouldn't spend his nights dreaming about his wife impaled on a hook in the underworld.

"You look so serious," Inanna teased. She lifted her hand to him, and he let her pull him down beside her in the grass. "Are you going to miss me?" she whispered against his mouth, kissing him.

"I will think of you every day," he said truthfully. Sometimes in love, sometimes in vengeance. Sometimes with kisses, sometimes with knives.

"This will be so easy," she giggled, burying her fingers in his hair. "The other pantheons are going to send burly warrior men, I'm sure. They'll never see me coming. Who'd pick a goddess of love, right? So I'll seduce them all, and then I'll rip their intestines out and feast on their power." She pulled his head to her for another kiss. "Don't be jealous when you watch me do it. You know I love you best."

For half the year, at least—who knows what you do in the winter, while I'm trapped below? *He propped himself up on one elbow and ran his hand down her arm.*

"If they know who you are, won't they know what you'll do?"

"We have such a wicked plan," Inanna said, stretching and clasping her hands behind her head. "My sister suggested it. We're going to shield ourselves from the other pantheons. They won't know who I am; they won't even know which gods I represent. I'll pretend I don't know either. They'll never see me

coming." She touched his nose playfully.

"And Ereshkigal will come help me if I need it. Don't worry, it'll be a quick victory. I'll be back in your arms in no time." Inanna smiled up at the sky, winding a strand of hair around her finger. "I hope the Egyptians send Amon. He's rather dreamy. Oooh, and maybe the Vikings will pick Njord—I wouldn't mind seducing him! They'll probably pick that oaf Thor, though. I can handle that. If you know what I mean by handle." She winked at him, and he wondered how he could love someone so much and hate her so much at the same time.

"I just hope the Aztecs pick an avatar that isn't too scaly," she went on.

"He'll be human," Dumuzi said. "With human skin. Like you." Easy to cut. Easy to bleed.

"Poor sweet worried husband," Inanna said, winding her arms around his neck again. "Don't fret so much. I'll have my objects of power to ward off the weakness of humanity. Ereshkigal promised she would come to me while I'm still young and start hardening me for the task. I won't be all sappy and emotional and human-ish like the other avatars. I'll win, and then I'll come back to you, and everything will be the same, only better because I'll be the most powerful goddess in the world."

"More powerful than your sister," he said, stroking her hair.

"Oh, don't," she said impatiently.

"Don't what?" His hand went still.

"Don't ask me again. I made a pact with her, Dumuzi. It's eternal. So please stop whining about it." She tugged on his neck, trying to pull him to her, but he stayed rigid, looking down at her face.

"You don't know what it's like," he said coldly.

"Sure I do," Inanna said. "I was there for three whole days,

remember? It's gross, but you survive."

"I have no choice."

"Oh, it's so hard to be immortal," she teased. He wondered how she could look into his face and not see the bitter ice of his hatred. It hadn't been there when she married him; he'd been only joyful, then.

"I haven't seen my sister Geshtinanna in three thousand years," he said. She took his place in the underworld for the other half of the year, and it made his summers painful, knowing she was down there suffering the way he did, for his sake.

"Sisters are horrible," Inanna said, laughing. "You're lucky. You should thank me."

"I want my freedom," he said, seizing her wrists and pushing her away from him.

"And I want valleys full of ponies and parties in the streets every night," Inanna said. "Which I might get when I'm the big supreme goddess, actually. Now stop fighting with me—I only have a little while before I have to be born. Do you think I'll be this beautiful when I'm mortal?" She stretched seductively, blinking at him with narrow, calculating eyes.

Dumuzi stood up, kicking her away as she tried to grab his ankle. He turned and strode into the trees, leaving a blackened path in the grass behind him.

"Fine, you big crybaby!" she called. "You'll regret it when you don't get to have me for seventeen years. And then you have to watch me with all those other gods. I'll enjoy it, Dumuzi! I hope you see everything! Maybe you'll learn something!"

Dumuzi wished he had his own gods he could pray to. He'd pray for his pantheon to lose. He'd pray for his freedom.

And he'd pray for someone to murder his wife . . . slowly and painfully.

CITADEL OF DARKNESS

There were no more sounds from below her. When Diana finally stopped, panting for breath, on a ledge halfway up the mountain, she couldn't hear the loud hissing or the crashing waves anymore. She held on to an outcropping and leaned out to look down.

The glowing green waters were still again, covering the valley, higher than they were before, but with no sign of the giant serpent . . . and no sign of Maui.

He's a god, she reminded herself and kept climbing. *He'll be okay.*

The rocks around her were black and pitted with holes, the edges sharp or curved and the rest rough like the pumice stones her stylists used to use on her feet. It reminded her of climbing volcanoes in Hawaii (a rare manager-approved side trip during a concert tour), and she sincerely hoped that she wouldn't find a seething lava pit when she reached the top.

At one point she slipped and fell, scraping her hands on the sharp rocks as she threw them out to catch herself.

"Ow," she muttered, brushing the dark pebbles off her hands as she walked forward. It took a moment for her to realize that she had reached the top of the mountain and could see the other side.

For a moment Diana thought she was looking at the same kind of valley she had just left, full of glowing water. But then her eyes adjusted, and she saw that the mistiness came from a bank of clouds that hid the valley below. Whorls and patterns of bright lights shone blurrily through the clouds, like gold and rubies and dark emeralds glittering in a treasure chest. To Diana, it looked like the view she'd seen a million times from an airplane window: a city below the clouds at night, homes and streets and individual lives compressed into swirls and spiderwebs of colors.

She wondered if this was how the gods saw Earth every day. It must be easier to dismiss humanity if you only saw them from this far away. You wouldn't feel so guilty, getting rid of all the people in the world, when you hadn't spoken to any humans in several hundred years, or watched them fall in love, learn to walk, sing karaoke.

Diana scouted along the edge until she found a part of the slope that seemed less steep. It was darker on this side of the mountain, without the iridescent water to light up the rocks. The city below cast a faint golden light, but much of it was blocked by the clouds, and she had to tread carefully.

It felt like she hiked for days, but gradually the light around her grew brighter and brighter, and finally she came out of the clouds and found a real path winding down the mountain, lit by freestanding torches as tall as she was that had been stabbed into the rock every few feet. The flames were a deep, glowering orange, and were embedded in the dark ends of the torches instead of rising from them, so they looked like giant cigarettes stuck in the ground with the lit ends still burning. They even flared occasionally, as if the earth itself was smoking them.

There was something Diana didn't like about the idea of walking between those torches. It seemed like taking the path would announce her presence. Instead she crept along beside it, staying behind the large boulders that were scattered in a long line beyond the torches like sentries. She saw no one on the path, nor any signposts that might have helpfully offered useful information, like THIS IS THE NORSE UNDERWORLD! THE BEST WAY TO RETURN TO LIFE FROM HERE IS TO EAT AN IMMORTAL GOAT! *Or something like that*, she thought wryly.

Before long Diana could see tall stone walls ahead of her, maybe a hundred times her height, with watchtowers and flapping black banners and—She shuddered, looking away quickly. Strange lumps of something were hanging on giant meat hooks on the walls, and she had a feeling they weren't hunting trophies . . . not animal-hunting trophies, anyway.

The path led straight up to a set of giant gates, carved with human-headed lions and fanged flies and snakes with clawed feet and winged things that Diana had never seen before. This didn't look like Hades.

Diana crouched behind a boulder, waiting for something

to give her a clue. Surely someone would come in or out eventually. She could see movement up on top of the wall, and she hoped that the shadows of the boulders hid her from view.

Suddenly something clattered on the path behind her, and Diana froze. Someone was violently kicking a rock along as they approached, muttering angrily. Diana wasn't close enough to make out the words, but she could see the outline of the figure as it came closer. It looked like someone short, with longish hair. A girl? The orange glow of the cigarette torches glinted off dark hair as she passed between them.

The rock she was kicking flew forward and hit the gates before she reached them. Diana slid lower and peeked out, hoping the extra torches around the gate would illuminate the girl's features.

Bang bang bang! The girl pounded on the gates much more loudly than Diana would have expected from her small size.

"NETI!" she shouted. "Open up!" She shoved the gates hard, and to Diana's surprise, they gave a little, bouncing back and forth with the clanking sound of chains. "NETI, curse your miserable skull and may it be eaten by maggots, open the gate RIGHT NOW!"

A square in the door slid open, and something blinked behind them.

"Oh. It's you," said a male voice, sounding tired and supercilious. "I should have guessed."

The girl shoved the gates again, and Diana hoped the gatekeeper had stepped out of the way before they hit him in the face.

"Let me in RIGHT NOW, Neti!" the girl demanded. "I have to talk to Ereshkigal, and since for some stupid reason she won't come up to me, I had to come all the way down here to talk to her."

Cold fire raced along Diana's skin. She felt as if someone had seized the back of her neck and yanked her into a suffocating closet, pressing a knife to her neck. She felt as if she'd been stabbed all over again.

It was Anna.

Diana had found the Sumerian underworld . . . and her killer.

Gus broke the silence. "So what's going to happen?" he asked. "Is Diana going to get to Hades? Is she going to die? How do I stop it?"

"Shh," Kali said, putting one hand on his shoulder. She could tell this was a god who didn't like a lot of questions.

"Yes," Orunmila said. "I'm afraid she is going to reach Hades, and she is going to die."

"What?" Gus cried. "That can't be right! There must be something we can do!"

"You asked how the future is written," Orunmila said.

"Pffft," Eshu contributed. Orunmila and Obatala both turned and glared at him. "What?" Eshu said. "You're not divining now. You're just giving your wrong opinion, as usual."

"Eshu, stay out of this," Orunmila commanded. "I will not argue with you in front of visitors."

"Great, then don't argue," Eshu said. "Just keep quiet while *I* tell them that the future isn't written in stone, and if they try hard enough, they can change it."

"What do I have to do?" Gus asked.

Eshu shrugged. "Oh, that's not my department."

"No, your department is causing trouble," Orunmila muttered. He stroked his chin, frowning at Gus. "There are many ways to the underworld," he said finally. "You may find different paths to it all over Africa. But all of them are perilous, and there is no guarantee you'll end up in the same place as her, or at the same time, or that you'll be able to find her and convince her to leave. You could easily get stuck there yourself, and then you'd both be dead, but distant underworlds apart."

Orunmila shook his head. "Almost every future path leads to greater danger and near-certain death for you both. It would be foolish to try and change this fate. If you ask me, you'd be better off turning your energies to *her* quest instead." He nodded at Kali.

"You mean getting back to our own time," Kali said. "Putting everything back the way it was."

"More or less," said Orunmila. "If that is what you want."

"So what do we do?" Kali said. Gus was staring bleakly at Diana now, and she guessed he wasn't even listening to them anymore.

Orunmila frowned at the nuts in his hand. "It's unclear." He clamped his hands together, shook them, and peered at them again. Kali noticed that his palms were stained a deep brownish-red. He looked up at her sharply. "Are you being followed?"

"Followed?" Kali repeated. "Not that we know of."

Orunmila rubbed his forehead, looking puzzled. "This indicates that there is someone on your path—one who goes before and after, one who watches you and meddles quite often, it appears. You haven't noticed a . . . a presence? Or anything strange happening?"

"Yeah, no," Kali said. "The last week has been pretty normal, I'd say." Orunmila turned over one of the nuts thoughtfully. "That was sarcasm," she pointed out.

"It is difficult to see your fate lines. Whoever it is has pulled them and tangled them and knotted them in such a way that nothing is clear."

"Just for me?" Kali asked.

Orunmila shook his head. "For all of you. His fingerprints are all over your childhoods as well."

Kali felt a cold chill, followed by a rush of anger. The gods had been trying to run her life ever since the change, but now it sounded like they'd been poking and scrabbling around in her real life, too.

She remembered the god who'd been appearing in Miracle's dreams in New York, making the subway dwellers offer him sacrifices. Miracle had only known him as "Dad," but she'd tried to describe him for Kali. She said he usually appeared as a dark-haired man or a large dog. Could he also be the one interfering with the avatars?

"Can you see any details?" Kali asked. "Is he a god? Which pantheon is he from?"

"He has godlike powers," Orunmila said. "He seems to be both an architect and a destroyer. But he hides very well—the answers fall through my fingers as I try to look at them. I don't understand it."

"Wow," Eshu said. "He must be very powerful. Maybe the most powerful god in the world, it sounds like."

"How do we find him?" Kali asked.

"He'll probably find you," Eshu said before Orunmila could answer. Kali wanted to punch his smug face. From Orunmila's expression, she guessed the divination god felt the same way. "Perhaps," Eshu went on, "while you are trying to figure out how the gods made the world this way."

"They didn't just snap their fingers and make it like this?" Tigre asked.

Eshu gave him a condescending look. "Is that how your powers work?" he said snidely. Tigre turned red and glanced away. "No, there was a very small amount of cleverness involved."

"Do *you* know what they did?" Kali asked Eshu.

There was an electric pause.

"Eshu?" Orunmila said with a frown, turning toward him. "You don't know anything we don't know about this, do you?"

Eshu moved so suddenly, even the gods in the room didn't have time to stop him. He leaped forward and knocked Orunmila's hand aside, scattering palm nuts across the floor. In the same moment, feathers sprouted along his arms and talons shot from his knees. He was a hawk almost before Kali could blink, and then he snatched two of the palm nuts from the ground, dove through the vine curtain, and sailed away into the sky.

Kali dashed over to the vines and yanked them aside,

but the Eshu-hawk was already a speck in the blue distance. The long drop to the ground below made her dizzy, and she stepped back, blinking in the darkness of the cave.

Orunmila and Obatala were on their feet as well, and they both looked angry.

"I knew we couldn't trust him," Obatala growled. "He'd never be content with a happy, peaceful world. He lives for trouble, Orunmila, I warned you."

Orunmila stooped, gathering the remaining palm nuts with a sigh. His long hair swung down, hiding his face, but his voice was glum. "I'm afraid this is typical of Eshu, visitors. There can be no more divination until I gather and enchant new palm nuts to replace the ones he stole."

"Well, where did he go?" Kali demanded. "You heard him—he knows something. If we can catch up to him, maybe we can make him tell us."

Obatala snorted. "Catch Eshu! You'll be lucky."

"They could try," Orunmila said. "After all, there are no more answers here."

"Is he the one who's been following us?" Kali asked. "I mean, why else would he run away, right?"

But Orunmila and Obatala were both shaking their heads. "How could he?" Obatala pointed out. "The African gods pledged not to leave the continent. He's sly, but I don't think he could have slipped through. You might be right that he knows something that could help you, though. He often knows more than he lets on."

"Where would he hide?" Kali asked. "Will he come back if he thinks we're gone?"

Obatala shook his head. "He is too clever to be tricked in an ordinary way. But perhaps he is not too clever to be hunted, if we gave you some help."

Orunmila was already nodding. "Yes, Oya would be a good choice," he said to Obatala, and Kali caught him tilting his head subtly toward Tigre. She wondered what that meant.

"Let's see if she is willing," Obatala said. "Back to the Earth, my friends."

They stepped, one by one, onto the flowing water, which had changed course so the steps now carried them down. Kali crouched a bit lower as they went through the vine curtain, feeling the large waxy leaves flap in her face and blinking in the hot sunlight as the watery escalator began its descent.

Tigre stood on the step above her, looking queasy and staring at the sky as if he were trying to ignore the long drop on either side of them.

"Chin up, soldier," Kali said. "We'll find Eshu and figure this out. And hey, they said you're the god you're supposed to be. That's good news, right?"

"I guess," Tigre said, shoving his hands in his pockets. "Although it doesn't seem to have done me any good so far."

"Maybe that's because you didn't believe in yourself," Kali said. She snorted. "Okay, that sounded a lot more self-help-y than I meant it to. I mean literally—gods need people in order to exist, and the more there are who know you, the stronger you are." *Like my beautiful followers*, she thought, *my vanished millions of faithful believers, lost when I wasn't looking—but I will get them back, whatever I have to do.*

"So, like, worshippers?" Tigre asked. He wobbled nervously as the stairs took a turn around one of the glittering waterfalls. "Like who? The gods we've met are too busy worshipping themselves to spare a thought for a useless, minor weather god who can't even create any weather."

"Worshippers might be too much to ask," Kali said, "but more than that, my guess is what you need is believers." She winced. Why wasn't there a way to talk about this without sounding like she was selling some kind of touchy-feely seven-step plan? They needed Diana—she could do the cheery I-*do*-believe-in-fairies stuff much more convincingly than Kali.

But if Orunmila was to be believed, Diana and her sincere enthusiasm were gone for good. And if Kali was stuck with Tigre on this quest, the least she could do was try to make him a bit more . . . useful.

"I'll sign up," she said, punching him on the arm. "It's the least I can do after you figured out there's more to me than destructo-goddess. So, I, Kali Nichols, do hereby declare that I believe in the Incan storm god Catequil. I believe that he exists. I believe that he can create storms. I believe that he's got mad weather-making skills. And I believe if he argues with me about it, I'm gonna push him off this escalator."

Tigre actually cracked a smile. "I believe that last part too," he said.

"Believe the whole thing," Kali said. "That'll make two of us. It's a start, anyhow."

Gus spoke up from the step below her. She hadn't thought he'd been listening.

"I think you might have a third," he said, nodding over Diana's body at the orishas who were crowding around the bottom of the tower. Kali followed his gaze and saw a short, round girl with reddish tones to her dark skin and a streak of coppery red waving through the shock of dark curly hair around her face. Unlike the other orishas, whose attention seemed focused on Gus and Diana, this one was definitely staring at Tigre. And perhaps Gus was right—her expression did seem entranced.

"Friend of yours?" Kali asked Tigre over her shoulder.

"I have no idea," he said.

The stairs deposited them at the bottom of the tower and Kali stepped out of the way as Tigre and Obatala jumped down beside her.

Several of the orishas pressed forward and took Diana from Gus's arms, laying her on a woven grass mat on the ground. Gus crouched protectively beside her.

Obatala clapped his hands. "Oya!" he said.

"Me!" the curvy, red-haired orisha cried in a voice that Kali found oddly husky for such a small person, as if she'd rolled all her words in honey and oats before speaking them. To Kali's immense surprise, the streak of red in the girl's hair shot to the edges of her Afro and became a much brighter cardinal red.

"Really? Me?" she said again, bouncing from one foot to the other.

"Yes, yes," Obatala said, waving her forward. Oya sprang to his side in one jump, pressing her hands to her hair. The red in it simmered down to more of a brick color.

It's like her hair is blushing, Kali realized, amused.

"Oya is our goddess of the hunt," Obatala said, "among other things—wind, hurricanes, change." Both he and Oya darted a look at Tigre, but Oya looked away quickly, pressing her hair down again. "She is our most skilled huntress, and if anyone can help you find Eshu, it's her."

"Oh, *what*?" Oya yelped. "We're hunting another god? *That* god? Do we have to? Why don't I just go sit in a trap right now and save him the trouble? Couldn't we hunt something else? I hear there's a were—"

"Oya!" Obatala interrupted. "Do you want to help or don't you?"

Oya seized two handfuls of her hair and tugged on them, stamping her feet for a moment. "Okay, okay," she said. "I do, I do, I will. But when you have to come help us out of a giant pit or cut us down from the trees or bring us back to life, don't say I didn't tell you so, because I am right now telling you so."

"You may leave the goddess's body here," Obatala said, casting Gus a sympathetic glance. "We will wait until her spirit is gone, and then I promise we will give her death rites befitting her status."

"No," Gus said, standing up. "I'm not leaving her, and I'm not going after Eshu."

Kali exchanged a glance with Tigre. She'd had a feeling this was coming. They didn't need to know much about Gus to guess what he'd say next.

Gus looked Obatala in the eye with a stubborn expression. "Tell me how to get to the underworld."

• • ● • •

"One moment please."

Diana heard the slot in the door slam shut. Anna kicked the gates, and the chains rattled again. "Neti," she yelled, "if you make me wait out here while you check with Ereshkigal, I will personally rip off your ears and feed them to vultures!"

The gates remained implacably shut.

Diana pressed herself closer to the boulder, feeling like her brain was beating against her skull as hard as Anna was pounding on the gates. She didn't know what to do. Part of her, a part that shocked and horrified her, actually wanted to run out there and stab Anna, pouring out her blood on the barren ground the same way Anna had done it to her.

But even if that didn't go against everything she believed in, it would still be a bad idea. This was Anna's territory, her world, populated by the gods of ancient Persia and Sumer. Diana did not particularly want to meet Ereshkigal again, either. She could clearly remember the last time she'd seen the death goddess, when Ereshkigal had cornered her and Gus in Central Park and hung Gus from a tree. She remembered Ereshkigal's gaunt, angry face and the pure hatred in her eyes.

Basically, there was no way Diana was going in there. She would find a way around. She would climb back into the mountains. She would even go back to the Polynesian underworld and face that serpent again before she'd go anywhere near those gates.

The slot slid open once more.

"Ereshkigal wants to know what you want," the dry voice said.

"What I—" Anna said in disbelief. She slammed her foot into the gate again. "Maggots and bloody eye sockets, WHAT IN IRKALLA DOES SHE THINK I WANT?" she yelled. "I want to know where the avatars are! I want to know what I'm supposed to do next! I want to find them, and I want to kill them, slowly and horribly, and I want to do it NOW!"

"Dear Inanna, I do believe this is the least seductive I've ever seen you," Neti said.

Anna picked up a rock and hurled it at the slot with perfect aim.

"OW!" the gatekeeper yelled. "That is *not* going to help your case!" He slammed the slot shut again.

Diana wondered what Anna would do if Ereshkigal didn't let her in. She hoped it wouldn't involve setting the whole plain on fire or blowing up all the boulders or anything like that.

Finally there was a loud creaking sound and one side of the gate inched open. From her hiding place, Diana saw a hand emerge and stop Anna in her tracks.

"You know the rules, Inanna," Neti's voice said. "One item of clothing at each gate."

"But I'm a freaking mortal right now," Anna protested. "What does she think I'm going to do to her?"

"Just do it." Neti sighed. "We all know you're wearing objects of power."

Snarling curses, Anna yanked off a gold bracelet shaped like a snake with its tail wrapped around its own throat.

She threw it to the ground and stormed through the gate, which slammed shut behind her.

Diana exhaled softly, taking deep breaths as she waited for her heartbeat to go back to normal. She peeked out at the gate again. The bracelet lay in the dust, gleaming. An object of power? What did that mean? Would it weaken Anna to lose it?

How risky would it be for Diana to try taking it?

Diana glanced up at the walls, but she couldn't see anything moving. Quickly she darted out from behind the boulder, seized the bracelet, and ran into the shadow of the wall beside the gate. Even if someone did come to patrol the top of the wall, surely they'd be looking out instead of straight down. They might see her running across the plain, but they hopefully wouldn't notice her skulking along the giant wall.

The bracelet was cold and heavy, but it didn't feel particularly magical, and it didn't seem to make her invisible or anything when she put it on. It just hung loose on her wrist, as if it might fall off at any moment. Diana pulled it off again and tucked it into her pocket. She pressed herself into the shadows, feeling the cold, damp stone scrape roughly against her skin, and slid along the wall as fast as she could, moving away from the gate. Her hope was that she could travel all the way around the citadel and escape into the mountains on the other side without being seen. And hopefully there would be another underworld on the other side of those mountains—a cheerful, sunlit underworld full of puppies and unicorns.

It would be nice if Maui were still with me. He'd probably know how to get out of here. She hoped her charming rescuer was all right.

As she moved away from the path of cigarette torches, the shadows grew longer and darker, and soon the only light came from inside the walls, shining occasionally through cracks or small slits of windows high up on the balustrades, or from the distant red glow of the mountains. There was no sign of life in the plain around her, and even the shuffle of her sneakers in the sand sounded too loud. The cliffs she could see were too sheer for her to scale, like panes of smooth glass rising out of the earth, so she had no choice but to keep edging around the citadel, hoping to spot another path into the mountains soon. The wall seemed to go on forever.

Perhaps it does, she thought anxiously. *I might never have gotten out of the Chinese labyrinth if they hadn't let me out. Maybe there is no way around, only through.*

She kept walking, her heart hammering against her ribs, as it got darker and darker.

Suddenly her fingers brushed something that wasn't stone. It felt like wood . . . maybe a wooden door in the wall. She paused, squinting into the darkness, running her hands along the outline of the door.

And then she felt warmth, the static spark of someone else's skin at her fingertips.

A match flared in the darkness, and in its brief glow she saw dark eyes, skin tinged with green, and short black hair tangled with moss. She froze with fear as the stranger lit a cigarette and inhaled, regarding her.

"Well," he said, in a voice like trees sighing, "who might you be?"

"No one," Diana said, taking a step back. "I'm in the wrong place, that's all. Sorry to bother you." She turned to run, but he seized her wrist abruptly. A vine snaked out of his clothes and wound itself around her arm all the way up to the shoulder. She fought the urge to scream, clawing at the leafy tendril, but it had fastened itself to her with tiny burrs that dug painfully into her skin.

"Keeping quiet," the strange man said. "A wise choice. I see you want no one to know you're here." He raised his cigarette to his lips with his free hand, sucking in the smoke casually as if there weren't a struggling girl in his other hand. "I suggest you stop moving," he said. "It'll only get more attached and cause you more pain." He let out a bark of laughter. "Well, I know what that's like." He fell silent again, staring out at the mountains as he smoked.

Diana stopped yanking on the vine. She felt ill with terror, her stomach prickling and churning as if her skin were turning itself inside out. The man's eerie calm was even more chilling than the serpent in the tidal wave. He reminded her of movie vampires, perfectly cold and still.

"Please let me go," she whispered. *Maybe Maui will come. Maybe he's right behind me and he'll show up and rescue me, like he did before.*

"Answer my question," he said, and she felt, more than saw, his eyes flick toward her, then back to the mountains. She hesitated, and with a gentle movement he turned her wrist ever-so-slightly. One of the burrs bit into the pale, fragile skin on the back of her hand, and she gasped in surprise at the pain.

"I'm—I'm—" she started to stammer.

"I suggest you not lie," he said, "as you were about to."

He was right. She had been trying to think of another name, an explanation for her presence, how someone her age could have died recently and found her way here by accident. But nothing she could think of sounded believable. He would see right through her.

The silences between his words were even scarier than what he said, as if each time he paused he were sliding his tongue along an invisible knife, debating whether to kill her now, without warning.

"I'm Diana," she said simply.

There was a pause. "Hmmm," said the stranger, lifting the cigarette to his lips again. She couldn't tell from his reaction whether he knew who she was, or what it meant that he'd caught her here. He inhaled for a long moment, and Diana bit her lip, trying to keep still so the burrs wouldn't dig further into her skin.

"M-may I ask who you are?" she said finally.

The man stubbed out his cigarette on the wall beside the door, and Diana saw a small black mark in the stone, as if he'd been pressing a cigarette to that exact spot for thousands of years. *That can't be right, though*, she thought to herself. *Cigarettes haven't been around for thousands of years, have they?*

"A vile habit," the man said reflectively. "For vile, loathsome people. But then, it's a vile place. And I cannot die." His last words dropped like stones down a well.

After a moment, Diana asked, "Would you want to?" *Perhaps if we can talk . . . perhaps he'll let me go.*

He reached over calmly and took her other wrist, steering her around to face him. She felt a new vine skate over her right hand and wrap around her forearm, and she tensed, ready to pull away, but his grip was locked and unshakable. As her eyes adjusted to the dark, she realized the vines were uncoiling from around his chest and shoulders, where they had been woven together like a shirt. Now glimpses of his bare chest showed through the unraveled gaps.

"I am Dumuzi," he said. "What does that mean to you?"

Diana searched her memory frantically, but she couldn't remember ever learning anything about Mesopotamian mythology or gods like Inanna and Ereshkigal. The name Dumuzi didn't even sound familiar.

"I'm sorry," she whispered. "I don't know who you are."

"No memories," Dumuzi said, touching one finger to her pulse without releasing his iron hold on her wrists. "But . . . a heartbeat." He gazed down at her wrists as if he might sink his teeth into them. "A trade I would gladly make," he said softly.

He stepped closer to her, breathing in her hair. Diana could smell the smoke on his breath and something else, like layers of forest floor, some leaves fresh and some decaying.

"You know my wife," he murmured in her ear. She shivered involuntarily, and he ran his fingertips over the cold goose bumps that prickled along her arms. "She would love to kill you again."

Inanna's husband. Of all the gods in all the underworlds . . .

"I could give you to her," he said, moss from his hair trailing across her cheek. "Or I could kill you myself." His nails dug into her skin. "Or . . . we could kill her together."

Diana drew in a trembling breath. Dumuzi's vines wrapped around her shoulders, squeezing tightly.

"I suggest," said the god, "that you choose wisely."

"Just tell me what to do," Gus said. "I've had enough of people I love dying. And there's a million myths about people going to rescue other people from the underworld, right?" The only one he could remember was about Orpheus, but Gus knew he'd be smarter than that guy.

"And usually failing," Obatala pointed out gently.

"I won't fail. Tell me how to get there."

"You're not going to change his mind," Kali said. Oya sucked in her breath.

"You're going to let him do this?" the little orisha said. She turned to Tigre, her eyes wide. "*You're* going to let him do it?"

Tigre looked bewildered, but Kali shrugged. "Gus is a god too," she said. "More or less. He can do whatever he wants. I'm still going after Eshu. Tigre, you can go with Gus if you'd rather."

"I wouldn't recommend it," Obatala interjected. "The journey to the underworld is always done alone."

"It's okay," Gus said to Tigre. "You don't have to feel guilty anymore. I'll go get Diana; you work on saving the world."

"Are you sure we should split up?" Tigre asked. "What if we never find each other again? Don't terrible things happen when people split up?"

"That's in horror movies," Gus said. "This is more of a supernatural action-adventure thriller." He winked at Tigre, trying to sound braver than he felt.

"Still, Africa is a big continent," Tigre said worriedly. "Even if you do make it back—"

"We'll meet back here," Kali said. "If that's all right with you," she added, bowing her head to Obatala. He rubbed his nose and nodded.

"If this is truly what you want," Obatala said to Gus, "bring your friend, and come with me. Oya will help these two."

"Bye, Gus," Tigre said.

"Good luck," Kali said, taking Gus's hand and shaking it. "I really do hope you succeed."

"You too," Gus said. He knelt to lift Diana's body in his arms. Staggering a little, he followed Obatala down one of the tree-lined roads leading away from the tower, farther out into the jungle and away from the ocean. The sun beat warmly through the palm leaves, but Diana's skin was icy cold against his hands. Ahead of him, the god's white robes brushed the ground, and yet stayed pristinely clean, whereas the bottoms of Gus's jeans were already muddy with red earth.

"I assume," Obatala said over his shoulder, "that you will want to keep her body close while you are on your journey."

"Yeah," Gus said. He hadn't really thought about how

that would work. Would he carry her all the way to the underworld and back? He didn't want to leave her, even though his arms already felt as if they'd been wrung out like wet towels.

"You cannot take her with you," Obatala said as if he'd read Gus's mind, "but I will take you to a guardian near the gates of death who will watch her while you are gone."

"There are gates of death?" Gus said. "So I can just walk in?"

Obatala chuckled. "They are not literal gates. What a mortal way to think." The trees were starting to thin around them and the houses were farther and farther apart. Soon they emerged into a clearing with a wide river running swiftly through it, encircling the gods' village. Obatala plucked a branch from a tree as he walked by and cupped it in his hands, breathing on it as he strode up to the river. Swinging his arm out, he flung the stick across the water, and as it shot through the air it got longer and longer and wider and wider. Within a moment, there was a long, wide wooden plank stretching from one riverbank to the other.

"For you," Obatala said politely, gesturing to the bridge as he walked straight out onto the water. Gus blinked, clutching Diana closer, and stepped out onto the plank, balancing carefully as he edged across. Once he was on the other side, Obatala tapped the end of the plank with his foot and it shrank into a stick again, disappearing into the foaming water.

The jungle seemed different on this side, more ordinary. The ground was covered in thick vines and grasses, and Gus saw a parade of giant ants marching along a tree root. The birdsong was more subdued as well, as if the most talented, most musical birds all lived in the city on the other side of the river, while the ones who'd been cut in the first week of auditions had to live out here.

Obatala pinched his nose together and made an enormous braying noise that didn't sound like it could possibly come from a human-shaped throat. He beckoned to Gus, and they wound through the trees as the sound echoed through the jungle. Gus ducked to avoid the trailing vines and spiderwebs that seemed to hang from every branch.

"There are many tales of going to the underworld, you're right about that," Obatala said. "You have to find the right path, but as I said, she may not be there when you arrive. From the pallor of her skin, I'd guess she is already very close to Hades, and she may bypass the African underworlds altogether."

"She's always really pale," Gus said, shifting Diana's head against his shoulder. "And I know she'll be trying to get back to life."

"Perhaps," Obatala said. "Some find that death is what they wished for all along. And some would like to return, but cannot find the way. My advice to you is be polite, listen to your elders, follow directions, and don't be impatient. This is not a world for blustering, weapons-waving war gods or aggressive video game heroes like the ones America likes so much." He gave Gus a stern look. "If you are imagining yourself in a futuristic martial arts movie where you burst in with guns blazing, grab the helpless maiden, and storm out, stop it right now. A different kind of valor is needed here, and my guess is that your human spirit is better suited for it than your god twin's."

Gus had, perhaps, been trying to picture himself as Neo in *The Matrix* or Captain Apollo on *Battlestar Galactica.* He felt Oro stirring under his skin, offended, and he tried to think of something besides battle and violence.

Luckily, just then he heard the sound of voices in the jungle ahead of him—quiet, cheerful voices, like friends playing cards on a Sunday afternoon. They passed between two boulders and Gus saw a village up ahead. Unlike the gods' city, this one was small and made of ordinary building materials. A thin trail of smoke drifted from one of the roofs, and a well stood in the center of the small circle of houses. Near the well, in the shade of a tree with spreading branches, two men and three women were sitting in rocking chairs, watching a monkey climbing above them as they talked.

The villagers' faces were lined with wrinkles and their hands, crooked with age, rested idly on their laps on top of brightly woven blankets. They reminded Gus of the residents he used to see gathered in front of the TV in his grandfather's nursing home, before his grandfather and then his parents had died.

As Gus and Obatala approached, one of the women lifted one shaking hand toward the well. Almost instantly, another monkey swung down from the tree, raced over to the well, drew some water into a cup, and ran back to the woman. It sat beside her as she drank, holding the cup gently in its tiny paws and patting at her mouth when she'd finished.

"Are these some kind of ancient, all-powerful gods?" Gus asked.

"No," Obatala said, stopping at the well. "They are some of the last mortals in Africa."

"Oh," Gus said. He had forgotten that Africa must have some people still alive, like New York did. But these did not look like the desperate, hunted subway dwellers he'd seen in New York City. They looked at peace, like they were well taken care of as they waited to die.

"It's interesting," Obatala said, leaning against the stones of the well. The villagers looked at them with mild curiosity, but didn't speak to them. "Long ago, when we created the mortal world, we lived very closely with people like this. The sky was down near the earth, and people climbed up and down to visit, or we shared their homes. Everyone got along. But then they angered us—I don't even remember exactly how. They took us for granted, perhaps. They cut off bits of the sky and used it in their soup. They whacked the clouds when they pounded grain, hurting our feet. Or they just demanded too much: bring my wife back to life, save my daughter from her sickness, give me wealth, give me love, give me children."

Gus crouched beside the well, using the stones to brace himself as he rested Diana on his knees. Obatala went on, gazing up at the sky.

"And so we left them. We packed up and moved away, taking the sky out of their reach and cutting the rope that had joined us. We stopped moving among them, stopped telling them where we lived and how to find us. If they tried to reach us, we ignored them or we killed them. I don't know what we did with our time—quarreled amongst ourselves, I suppose.

"Is it any wonder, then, that they turned around and started ignoring us? Or that they fought each other so much, trying to get from their neighbors what we would not give them?" He pressed his hands together, looking at the elderly group with a sad expression. They had gone back to watching the monkey, laughing as it nearly missed the branch it was jumping for.

"Now that the continent is ours again, we have come back down here to live, and it's made us realize how much we missed it. How much we missed *them*. We gave them these homes as they grew older and more alone, and we look after them now, when most of them are too weak to take care of themselves. They're not our elders, but they would have been somebody's, in a different world, and they deserve respect."

Obatala rubbed his chin. "I think, if we had it to do over again, we would have done things differently. We would have come back sooner, cared for them more, instead of staying in the sky complaining about why no one seemed to think about us."

He paused and glanced down at Gus. "Well, perhaps we will have a chance. If your friend Kali succeeds, maybe we will get to do it over again, and better this time."

"Is that why you're helping us?" Gus asked.

Obatala smiled. "Oh, let the orishas think they convinced me. They love having their voices heard. And they seem very fond of the two of you and your twin spirits." He nodded at Diana.

Something rustled in the trees on the far edge of the clearing, and a few of the old villagers leaned forward curiously to see what was happening. Gus peered around the well and saw something long and gray part the bushes.

Two elephants stepped into the clearing, one of them holding back the branches with his trunk so the other could step through. Their skin was wrinkled, their ears were enormous, and their eyes were dark and kind. Gus had seen elephants at the Los Angeles Zoo and once at a circus when he was very young, but he'd always thought those elephants looked sad and dusty and tired. These elephants seemed radiantly happy. The larger one's face crinkled in what looked like a smile as it waved its trunk at Obatala.

"Hello, Abidemi, my friend," Obatala said to the bigger elephant. He crossed toward them, holding out his hand, and Abidemi touched it ceremoniously with his trunk. Obatala turned and bowed toward the smaller elephant. "And Kayode, thank you for coming with him. I have a great favor to ask of you both." He beckoned to Gus, who stood, carrying Diana.

Kayode lifted his trunk curiously, but Abidemi stepped back, the light going out of his eyes. He lowered his tusks and made a low noise at the other elephant.

"It's all right, Abidemi," Obatala said gently. "He is not the kind of man you fear. Stand still, Gus." Abidemi came forward reluctantly and passed his trunk over Gus's shoulders and head. Gus felt the tip brush his face, like the hand of a blind person learning his features but with a snuffling breath that smelled like bananas.

The elephant snorted and shook his head so his ears flapped.

"He says you smell like war and bloodshed," Obatala said. "Now the girl, my friend."

Abidemi did the same thing to Diana, touching her hair and her neck lightly with his trunk. The smaller elephant pressed closer, brushing Abidemi's trunk with his own. His large dark eyes blinked at Gus.

"Yes, it's true," Obatala agreed, "she has a hunter's spirit."

"I promise she'd never hurt an elephant, and neither would I," Gus said. He hated the fact that the sight of him seemed to have made the big elephant so sad.

"Abidemi can remember a time when men still blazed across this territory killing his friends and family," Obatala explained. "He is much older than his companion, Kayode, who was born after humans were too old to hunt, when the elephant population was beginning to recover. In the last few decades, the elephants here have lived happy, peaceful lives." Abidemi snorted again. "Yes," Obatala said. "Abidemi says Kayode doesn't know enough to fear you."

"Please tell him we're harmless," Gus said. "We would never ever hurt them."

Obatala murmured in the bigger elephant's ear. Gus met Kayode's eyes, and the elephant did a shuffling step in the dust, his eyes shining.

"Abidemi, I am only asking you to protect this girl

while her spirit travels," Obatala said. "The boy is going in search of it."

The elephant's ears swung forward and back and it tilted its head.

"Because you are strong enough," Obatala said, "and because you won't forget and wander off and leave her alone, like certain animals might. Baboons? Impalas? I shudder to think."

Abidemi and Kayode both trumpeted, as if they were laughing. Kayode stroked the older elephant's face with his trunk, moving his feet. Abidemi shook his head slowly for a long time, but finally he looked at Obatala and nodded.

"Thank you, my friend." Obatala bowed and the elephants started toward a path that wound away from the village into the jungle.

"Where are we going now?" Gus asked, following them. He glanced back at the old people, most of whom were asleep in their chairs.

"You want to visit the land of the dead," Obatala said. "So we must begin where all such journeys begin . . . at the graveyard."

The orishas seemed to press closer as Obatala disappeared from view. Their strange eyes were fixed on Tigre and Kali now. Oya stepped forward, flapping her hands at the crowd.

"Shoo!" she scolded. "Go on now, back to your business, you gossipy hens."

"Hey," protested a woman with a long scrawny neck and beady eyes.

"It's just a phrase, don't get offended," Oya tut-tutted. "Now off, shoo!" She bounced a step toward them, the red color flaring brightly in her hair, and the whole pack of orishas turned and scattered into the city.

"Oh yes, that's right," Oya sang, waggling her hips as she turned back to Kali and Tigre. "No-bo-dy messes with Oya!" She sank her hands into her hair and looked up at Tigre, who towered over her. The top of her Afro barely came up to his shoulder.

"So you're Catequil?"

"Yup," Tigre said awkwardly.

"Really? You're really him?"

"That's what they tell me," Tigre said, shooting Kali a wry look. "But you can call me Tigre."

"Oh, no way!" Oya protested, her eyes shining. "Names have so much power. I should call you 'Catequil Catequil Catequil' for extra oomph."

"I—um, okay," Tigre said.

"It'll take you all day to have a conversation," Kali said with a grin. "But maybe she has a point. Catequil."

"It's weird," Tigre said with a shiver. "Nobody's called me that since I was a kid." His father had never liked the name, but then, his father had never really liked *him* much, either. His mother had tried using it for a while, but gave up when his sister Claudia started calling him Tigre, which seemed to work for everyone. Even in school, half of his teachers hadn't known his real name. When his ex-girlfriend found out what it was, she'd made fun of him for weeks. Vicky pronounced it "Catty Quill," which made it even worse.

But when Oya said it, it sounded majestic and ancient. "Kah-te-keel." He realized it was the same *qu-* sound that was in Quetzie's name, and he glanced up at the sky, wondering again where his neoquetzal friend had gone.

"So this is all very fun and civilized," Kali said, "but shouldn't we be chasing Eshu? He's already got about half an hour's head start on us."

"Oh, we will so catch him," Oya said. She closed her eyes and pressed her palms together. "Although I bet we'll regret it when we do. That guy is a pain in the toe." With her eyes still closed, she lifted one bare foot forward and wiggled her big toe at Tigre. "He went north, didn't he?"

Kali looked up at the tower, shading her eyes, then turned to get her bearings. "That way," she said, pointing.

"North! Yes!" Oya said, jumping in place. "I win! Let's go!" She sprang into action, racing straight through the trees and gardens, ignoring the roads. Tigre watched, astonished, as she leaped nimbly over several fences and stormed right through a herd of goats, who bleated angrily at her.

"Looks like it's time for a run," Kali said. "Quick—I'm not entirely sure she'd notice if she lost us." She set off after Oya, and Tigre followed her, feeling awkward about running through people's yards and goat herds. He tried to go around the first garden, but Kali shouted: "Come on, Tigre!" and he had to sprint to catch up.

As they ran through the herd, one goat suddenly made a popping sound and changed into a long, scraggly-looking man with a tuft of white hair on his chin. "Baaad children!" he scolded, thumping Tigre on the head as he ran by. "Quit mehhhssing around like you're bewitched."

"Sorry," Tigre called, throwing himself over the next fence. "Really, very sorry!"

Running on level ground, even with houses and streams and fences in the way, was much easier for him than climbing stairs; after all, he had done this a hundred times when the storms in South America took him over. Soon he was running alongside Kali, stride for stride. Ahead of them he could see a large river, several houses wide, that seemed to run along the outer edge of the town, foaming green and brown with muddy banks. On the other side there were no buildings, only clusters of fruit trees.

They skidded to a stop at the river's edge, where Oya was racing around gathering smooth, round river stones.

"Isn't this brilliantly exciting?" she called as she heard them approach. "I love hunting. I *love* it. It feels like my veins are turning into leopards, racing below my skin, leaping out through my feet. How about you? I feel like I can smell the whole jungle!"

"That doesn't sound so pleasant," Kali remarked.

"Don't you talk about the jungle like that," Oya retorted with her hands on her hips. Tigre honestly couldn't tell if she was really mad or just kidding. The red streak in her hair went darker and quivered, but the next moment her sunny smile returned.

"Come on, we need more of these," she said, flipping one of the river stones in the air and catching it behind her back. She dropped it on a small pile at the edge of the river.

"What for?" Kali asked, picking up another one and adding it to the pile.

"Well, I'm guessing you don't want to swim across the

river," Oya said. Kali shuddered, and Tigre remembered that she didn't know how to swim.

"Isn't there a bridge somewhere?" Tigre asked.

"We're making one, aren't we?" Oya said brightly. "Psht, we can't have any permanent bridges, silly. Or else it'd be much too easy to attack us; we have more sense than that."

"Attack you?" Tigre repeated, startled. "Who attacks you?"

"Other African cities," Oya said, as if that were obvious. "You didn't think the Yoruba were the only gods in Africa, did you? We fight the Fon all the time because they're closest, but that's boring—like, it's so obvious how I'm going to die every time. I prefer the Ashanti—battles with them are totally wild. But the best are the San, if we can get them all the way up here, because it's the kind of hard-core fighting that just gets inside your blood, you know?"

"What are you talking about?" Tigre said. "You sound like you think war is fun."

"Of c—oh!" Oya grabbed fistfuls of her hair, which flared iridescent red at the tips. "I can't believe I just said that! I'm sorry! I totally forgot about you guys being mortal! No, of course it wouldn't be fun if anyone *actually* died. Good grief, that would be *horrible*." She pressed her hands to her mouth. "Ack! I should stop talking. Just ignore me. Seriously, we only do it to keep ourselves amused. Like you have TV and sports, we have epic battles to the death, and then we all come back and start again. It's *so* much fun, but no, no, it wouldn't be for you, of course. I'm sorry."

Tigre noticed that Kali was hiding a smile. He had a

suspicion that the Indian avatar knew exactly what Oya meant when she talked about battle being exciting.

"So, Oya, how do you know Catequil?" Kali asked, scooping a trio of stones out of the river.

"Oh, *everyone* knows about Catequil," Oya said.

"Really?" Tigre asked.

"No, not at all," she said, smothering a giggle. "Sorry, I'm probably the only one in Africa who's heard of you." *You and perhaps Eshu*, Tigre thought. "I have this weird obsession with knowing stuff about my competition," Oya went on, "so I learned everything I could about all the weather gods in the world. I never thought I'd get to meet you, though! I tell you, this apocalypse is a great way to meet people. You were so cool for a while there, before the Incas came along. I liked how you were more than just a weather god. Now Tlaloc, for instance, can do weather really well, but that's all he can do. I BRING THE LIGHTNING! I BRING THE THUNDER!"

Tigre jumped; Oya's imitation of the Aztec storm god was uncannily on target.

"You've met Tlaloc?" he asked.

"Not in person, but I've studied him over the last several centuries," Oya said. "Anyway, he's tough, but he's no you. No prophecies, no visions—no imagination, if you ask me. Just a lot of shouting and wetness."

"Sounds about right," Kali said, giving Tigre a grin. He returned it, feeling pleased. He'd never thought of himself as having vision or imagination before.

"All right, that's enough," Oya said, pushing away his hand.

As they'd talked, Oya had been piling their stones until the stack was as tall as she was. Now she stood next to it and put one hand on top, burrowing one of her bare feet further into the mud of the riverbank. Tigre expected her to chant or something, but all she said was:

"Bridge, please!"

The stones rattled in polite response, and then one by one they started to bloom into larger rocks, like balloons being blown up in quick bursts. The ones closest to the ground settled into the bank, squirming in the mud until they were firmly entrenched. The rest began to shoot out over the river, unfolding until they reached the other side, where the far end of the bridge lodged itself in the ground. Several fish popped their heads out of the water to goggle. Tigre could have sworn they were nodding admiringly to each other.

"Perfect! Thanks!" Oya chirped, leaping onto the bridge and padding over to the other side. Tigre watched dubiously as Kali followed. There was no rail or wall along the edge; nothing between him and the river.

"Hurry up, Catequil Catequil Catequil!" Oya hollered, cupping her hands around her mouth.

Carefully he climbed onto the bridge and wobbled across. From the corner of his eye he could see the fish watching him. He wondered if fish could giggle, because he was sure they'd never seen anything so awkward before. He was relieved when he finally jumped down on the other side.

Oya snapped her fingers, and the rocks shrank instantly back to their regular size, dropping into the river with a series of plops.

"Still north, I think. Come on!" Oya ran lightly up the muddy bank into the trees, her curves and rolls looking weightless and graceful. She turned at the edge of the jungle, looking back at them mischievously.

"Let's go catch a god."

"Why—why would you want to kill Anna?" Diana asked, hating the way her voice shook.

"Why wouldn't you?" Dumuzi asked, his tongue flicking between his teeth. "She killed you first."

"I'm not dead," Diana said, tugging her arm and wincing as the burrs sliced into her.

"We could fix that," Dumuzi said. "Inanna and Ereshkigal could make your death last for centuries."

"And I'm not a killer," Diana said. "I just want to get out of here. Please, please let me go."

"I'm not going to do that," Dumuzi said. "I suggest you stop asking." He released one of her wrists, and the vine twisted to allow him to reach up to her face. Dumuzi ran his thumb along her jawline, and Diana felt her trembling get worse. "It will be easy," he hissed. "You have already begun."

Abruptly he shoved his hand in her pocket and pulled out the bracelet. He pressed the cold metal to her cheek. "All you need is the other six. Then she will be trapped here. Her body in the upworld will die. You can take her power."

"I don't want her power," Diana said. "And what's in it for you?"

"These," Dumuzi said. The metal began to feel warm against Diana's skin. "And freedom."

Diana didn't know what to do. Could she really kill Anna? Even if it was by stealing things, and not by actually stabbing her? Was that the same thing as killing her? If Anna's soul was trapped here, at least it would still exist, and she'd be with her fellow gods, even if she hated them. And if Diana didn't do this, either Dumuzi would kill her now, or Anna would hunt down Diana and Kali and Tigre and Gus and kill them all. So it was sort of like self-defense. Retroactive self-defense . . . post-murder.

The bracelet was beginning to burn, and Diana tried to turn her face away, but Dumuzi pressed it harder into her flesh.

"Okay," Diana gasped. "I'll—I'll try."

The god lifted the bracelet away, and a chilly breeze swept across the burn.

"Good," he said. The vines gracefully unwound from her arms, weaving back into his shirt, but at the same time another one snaked out and coiled around her ankle. Instead of burrs, this one had thorns as long as her thumbs, and when Diana moved too much they stabbed her viciously.

Dumuzi opened the wooden door behind him and stood back for Diana to walk through. She wished he would talk more, tell her anything. Why did he hate Anna so much? What did he expect Diana to do?

The door opened into a rough stone tunnel that seemed to run along inside the citadel wall. Guttering torches like the ones she'd seen outside at the gates sprang from the wall at distant intervals, leaving dark patches of shadow in between. It smelled like a meat locker, cold and bloody.

The god closed the door behind him and stood in the

dim light for a moment, his expression suggesting that he found this place as horrible as Diana did—maybe even more so.

"Why do you stay here if you hate it so much?" Diana asked. She pressed her hand over the small cuts along her arms, trying to stop the stinging pain. "I mean, aren't you a god? Can't you do anything you want?"

Dumuzi put his hand on her shoulder and turned her in the direction that would take them back to the main gate. "Ask your Persephone that," he said. "Now walk."

Persephone? Diana thought as she walked with the pressure of Dumuzi's hand against her back. She searched her brain. *She was . . . she's the one who married Hades, wasn't she? Queen of the underworld.* The myth started coming back to her. *He abducted her—she's the one who ate while she was in the underworld. And then she had to stay with him for as many months of the year as pomegranate seeds she'd eaten, but the rest of the time she spent on Earth with her mother.*

She tried glancing over her shoulder, but Dumuzi firmly pushed her forward. "So you're stuck here?" Diana asked. "Is it for only part of the year, like Persephone?"

"Yes," Dumuzi answered. "But that is because my sister takes the burden of the other half. Half a year every year in this place for all eternity . . . " He fell silent. Diana waited a moment before she spoke again.

"That myth was about seasons, wasn't it?" she asked. "When she was in Hades, it was winter, but when she went back to her mom, it was summer. Is yours like that?"

"Yes," he said. "I suggest you not call them 'myths' if you prefer to live."

"Oh," Diana said. "Sorry." She stumbled on the uneven

stone floor, and he seized her elbow, keeping her from falling. His hand was warm, and where he touched her, the little slices from the burrs seemed to disappear. Once she was upright again, he took it away and pushed her back into walking.

"So what did you do?" Diana asked. "To get stuck here?"

"I did nothing," Dumuzi said. "Inanna was the one who angered Ereshkigal."

"So Ereshkigal demanded you as revenge?" Diana guessed.

"No. Inanna chose me to take her place here." Dumuzi's voice could have frozen an ocean. "She felt I did not mourn her well enough."

"Oh," Diana said again. "Wow." She passed a door in the wall leading into the citadel, but Dumuzi didn't stop her, so she kept walking. "Yeah, I guess that would make me pretty mad too." Anna should have been the one being punished all this time, but she'd condemned her own husband to suffer instead. *She must be really powerful in her pantheon. No wonder he wants her dead.*

"So if we kill her—you'll be free?"

"If she is here," he said, "and if I have these." He held out his arm, now with the bracelet clasped around it.

"What do the objects do?" Diana asked.

"They do nothing," Dumuzi answered. "They are power. She stole them herself, originally, from Enki." His hand closed over Diana's shoulder, bringing her to a stop. To their right was another wooden door, opposite the wall they'd come in through. Diana couldn't tell how close they were to the main gate.

Dumuzi opened the door and looked out, keeping a hold on Diana's wrist. After a moment, he pulled her forward and shut the door behind them.

They were standing on a paved walkway. Above them towered the citadel walls; ahead of them was a maze of streets and buildings and gates rising to a dark fortress in the center. Everywhere there were people, but the lights shone right through them, and they looked aimless and slow and decomposing, like zombies. None of them turned at the sound of the door closing, and one walked straight past only a few inches from Diana without even glancing at her.

Dumuzi started down the street in the direction of the main gate, keeping close to the wall so none of the rotting ghosts would touch him. Diana imitated him, hurrying to keep up and wincing as the thorns sank into her ankle.

Soon she saw that they were circling another wall, built inside the first and parallel to it, and a shade closer to black than the gray of the exterior wall. Ahead of them was a set of gates in this wall, like a slightly smaller replica of the ones outside. Hanging on a hook just outside the gate was a necklace of blue stones.

Dumuzi stopped under an eave. "Take it," he said.

"Why can't you take it?" Diana asked.

"My wife is cautious," he said with a thin smile. "They're enchanted so I cannot steal them. But she is not cautious enough. She knows no one else here would dare." He jerked his chin at the necklace.

This is weird, Diana thought as she crept forward. *I'm just taking her jewelry. How could this kill her?* If she were really going to do something that huge, it felt like it ought to be epic, violent, and face-to-face. This was too sneaky.

Like pretending to be your friend and then stabbing you in the gut?

Diana lifted the necklace off the hook, the blue stones rolling between her fingers. She hurried back to Dumuzi, who settled it around his neck with a bright look in his eyes.

"Will you really let me go if I do this?" Diana asked. "You promise?"

"I will," Dumuzi said. "I will name constellations after you. I will grow groves of lilac trees in your honor. I will send genies to protect you for the rest of your days."

Diana was taken aback. It almost sounded like there was joy in his voice. This was more than he'd said all at once so far. His attention was on the necklace, so Diana could study his sharp, handsome features, and she saw that his hands were trembling as they stroked the beads, almost as much as hers had been. This was something he cared about very much.

"Okay," Diana said. "Take me to the next one."

Dumuzi pressed something in the wall, and a small door revolved out of the stonework. Diana squeezed through with the god close behind her.

She could see the next gate from here, in yet another, darker wall. Dumuzi had said there were seven objects, so Diana guessed that there were seven gates Inanna had to pass through before reaching her sister—leaving a piece of her power at each threshold along the way.

A round stone bulb jutted out of the stonework by the third gate, and perched on top of it, unfolded to rest around the globe, was a pair of sunglasses.

Diana picked them up doubtfully. They were sleek and modern-looking, like something a movie star would wear. She should know; she'd owned several pairs like this herself. It didn't have a label inscribed in it, but she thought she recognized the designer.

"This doesn't look right," she said, returning to Dumuzi. "This can't be an object of power, can it?"

Dumuzi took the sunglasses reverently. "You don't feel it?" he asked. "She has changed its shape to suit your world, but the core stays the same." With a solemn expression that would be funny if Diana weren't still so scared of him, he slid the sunglasses onto his nose.

"I think it works for you," Diana said. "You'd fit in well on the red carpet."

"Ereshkigal's carpets are red," Dumuzi said, his eyes hidden. "With the bl—"

"Please," Diana said, interrupting, "please don't say 'with the blood of her victims.'"

Dumuzi kept silent, the corners of his mouth twitching.

"Okay," Diana said. "Thanks. Number four?"

This gate was farther away; they had to walk in a curving line a quarter of the way around the city before they came to it. Diana thought she saw a ghostly market down one of the side streets, and the figures here seemed a little denser, but they didn't look any happier or more active.

The fourth object was a pair of small silver ball earrings,

and Diana actually remembered seeing them in Anna's ears. Had she had these objects of power with her the whole time? Was that how she'd communicated with her pantheon, planning the trick with Ereshkigal?

Dumuzi pushed the sunglasses up on his head, took the earrings from her, and stabbed them into his ears, creating holes where there hadn't been any before. Two vines swarmed up from his shirt to dab away the blood from his earlobes.

Diana was starting to get really tired; her feet ached the way they always did at the end of a long concert tour, and the cold air of Irkalla seemed to be settling into her bones, squeezing everything inside her painfully. She took deep breaths, concentrating on putting one foot in front of the next as they went through the fourth gate and walked to the fifth.

Here a gold ring was sitting on a stone ledge. Diana picked it up, surprised at how heavy it was. She walked back to Dumuzi, wondering if Frodo had been this tired on his trip to Mordor. Probably more so. She should count herself lucky there weren't orcs chasing her, at least.

"One ring to rule them all," she joked, dropping it into the god's outstretched palm. *Gus would be so proud of me for that reference.* She thought of Gus laughing, pushing up his glasses, mocking her sci-fi knowledge. *If only I could get just one more hug from him.* A wave of longing hit her, and she swayed, feeling dizzy.

Dumuzi caught her shoulders, turned her toward him, and studied her face. He put two fingers lightly against her cheek, and the pain of the bracelet burn faded. Then he ran his hands firmly down her arms, and her cuts vanished in a rush of warmth.

"There," he said.

"Thank you," she said, lifting her hands to look at the unbroken skin with surprise. It felt odd to be thanking him for healing the pain he'd inflicted himself, but the god standing before her now looked very different from the one that had cornered her outside the walls. With each item, he stood up straighter and looked years younger. His eyes were shining; Diana thought he almost looked like he was holding back tears.

"Thank *you*," he responded, turning the ring so it glinted in the lamplight.

Another hidden door took them through the fifth wall, and Diana noticed how close they were now to the fortress. The smell of rotting meat was stronger here, and the fortress cast a shadow on the streets around it so that she felt almost like she was walking through a dense fog.

Stalls were set up along the main road here, and crowds of ghosts were gathered around each one, poking the decaying fruit and holding rusted metal things up to the light to examine them. Diana stayed as close as she could to Dumuzi, shivering as she brushed past chilly gray shoulders and threadbare robes. She could see the holes in their faces, the hint of things crawling behind their sunken eye sockets.

Dumuzi took her wrist and steered her toward the wall behind the stalls, where they stepped over a few scrawny, lounging cat spirits and around piles of stinking gray hay that made Diana feel even sicker. This was no place to be trapped for all eternity. *If I were him, I'd probably do just about anything to get out of here too.*

At the sixth gate, which was the blackest of all of them, Diana had to search for a moment before she found the next object. She scanned the wall around the gate with her eyes, feeling the thorns tighten around her ankle. *What will he do if I can't finish the task? What if she's already come back and taken it?*

Then something glinted against the dark stone, and she spotted a chain-link belt fashioned of black metal, hanging by the buckle from a high nail driven into the mortar. Diana stood on tiptoes, reaching to knock it down, and after a minute of tugging, the links cascaded down on her head and she poured them all into one hand.

"Interesting," Dumuzi said as she handed it to him. He ran the belt around his leafy tunic, which looked odd and incongruous, but Diana wasn't about to point that out.

"Here we must go through the real gate," Dumuzi said. "Keep your eyes closed and do not pull away from me." He wrapped one arm around her shoulders, pressing her back against his chest. She could feel his heartbeat through the rustling vines. Diana closed her eyes and let him guide her forward. She felt a rush of cold air across her face, and then it turned and rushed back, whipping her hair around. It seemed like they were walking for much more time than it should have taken to get through the gate, but finally Dumuzi let go of her and said, "We are here."

Diana blinked. They were standing in front of the seventh gate. It was so black that it seemed as if it were a hole in space instead of something filling space, and she couldn't see any doors or handles. She also couldn't see anything that looked like it might have been left by Inanna.

She glanced up and saw that Dumuzi looked puzzled too. "Where is it?" she asked.

His hands curled into fists. "So close," he murmured. "What did she do?"

Diana touched the wall beside the gate, running her hand up the freezing marble in case there was something she couldn't see. It felt like she was plunging her hand into black, icy tar. Shuddering, she moved her hands quickly across the gate and the wall on the other side, and then stepped back, pressing them together to try and wipe away the sticky feeling.

"I'm sorry," she said, her teeth chattering. "I don't see anything." She didn't know whether to feel relieved or terrified. This way she didn't have to kill Anna—but what would Dumuzi do now?

He stared at the gates, frowning.

"What should it be?" Diana asked. "Do you know?"

"The first time, it was a dress," he said, making a gesture to indicate something floor-length.

Diana shook her head. "There's nothing here like that."

He was silent, scrutinizing the black stone with eyes nearly as dark.

"Maybe six will be enough?" Diana said hopefully.

"We must go in," he said, "and take it from her."

Diana looked up at the looming fortress, dread seeping through her. "They'll kill me in there," she said. "Like, really, permanently dead."

"Then at least I'll have company," he said.

Diana glanced at him sharply. It was hard to tell, but—"Was that a joke?" she asked. "Were you just funny?"

"Apparently not very," he said.

She hid a smile. Her gaze traveled down to her ankle. "All right." She took a deep breath. "I'll go in there if you unchain me."

Dumuzi touched the vine, hesitating. "What if you run?"

"I won't," Diana said. "Trust me."

"I do not like trusting," he said. But he knelt and pinched the vine until it let go of her and coiled itself back to him. He placed his other hand around her ankle—it was big enough to reach all the way around—and soon she felt the warmth again, and the cuts from the thorns disappeared.

"That is a great trick," Diana said. "I wish you could come back to the real world and fix the stab wound your wife gave me."

"It only works on plant-inflicted injuries," Dumuzi said, standing up again.

Diana had a fit of giggles. She couldn't stop herself. He folded his arms with a frown. "Plants can be very dangerous," he said sternly.

"I'm sure," Diana said, burying her face in her hands to contain her laughter.

"You're going to offend my shirt," he said, and she cracked up again, bending over with her hands on her knees.

When she finally composed herself, she saw that he

was smiling but trying not to. "No one has found me funny in a long time," he said. "You remind me of her in happier days."

That sobered her up. "I'm not like her," she said.

"Venus was just a later version of Inanna," he said. "But you're right. She is much less human than you." He paused. "She would take that as a compliment."

"That's how I take it," Diana said.

There was a moment of silence, and then he stepped toward her with a look in his eyes that made her think he might try to kiss her. But he just turned her shoulders, pulled her close to him again, and walked her forward the way he had at the last gate. With his other hand he covered her eyes.

This time the cold wind was stronger and busier, so it felt like she was walking through a swarm of ice bees that stung the exposed bits of her face and hands. Without Dumuzi's strong arm around her, Diana thought she might have been blown away, or shredded into small pieces.

Then the wind dropped suddenly, and her ears rang with enormous stillness, as if she'd been flung into an abandoned mausoleum.

Dumuzi took his hand away from her eyes and touched her lips briefly with one finger—*don't talk*. She nodded, and he let her go.

The room was enormous, and empty apart from a huge, sweeping black marble staircase ahead of them. A dim red-and-silver light came from the line where the walls met the ceiling. A long, worn-down carpet rolled from the door all the way up the stairs, and it was stained with different shades of red. Diana remembered what Dumuzi had said and stepped off it, feeling sick.

Dumuzi crouched and touched Diana's sneakers, one after the other, and she lifted her feet as large, hairy leaves wrapped themselves around her shoes, padding her footsteps. The god stood and led her toward the stairs. They both stayed off the carpet.

At the top of the slippery stairs, Dumuzi turned left, and Diana followed him down a long, narrow hallway with high ceilings. Soon she heard voices ahead of them and Dumuzi slowed down, creeping softly along the wall.

"What is WRONG with you?" Anna's voice shouted. "Don't you want to win this stupid contest?"

"So you can have all the power?" Ereshkigal answered in a dry, papery voice. "Oh yes, I can't wait."

"Better me than that useless Incan weather god," Anna spat, and Diana winced. *Poor Tigre.* "Or perhaps you'd like to be subservient to Kali, or Thor, or some Polynesian war god?"

"I'll be down here, minding my own business," Ereshkigal said. "Why should they bother me?"

"People will forget you," Anna said. "I've been in the mortal world, remember? Nobody knows who you are, sis. You're nobody. One day you'll disappear completely."

"You've always wanted my throne," Ereshkigal hissed. "I knew you'd be back to try and get it again one day."

There was a crash, as if Anna had kicked something over in a rage. "I don't want your stupid throne!" she yelled. "I want you to help me kill the other avatars!

What's so confusing about that? Why didn't you gut Diana when you had the chance?"

"Shamash stopped me," the goddess of death answered. "He forbade me to meddle."

"GODS!" Anna shouted. "When I'm queen of the world, I'm going to stuff him into a buffalo and sew up both ends so he's stuck there forever!"

Dumuzi darted across an open doorway and crouched on the other side, beckoning to Diana with two fingers. She pressed herself to the wall and peeked in quickly, getting a glimpse before pulling back out of sight.

It looked like a throne room, with two dirty white skeletal thrones at the far end. Ereshkigal was seated in one of them, and a bored-looking man sat on the other. Hooded figures stood around the edges of the room. And from what Diana could see, there were enormous hooks embedded in the ceiling and walls. She didn't want to look too closely at what was hanging from them, although the smell of death coming from the room was a strong clue.

"All right, fine," Anna snarled. "I'll go back and find them and kill them myself. Just give me back my stuff."

"You think you're very clever, sister," Ereshkigal said. "We know what you did. We know that you gave Neti a piece of clothing at the last gate that was not an object of power."

"I must have forgotten what was what," Anna said. "Mortal brains are very busy."

"It was a pointless attempt to hold on to your power," Ereshkigal hissed. "We know it doesn't work without the other six."

"So who cares?" Anna said.

"You will show respect to this throne!" Ereshkigal said. "Seize her!"

Suddenly Dumuzi threw something into Diana's arms. She shook it out quickly and realized it was a long hooded cloak.

"Oh no," she whispered, and then he was next to her, flinging it over her head and tugging it into place. The hood was barely over her face when he shoved her into the throne room, alone.

The other hooded figures were converging on Anna, who was screaming curses at them. No one seemed to notice another cloaked shape joining them. The coarse wool of the cloak scratched Diana's arms as she tried to look menacing, ducking her face away from Ereshkigal's throne.

"Get off me!" Anna screamed. "Don't you touch me!" One of the figures grabbed her arm and she kicked him solidly in the chest, knocking him to the ground. The others hissed, pressing closer, and Diana slipped between two of them, edging toward Anna.

She scanned Anna quickly, looking for something that might be an object of power. Anna was wearing ordinary brown sandals, a knee-length flowered skirt, and a short-sleeved green silk blouse. She didn't look like a vengeful, murderous goddess. She looked like any of the attractive actresses that waited tables in LA, waiting to be discovered.

But her face was contorted in rage. Diana remembered that was one of the last things she'd seen before dying. She could almost feel the silver slice of the knife plunging into her again.

There was no other jewelry on her; her wrists and neck and ears were bare. The hooded figures hesitated, and then one of them seized a corner of her skirt and another snatched at a sleeve, tugging her in two directions.

"That's not *it!*" Anna yelled at them, shoving them both away. "Don't you think I learned my lesson last time when I had to stand here naked?"

As she whipped around to scream at them, something flashed in the light. Diana squinted, then jumped forward, grabbing a handful of Anna's hair and pulling hard. She felt a stab of glee as Anna shrieked with pain.

Diana stepped back and opened her hand. Nestled in her palm was a small black ebony comb the same color as Anna's hair, with one small diamond in the center of it. That was the flash Diana had seen. Anna could have made the comb look any way she wanted, but her vanity had added a diamond; otherwise no one might have found it.

"Well done," said a voice like bones rubbing together. Diana looked up and saw the king of the underworld gazing at her from his throne. He clapped his hands once, twice, three times, and she had the eerie feeling that he knew exactly what had really happened here.

"Yes, good work, minion," Ereshkigal said. She held out her hand commandingly. "Bring it to me."

Diana closed her fingers around the comb and stepped back toward the door, keeping her head lowered below the hood. Should she run? How far could she get before Anna and her sister caught her and hung her from one of those hooks?

Ereshkigal's eyes narrowed. "I said bring it to me. Who

are you, daring to disobey me?" As Diana took another step back, Ereshkigal threw back her dark, matted hair and raised her other hand, as if she were about to throw something invisible and deadly at Diana.

"You will be punished for this," Ereshkigal hissed.

"I think not," said a strong voice behind Diana.

A warm hand encircled Diana's, and with a feeling of relief, she let go of the comb, letting it drop into Dumuzi's fingers. It was done. Diana sank to the floor, pulling the cloak around her.

"Dumuzi?" Anna gasped. She pushed through the crowd of cloaked figures and ran to him, throwing her arms around his neck. "Thank *gods* you're here, darling. I've missed you so so so so so so SO terribly much." She covered his face with kisses on each "so." "And they're being just horrible to me! I'm so glad you came to stop them. My big handsome hero." She snuggled into his chest, and Diana saw him lift his free hand to rest it lightly, tenderly, on her hair for a moment.

Anna opened her eyes and spotted the bracelet on his wrist. She stared at it for a moment, and then jerked back, pushing him away.

"How did you get that?" she said through clenched teeth. Her eyes scanned him. "And that." She pointed to the necklace. "And that, and that, and—" She motioned to the sunglasses, and the earrings, and her face grew more and more shocked and wrathful. With a smile, Dumuzi flourished the comb at her.

"Admit it," he said. "They look better on me."

Anna whirled, glaring around her. "Who helped him?

Who did this? Ereshkigal—Nergal—if you—"

"We would never help our little pet to escape," Ereshkigal said. "But what a smart little pet he is. And of course, now we'll have a new one." She smiled thinly at Anna.

"NO!" Anna screamed. "No, I won't, I won't stay here!"

"You shouldn't have come back in the first place," Dumuzi said, pushing her away as she lunged at him.

"I thought you loved me!" she howled. "How could you *do* this to me?"

"You did it to me," he said coldly. "And I love you far more than you ever loved me. But you cannot be cruel to something forever and still keep it, Inanna."

"What about the summers?" Inanna whispered, clutching the vines of his shirt. "Weren't they always wonderful, Dumuzi? Didn't we always have more fun because we'd missed each other for so many months?"

"That reminds me," Dumuzi said, twisting her hands off him. "Queen Ereshkigal," he said formally, "with the power I am wearing I am the most powerful god in Irkalla right now, true?"

"True," Ereshkigal said warily. "Are you going to try stealing my throne, too?"

Dumuzi snorted. "I would rather eat a whole forest," he said. "No, I have only a few requests . . . or you could call them commands, if you prefer."

The queen of the underworld bared her teeth, but nodded, linking her hands together in front of her.

"First, I ask that you take Inanna in my place here for the rest of eternity," he said, "and that my sister

Geshtinanna be freed from her yearly six months as well."

"So I have to stay here ALL YEAR?" Anna wailed. "That's so mean! Dumuzi, we'll never be together!"

"Exactly," he said. "I know your ways. You might wile your freedom out of me, although I could never have gotten it from you."

"In any case," Ereshkigal interjected, "Inanna's a mortal now. She can't return to her human form without the objects of power, so when it dies, she'll be like any other mortal in Irkalla—trapped here forever."

Diana pulled the cloak closer, shaking. Was this any better than driving a knife into Anna's heart? Did anyone deserve this? Diana had killed her. Diana was a killer.

"Second," Dumuzi went on, "I ask for safe passage for my friend." He put a hand on Diana's shoulder, and she started to get up, but he pressed her down again, keeping her face hidden.

"Who's that?" Anna snarled. "Who helped you? Who dared? Was it one of the demons? Have you been planning this all along?"

"It was more of a lucky accident," Dumuzi said. "Ereshkigal, I want your word."

"I'd like to know who it is too," the queen said.

"First swear," he insisted.

Ereshkigal sniffed. "All right. Your friend may leave safely. No one in Irkalla will harm them—not even you, sister."

Dumuzi helped Diana to her feet and pushed back her hood.

Anna made a wild animal noise, half a growl and half

a howl of anger, and fell to her knees, tearing at her hair. Ereshkigal clenched her fists, her face going so pale it was almost translucent.

"You," she snarled.

"Let me kill her!" Anna screamed. "Let me rip her skin off and dig out her eyes!"

Diana was shaking so hard, she could barely stand. Dumuzi put his arm around her, supporting her. "You gave your word," he said to Ereshkigal.

"I know," she said. "Get out. Now."

"What about the judges?" the king interjected from his throne. He was sitting back with one leg thrown over the arm of the chair, as if he were watching a sports match he'd seen before. "Shouldn't we summon them so they can give the girl Inanna's powers? I know the setting is a bit unorthodox—"

"No," Diana interrupted. "I don't want them." She put her hand over Dumuzi's. "You can have them. I want to leave."

"Dumuzi, you fool," Anna spat. "Falling for another goddess of love. She'll never love you like I did! She's in love with a Polynesian war god! She likes armor and swords clashing and sweaty men running through forests. She'd never love a shepherd like you."

"I'm not in love with Oro," Diana said. "I'm in love with Gus."

"And I'm not looking for love anymore," Dumuzi said to Anna. "I know better now." He steered Diana around and started walking her to the door.

"This isn't over!" Anna screamed.

"Yes, it is," Dumuzi said, and stepped out of the throne room without a backward glance.

Halfway down the hall, Diana's trembling made her slip on the marble floor, and Dumuzi stopped and scooped her into his arms. Vines unfolded from his tunic, stroking her face and hair and rubbing her shoulders comfortingly as he walked down the marble staircase. Diana closed her eyes, keeping them shut as wind tugged at her hair and gates slammed behind them and sand swirled against her eyelids.

Finally Dumuzi set her down on her feet, and she opened her eyes to find herself standing outside the walls of Irkalla. Ahead of her was a path winding up into the mountains. She looked back and saw only a blank wall instead of gates; this was not the path she had come down from the Polynesian world. This one led somewhere new.

"That is the way you want to go," Dumuzi said. "Trust your instincts. And thank you, Diana." He touched the bracelet on his wrist. "You did the right thing."

"I hope so," Diana said. "It doesn't feel right."

"You spared the world—and me, and my sister—much suffering," he said. "I hope you win the battle. You would be my choice for ruler of the gods."

"I'm glad you're free, Dumuzi," Diana said. "Just, hey . . . next time you need a favor, try to be less terrifying about it."

He laughed, a surprising sound like waterfalls in a forest. "I promise," he said. "Good luck."

"You too." Diana held out her hand, but he stepped forward and hugged her. The warmth and life of green things growing seemed to envelop her, and she felt stronger, her exhaustion and hunger evaporating. He let go, and she turned, walking toward the path.

Halfway up the mountain, she looked back and saw that he was still standing there. He had his arm around a small girl who looked very much like him, and they both raised their hands to wave good-bye.

Diana waved back and kept climbing.

Tigre was not having the best day. In fact, he was not having the best month, or the best year, or the best life. Not only was he a thoroughly incompetent avatar, but he was pretty sure he'd offended half the orishas in Africa by accidentally stepping on their spirit plant homes or swatting at their spirit animal forms. But seriously, how was a person supposed to take a normal walk through a jungle when the vines and trees and frogs and lizards and butterflies kept suddenly turning into people and back again?

It was rather unfair.

Plus he was pretty sure there was a tortoise stalking him.

This didn't make a whole lot of sense; there was no way an ordinary tortoise could keep up with the pace they were setting through the jungle. But he'd seen a tortoise sitting on a tree stump in the square in the city, staring at them, and he was pretty sure he'd seen the exact same tortoise watching them go by from the bank of the river. And then, just now, he thought he'd seen it again, looking down at them from a moss-covered boulder.

He might not have noticed it except that it had a

strange dark red pattern on its shell—like a spider, with a central oval and eight legs branching off from it. Its eyes were very bright, and it seemed to always be staring directly at Tigre.

But that was crazy. Surely he was being crazy. It must be a kind of turtle that was everywhere in Africa, and he was just paranoid to think it was staring at him. Kali and Oya would laugh their heads off if he mentioned it.

So he kept running instead, sweat rolling down his face and back. There were insects everywhere. It felt like half the insects in Africa kept trying to fly up his nose. He slapped at a mosquito and it popped into a tiny-boned girl with sharp features and short hair that looked like electric wires.

"Ouch!" she yelped, stamping her foot. "That is SO RUDE! I was just trying to drink your blood! There's no need to try and *kill* a person! Sheesh!"

"Leave him alone," Oya said, crashing back through the trees and poking the girl in her bony arm. "Not for you."

"Oya," the girl whined, but Oya pointed back to the city and the girl shifted back into a mosquito and flew away.

"Some orishas," Oya said, rolling her eyes. She saw him eyeing another mosquito that was circling his face and waved it away for him. "Keep on swatting; don't worry, they're not all gods."

"Um . . . okay," Tigre said, although he knew he wasn't about to risk it.

"I hear water," Kali called from up ahead.

"YAY!" Oya sang out. "It's my river, Catequil Catequil Catequil!" She threw her arms around Tigre in an impromptu hug and then ran off in the direction of Kali's voice.

"She has a river," Tigre said as he caught up to Kali.

"So I see," she said.

Oya was frolicking in the shallows of the river, where the water came up to her knees. The river was huge, ten times the size of the one around the Yoruba city, and it wound away from them toward the north, clear and still and peaceful in the fading light. Tigre realized that the sun was setting; they'd been running for half the day.

"Come on in," Oya called, laughing. "Isn't it the most beautiful river in the world?" She splashed out and ran up the bank, grabbing Tigre's hands. "Come on, you'll love it."

"Oh no, no, I shouldn't," Tigre said, leaning back. "My shoes—there's mud—"

Oya knocked him onto the grass and tugged his shoes and socks off before he could stop her. Briskly she rolled up his pants and yanked him to his feet again.

"Um, Kali?" Tigre called as Oya dragged him bodily down to the river. "A little help?"

"Looks like a weather god thing to me," Kali said, grinning and lifting her palms in a *What could I possibly do?* gesture.

"Isn't it great?" Oya said, beaming, as Tigre's toes sank into the thick mud. The cool water lapped around his knees, soothing his tired legs and feet. "It's mine, you know. I'm the goddess of this whole river."

"I thought you were a hunting goddess," Tigre said.

"Or winds or hurricanes or something."

"I'm a lot of things," Oya said. A branch swirled by, bumping against her, and she caught his arm to stay upright. "Depends on who you ask. Some people think I'm just another orisha, but hello, I have this whole big river, don't I? So other people say I'm more important, like Orunmila and Obatala. Anyway, I'm complicated." She smiled.

"Like most girls," he said. "But you have orisha eyes."

"Oh, these?" She touched the white circles around her dark eyes. "That's just because they're pretty." She blinked several times quickly, and the white bit seemed to collapse in and rejoin her eyeball until she stood there looking up at him with normal brown eyes. Now she seemed a bit more human, despite her temperamental hair. "It's the latest fashion trend here," Oya explained. "You might have noticed we're easily bored. Always looking for something new and crazy to do. Want to see a trick?"

"Sure."

Oya let go of him and scooped a handful of water into her palms. She lifted it to her face and blew on it in a circular motion, sending tiny waves around and around until suddenly she threw the water up over her head.

A tiny, perfect cyclone sat in the air, rotating busily. It swirled for a moment, and then the bottom tip began to reach down toward the water, stretching the cyclone longer and thinner. When it touched the river, the whole thing collapsed into the water.

"Wow," Tigre said, impressed.

"Isn't that cute?" Oya said. "And it's so easy. Here, you try."

"No, that's, like, magic stuff," Tigre said. "My powers aren't that strong."

"Yeah, right," Oya said, as if he was joking. "You forget I have better resources than library books. I know all your secrets, Mr. Catequil, so don't play powerless with me." She took his hands in hers, cupped them together, and dipped them into the water. He lifted it to his face the way she had.

"Now blow," Oya said, "like you're trying to whistle but no sound is coming out. Quick, before you lose the water!"

Tigre followed her instructions. He didn't even have time to think *Now she'll see what a loser I am* before he felt something moving inside his hands, like a trapped animal. He let go quickly, jumping back.

The tiny storm hanging in the air wasn't as neat or symmetrical as Oya's, but it was bigger, and drops of water were raining from it onto the river below. Slowly it stretched out like Oya's had, but just before it hit the water, Tigre thought he saw a flash and heard something like a miniature clap of thunder.

"Awesome!" Oya cried. "That was so cool! Wasn't that cool?"

"That," said Tigre, "was really, really, *really* cool."

Oya's hair turned light pinkish-red all the way through, from the roots to the tips. She started dancing, kicking up splashes of water and singing, "We made some mini-storms, yes we did, yes we did."

"Sorry to interrupt whatever you're doing," Kali called, "but it's getting dark. Are we staying here tonight?"

Oya looked up at the sky. "Oh my gosh!" she yelped. "How did the sun get so far down?" She grabbed Tigre's hand and ran back to the shore, dragging him along behind her. As her feet hit the pebbles she dropped his hand and started running around the edge of the forest line, gathering branches and twigs and loose wood.

"Quick!" she said. "We have to make a fire. Come on, QUICKLY!" She dumped a pile of wood on the beach and raced back to the trees. Kali looked from the wood to Oya and back again. Then she knelt, stacked the wood in a triangle, and touched it with her hand.

Flames flared out of the branches instantly, crackling and spitting. Tigre looked at his hands. Making fire would probably be more useful than tiny storms that only lasted a minute or two.

Still . . . it's better than nothing.

He joined Oya at the tree line and realized she was trying to pull an entire thorn bush out of the ground.

"Ow," he said, flinching as he saw spots of blood appear on her arms. "Wait, don't hurt yourself."

"We need enough of these," Oya panted, "to build a circle around us for the night."

"Seriously?" Tigre said. She kept tugging without answering, so he ran back to Kali. "We need the axe," he said.

"Awesome," Kali said. "I'm so glad I didn't drag this thumping Viking weapon all over the jungle for no reason. Here, watch the fire." She pointed to a pile of firewood and went to help Oya hack the thorn bush free.

Darkness fell swiftly, and Tigre spotted several strange

small lights in the jungle and out over the river. Were they fireflies? Eyes in the dark? Gods lighting their way home? He fed the fire while Oya and Kali stacked thorn bushes all around it.

"Okay, ow," Kali said, dropping to the sand beside him after the last bush was in place. She examined her hands in the firelight. Long scratches ran up her arms and she was covered in dirt and tiny spiders.

"Where's Oya?" Tigre asked.

"She ran back into the jungle. She said she was going to get us something to eat." Kali's stomach growled loudly and she grimaced. "I'm going to throw myself in the river for a second and try to get clean."

She gingerly scooted one of the thorn bushes aside and went out, closing the circle again behind her. Tigre threw another stick on the fire. The heat of the day had faded with the light, and a chilly breeze was coming off the river.

A rustling came from the thorn bushes and Oya scrambled through, shoving them back into place behind her. She crouched beside Tigre, triumphantly laying two hares onto a flat rock beside him.

"Dinner!" she announced. Seeing his expression, she added, "Don't worry, they're just regular rabbits, not orishas. That'd be pretty awkward, huh?" She reached for one and then tensed, looking around. "Where's Kali?"

"At the river, washing up," Tigre said.

"Oh gods," Oya said, leaping to her feet. "Stay quiet." Tigre didn't even see her move the bushes; she seemed to bound right over them. He stood up, but the firelight blinded him and he couldn't see into the darkness beyond the thorn bushes. He strained his ears instead, and realized that it was eerily silent. The insects and birds that had been chattering away all day had fallen quiet. In the stillness and the darkness, Tigre almost felt as if he'd drifted away from the rest of the universe.

Suddenly a wild roar split the air, full of rage and danger. It sounded like it was right at Tigre's elbow, and he spun in a panic, but there was nothing inside the circle of thorns.

He wanted to call out, but Oya had said to stay quiet.

Another roar sounded, and then snarling and a sound like a cat hissing, and then the thump of something fleshy against stone, and a shriek and more snarling and another roar, and then footsteps—or was it pawsteps—running straight at the bushes, straight toward Tigre—

Kali and Oya dove over the top of the bushes, tumbling to the sand. Tigre jumped between them and the fire, and Oya crashed into him, knocking him over on top of her. Kali scrambled to her feet, spinning toward the thorns, but nothing followed them over.

The roar came again, and then loud snuffling around the edges of the bushes.

"Holy teeth and claws," Kali said, putting her hands on her knees and breathing deeply. "What was *that*?"

"A lion," Oya said from under Tigre. She wriggled, shoving him off of her. "Obviously. Most people know better than to go wandering around in the dark by a river."

"Okay, maybe you don't know this, but I'm, like, the

pure embodiment of destruction," Kali said. She brushed sand off her clothes and pulled her hair back into a ponytail again. "I think I can take one lion."

"Could have been a crocodile, too," Oya said, jumping up to face her. "And don't forget that your gods can't protect you here. They might have watched over you in your own places, but they can't come here. Maybe that invincibility you're so proud of is just a couple of four-armed guys pushing you out of the way whenever something comes at you."

Kali bristled. "Those 'four-armed guys' are very powerful gods. And my friends," she snapped.

"Even so, they can't come to Africa," Oya said, hands on her hips. "I'm not saying I care if you live or die, but I never leave a hunt unfinished, so do me a favor and wait until we're done to get yourself killed, okay?"

"Hey, nothing's managed to kill me yet," Kali said. "I doubt one measly lion is going to do it."

"It's not just a lion!" Oya yelled. "And if it can't do it, then maybe I'll give it a shot!"

"I'd like to see you try!"

"Kali, Oya," Tigre interjected, alarmed. "Please don't fight. We're on the same side."

"She's only ever on her own side," Oya said, wagging her finger at Kali.

"Yeah, that's why I'm here trying to save the world instead of just killing these guys in their sleep," Kali said. "I guess you figured me out."

"All right, enough," Tigre said, standing between them. "Kali, you go sit over there. I'll help Oya make dinner for all of us, and then we'll go to sleep, and no more fighting tonight, okay? I mean it."

He tried to look as stern as he could, although Kali's amused expression didn't make him feel very tough. The red streak in Oya's hair was flaring up and down.

"Yes, boss," Kali said finally, stepping back into her corner and sitting down. She unhooked her axe and began sharpening it on a stone, her eyes glittering as she glared at Oya.

"Hmph," Oya said, flouncing over to the fire.

Tigre sighed, rubbing his forehead. Girls were complicated enough without superpowers. He'd seen Vicky pull another girl's hair and scratch her face in a catfight once. Kali, on the other hand, might actually disembowel Oya if she got angry enough. And then Oya, being immortal, would probably come back and shove Kali off a waterfall. And what exactly was he supposed to do to stop them? Make a tiny cyclone out of river water? Wouldn't that be useful.

He really, really hoped they'd catch Eshu soon . . . and that the god of mischief would have the answers they were looking for.

The graveyard seemed small at first: several piles of stones arranged ceremoniously over a few burial mounds, surrounded by leaning trees and covered in crawling vines. But as Gus looked around he realized that there were more rock piles in the jungle around them, and that in fact the graveyard stretched for at least a mile in each direction. Perhaps it had once been cleared and the greenery had grown back over it, or perhaps they had buried their dead among the trees. He couldn't tell.

His arms tightened around Diana and he breathed in the lilac smell of her hair. He didn't like bringing her here, to a place of death and spirits. It felt like offering her to the ghosts.

The elephants brushed their trunks over the stones with quiet reverence, stepping carefully between the burial mounds. They stopped at a clear spot in the center of the graveyard and turned to look at Gus. He wondered if he was imagining the sadness in their eyes.

Obatala nodded. "Leave her here with them," the god said. "She will be safe."

Gus knelt and laid Diana on the ground, on top of a tangle of soft leaves and vines. Her fingers were half-curled, as if she had fallen asleep holding a teddy bear but someone had taken it away. Her bright hair and pale skin stood out like fire and ice in this green and gray place, and it seemed to him that her eyelashes were trembling, as if she was dreaming. He hoped they were good dreams, peaceful dreams, and he hoped she would wake up from them soon.

He stood up, wishing he didn't have to leave her here.

"What do I do?" he asked. "How do I save her?"

Obatala sighed. "I cannot promise anything. Getting to our underworld is not impossible, but she might not be there. She might have come through and left already. She might never enter it. She may already be on the path to Hades. You may arrive too late."

"Especially if we keep talking about it," Gus said.

"Please just tell me where to go."

Obatala pointed to the far side of the graveyard. "Start walking. Keep walking. Think upon death. The more dead people you know, the sooner you'll arrive. There are many paths; you'll find your way there eventually, no matter which you take. Be courteous and respectful; it will get you as far as—perhaps further than—courage or strength. Now go."

Gus looked where the god was pointing, but all he saw was more jungle, more trees, more of the same landscape they'd been walking through. He was about to argue with Obatala for more of an explanation, but he stopped himself. *Courteous and respectful. Have faith in his instructions.*

He took a deep breath and started walking. He heard the elephants shuffle their feet behind him, and he heard Obatala turn and start back up the path to the village. He wanted to run back and kiss Diana one more time, in case he never saw her again, but he made himself keep walking without looking back.

Think about death. I've certainly done that enough in my life. What happens afterward? I don't believe Mom and Dad and Andrew are in an underworld somewhere, living with gods like the ones we've met. But maybe I believe in Heaven . . . only, if God is real, like I think he is, then why hasn't he gotten involved? Why did he let the gods do this? Maybe it makes no difference to him.

I love death, whispered another voice in his head. *I love the snap of necks breaking and the wet thud of spears sinking into flesh.*

"Go away, Oro," Gus said.

He looked up at the blue slivers of sky visible through the branches. Was it getting darker? Surely it was only late afternoon. And yet the light was definitely fading. Colors were disappearing as everything shifted to shades of gray, then darker gray, and then darker still. Now he couldn't see anything beyond the trees immediately around him; it seemed like he was surrounded by an empty black night that was slowly moving in closer and closer.

The sounds of the birds and insects had stopped too, leaving a stillness behind that seemed to spread further with every step he took. He walked and walked, thinking about his parents, about Andrew, about Diana, about having a person and then suddenly not having them anymore, about not being able to say good-bye, about things cracking inside you and wishing you'd said what you meant, about shiny wooden coffins and uncomfortable suits, about blood spilling over your hands, about loneliness.

A new, pale light was growing that was completely different from the warm, beating African sun. It came from nowhere, saturating the land around him, and it felt like nothing, barely registering against his eyes as it skimmed the surface of the white-gray sand that now stretched before him. The trees were gone. The jungle had vanished. He was walking through an empty landscape. He wanted to turn around and look back to see where he'd come from, but he thought of Orpheus and kept his gaze straight ahead, just in case.

He seemed to walk for a long time. His senses were muzzy and he was starting to lose feeling in his fingers and toes. Half-asleep, he felt his mouth twitch, and suddenly it opened and began forming words, although he hadn't planned to speak.

"This," he said, moving his lips as if experimenting with them. "This is a waste. Of time." His mouth stretched into a ghastly smile.

"Stop it," Gus said, shaking his head as hard as he could, trying to wake himself up. "Oro, leave me alone."

"Why would we. Want her alive?" the god said, the words coming awkwardly and sounding funny. "We should be. Killing."

Gus drove his feet into the sand, pinching his arms. "I'm not listening to you. Go away. This is *my* body."

"For," the god said. "Now."

He felt Oro retreat again, and with a new burst of strength he started walking faster. If Oro kept trying to take over, Gus didn't know what would happen. He didn't want to find out.

In the distance he could see something like a silver ribbon across the sand. A river? As he got closer, he realized the river wasn't making any sounds—no gurgling water or splashes or murmuring over the stones. It just slid by silently, quiet and still and very wide.

An old woman was standing in it, not far from the bank. Her skin was wrinkled and the color of coffins. She watched him come closer with round, unblinking eyes.

Gus stopped on the riverbank and bowed politely to her. He noticed a brass pot by his foot, full of brightly colored cloths.

"I haven't seen one like you in a long time," the

woman said in a husky, curious voice that sounded as if she hadn't spoken in a long time either. "One of the living who wishes to visit the dead. Nowadays people fear death so much more. They won't even risk the journey."

"I am looking for someone," Gus said.

"Ah," she said, a long breathy sound. "You're one of those. Seeking a lost love."

"Yes," Gus said.

"Many used to come for that purpose," she said. "One man lost four wives in a row. He grieved so deeply for them all. He came this way looking for them. Your heart hurts from only one loss—imagine so many."

"I've lost others, too," Gus said. "But I won't lose Diana. If she's here, I'm going to bring her home."

The old woman was shaking her head, her eyes glistening with tears. "It never works, I'm afraid. The dead are gone, and you must mourn them, but keep living. I'm sorry." She touched the water beside her, and the river seemed to get deeper and wider and stronger. "You may not pass this way. You must let go of your love.

"Your journey ends here."

EIGHTEEN YEARS AGO . . .

The earth buckled and shook under his feet, and Odin grumpily jabbed it with his staff.

"Stop writhing, Loki," he snapped. "Stay still.*"*

The god of mischief lay chained to three great rocks, panting with exertion and pain. He glared at Odin. "This is your fault," he snarled. "You could just let me go. Then the earthquakes would stop."

A low hiss came from above him, and the poisonous serpent leaned over the top of the rock, dripping more venom into Loki's eyes. The god screamed in agony and jerked at his chains, straining to break free. His movements made the land around him jump and crack. Odin rolled his eyes. Drama king.

"Sorry, sorry," Loki's wife, Sigyn, called, running back from the cliff edge with her wooden bowl. She shoved the bowl under the serpent, catching the venom, and used a handful of her dress to wipe Loki's face clean. Odin could see the burned, ravaged skin healing already, smoothing out the wrinkles left by the acid.

He couldn't believe that Sigyn had stayed with Loki for all these centuries. If she hadn't, the drip of venom would be constant; as it was, Loki only had to suffer for those few moments when she ran to empty her bowl over the side of the cliff.

It's as much a punishment for her as him, *he thought,* which we did not intend. Perhaps worse, since she also has to put up with his personality. *Loki was the one who'd killed Balder, everyone's favorite god, but Sigyn was loyal to him despite everything.*

A cold wind whipped off the sea and the assembled gods huddled into their fur-lined cloaks. "We are gathered here at Loki's particular request," Odin said, "to choose our avatar for the contest of the gods."

"ME!" Thor bellowed from the front of the crowd, thumping his chest. "I shall go!"

"I know, you've been volunteering for months, Thor," Odin said with a sigh. "But we're going to do this by a proper vote. And Loki asked to be allowed to address us before we decide."

"Why?" Frey asked. "What's he got to do with anything?"

"How do you even hear about these things?" his sister Freya asked Loki, her hands on her hips. Despite the freezing winds, she was wearing low-cut armor and the slits on the sides of her fur skirt came almost to the tops of her thighs. "I know you wouldn't let poor Sigyn leave just to gather gossip."

"I have my ways," Loki said, grinning toothily.

His children, *Odin guessed. Two of them—the World Serpent and the wolf Fenrir—were bound like their father until Ragnarok, but his daughter Hel could still visit him from the underworld. She must have told him their plan.*

Sigyn pushed back a loose strand of her long blond hair and the bowl of venom wobbled. Loki shot her a look, and she went back to holding it with both hands. Odin noticed a couple of burns on her fingers, which had probably been caught accidentally in the venom drip.

"Well, get on with it," Odin said. "The sooner we send our avatar to be born, the older and stronger he'll be when the battle begins."

"I have a proposal for you all," Loki said, his dark eyes glittering. A hush fell over the gods, and Odin marveled again at Loki's powerful charisma. Here he was, stretched out on a pile of rocks, almost horizontal, his cunning hands trapped and his legs pinned so he couldn't shape-shift and escape. And yet, with just a few words, he could mesmerize them all.

"I know why you're doing this," Loki said. "You say it's just a game, but I've seen the fear in all your eyes. You have been waiting for Ragnarok for centuries. Why hasn't it come? Why the long delay, the fading glory? Will you have any power left when the end of the world finally arrives? Ragnarok, the Twilight of the Gods, could come at any moment. And you know that this time, when you die, it will be forever."

Freya leaned against Frey and he put his arm around her. Even mighty, dim-witted Thor looked uneasy.

"But perhaps there's still a chance," Loki said smoothly. "Perhaps there's a way out. Perhaps it isn't coming. Perhaps you could change your fate after all." He turned his head to give Odin a piercing look. "That's what this is really about. You are entering this contest to steal the power of the other gods. You hope to win, and then, with all that power, you'll be too strong for my giants to defeat you at the end of the world. Odin and Thor and Heimdall and Frey won't have to die after all." His smile could

slice glaciers in half. "A happy ending for everyone.

"However . . . I have a different suggestion." He twisted his wrists in his chains, unconsciously, as if he had forgotten he couldn't use his hands to hypnotize them. "You all know how Ragnarok begins, right?"

His voice lowered, drawing them closer. "It begins when my son Fenrir and I break free." Several gods shuddered. "Violent earthquakes will tear apart the land and these rocks that hold me now will crumble to pieces. I will be free to walk the Earth, and you know what I will do, because it has been foretold. I will gather my monstrous children and my friends—your enemies—the giants and all the weary souls of the dead, and we will march on Asgard. You will die first," he said to Frey, who scowled. Loki turned his gaze to Tyr. "You will die." He searched the crowd until his eyes met Heimdall's. "You and I will kill each other," Loki said, his mouth twisting.

"Yes, all right," Odin interrupted. The spell Loki wove over them was a little too potent; Odin could feel their courage sagging and the long despondency that they'd suffered for centuries returning. "We've all heard the prophecies. What's your point?"

"What if it doesn't have to be like that?" Loki said. "What if there is really a way to change everything—guaranteed? I'm not talking about storing up a little extra power for the fight. I'm talking about taking our fate and snapping it in half and throwing it over this cliff, saying; 'No! We shall not die this way! We choose a completely different path!' "

"How?" Freya asked, lifting her chin defiantly.

The scar tissue around Loki's eyes shone like the snow as he raised his head. "Set me free," he hissed.

In the stunned pause that followed, Odin nearly leaped

forward to stab Loki with his invincible spear. It would only shut him up for a short while, but it would be very satisfying. Had Loki really called them out here to this freezing cliff for this lunacy?

"Make me your avatar," Loki hurried on before Odin could speak. "Send me down to fight the other gods."

"WHAT?" Thor shouted. "No, I *am the avatar! I am the warrior of the gods!"*

"Listen to me," Loki said quickly. "It's perfect. It won't set off Ragnarok because my wolf son will still be bound, and you'll shove me straight into human form so you can be sure I won't try anything. And if anything goes wrong, who's more expendable than me? I could easily die, and then Ragnarok couldn't possibly happen. The whole chain of events would be broken. There'd be no way for it to unfold as foretold. The future would be wide open, and you all might truly live forever."

"But we don't want a god from somewhere else ruling over us," Frey pointed out. "If you lost, we'd have to deal with Amon or some toothy bloody thing from South America."

"Perhaps I won't lose," Loki wheedled. "You have often seen cleverness defeat force. What other pantheon would send their trickster? And yet, who better to win a contest, especially in mortal form? I can outwit the top warrior of any pantheon on this planet. I would deliver them to you on a gold platter."

He's probably right, *Odin thought.* Loki is smarter than the entire Greco-Roman pantheon combined. Perhaps he really could defeat them all. If anyone else sends someone clever, Thor might be doomed.

"No, no, no!" Thor shouted, waving his hammer. "I am the avatar! Warriors win lots of things! I'm good at winning! Me!"

"Besides," Loki said, ignoring Thor and turning his broken eyes to Odin and Odin's wife, Frigg, who stood beyond him in the swirling snow, "haven't I been punished enough for the death of your son? Frigg, you see how I suffer, how I have suffered for centuries. You two killed one of my own sons and used his entrails to bind me here. I have known nothing but pain and captivity for far longer than Balder was even alive. Couldn't you find it in your great hearts to forgive me at last?"

There was a long silence, punctuated only by the howling of the wind over the mountaintop high above them and the waves crashing far below. Odin turned to look at his wife.

Frigg closed her eyes slowly. The pain of Balder's death was still etched on her beautiful face. "No," she whispered. "I can never forgive."

Loki's face twisted in a strange look; Odin didn't know if it was fury or grief or desperation.

"But he has a point." Tyr, the one-handed god of war and justice, spoke at last. "If we set him free and chose him as our avatar, it would rewrite our whole future. We would be like humans—anything could happen to us, except death."

"No Ragnarok," Freya said with shining eyes. "No more nightmares, no more fear."

"I'm not afraid!" Thor yelled. "Ragnarok is our destiny and I face it with courage!"

"But we couldn't spare you at Ragnarok," Frey said to him. "If you died in this mortal form, the battle could go horribly wrong and things could be far worse for us. If he *dies, that's several problems solved right there."*

All the gods started talking at once.

"He has been here a long time—"

"Remember when he tricked the giant who built our wall? That was pretty smart—"

"A mortal death would be perfect for him—"

"No more Ragnarok—"

"No more Ragnarok—"

"I should be the avatar! ME!"

A trumpet horn sounded that was earth-shatteringly loud, and the gods yelped in protest, covering their ears.

"Fools," said the god with the trumpet, striding forward to stand beside Odin. Loki's face twisted in a snarl as he recognized Heimdall, the god foretold to fight him to the death at Ragnarok. Heimdall was the watchman of the gods, guarding the bridge to Asgard. His sight and hearing were so acute that he could spot a seagull off the shore of North America from here and listen to the sound of its wings beating. He faced the gods with a look of disgust, his cloak swirling around him.

"What are you thinking?" he demanded. "Have the last thousand years withered your brains so much? Have you all completely forgotten who we're dealing with, just because he's been chained to a rock all this time?"

Odin stroked his beard, looking down at the ground. Heimdall was a strong and true warrior of the gods. He often saw things the others missed.

The watchman pointed at the chained god. "This is Loki," he said. "Perhaps he was once just an amusing mischief-maker, but we saw him grow more and more evil. We should know what he is capable of. He hates us all, and his hatred for us has been growing stronger all this time, with every drop of venom.

"And now you talk of setting him free—and not only that, making him our avatar? Does anyone remember what happens

to the avatar who wins? The amount of power that one god would have?"

"Me!" Thor shouted again. "It should be me!"

"Imagine Loki with that much power," Heimdall said intensely. "Imagine a god who hates us that much suddenly being so much stronger than we are. Imagine his vengeance."

"I don't hate you," Loki interrupted. "Maybe I've learned the error of my ways. Maybe this punishment has really taught me a lesson and I'm a wiser, gentler, kinder god now."

"The King of Lies." Heimdall sniffed. "If we've learned anything in a thousand years, it should be not to trust anything Loki says."

"All right, I'll be honest," Loki said. "I do hate you *quite a bit right now, dear watchman."*

"Heimdall and Loki have both made good points," Odin said. "We are going to do this fairly, as I promised before. We will put it to a vote."

"What about me?" Thor bellowed. "Shouldn't I get to speak?"

"Really?" Odin said. "What would you like to say?"

Thor banged his hammer and shield together, making thunder rumble over the mountains. He puffed up his chest, threw back his long red hair, and tensed his arms to make the muscles stand out. He took a deep breath.

"ME!" he roared. "I should be our avatar! I am strong and fearless! I am the mightiest of warriors! I will defeat them all! Send ME!"

He bowed, and Odin sighed. "Yes, thank you, Thor. That added a lot to the discussion." He spread his hands to the crowd of gods. "Now we will vote. All those in favor of releasing Loki and making him our avatar, raise your hands."

The bowl of venom was nearly full again, but Sigyn balanced it carefully in one hand as she raised her other. To Odin's surprise, Tyr's hand was among those lifted. He studied the raised hands, counting quietly.

"All right—all those who vote for Thor?"

Thor's hand shot into the air and he waved it a few times. "ME!" he yelled. "I VOTE FOR ME!"

Odin nodded, counting. "It is a tie. And I cast the deciding vote."

"Don't I get to vote?" Loki said. "I can't exactly raise my hand, after all."

"Prisoners don't get the right to vote," Odin said, and Loki's face darkened. He knew what was coming. "Heimdall is right, Loki. You cannot be trusted. We cannot risk releasing you for any reason." He nodded at Thor. "Thor shall be our avatar."

"HOORAY!" Thor shouted, flinging his helmet in the air. "Victory is mine, as always!"

The snowstorm was picking up. Gods and goddesses began throwing their hoods over their heads and disappearing into the wind, vanishing back to Valhalla, where it was warm and there was always plenty to drink. One by one, they left. Some of them nodded sympathetically to Loki before disappearing. Frigg put one hand on Odin's arm and kissed him lightly, her eyes full of trust as she faded into the air. I made this choice for you, my heart, *Odin thought.* I hope it was the right one.

He leaned on his staff and looked at Loki. Now they were the only ones left, along with Sigyn.

"Too bad, old friend," Odin said. "Better luck next time."

"I will have better luck one day," Loki said in his voice of ice

and glittering knives. "The day when I kill you all. You made a mistake, old man. This was your last chance to change things. Now my revenge will be even more terrible."

"I have no doubt," Odin said. "Good-bye, Loki. See you at the Twilight of the Gods."

He opened a gap in the air and stepped forward, walking through the swirling snow back to his warm, safe hall. Behind him he heard Sigyn get up and scurry to the cliff to empty the bowl.

"You'll regret this, Odin!" Loki shouted. "I promise you that!"

The venom splashed into Loki's eyes and he began to howl and twist, shaking the Earth harder than ever before. Somewhere far above, a chunk of snow broke free of the mountain and crashed down into the sea.

Odin took another step and was gone.

Palace of Sleetcold

The mountain was much higher than it looked from the ground, and the wind shrieked wildly around Diana as she climbed, tugging the hooded cloak around herself. The light up here was silvery and pale. It seemed like it might be coming from the drifts of snow or the icicles hanging from the cliffs above her.

She'd been edging along a narrow ledge for a while when it turned and ended at a narrow gap between two tall rock walls. Diana hesitated. She didn't like confined spaces, but going back would be almost impossible.

She inched sideways into the gap, sliding between the cliffs. The rocks scraped painfully at her elbows and knees, but soon she saw something glittering ahead of her, and her forward hand felt space instead of rock. She squeezed herself through the last few inches and stumbled out into a wide, flat, snow-covered terrain surrounded by towering cliff walls. Ahead of her was a frozen river spanned by a glittering bridge of ice, and beyond it she could see an enormous fortified town enclosed by a high wall. Seated at the gates to the wall was a really, really, *really* large dog with ridiculously gigantic teeth.

Diana pushed back the hood of the cloak and stared at the scene.

What do I remember about Hades? A river and a dog. But this can't be it, can it? I thought you used a ferryman to get across the River Styx, not a bridge. And doesn't the dog at the gates of Hades have three heads?

Maybe she was remembering wrong. And if this was Hades, this might be the place where she could bargain for her life.

She walked slowly down to the river, her sneakers crunching in the snow. As she got closer, she could see things shining in the river that weren't pieces of ice. *Fish? Frozen in place?* she wondered, but then she realized that they were knives. Thousands of knives were encased in the ice of the river.

Creepy.

She approached the bridge cautiously, but she couldn't see anyone except the large dog on the far side. The railings were smooth and shimmering silver, and the floor of the bridge was ice so clear she could see straight through to the river. It would be like walking on air. Taking a deep breath, Diana stepped onto the bridge.

A loud noise sounded, like gongs being struck and statues being pushed over and glaciers crashing together. Diana froze.

A giantess unfolded herself from below the bridge and stuck her chin over the railing to stare at Diana. She had lanky white hair and a bright red, bulbous nose, and she gazed at Diana with watery, bewildered eyes. She was as tall as a stadium. Diana had no idea how she could have missed seeing her before.

"Hello," said the giantess. "What in the realms are you?" Her voice was stuffy and thick, as if she had a bad cold.

"I'm sorry to intrude," Diana said, backing off the bridge.

"You're not dead," the giantess said. "That's obvious, because the bridge sounded when you stepped on it. But you're not quite alive, either, because it wasn't as loud as it would be if you were. And you died in battle, so you should have gone to Valhalla, perhaps, but then the Valkyries would have taken you there." She blinked slowly. "I'm too old for strange things like you."

"I'm trying to get to Hades," Diana said, nodding at the town across the river, "so that I can be sent back to life."

The giantess snorted. "That's not Hades. That's Hel."

Diana rubbed her cold ears. "Did you say 'hell'?"

"The Norse underworld," the giantess sniffled. "Ruled by Hel, queen of death."

"Oh," Diana said. *How odd.* She'd never known that that was its name. "Well, then I'm probably in the wrong place." She took another step back.

"You certainly are," said the giantess. "But you can't leave now, not after all that noise. Hel will be expecting you." She turned her eyes slowly to the fortress walls. Diana followed her gaze and realized with horror that there was a woman with long, limp, reddish-blond hair standing with her arms crossed on the wall above the gate. Her top half looked normal, but from her waist to her feet she was a bluish-black, rotting, decaying color, and so was her robe. Through the holes in her robe, it looked like her flesh was about to drop off with a sickening plop.

The hound before the gates had rolled onto his back, and was looking up at the woman submissively. Slowly Hel raised one hand and beckoned to Diana.

"I'd rather you didn't go over the bridge," the giantess said. "It'll make a fearful noise, and my head is already pounding."

"Can I walk on the river?" Diana asked. "Or might it crack?"

"I've been sleeping on this river for hundreds of years," the giantess answered. "I think it can hold a little tuft of goat hair like you." She unhooked her chin from the railing and sank back under the bridge, curling into a ball. Her robe matched the greenish-white of the river, and when she was still, it was almost impossible to see her.

Perhaps Hel would be able to help Diana. After all, Thor had turned out to be nicer than anyone expected. There was no reason for Hel to hate Diana the way Ereshkigal did.

Still, Diana felt her heart pound nervously as she slipped and slid across the ice, trying not to think about the river of knives just below her feet. She reached the bank on the other side and scrambled up. The wind tugged viciously on her cloak, getting stronger and snowier as she approached the gates.

The dog jumped to its feet and growled at her.

"Down, Garm," Hel said from the top of the wall. The hound snarled, but crouched low, eyeing Diana.

"Hi," Diana said nervously.

"The Greek avatar, am I right?" Hel said in a voice like snowstorms and petrified forests.

"Yes," Diana said.

"How is our Thor doing?" Hel asked. She said "our Thor" the way someone might say "our leprosy."

"Um," Diana said, "he's great. He's very strong. He seems like a good guy."

"He is a good guy," Hel said, her voice dripping with disdain. "What about my father?" Diana tried to focus on her face. It was hard to talk to someone whose body was decomposing.

"Your father?"

"Loki," Hel said. "Any sign of him?"

Here was a name Diana recognized. He was a famous Norse god. Why hadn't he been with the pantheons in New York? Surely she would have seen him. "I don't think he's been around," she said. "He wasn't with Odin and the others, as far as I saw."

"Of course not," Hel said. "He is suffering an eternal torment." She said this in a bored tone, with the inflection of "He is at home writing Christmas cards." "But he is planning something. I can tell. He won't tell me what it is. So I thought perhaps you might know."

Diana was about to say "I don't think so" when Hel continued: "If not, I suppose I'll just kill you."

"Oh," Diana said, stepping back. She didn't like how close she was to Garm's slavering jaws. "Do you have to?"

"I'm not in the habit of letting souls leave," Hel said.

There was a loud growl from somewhere close by. Hel and Diana both glanced at Garm, but the hound was crouching even lower, sniffing the air, and looking terrified. It hadn't come from him.

"Strange," Hel said. She sniffed the air too, inhaling deeply, and her brow furrowed. "Fenrir?" She shaded her eyes and squinted at the landscape.

"What is it?" Diana asked. She spun to look around, but the snowstorm had picked up, and all she could see was fog and flurries of white.

"My brother," Hel said vaguely. "It smells of him and sounds of him. But that can't be—he is bound like my father. Is it a shadow of him? Fenrir?" she called.

The growl came again, closer now, and Diana shivered.

"Perhaps I won't have to kill you myself after all," Hel said.

Crunch, crunch, crunch. Pawsteps in the snow padded softly toward her. Diana whirled and saw a dark, four-legged shape. It was impossibly huge, even huger than Garm. Its fangs were bared and its hungry eyes glittered.

The wolf paced toward her, and Diana knew with terrible certainty that she was about to be ripped apart with sharp claws and devoured, and then she really would be very, very dead. With a pang of grief, she thought about Gus, and then something made her think of her dad, and how she never had a chance to tell him she was sorry for leaving with Mom and that she loved him.

"Diana!" shouted a voice in a flutter of wings.

She looked up and saw Maui dropping from the sky.

He seemed to be in the middle of turning from an exotic pigeon into a man; emerald wings sprouted from his back and white feathers covered his chest. He held out his arms to her and she bent her knees and jumped, springing up into them.

The wolf howled and lunged, his snapping teeth closing on the air just below her sneakers. Diana wrapped her arms around Maui's neck and buried her face in his feathery chest, holding on for dear life. Maui beat his wings and rose higher as the snow buffeted them with more and more force.

Diana peeked out and saw the dark shadow of the wolf disappearing around the back of the fortress. Hel was still standing on the wall, rubbing her chin thoughtfully as she stared at the snow where Fenrir had been. She didn't seem concerned about a winged stranger dropping out of the sky to snatch Diana away.

"That," Diana gasped, "was pretty amazing timing."

"One of my many talents," he said with an adorable grin, squeezing her reassuringly.

"Not that I'm ungrateful," she said, "but I wouldn't have minded your help in the Sumerian underworld, too. This god kind of grabbed me and it was maybe the scariest thing ever."

"I'm sorry I missed it," Maui said, sounding genuinely regretful. "Is that where this stylish cloak came from? Hang on, we're going over the top."

Diana closed her eyes, feeling the driving sleet pelt her face like wet needles and melt into her hair. The cloak flapped around her legs and the muscles in Maui's shoulders tensed as he soared over the top of the cliff wall.

The wind abruptly dropped as they cleared the cliff, and for a terrifying moment they fell like stones, Maui's wings flapping desperately. But then he caught a current of air, and they straightened again, floating down the long, rocky slope below them.

Soon Diana felt her feet brush the Earth, and Maui touched down lightly, holding her arms until she got her balance. Then he stepped back with a smile and shook himself, his wings folding up into his back and his T-shirt reappearing in place of the feathers.

"Fancy meeting you here," he said. "Nice to see you again."

"You too," she said fervently. "Thank you so much."

"Of course. Happy to help," he said. "You trust me, right?"

"I—sure, of course," Diana said, thinking, *That's an odd and kind of unsettling question.*

"Great!" Maui said, beaming. "I love proving Rohe wrong." He offered her his arm. "Now," he said with a cheerful wink, "why don't I take you straight to Hades?"

When Kali woke up, squinting in the hot morning sunlight, there was a man standing on the other side of the thorn bushes, looking down at her.

No, wait, it was a woman.

Kali sat up and rubbed her eyes. Okay, that was definitely a man. Was she losing her mind? She started to stand up; then the man turned around, and she nearly fell over.

The *other side* of the man was a woman.

He/she had two faces—one male, one female, facing in different directions.

"What do you think?" said the man half. "Here, let me look again." The person started to turn around, and then jerked back.

"I'm still looking!" the female side said. "Stop squirming!"

"I'm not—I just want to—hey, quit it," said the male face, gritting its teeth. Kali watched, fascinated, as the man/woman flailed in place, one side trying to stay put while the other side tried to turn around.

Finally the male side lost, and the stranger stood for a moment, gasping as if he/she had run a marathon or two. The female face—which was very beautiful, apart from the male face stuck on the back of it—stared at Kali, tapping its chin and holding its elbow in its other hand. From this angle it looked like the hands faced this way, fitting the female side, but when he/she turned around, they still looked right, as if the hands had flipped halfway through the turn.

"Mawu-Lisa!" Oya cried, bounding over to the circle of thorns. She shoved the bushes aside and threw her arms around the female half, hugging her happily.

"Careful, watch the hands," said the male face.

"These are my new friends," Oya said, stepping back. "That's Catequil, and this is Kali. They're avatars."

Kali was mildly amused to be referred to as a friend after the fight the night before, but she didn't argue. Tigre came to stand beside her. He smelled like soot and his fingers were burned from trying to pull the cooked rabbit out of the fire last night. She could have retrieved it safely, but she had decided to let them fend for themselves and see how they liked it.

"Ah," said the female face. "The pawns in that little game."

Kali was going to make a snide rebuttal, but Tigre pinched her arm and she restrained herself.

"This is Mawu-Lisa," Oya said. "Or Mawu and Lisa. They're Fon creator gods."

"So you're Lisa?" Kali said to the female side.

"No, I'm Mawu," said the female face.

"I'm Lisa," said the male face.

"Okay. That's not confusing at all," Kali said.

"Can I turn around yet?" Lisa asked gruffly. "I'd like to be part of this conversation too, if you don't mind."

Mawu rolled her eyes at them, making a *blah blah blah* gesture with her hand.

"I know what you're doing!" Lisa said. "That's my hand too!"

"Mawu-Lisa," Oya interrupted, "we're looking for Legba."

"We are?" Kali said. "Who's Legba? We're looking for Eshu."

"Eshu and Legba are the same person," Oya said impatiently. "The Fon just have a different name for him. Have you seen him?" she said to Mawu-Lisa.

Both faces tried to look up at the sky at once, but since lifting one chin meant lowering the other, Mawu-Lisa's head bobbed back and forth for a moment before Mawu huffily tucked her chin in and let Lisa stare at the sky. Kali glanced up too, but all she could see was a cloudless wall of bright blue.

"Uh-oh," Lisa said in an odd tone of voice.

"What uh-oh?" Mawu said, forcing his head down so she could look up. "What's he doing now?"

"I don't know," Lisa said. "According to my sun records, I haven't seen him in our territory for several days."

"Uh-oh," Mawu echoed.

"If he's also Eshu, then hasn't he probably been in Yoruba territory, being Eshu?" Kali said. "What's the big deal?"

"It's better to keep an eye on Legba," Mawu said. "Otherwise he's liable to start some kind of zebra-giraffe feud or teach crocodiles how to make fire or something."

"I thought *you* were watching him," Lisa snapped.

"My job *clearly* only covers nighttime responsibilities," Mawu said, crossing her arms. "That's implied by 'goddess of the moon,' don't you think? I figured he was sleeping, and that you had him under guard during the day."

One hand came up and smacked the side of their head.

"Ow!" both faces cried.

"I've told you to stop doing that!" Lisa shouted.

Mawu rubbed her head, looking indignant.

"Thank you very much for checking," Oya said, bowing to the creator gods. "We'll head upriver and keep looking for him."

"Let us know if you need help," Mawu said with a serene smile.

"Yes, good luck!" Lisa said, waving and trying to look back over his shoulder at them.

He/she walked off into the forest in an odd spinning way that seemed to involve taking turns walking forward.

Kali let out a breath. "That looks difficult," she said. She had a hard enough time figuring out what to do with herself; she couldn't imagine having another person attached to her.

"They've been together a long, long, long time," Oya said. "They have to be opposites to maintain the harmony and balance of the universe. Thanks to them, the Fon cities are very peaceful and happy. Really, they're very powerful. I just love them. Except in battle—there's no way to sneak up on them!"

Oya seemed to have forgotten their fight the night before. She fluffed up her hair and headed down to the river. Tigre hesitated before following her.

"Hey," he said to Kali. "Um, this is going to sound weird, but—did you see a rabbit watching us while we were talking to Mawu-Lisa?"

"A rabbit?" Kali echoed.

"It was over there, but now it's gone," Tigre said, pointing to the edge of the forest. "It looked like it was listening to us."

Kali tilted her head at him. "Do you think it's planning revenge on us for eating its brother and sister last night? Should we be worried?"

"Ha ha, very funny," Tigre said. "I just wanted to see if you'd noticed."

Kali shook her head. "Sorry. Maybe it's a friend of

Oya's. You should ask her."

"Maybe later," he said, shoving his hands in his pockets and shuffling down the shore to the river. Kali kicked out the last embers of the fire and scattered the thorn bushes before following them.

She left her shoes on the riverbank and waded into the cool, clear water. It was shortly after dawn, and already the heat was plastering her clothes to her skin. Tigre was standing in the river close to shore, blowing on something in his hands. As she came up, he opened his palms and revealed a tiny whirlwind in the air.

"Look at you," Kali said admiringly. "I bet Tlaloc can't do that. He doesn't have the finesse."

"Catequil is much more stylish than Tlaloc," Oya said. "Plus cuter. Have you seen that storm god? His eyes look like they're going to pop out and bonk you in the head."

"I'm probably a bit gruesome in my real form too," Tigre said.

"Nope." Oya shook her head. "You look a lot like you do now. Maybe a little more dark and mysterious and swaggery."

"Really?" Tigre said.

"So work on that," Kali said, shoving his shoulder. "More swaggering. More mystery. Like, try talking less. I mean, sheesh, the way you yap yap yap all the time, how will a girl ever get a word in edgewise?"

Oya giggled.

"My last girlfriend got plenty of words in," Tigre said. *Anna?* Kali wondered, and he must have seen her expression because he added quickly, "Back in the real world. Her name was Vicky. She thought I was too quiet. She would definitely not buy me as a thunder god."

"I like quiet gods," Oya said flirtatiously, and Kali raised an eyebrow at Tigre over her head.

"You should do that trick again," Kali said, pointing at the spot where the cyclone had collapsed into the water. "But try making it a rainstorm instead of a cyclone. I bet if you whistled in quick puffs instead of a circle you'd get something different."

"Oooh, good idea!" Oya said. "His mini-storms are already so much cooler than mine. Do it, do it!"

Tigre scooped up a puddle of water, grinning, and began puffing on it.

Something prickled at the back of Kali's neck—the strong, creeping sense of being watched. She rubbed the base of her skull and turned around.

A man was standing on the shore. She thought she caught him standing up as she turned around, and she wondered if he had really been sniffing her shoes, and why he would do that.

He was young and handsome, with long, glossy dark hair, and when he saw her turn around, he smiled, his sharp white teeth glinting in the sunlight.

"Hello," he said, bowing slightly. "I'm so sorry to intrude."

Oya gripped Kali's elbow. "Who are you?" the orisha asked suspiciously. Tigre stepped up on Kali's other side, and she tried to guess where on the scale they fell between menacing and ridiculous. Given their rolled-up trousers, wet hair, Oya's size, and Tigre's scrawniness, Kali had a feeling it was closer to ridiculous.

"My name is Tan," the stranger said politely. "I wouldn't have bothered you, but I couldn't help but overhear that you are looking for the one they call Legba."

"That's right," Oya said in a guarded voice.

"Do you know where he is?" Kali asked.

"I believe I saw him this morning," Tan said. "He was traveling upriver as I was coming down, and he was shaped like a tortoise. That is possible for him, is it not?"

Tigre started beside her, and Kali looked at him curiously.

"It is possible," Oya said. "But we don't need any help finding him."

"I'm sure you don't," Tan said charmingly. "Your skills as a huntress are known throughout these parts. I wouldn't even offer myself as a guide, as I would certainly not wish to offend you by suggesting that I might be of any use, only I saw the cave he went into, and I thought it might save you some time if I took you there, even though I am quite certain you would easily find it on your own eventually."

"We will," Oya said. "Don't worry."

"Why wouldn't we let this guy take us there?" Kali asked. "What if Eshu escapes while we're sniffing around trying to find his trail?"

"Far be it from me to intrude," Tan said, "but I believe the succulent young lady is correct. My impression from his behavior was that he intended to take but a brief rest in the cave, although I also have no doubt that the bountiful orisha could find him under any circumstances, even if it took a modicum longer."

"I don't trust this guy," Oya said, loud enough for Tan to hear. "I've never seen him before."

"Still," Kali said, "it's the three of us against one of him, right?"

Tan bowed again. "It would please me to be of use, and also to inform you of the particulars of my existence for your reassurance. I am a desert god from the western Sahara, and I have taken to traveling recently out of a desire to see the whole continent, now that it is ours alone and the delectable mortals have gone, much to all our delights, I'm sure."

"I vote let's get this over with," Kali said, ignoring Tan. "I'd like to get my hands on Eshu and ask him a few questions."

"I vote we keep looking *my* way," Oya snapped. "*I'd* like you to not *die* before we find him, as I believe I've said before."

"Looks like you're the tie-breaker," Kali said to Tigre. "What do you want to do?"

Tigre shifted uncomfortably as they both stared at him. "Um, I, um," he stammered. "I guess I agree with . . . Kali?"

Nice question mark at the end there, decision maker, Kali thought. "Democracy wins," she said. "Lead on, Mr. Tan."

Oya shook her head, muttering, but she waded out of the water with Tigre and Kali without protesting any further. Up close, Kali saw that Tan's eyes were a strange yellow color, like the desert with ripples of black running across it. He blinked very rarely, which was a bit unsettling. Maybe desert gods had different kinds of eyes.

"Wonderful," he said as Kali and Tigre put on their shoes. Kali checked hers carefully first, but found nothing weird about them or inside them. "I am so pleased to be of service. It really delights me to be able to come to the aid of such charming and well-fed young people."

Er . . . what? "Are you hungry or something?" Kali asked. "We have some rabbit left over from last night."

Something flashed in his eyes, and then he shook his head. "No, thank you kindly, that is most generous of you. I am hungry, yes, but I'm afraid I'm saving my appetite for a great feast I will soon be celebrating in honor of my birthday."

"I don't know many gods who celebrate their birthdays," Oya said.

"A human fancy I picked up," Tan said, smiling, showing his sharp white teeth again. "Are we all ready? Shall we walk this way? Please inform me if you have any trouble with the terrain or the pace I set. I have not encountered real humans in quite some time." His tongue flicked out and back in, and then he turned and started walking upriver in long, loping strides.

"Are you sure about this?" Tigre whispered to Kali. "He's a little bit creepy, don't you think?"

"So are most of your gods," Kali said. "But they're not all bad, right?"

"I have no idea," Tigre said. "They're not showing up in my nightmares here."

"Nice," Kali said. "That's great news."

"Yeah. Funny, I slept better last night—on the sand in a ring of thorns with lions prowling outside—than I did in a real bed in New York."

The river slid by, murmuring softly, as they walked through marshy grass and stretches of sand and pebbles. Soon the forest beside them began to spread up a hill, and in the cliffs below the trees Kali could see sandy caves.

"There," Tan whispered, turning to them and pointing at a tunnel that disappeared into the rocks of the cliff. "Your prey went in there."

"You're sure?" Oya said.

Tan's nose twitched. "You could go inside and look. I would gladly stay out here and keep watch so he cannot escape. I can be swift when I need to be." He turned his head back toward the cave, and something moved below his hair, on the back of his skull.

Kali's heart skipped a beat, and she glanced at Tigre, but he didn't seem to have noticed. Oya was advancing on the cave, padding softly over the rocks. Tigre tiptoed after her, and Kali deliberately let herself fall back a bit, crouching to tie her shoe so Tan would walk ahead of her. His strange yellow eyes were fixed on Oya and Tigre, so Kali was able to stare at the back of his head without him noticing.

There was something weird about the shape of his skull. And when he stepped forward and his hair shifted, Kali was sure she saw it again . . . something moving on the back of his head.

Risk offending a perfectly innocent desert god, or possibly take out a creepy monster? The image of Tan burying those sharp teeth in her neck sprang too easily to her mind. She leaped forward, grabbed his arms, and slammed him into the rock wall beside the cave entrance.

"What are you doing?" Tigre shouted.

Tan snarled, a feral, familiar sound, and twisted in Kali's arms. He was unnaturally strong, but so was she. She kneed him hard in the back and banged his head into the rocks again. He staggered, going limp for a moment.

"Kali!" Tigre yelled. "Kali, stop! What did he do?"

"Tigre, quick, pull up his hair," Kali panted.

To his credit, Tigre didn't waste time arguing with her. He ran over and took a handful of Tan's hair, lifting it off his skull.

They both stared, horrified.

Tan had a second mouth on the back of his head—this one with long fangs and strong, furry jaws. It snapped at Tigre and he just managed to pull his hand back before getting bitten.

"It's the were-lion!" Oya gasped. "I heard there was one prowling these parts. I *knew* that was what attacked us last night. I've been planning to hunt him down to protect our old mortals."

"Well, here he is," Kali said just as Tan regained full consciousness. He jerked up, trying to smash his head back into her face, but she dodged, still gripping his arms, and swung him around to slam him down on the ground. The hidden mouth roared up at her, its breath reeking of meat and death—a smell that brought back a wave of ancient memories. She could remember riding a lion into battle, clutching its thick golden fur, her knees gripping its powerful flanks.

Tan bucked and kicked, his teeth snapping inches from her face. "Any ideas?" Kali shouted to the other two, trying to kneel on his back to keep him still. He writhed, nearly throwing her off, and she had to bang his head into the rocks again. Blood spurted from his forehead, and she felt a thrill of power. "Should I just kill him?" she asked. She looked up and saw a horrified expression on Tigre's face. He looked as if he'd never seen her before.

Something about "goddess of death and destruction" confusing you, Tigre?

Oya ran to the river and came back, blowing on a handful of water. "Here," she said, kneeling beside the were-lion. "Try to keep him still." Kali grabbed a hank of hair as far from the snarling second mouth as possible and yanked Tan's head back. Blood poured down his face, and his regular mouth lolled open. Oya leaned forward and popped her mini-cyclone inside, closing his jaw with her other hand.

Tan's yellow eyes went wide, and his face contorted. Kali could see the cyclone working its way down his throat and into his chest. He made a weak croaking sound and keeled over.

"Cool," Kali said, letting go of him and sitting back on her heels. "Not as bloody as I usually go for, but cool." She gave Tigre a hard stare. *This is who I am. Deal with it.*

"Is—is—is he dead?" Tigre whispered.

"No," Oya said, whisking her hands together. "But he's feeling very, very sick. Obatala can deal with him now." She pinched a piece of the air and whispered into it for a moment, then let it go. "He'll be here soon."

Tigre was leaning against the cliff, clutching his stomach. Kali frowned at him. "You do know he was planning to eat us, right, Tigre?"

"Not helping," Tigre muttered, pressing one hand to his mouth.

Kali rolled her eyes. "So, okay," she said to Oya, "I admit it. You were right. He was really, totally not to be trusted."

"You were right too," Oya said. "You're pretty tough—for a mortal. I think maybe I won't pick a fight with you after all."

"And I vote no more lion wrestling," Kali said. "And maybe a *little* more listening to you." At least Oya wasn't sitting there judging Kali for what she had to do to protect them. If anything, Oya respected her more. Why did Tigre have to be all lame and moralizing and human about it?

"I guess Eshu isn't really in there," Oya said, nodding at the cave. "It didn't smell like him, anyway."

"Is it true he can be a tortoise?" Tigre asked, taking deep breaths.

"Of course," Oya said.

"What about other animals?" Tigre asked. "Like, say, a rabbit?"

Kali and Oya both looked at him intently. "He often travels as a hare," Oya said. "What are you saying, Catequil?"

"Um," he said, "I think—I think maybe he's been following us."

EIGHTEEN YEARS AGO . . .

Huitzilopochtli and Inti were arguing about who should get to stand on the altar and address the other gods.

Again.

"This is my sanctuary!" Inti protested. "This altar was built for me!"

"We agreed to meet here because it isn't covered by jungle or city," Huitzilopochtli snarled at him. "But I am the supreme Aztec sun god, and I should get to stand on the altar of the sun." The bird feathers that ran down his left leg quivered angrily, and the snake he had in place of a right foot hissed. "Besides, you don't even have legs to stand on. You can just float beside me."

Inti's flat gold face scowled, glinting in the moonlight. Beside him, the silver disk of his wife, Quilla, hustled closer, frowning menacingly.

"Why should the sun gods get to speak first anyway?" Tezcatlipoca called out from the crowd. "While the sun is down,

the night gods should lead the meeting."

"Oh, yes, let's hear from the god of evil, please!" snapped a goddess swathed in rainbows.

"Why are we lumped in with the Incas and the Mayas, anyway?" Tezcatlipoca cried. "The Aztec gods were much more powerful. We can stand on our own!"

"All right," Xochiquetzal, the Aztec goddess of love, interjected soothingly. "Don't be rash now. If we fight amongst ourselves, we'll only end up as weak as the other pantheons think we are. We have to stick together."

"But who are we going to choose as our avatar?" the dark god of night insisted. "I don't want to be ruled by a Mayan god—or worse, an Incan!"

Cries of outrage came from several of the gods.

On a low wall near the Path of the Sun that came down from the mountain, a minor local weather god sat with a chinchilla in his hands, stroking its soft fur gently. A lizard ran up his back and stopped on his shoulder, its tongue flicking in and out as if it were whispering to him. The god nodded, his dark eyes fixed on the squabbling pantheons that filled the moonlit grounds of Machu Picchu.

"It doesn't matter who we choose," said a gloomy voice. The Aztec god of the dead, Mictlantecuhtli, stepped up to the altar beside the sun gods. His bones rattled as he breathed in, and the collar of eyeballs around his neck jiggled. Several gods in the crowd shifted nervously, as if the eyeballs might be staring at them.

"We're going to lose anyway," said the skeletal figure. "Everyone can see that this cycle is written that way. We never win at anything. Why should this be any different?" The owl feathers on his head swayed, bumping the blue-green humming-

bird feathers on Huitzilopochtli's headdress.

"That's true," murmured Coatlicue, the Aztec earth goddess. The snakes in her skirt nodded in agreement. "It is an unlucky time."

"So why play at all if you feel that way?" Quilla challenged them. "Why not stay out of it?"

"They need me," Tezcatlipoca smirked. "Odin said so. He promised that if I help, he'll make sure whoever wins will keep the names of the Aztec gods alive."

"Just the Aztec gods!" cried Quilla.

"How can we trust him?" Huitzilopochtli asked at the same time.

"We can't," Inti said. "We have to win if we want to be sure of our safety."

"Odin will owe me a favor," Tezcatlipoca said. "I like the sound of that."

"But what about the poor avatar?" Quilla asked. "Are you telling a god to throw away his life for a game none of us think we can win, just because we want to play anyway?"

"There are several unimportant gods here," Huitzilopochtli said, his eyes scanning the crowd. "We could sacrifice one of them. We know all about sacrifice, don't we, my friends?"

From his perch on the wall, the weather god was amused to see a number of figures in the crowd melt quietly into the air. He held the chinchilla up to his other ear, her feathery whiskers tickling his cheek.

It's a lot of power . . . a great deal of power, *the chinchilla whispered to him.* More than any god here has ever felt. Enough to show them what you're really capable of. Enough to take back the mountains and the sky.

"Well, it's not going to be one of ours," the rainbow woman said stoutly.

"Shouldn't we talk about this?" Inti pleaded. "There are a few strong gods among us. Huitzilopochtli, you might have a good chance of winning."

The Aztec god snorted. "And throw away my immortality? This life is thin and unsatisfying, but it's better than no life. I don't see you volunteering either, Inti."

"We'll pick a nobody god," Tezcatlipoca said. "We'll force him into it. Huitzilopochtli and I can do that. Someone nobody will miss."

From the expression on Quilla's face, if she'd had hands, she'd have been wringing them. "We'd be killing him," she cried. "Killing a god. *Taking his immortality. It's so much worse than murdering a mere human. How could we choose someone to do that to?"*

"There's no need."

Gods and goddesses shuffled aside in a flurry of feathers and snakes and bones. None of them recognized the young man walking up to the altar. He wasn't even interesting-looking. His skin was just brown, not blue or green or black or bright white. None of his limbs hissed or thrashed. He wasn't wearing anything bloody at all. He looked like a boring mortal.

The chinchilla and the lizard were back on the wall, and none of the gods spotted the glass-winged butterfly tucked behind his ear, antennae trembling.

The god stopped at the stone altar, laying one hand on it lightly. "I volunteer," he said.

Several gods gasped. Quilla's mouth fell open.

"Haven't you heard our conversation?" Inti asked worriedly.

"Don't you know what this means?"

The young man nodded, touching one of his ears in a thoughtful way.

Huitzilopochtli squinted at him. "Are you Mayan or Incan?" he barked. "You're not one of ours."

"He is Incan," Inti answered. "More or less. A weather god that we adopted. Son, aren't you also a god of proph—"

The god brought one finger to his lips, giving Inti a significant look, and the sun god fell silent. Huitzilopochtli was already talking over him and didn't notice.

"Perfect," he said. "A silly little weather god from the Andes. Nice and expendable. We'll run out the cycle, take Odin's favors, conserve our strength, and wait for our next chance. Done." The blue and yellow lines on his face wrinkled as he smiled and clapped the volunteer on the shoulder. "This is the kind of courage I love to see in my warriors. Maybe your spirit will return one day as a hummingbird, like the bravest of mortals."

"Maybe," the weather god said inscrutably.

"So," Huitzilopochtli said, "what's your name, avatar?"

"My name," said the god, "is Catequil."

VILLAGE OF GHOSTS

Now that Diana had a guide, the darkness between underworlds seemed less terrifying. Maui kept her arm in his and chattered about light, funny things, making her laugh. When they heard wild howling in the distance, he steered her away confidently, and soon it faded. They'd get to Hades in no time, and she wouldn't have to go through a bunch of other scary underworlds on the way.

She stopped, holding Maui back for a moment.

"Do you hear a river?" she asked. "Maybe over that way? Do you think it's the River Styx?"

"The underworlds shift around a bit," Maui said, "but I doubt it. Last I checked, it was farther this way." He tugged her away from the sound. Diana walked a few steps and then stopped again.

"Are you sure?" she said. "I just . . . I have this feeling. I know it sounds weird, but there's something about it. . . . "

"You're probably just woozy from being nearly dead for so long," Maui said, patting her hand. "Trust me, Hades is this way."

"Can we check?" Diana said, pulling her hand free. *Trust your instincts*, Dumuzi had said. Her instincts were saying *go that way.*

"Well, it's no skin off my nose," Maui said affably, "but you know what could happen if you get trapped in the wrong underworld—or by the wrong death god."

Diana walked away from him, back toward the sound of the river, her head lowered as she listened. Maui glanced in the direction of Hades, tugging a lock of his hair, and then trailed after her.

"The Egyptian underworld, for instance," Maui said with a shiver. "It's bloody horrible! Especially if you don't come loaded with treats and expensive things like the pharaohs. They'll want to weigh your heart down there, you know. They'll rip it right out of your chest, and if it weighs more than this feather they've got, they feed you to a crocodile creature. Snap snap." He clacked his teeth together with a sound uncannily like monstrous jaws closing.

"Hmm," Diana said.

"Or there's Xibalba," Maui said. "The Mayan underworld. You do *not* want to end up there. There's this river of scorpions, right? And they love testing their visitors with crazy trials involving jaguars and bats and ball games. How are you at basketball?"

"Um . . . terrible," Diana said. Were those shapes in the darkness up ahead?

"Right, now imagine playing basketball . . . WITH YOUR OWN HEAD," Maui said dramatically. Distracted, Diana didn't react, and he looked disappointed.

"Those look like houses," she said, pointing.

"Hades doesn't have any houses," he said. "It has Elysian Fields, though. Big shiny gold fields for nice people and brave people and good people. Like you. Wouldn't you like to run around some pretty fields for the rest of eternity?"

Diana had reached the first house, with Maui close behind her. She walked around it curiously. It was low and long, made of stone with a thatched roof. There were curtains fluttering at the windows and a pair of sandals lying by the front step, but she couldn't see anyone inside through the open windows.

A vegetable garden was growing in the back and around one side of the house, separating it from the house next door, which looked much the same, except that smoke was coming from its chimney. All the houses faced onto a dirt road, with more houses across the way.

Everywhere there were signs of life, but no people. It was so much like the world right after everyone disappeared that Diana almost wondered if she'd crossed out of the underworld somehow. There was even a sky, with a full moon floating peacefully in it, but she couldn't see any stars. And the light from the moon was strange, brighter than a normal moon.

She could still hear the river, but she couldn't see it. She tried to figure out which direction its noises were coming from, and she realized she could hear something else, too—the murmur of voices. The voices were friendly and ordinary, like the sounds of a quiet country village on an ordinary day.

"Where are we?" she asked Maui.

He shrugged. "Beats me. Definitely not Hades, though."

"You've never been here before?"

"Not that I can recall. Looks rather dull, doesn't it?"

"I think it looks kind of sweet," Diana said. "But where are all the people?"

"Maybe this is where people go who died of boredom," Maui guessed. "Don't you want to get on to Hades? There's no one here to help you, and your body could be dying up there."

"I know," Diana said. "I guess you're right." She turned to follow him back down the road.

"Help!"

Diana caught Maui's elbow. "Did you hear that?"

"Um, nope," he said. "Come on, this way."

"I thought I heard someone calling for help," Diana said.

"In the land of the dead? Go figure. Probably someone being tortured. Nothing we can do."

"This seems like such an un-torture-y place," Diana said.

"Help!" the voice cried again, just at the edge of her hearing.

"I'll just check quickly," Diana said, backing away from Maui.

"Diana," Maui said impatiently, "don't be silly. How many tortured souls have you seen so far? Could you help a single one?"

"I helped Dumuzi and his sister," Diana said, lifting her chin.

"By killing Anna," Maui pointed out.

Diana's mouth dropped open. "How did you know that? I didn't—were you watching me?"

Maui looked guilty.

"Help!" the voice came again.

"We'll discuss this in a minute," Diana said. She turned her back on Maui and ran up the dirt road toward the voice.

Broad-leaved trees grew between the houses, shading the road, and now and then she could hear tinny bells, like the kind someone might put on a goat or a cow. The air was warmer than she'd expected, nothing like the freezing wasteland of Hel or the chilly walls of Irkalla.

She came to a place where the road divided, criss-crossed by other paths, and she followed the fork to the right, where the trees grew more thickly. Now she thought she could see the river, glimmering in the moonlight at the end of the road. But the voice was closer than that.

Suddenly she crashed into something warm and yielding, with two arms that grabbed her shoulders for balance.

Something that went "oof."

Diana wobbled, startled, and stuck her hands out in front of her. She couldn't see anyone, but her hands definitely hit a person.

"Careful, child," said a woman's voice. "No need to hurry so."

"I heard someone calling for help," Diana said, her mind shouting, *Invisible people! The village is full of invisible people!*

"Ah, yes, that be me," said the voice with a chuckle. "I

got my basket stuck again. Ev'ryone else be so used to it, no one comes runnin' to help anymore. They say, that old lady, she fend for herself. Maybe if she stop carryin' her basket on top her head while walkin' under low-hangin' branches, she not be havin' this problem."

"Can I help?" Diana asked.

"That depend," said the woman, patting Diana's arms. "How you be at climbin' trees?"

Warm, callused hands encircled her wrists and pulled her to one of the trees that hung over the road. Hooked on a branch overhead was a basket that looked heavy and full. If this woman had been wearing it on her head, she was probably quite tall.

"I can get it," Diana said, dropping her cloak at the foot of the tree. She found a foothold in the trunk and pulled herself up, gripping the closest branch in her arms. Soon she had reached the branch with the basket, and she clambered out to it, unhooking the handle from the tree. She held on with her legs and leaned down, lowering the heavy basket, and then felt silly, because she couldn't see the person she was handing it to.

But she felt the basket get lighter, and then the woman's voice said, "Thank you, honey," so she carefully let go. It was weird to see the basket float lightly to the ground, as if it was moving by itself.

Diana climbed back down and saw the basket hopping a little in place. It took her a moment to figure out that the woman was trying to lift it.

"Can I help you carry it?" she asked. "Where are you taking it to?"

"That would be a great kindness," the invisible woman said. "My home be close."

Diana tried lifting the basket by the handles, but it was loaded with yams, and she could barely budge it that way. She crouched and wrapped her arms around it, lifting with her legs as she stood up, trying not to stagger too much.

There was a silence, and she realized with a stab of worry that the woman could have walked away without Diana noticing.

"Hello?" she said.

"Just along this way," said the woman, her footsteps shuffling in the dirt.

"Wait, I'm sorry," Diana said, "I should have mentioned . . . I, um, I can't see you."

The woman chortled. "You must be new. I can see you well enough. You be able to see us all soon." She touched Diana's hand and guided her onto the path, then led her back the way she'd come, keeping a light touch on Diana's skin.

"I'm just passing through," Diana said. "I'm not really dead. Which underworld is this?"

Her invisible companion chuckled again. "It not be havin' a name. I was an Ashanti in my life. You can call me Afua."

Ashanti. Isn't that African? Diana thought. "I'm Diana," she said.

"Have you been long dead or shortly dead?" Afua asked.

"I'm not dead at all," Diana said. "I'm trying to get back to my life."

"I been dead a long, long time," Afua said thoughtfully. "It's not so bad. You'll see." They reached the crossroads, and Diana looked back to where she had left Maui. He was gone, but somehow that didn't surprise her. Afua's touch guided Diana down a new path, leading her up to one of the low houses.

"This be mine," Afua said. "My lazy husband, he send me out for yams. And where he is now? Probably asleep in a field somewheres instead of here to help me put dem all away. It's good you died while you young, child. I be an old lady forever now. Can't even reach de yam shelf without my bones creaking."

There was kindness in Afua's voice, even if she couldn't seem to remember that Diana had said she wasn't dead. Diana wanted to keep going, to go back and find Maui or continue looking for Hades, but she felt sorry for the old woman, and she felt she would be rude to leave. "I'll help you put them away," she said, "if you like."

Even though Afua was invisible, Diana could hear the smile in her voice. "What a good spirit you are," she said. "You be much beloved in the village afore long. They love new friends around dese parts." The door to the house swung open and Diana followed the woman's footsteps inside, maneuvering carefully to set the basket down on a table. She rubbed her arms, her shoulders aching.

"Dey go up in dat basket," Afua said, and then, remembering that Diana couldn't see her, she lifted Diana's hand to point at a basket on a shelf. Diana climbed up on a bench below it and began transferring yams from one basket to the other as Afua handed them to her. After a moment of this, Diana laughed.

"What be amusin' you, child?"

"It's just," Diana said, "I've been to lots of underworlds now, and I thought being chased by horse-headed guys or lowered down dark chasms were the weirdest things that could happen to me, but actually, this kind of feels weirdest of all. I mean, it's just so . . . normal." She hadn't done anything this everyday in a long time—probably since before she got famous. Pop stars never unloaded their own groceries, according to her mother, who was happy to spend Venus's money on innumerable untrustworthy assistants and other help. Diana liked the way this reminded her of helping her dad, back when she was a kid.

"Death be not so different from life," Afua said. "At least for us."

"I like that," Diana said. She reached down to take a yam, and for a moment she thought she glimpsed a brown hand holding it up to her, and a corner of bright red skirt brushing the floor. "Hey, I think I'm starting to see you."

"That's good," Afua said with the smile in her voice again. "That's very good. It won't be long now."

"Please," Gus said, forcing himself not to shout and argue and demand things. He knelt on the riverbank, his jeans squishing in the soft mud. "Please, please, I need to see her."

"I know you do," the old woman said kindly. "You never said good-bye. She died too young. It isn't fair. It should have been the other guy. It should have been you.

I need her, I can't live without her, there are hungry children at home waiting for her, the world depends on her—do you think I haven't heard it all before? Everyone who dies has someone who loves them. If they all came to me and begged for their loved ones back, what should I do? It would be unfair to say yes to some and no to others. And we cannot let the dead crowd back into the world. I'm sorry. It must be no for everyone."

"I'm not asking for everyone," Gus pleaded. "I'm not looking for my mom and dad. I'm not asking you for my brother. I know I can't end death and bring everyone back. I'm only asking you for one girl—and she did die too young, and I can't live without her, and the fate of the world *does* depend on her. She might not even be here, but I have to look."

The old woman sighed. She waded closer to the riverbank. "Hand me that pot."

Gus picked up the brass pot and stepped into the river, handing it to her. *You could take her*, whispered a voice in his head. *She's just an old woman. You could grab her and force her to let you cross the river. She might be all that's standing between you and Diana. Doesn't that make you angry?* His fingers itched as if Oro was trying to wrest control of them and strangle the woman himself.

I would never do that, Gus thought, letting go of the pot and pulling his trembling hands back. *You're fighting a losing battle if you think you can make me attack harmless old women.* The deep furrows of the tattoo along his arms stung with pain and he pressed his hands together, trying to push the pain—and Oro—back down.

The woman pulled a bright yellow square of cloth out of the pot and held it, the sunny color pouring over her fingers.

"There's something else," Gus said. "She isn't dead. Not yet. Her spirit is trapped in the underworlds, but her body is alive. That's why I think I can bring her back."

"Really," the old woman said, lifting the yellow cloth so she could look through it at the sky. "That does help."

"I'll do anything," Gus said desperately. "I'll stay here in her place if that's what you want. Take me instead."

She laughed in a bubbling way, like the river. "We don't need any living souls here," she said. "But it is generous and brave of you to offer." She let go of the yellow cloth and it fluttered down to the surface of the river like a drunken butterfly.

"Please," Gus said. "I love her."

"One day they're going to realize I'm far too soft," the woman said, "and then I'll be fired from this job. Go find her." She took another handful of cloths and tossed them out into the river. As they touched the water, parrot greens and leopard spots and desert oranges, each cloth hardened and froze in place, becoming a brightly colored stepping-stone. In a moment there was a path stretching across the river.

"Thank you," Gus said, hoping she could hear the awe and gratitude in his voice. He took her hand and kissed it. "Thank you so much."

"Go while the path is strong," she said, squeezing his hand.

He hopped up onto the yellow stone at the beginning,

and then stepped from cloth to cloth all the way across the river, holding out his arms for balance. The last few rocks were wobbly and a little squishy, as if they were starting to turn back into cloth. He jumped off the mottled red and black one at the end and landed on the riverbank.

When he turned around, the old woman was tugging the cloths back to her, folding them and replacing them in the brass pot. He waved good-bye, but she didn't look up.

On this side the pale sand became reddish dirt and the light was more like moonlight. A path wound up from the river between thick trees and low stone houses. He followed it, looking for signs of life.

A door swung open on one of the houses, and Gus spun around, but no one came out. Could it have been the wind? But there was no wind that he could feel.

Something brushed across his cheek and he jumped again. A leaf was spiraling gently to the ground, but it was long and dark green, unlike the small pale leaves on the trees above him. He heard something that sounded like a giggle.

With a small thump, a coconut came bouncing down the steps from one of the houses and rolled across the road in front of him. It seemed to roll for longer than it should, changing course as if people were kicking it back and forth.

Gus kept walking cautiously, watching the houses. Curtains moved as if eyes were peeking out at him. The murmur of the wind—*except there is no wind*—dropped as he went by and picked up again behind him. He saw leaves rustling as if monkeys were racing through the trees beside him, and now and then he thought he could hear bells, or the distant patter of footsteps.

The village was bigger than he'd expected, with roads crossing each other and leading farther in. At one point he thought he saw a spade moving by itself in one of the gardens, digging a small hole in the ground, but when Gus stopped to look at it more closely, the spade stopped too, stuck upright in the ground. Had he imagined it?

He felt a sharp tug on his hair and turned, hearing the ghostly giggles again. Again, there was no one behind him. The street was empty.

"Hello?" he said. No one answered.

Farther up the street he saw a movement. It looked like a bucket of water floating through the air by itself. Gus ran toward it, but it turned down a path and disappeared into a house before he could catch up, and the door shut firmly behind it. Gus tried knocking, but no one let him in. He thought about just walking in, but he didn't think that would qualify as courteous and respectful, so he went back to the road and stood there, lost in thought. He was beginning to get the strong sense that there *were* people here, all around him, but they were invisible, and they were deliberately staying out of his way. Except, perhaps, for a couple of kids, who were having fun teasing him. The giggle he'd heard had a young quality to it.

Reluctantly, he reached down into himself and tapped for Oro. *If you fight in the forest,* Gus thought, *and you're a god, perhaps your hearing is better than mine.*

"Of course. It is," his mouth said in Oro's strange, stilted way. At the same time Gus felt an odd tingling in his head, as if the god were climbing up into Gus's brain and poking around in his eardrum. Suddenly the sounds around him became sharper, like an image coming into focus. He could hear footsteps clearly now, tiptoeing through the sand, and the squeak of a gate farther up the road as someone hurried out of the way. And if he tilted his head carefully, he could just make out voices on the edge of sound.

"He's cu—"

"—eep him."

Something poked him hard in the arm and he reached, trying to grab whoever it was, but they dodged out of the way, laughing.

"Slow."

"—live."

Then he heard footsteps running, and he looked down to see puffs of dirt as someone raced toward him from the top of the road.

"She's com—"

"Qui—"

"—ide him."

Invisible hands grabbed his arm and tugged him toward a house surrounded by a grove of banana trees. He tried to resist, and more hands appeared at his back, shoving him along. It felt like maybe four or five invisible people were bundling him onto the porch of the house. The door swung open, and a whiff of frying bananas spilled out.

Gus twisted, trying to see the road. Why were they getting him out of the way? Had they said "hide him"? From what?

Strong arms yanked him into the house and the wooden door slammed behind him. He was standing in a kitchen. A fire flickered in the fireplace and half-chopped vegetables lay on the wooden table. There was a window over the copper sink, with filmy white curtains that billowed lightly in the breeze.

Hoping there was no one in his way, and that they were all trying to block the door instead, Gus made a dash for the window. To his surprise he made it onto the sink, and then he felt a hand on his ankle, trying to pull him back. With a lunge, Gus grabbed the sill and threw himself out into the air, jerking his foot free. He crashed to the ground below the window, rolling in the dirt.

He heard the door open behind him, but he jumped up and ran to the road before they could reach him.

Puzzlingly, there was nothing there.

Not that he could see, anyway. But he could feel . . . something, like a presence . . . couldn't he?

"Diana?" he called.

He thought he heard a ghostly gasp behind him. Not too far up the road, something moved—a sleeve fluttering in the air, or a wayward red-gold curl, and then it was gone.

He stepped toward it, reaching his hands forward but finding only air.

"—us?"

Was it Diana's voice? How would he even know if he

did find her here?

"Diana," he said. "It's me. It's Gus."

"—ssible."

"You be imagin—" said another voice, soft and female.

"No, you're not imagining things," Gus said. "It's me, Diana, it really is. It's Gus."

Silence drifted down the street. He stepped forward again, feeling around in the emptiness. "Please," he said, his voice cracking. "Please let me talk to her. I'm her friend. I love her."

"—to take her away fr—" whispered the voices at the gate behind him.

"Yes," Gus said. "I came to take her home. She shouldn't be here. She shouldn't be dead. Please, don't you remember what it was like to lose someone you love? She doesn't have to be lost, she doesn't have to be gone—not if you let her talk to me. Please, please help us."

"—is Gus," said the shadow of Diana's voice. *"I know it—"*

Gus felt a hand take his—not Diana's; it was too big and knobbly for that. It lifted his hand tentatively and then gave a little pull, like it wanted him to walk forward down the road. Gus obeyed, taking a step, and then another, as the hand led him up to a mango tree glittering with dew-speckled cobwebs. There it stopped him, and then, after a moment, Gus felt his invisible guide place something in his hand—another hand, this one small and cold and, Gus was sure, pale as moonlight.

"Diana?" he said.

"Gus? Is it rea—"

Her voice faded out, but he could still feel her hand in his, squeezing with impossible strength, as if she might never let go ever again. He pulled her toward him and wrapped his arms around invisible shoulders, feeling invisible arms go around his neck, knowing exactly where she was. He didn't need to see her to know for certain that it was Diana.

"I came to take you back," he said, crying into her invisible hair, which still smelled like lilacs. "I came to save you." He took a ragged breath. "For once." Her shoulders were shaking too, and he felt wet spots appear on his shirt as invisible tears fell.

"—y can't I see y—" her voice whispered in his ear. *"—you dead?"*

"I'm not dead," Gus said, "and neither should you be."

He felt one of Diana's hands lifted off his shoulder for a moment, as if someone had picked it up to show it to her.

"—'m invisible!" her ghostly voice said with surprise.

"Yeah, you are," he said, hugging her closer. "You hadn't noticed?"

"—eally weird."

"Let's get back to the real world," he said, "before I lose you again." He kept one arm around her shoulders and took her other hand, steering her back to the road that led down to the river.

"—ye!" he heard Diana call over her shoulder. *"Nice to mee—"*

"Bye."

"Bye."

"Good l—" whispered the spirits around them.

"—anted her to stay." Gus heard one of them say sadly. *"We all d—"*

Diana leaned into him, her invisible arms hugging him tightly. He brushed the air where her hair would be, and felt his hand accidentally hit her nose.

"Ow," she said, and started giggling, her shoulders shaking with laughter. *"—y hero."*

"Sorry," he said with a smile. He was sure he saw a flash of white teeth as she smiled back. And when he looked down, he could see her footprints appearing next to his in the dirt, the unmistakable outline of sneakers.

"Have you been here long?" he asked.

"—on't think so. Maybe. I think I was going to meet Afua's frie—" Even the shadow of her voice sounded puzzled, as if she couldn't remember why she'd been doing something so ordinary.

The river appeared before them, wide and bubbling, with the old woman standing in it as before. Gus waved to her. "She's alive!" he called. "Look, I found her!" He squeezed Diana's shoulder, and he felt her lift her arm and wave it too. The ghostly shape of fingers wavered in the air, and he saw a flash of red that he was sure was her hair.

The old woman waved back, shaking her head in pleased disbelief. She shook out the pot of cloths and once again the stepping-stones appeared. Gus slid his hand down to take Diana's hand, holding it firmly. "Don't let go of me," he said. "Whatever you do."

He stepped out onto the first stone, then the second, as she moved out behind him, stepping where he'd stepped, from one cloth to another across the river.

On the far side, he put his arm around her again and turned back to the old woman. "Thank you. If there's ever anything I can do to help you," he said, "just let me know."

"You can save the world," the old woman said with a twinkle in her eye. "I hear she's necessary for that."

"Yeah, she is," said Gus.

"Pshaw," Diana whispered.

They walked across the sand in the pale light, holding each other close. If he didn't look to the side, it was easy to forget she was invisible; she felt so real, so alive under his hands. The dreaminess of the underworld was beginning to fade, and electric excitement shot through him. He'd found her! He just had to get her soul back to her body, and Diana would be alive again.

"Say something," he said. "I can't believe you're really there."

"—sure am . . . never been happier to see—well, not see—someo—"

She stopped walking and turned in his arms toward him. He felt her lips hit his chin.

"Oops," she whispered. *"—ot quite as romantic as I'd plan—"*

He took her invisible face in his hands and kissed her. With their eyes closed, their lips found each other perfectly.

They walked back across the sand hand in hand, the light fading around them until they were walking through darkness, and then gradually green shapes began to appear, and soon they were in the jungle, with monkeys chittering in the trees and brightly colored birds flashing through the branches.

Diana's hand gripped his more tightly as they stepped into the graveyard and she saw the elephants standing over her body. He led her up to it, and then, with one last squeeze, she let go. When he reached out again, there was nothing in the air beside him.

Gus knelt beside Diana's body. The younger elephant wound his trunk through Abidemi's. The elephants leaned toward each other, watching.

Slowly, Diana's eyes opened. She blinked up at Gus, at the jungle, at the elephants with their wide, dark eyes.

"Hey," she said with a smile, reaching for Gus's hand, and then winced, touching her stomach. "Ow. Man. That didn't hurt quite so much when I was dead." Her smile spread, looking like it might sail off her face. "I guess that means I really am alive again." She rested her head back on the ground. "After all that. Maybe I just needed someone to lead me out." She lifted her hand to Gus's face.

"Thank you for coming to get me."

"Thank you for being there when I got there," he said, taking her hand in both of his.

"Thank you for bringing my body with you to Africa."

"Thank *you* for not dying when you got stabbed."

Gus caught the elephants rolling their eyes at each other. Diana laughed, then winced again, pushing herself up to sitting.

"So now what?" she said. "We still have to save the world?"

"Kali's working on that," he said.

"Of course she is," Diana said. "And—the other avatars?"

"Tigre's with us. Thor and Anna are still back in New York. She was pretty mad when we took you. I'm afraid she's going to come after us," he said.

A shadow crossed Diana's face, and she shook her head, no longer smiling. "She's not coming after anyone." She started to stand, and he took her elbows, helping her up. "I have a lot to tell you," she said, looking into his eyes. "Bad things. I don't know if you're going to like me much anymore when I'm done."

"You never have to worry about that," he said, supporting her weight. "You can tell me everything while we wait for Kali and Tigre to come back. And then we'll all go save the world together."

"This really could have been brought to my attention a little sooner," Oya muttered. "You didn't think it was worth mentioning that there was someone spying on us?"

"A turtle?" Tigre protested. "In what universe is a turtle a potential spy?"

"THIS one!" Oya and Kali said simultaneously.

"All right, all right," Tigre said. "I said I was sorry." He handed Kali another branch and she hammered it into place with a rock.

Oya tilted her head, listening, and then she pointed at Kali with a nod.

"This is totally pointless," Kali said loudly. "You guys, if another were-lion comes along, I can just kill it like the last one."

Tigre shifted uncomfortably. He hadn't liked the look on Kali's face as she wrestled with Tan, like she'd been waiting to fight something for far too long.

Kali kicked him, jerking her head at the thing they were building, and Tigre realized that he'd forgotten to say his line. "Oh," he stammered, "well, I, I think it's safer this way. It's better to be, um, safe."

Kali rolled her eyes at him.

"Yeah," Oya added at top volume. "This is just a precaution while we sleep. It'll yowl if anything dangerous approaches."

"Oh, great," Kali practically shouted. "So every time anything goes by it's going to wake us up? Monkeys and rabbits and butterflies and everything?"

"No, no," Oya cried, and Tigre waved his hands at them. *A bit much, ladies*. She lowered her voice a little bit. "This is only for *really* dangerous things. It's enchanted to ignore anything unimportant."

"Ah," Kali said. "So it'll ignore anything that we don't have to worry about? Trivial, impotent, useless creatures?"

"That's right," Oya said brightly.

He's going to see right through this, Tigre thought. *He's probably out there laughing at us right now.*

They'd spent the afternoon building their "guard," which was vaguely man-shaped. Oya was boiling something nasty-smelling over the fire, and the heat and the smell were making Tigre feel really sick. Although the memory of the were-lion's blood spattered over the rocks didn't help either.

How can I judge her? he thought, glancing at Kali. *She was protecting us.*

Oya brought the pot over from the fire, holding it in her bare hands. *A neat god power. No need for potholders, ever.* Tigre watched as she poured the contents carefully all over the wooden man, coating him in a black, viscous substance.

"All right," she said, looking up at the darkening sky. "Time for bed!"

"I know!" Kali said, letting out an exaggerated yawn. "I'm *soooo* tired. I'm sure I'll fall asleep *right away.*"

Tigre nearly said, "Now? Without dinner?" but he saw the looks on their faces and realized they wanted to get on with the plan.

Oya shook out three blankets around the fire. They were camping on the shore of the Niger River again, farther upstream from where they'd been the night before. They had pretended to search for Eshu for part of the day, hunting through the caves and whispering plans to each other whenever Oya was sure no animals were nearby. This particular trick was Oya's idea—she said it had worked on someone called "Anansi," who was apparently another version of Eshu/Legba. Kali had heard of him, but Tigre hadn't.

They all lay down and closed their eyes, although Tigre was sure the other two were as restless and far from sleep as he was. He stared at the sky for a while, watching the stars come out one by one, and then he closed his eyes, trying not to remember the crunch of Tan's skull on the rocks.

He was nearly asleep when he heard a light *thump thump thump* near the guard. This brought him fully awake, and he listened, keeping his eyes closed.

Thump thump thump it went again. It sounded like footsteps, but strange ones, not human. *It could be a hare. The Eshu-hare.*

Thump thump thump. It sounded like he was loping back and forth across the sand in front of the guard.

Thump thump. The pawsteps paused. Tigre could imagine the hare sitting up in front of the guard, its nose twitching as it stared up at it.

"Oho!" a voice whispered. "So you don't think I'm important, ha?" There was a scuffling sound, as if the hare was turning around and around in the sand. "Don't you know who I am?" the voice muttered.

The guard, of course, did not respond. There was no enchantment on it like Oya had described. It was just sticks and tar. But Eshu the hare didn't know that.

"Psst!" the hare said boldly, a little louder. "Aren't you watching for dangerous things? I tell you, you're off your game, my friend. There's nothing more dangerous than me in these parts." The pawsteps strutted back and forth for a moment, then stopped again.

"Really? Can't you see how powerful and important I am?" Eshu demanded. He was barely keeping his voice down at all now, as if he'd forgotten that the three of them were sleeping nearby. "You could at least speak to me! You're being very rude!"

More silence from the guard.

"Are you calling me trivial and impotent?" Eshu snarled. "I'll show you! I'll show you useless!"

There was a loud *THUD.*

"Ow!" Eshu yelped. "Hey, let go! Let go of me! I'll hit

you again, I swear I will! And my other paw is even stronger!"

THUD!

"Unhand me! Give me back my paws!" Eshu cried. "Don't make me kick you!"

THUD! THUD!

"What?" Eshu squawked. "How are you doing this? Let me go! Or so help me I'll—Oh, feather monkeys."

Oya had risen to her feet, lifting a branch from the fire. She carried it over to the guard as Tigre and Kali scrambled up to join her.

There was a hare hanging from the scarecrow, all of its paws trapped in the sticky tar. It looked completely stuck and rather pathetic. Tigre was astonished.

"I cannot believe," Eshu said, enunciating each word, "that I fell for this *again*." He let his head fall back, his long ears drooping.

"Your ego always trumps your cleverness," Oya said. "Silly rabbit." She sounded very pleased with herself.

"How do we know he won't shape-shift and get away?" Kali asked.

"The tar has a binding spell in it," Oya said. "It keeps him in this shape as long as we have him captive."

"Bo-ring," Eshu said, rolling his head from side to side. "Couldn't you come up with something new, at least?"

"Why bother," Oya said sweetly, "when you're dumb enough to fall for the same trick twice?"

"I'm not dumb," Eshu bristled. The torch cast flickering shadows across his fur, and on the sand behind him, the shadow of a giant rabbit danced with the shadow of a man, long ears stretching into the dark.

"I thought you said this trick was played on Anansi," Tigre said.

"And wasn't he a spider?" Kali asked. Eshu smirked.

"They're all the same," Oya said. "Eshu, Legba, Anansi, all the same trickster in different shapes. He crisscrosses Africa like that all the time."

Kali rubbed her forehead thoughtfully.

"Come on," Eshu whined. "Let me go. I don't like being stuck." He tugged on his paws. "Ew, it's making my fur all sticky. Let me off and I'll tell you whatever you want to know."

"I don't think so," Oya said, "Mr. Untrustworthy. You tell us first, and then maybe we'll let you go."

"Oh, *fine*," Eshu grumbled.

"And don't lie," Tigre said.

"Why would I bother?" said Eshu. "This game is tiresome anyway."

"Go ahead and interrogate him," Oya said. "I'll watch for signs that he's lying."

"I want to know how to fix the world," Kali said. "You said you know what the gods did, or something like that. You mean how they stopped people from reproducing, or how they brought us forward in time?"

Eshu giggled, a weird sound coming from a hare. "You're thinking about it all wrong," he said. "That's exactly what they wanted when they set this up."

"So tell me how to think about it right," Kali demanded, sounding exasperated.

"You're all so easy to play with," Eshu said. "They

didn't pick any clever avatars, did they? Typical gods, thinking they can win with brute strength instead. Such limited imaginations."

"So they were lying to us?" Tigre guessed. "About what? Jumping us forward in time? Wiping out all of humanity?"

"If they could really get rid of all the mortals that easily," Eshu said, "don't you think they'd have done it a long time ago? Out of revenge, if nothing else?"

"But why would they?" Kali said. "They need them to survive. What's the point of being a god without worshippers?"

"True," Eshu said, rolling his head from side to side. "How astute of you."

"So they're not gone," Tigre said, trying to puzzle it out. "Did they send them somewhere? Like a parallel world or something?"

"Hee!" Eshu cried. "That's a theory worthy of your little friend Gus. Perhaps you watch those science fiction movies too?"

"But he's close, isn't he?" Kali said. "You're nervous, aren't you? Your ears are flicking."

"I'm not nervous," Eshu said, shaking his head so his ears flapped. "I don't care what you know. I like seeing things fall apart. It'll be so entertaining to watch the pantheons scramble to stop you from entering the Cave of Illusions." His mouth snapped shut, as if he'd said too much.

"The Cave of Illusions?" Tigre echoed, confused.

Kali clapped her hands to her face. "Oh my God," she said. "We're idiots."

"Finally, something I agree with," Eshu said.

"None of this is real," Kali said in a wondering voice.

"Hey," Oya protested. "I've been around for centuries. I think I'm quite real."

"You are, because you're inside the illusion," Kali said. "They must have cast it on the African gods, too. I'm right, aren't I?" she said to Eshu. He shrugged a rabbity shrug. "Tigre, think about it," she said, seizing his arm. "We're not in the future. They never cast an infertility spell. They didn't bring us forward in time. They just—moved us. They wrapped the illusion of this world around us because they wanted a proper playing field for the avatar games."

"With no humans," Eshu pointed out. "Humans muck things up. Always getting in the way and changing their fate. The gods like things clean and simple. Of course, you lot have to be the most ornery, destiny-poking, stubborn humans they've ever dealt with. Guess they didn't see that coming." He sounded quite satisfied.

"But that's so complicated," Tigre said. "Making this whole world? The Forever Youngermen and the Eternally Me kids and the crystal hunters and Quetzie and everything?"

"Well," Eshu said, "they didn't invent all that. They set up a scenario—humans can't reproduce anymore—and stepped back to see what would happen as the rest of the illusion played out. You can try it yourself, if one of you wins. Try taking away human fertility, and you'll see things happen exactly this way."

"Yeah," Kali said. "We're not going to do that."

"And they lied to us, too?" Oya asked. "Giving us Africa?"

"To keep you out of the competition," Eshu said. "I mean, us. Once somebody wins, they're going to break the illusion and take us all back to the real world. Africa would be fair game again, but this time there'd be one supreme god so powerful, none of the African gods could fight him."

"Or her," Tigre said, his eyes on Kali.

"Well, I never," Oya said, sounding really angry.

"I know," Eshu said. "Imagine gods lying and cheating to get their own way. Unheard of!"

"When I get my hands on Zeus . . . " Oya said.

"And that's why they keep saying we can't go back in time," Kali interrupted. "But we don't have to! Our world is right there, just behind the illusion. We've only lost a couple of weeks—however long we've been in here. If we can break it, we can all go back to our lives."

"Er," Eshu said loudly. "Not exactly."

"How do we break it?" Kali demanded. "Where's the cave?"

"I'm glad we're having this conversation here," Eshu said. "Otherwise Zeus and the others would be swooping in and stomping around bellowing a lot. They can't even *see* this. That was dumb of them, wasn't it? Sticking a continent-shaped blind spot into their plan?"

"Answer her questions," Oya said, pulling on his ears.

"OW OW OW," Eshu protested. "Sheesh, you don't have to be all brutal about it. Fine, okay. There's a mirror—it belongs to one of those goofy-looking Aztec gods. It's indestructible, but if you can break it, the illusion will shatter."

"Oh good," Tigre said. "Just break an indestructible mirror. No problem."

"BUT," Eshu said portentously, "you can't break it without consequences. Someone still has to win. A lot of power will be released, and if an avatar doesn't grab it, someone else will. Or the universe will descend into chaos. Either way—fun!"

"How do we do that?" Kali asked. Eshu rolled his eyes.

"I don't know *everything*," he said. "In fact, that's pretty much all I know. So can I go now? My poor pretty paws will never be clean again."

"One more question," Kali said. "Where is the Cave of Illusions?"

"Oh, clever clogs," Eshu said. "Where would you put it?"

"If it belongs to an Aztec god, it's probably in Mexico, right?" Tigre said. "Don't they have big caverns there?"

"Yes, yes," Eshu said. "It's in a big old cave in Mexico. You're ever so clever. Will you *please* let me go now? Hanging here is much more tiring than it looks."

"What do you think?" Oya asked them. Tigre liked the way she looked at him as well as Kali, as if he had equal say. "Should we cut him loose? I think we've got a fair amount of information out of him."

"I agree," Kali said. "Tigre?"

"Sure," he said. He felt stronger than usual, ready to fight. Eshu had said that humans liked to mess with their own destiny. Maybe his fate really was up to him. "Let him go. And then we'll go end this thing."

FOUR YEARS AGO . . .

"We have to work quickly," Dionysus said, dropping down from the sky with a thump. Gold sand puffed in a cloud around his feet. "I drugged his drink, but Apollo won't sleep for long."

"Come on then, my dear," Zeus said, taking Venus's elbow. "Let's show you off to your new family."

Venus shook back her long golden hair, smoothing her silky robes. The Egyptian sun was hotter and drier than she was used to, and she hoped that she didn't look sticky or blistered. She needed to be at her most gorgeous right now. She smiled to herself. When don't I look gorgeous? They'll love me no matter what.

"I don't like this," Vulcan said, stomping along behind them.

"You don't have to," Venus said breezily. "It has nothing to do with you."

Vulcan snorted. "My wife being handed over to another man? I think it does."

"Zeuuuus," Venus whined.

"Vulcan, you've barely been married for the last several centuries," Zeus said. "And she's what the Egyptians demanded. We've all agreed that it's the best thing for our pantheon."

Venus fluffed her hair again, pleased. She was so beautiful that another pantheon wanted her. And now she could get away from both her lumpy, misshapen husband and the sweaty, red-faced war god she was cheating on him with. She'd have a brand-new admirer to adore her, and he was really hot. Like, sun-god-hot. Even hotter than Apollo, who had always rejected her advances. Hrmph. This would serve him right. By the time he woke up, Diana would be gone and Venus would be their new avatar. It was perfect. She'd get all that power when Amon won, but she wouldn't have to do anything for it. No risk, lots of reward. Just the way she liked things.

Even so, her stomach felt queasy as they walked across the desert to the gathering of Egyptian gods. They were all so strange-looking. One had the head of an ibis, one a jackal, one a falcon. One large, underdressed woman appeared to be part hippopotamus. And one goddess was half cat, her whiskers twitching as she licked her hands. Venus didn't even know if the cow was a goddess or just a hapless animal that had wandered along with them.

She recognized Isis, who at least was all human, by the tall headdress and dark eye makeup. Venus wasn't very good at remembering people's faces or names or anything much about their lives, but she usually remembered what they wore and what their makeup looked like. Isis was very pretty. If she ever smiled, she'd probably be able to get her own way without having to be so bossy all the time. Venus had known from the moment she was born that if she batted her big blue eyes enough, most people would eventually do what she wanted.

Beside Isis was a woman whose skin was entirely blue, with little stars twinkling in it. She nodded as the Greeks approached.

"Yes," she said. "Amon will be pleased."

"She's just what he's always wanted," Isis said disapprovingly, her gaze traveling from Venus's high white forehead down to her perfect, sandaled feet.

"She's just what everyone's always wanted," Hera said in the same tones of disapproval. "That was the point."

Venus preened, shaking out her hair and showing off her glorious smile. Hera had never said anything that nice about her before. Venus had always suspected that the queen of the gods was just jealous of her. But maybe Hera did like her a bit, despite herself. She smiled dazzlingly at Hera, but the other goddess just scowled back, as usual.

"We should get on with it," Dionysus said nervously. He must be afraid Apollo will wake up and come after him, *Venus thought, but she was disappointed. This was her favorite part—when everyone stared at her and talked about how beautiful and special she was. She'd been looking forward to this.*

"Nobody told Maat, right?" the blue woman said. "Or Athena? The judges can't know—they might disqualify both of our avatars."

"We'll keep the alliance hush-hush, don't worry," Zeus boomed. Isis narrowed her eyes at him as if she was sure he was incapable of doing any such thing.

"You have an explanation prepared for why your avatar has two goddesses in one body?" she said coldly.

Venus tilted her head at them. What?

"Of course," Zeus said quickly. "We'll say we just think Venus

will be a useful addition. Now, let's get on with it." He shoved Venus forward and all the gods began to form a circle around her.

"Wait," Venus said. "What do you mean, two goddesses in one body? It'll just be me, won't it?"

Isis cackled. "And where do you think Diana is going to go?"

Some of the animal-headed gods were already chanting. Zeus seized Hera's hand and joined in.

"I thought she was going to disappear!" Venus said. "I thought I *was going to be the only avatar."*

"Human souls are a little harder to dislodge than that," the blue woman said. "You'll have to find a way to entwine your spirit with hers." She took Isis's hand, closing the circle, and all the gods took a step toward Venus, penning her in.

"And then what?" Venus cried. "What happens when we win? Do we split up again?" She looked around the circle wildly. "Zeus, what happens then? I'm not going to be stuck with her forever, am I? Then I won't even be me anymore! Wait, please, I want to be me! I don't want to lose myself!" She threw herself to her knees at his feet. "I've changed my mind, please, don't do this!"

"It's too late," Hera said, shoving Venus back with one foot. "You agreed. We all agreed."

Venus felt her hands go wobbly, like they were being melted down on Vulcan's horrible furnace. Her whole body was being melted down. She was going to be melted down and poured into a cauldron with Diana, stirred and blended until they were one mixed metal together instead of the pure, shining, soft, breakable gold she was right now. She clenched her fists, trying to fight back.

She saw, like a hallucination overlaying the desert in front of her, a bedroom that Venus, goddess of love, would never enter, the walls covered in sports things and nature calendars, the colors all green and brown instead of pink and yellow. She saw a mirror and a face—Diana's face, but thirteen years old, and Diana's hands, touching her forehead and cheeks with concern.

"Come on, Diana!" a woman's voice called from downstairs. "We'll be late for the image meeting! This is your big break!"

"What am I doing?" Diana whispered to the mirror, and Venus felt her own lips forming the words. "I don't want to be a singer. I don't want to be a superstar."

Yes, I do, *Venus thought,* I do want to be a superstar. Me. Venus. Me. *And the last of her resistance wavered, and then, with a shove she felt physically all the way through her, she was here and nowhere and herself and no self all at once.*

Venus screamed.

The Water Crossing

Diana lifted her shirt and peeked at the long jagged scar running across her abdomen. *Mom and Doug are not going to be happy about that. No more of those hooker outfits that show off my abs. How will they ever sell albums now?* Coming back from the dead seemed to have sped up the healing process, although it still hurt when she made sudden movements or tried to reach up.

Kayode, the littler elephant, leaned down to touch her scar gently with his trunk, and she scratched behind his ear. His tail swished appreciatively.

Diana was feeling a bit like Venus again—the pop star, not the goddess—perhaps because the crowd of orishas peering at her through the trees was so much like the crowds of fans that seemed to gather every time she ate in a restaurant. Of course, she wasn't usually sitting at a stone table by a stream with two elephants standing over her.

Gus wove his way back through the tables, carrying a banana leaf with some kind of grilled fish on it. Behind him was the god he had introduced as Obatala, when he'd explained about the orishas being nature gods. The leader of the orishas stopped beside Diana's table as Gus sat down.

"Thank you so much," Diana said. "I'm absolutely starving." She'd never felt anything quite like the pit of hunger in her stomach right now.

"I believe your friends are returning," Obatala said with a nod at the path that led north from the city into the jungle. Diana turned and saw three figures walking through the sun-dappled shadows. One of them was small and round and unfamiliar, but she recognized the other two. She scrambled up as they spotted her and ran across the square toward her.

"You're alive!" Tigre cried. Diana hugged them both. They smelled of soot and tar and singed fur.

"Rock *on*," Kali said, sounding more pleased than Diana had ever heard her. "Okay, I'm impressed."

"I'm so sorry, Diana," Tigre said. "It's my fault, I should have known Anna—"

"No way," Diana said. "Don't you dare apologize to me. No way is it your fault. Besides, I hear this neat work is thanks to you." She pointed at her scar. "So cool, Tigre. You should see my sewing; it's *hopeless*." He smiled bashfully.

"Diana, this is Oya," Tigre said, indicating the small red-haired woman with them.

"Wow," Oya said. "You're even prettier when you're awake."

"Nice to meet you," Diana said, blushing.

"I figured you'd make it back," Kali said. "If you wanted to."

"I really wanted to," Diana said. "But I'm lucky Gus came for me."

"Nice work," Kali said, giving Gus a high five.

"Can you believe we made it?" Diana said. "That we're all back together?" She sighed happily. "I really really thought I'd never see any of you again. Especially in the Norse underworld. What a terrible place to die—or to go when you die, or whatever."

Kali and Gus exchanged looks. "Long story," Gus said. "Tell you later."

"First I have to eat," Diana said, sitting down again. "Or I might eat one of you."

"All right," Kali said, swinging her leg over the bench opposite Diana's. "But then we have some stuff to do." Diana saw Oya pull Obatala aside and start talking to him, her hands waving frantically.

"Like what?" Gus asked as he and Tigre sat down.

"Like get to Mexico," Tigre said. "And break an unbreakable mirror."

"I have an idea about that," Kali said. "The bad news, at least for me, is that it might involve swimming."

Kali explained what they had learned from Eshu about the Cave of Illusions and the Aztec god's mirror.

"I think he must mean Tezcatlipoca," Tigre interjected. "He's actually called the 'lord of the smoking mirror,' although I don't know much more than that. Do you really think there's a way to break it?"

"Well," Kali said, "I know this god who has this trident, see, and he claims it can shatter anything. He called it his invincible trident. He was kind of loud and boom-y about it."

"Poseidon," Diana said, snapping her fingers. "He was carrying it around the Metropolitan Museum, looking all stormy and wet."

"So we're going to steal Poseidon's trident?" Gus said disbelievingly.

"We have to find him first," Diana said. "He takes it with him everywhere."

"I'm hoping our new friends will help," Kali said, nodding at Obatala and Oya. "If they're mad enough about all this, I think they might. Right now I assume Poseidon is in his own palace, but he'll come after us once we leave Africa."

"Him and about a thousand other sea gods and storm gods and such," Gus said.

"Right," Kali said. "Which'll make it harder to steal the trident without alerting everyone to what we're doing. So what we need to do is find a way to sneak into his palace and steal it *without* him noticing."

A flutter of wings caught Diana's eye, and she looked over to see a bird with bright feathers and a long beak land on Obatala's shoulder. It looked like it was whispering in his ear. Obatala nodded and walked over to the avatars with Oya trailing behind him.

"Oya tells me we've been lied to," he said grimly.

"Not by us," Kali pointed out. "But we're going to try to fix it, if you know any underwater gods we could talk to."

"I'd like to see their plan ruined," Obatala said, narrowing his eyes. "I'll take you to Olokun. She's a little tempestuous, but I think she'll help." The bird on his shoulder squawked, and he raised one hand to stroke its beak. "Yes, I know. My friend comes with an interesting story. Several miles northeast of here there is an orchard of avocados that has grown wild, with our help, as our birds love it. In the last couple of days it seems it has been invaded by a very unusual trespasser."

He looked at Tigre. "Do you by any chance have a remarkably large feathered friend with a fondness for avocados?"

There was a lighthouse under the sea, which seemed a little pointless at first, until Obatala explained that it used to be one of the Seven Wonders of the Ancient World. Kali supposed that if she could have her pick of the world's treasures, she wouldn't sneeze at an Ancient Wonder either. She did wonder how Olokun had transported it from the Egyptian harbor—as far as she knew, it had fallen into ruin and there were only bits of it left. But here it was, whole again, and Kali had too many other questions to bother her with that one. Questions like, "How do you steal a trident from a god?" and "Do you by any chance have a secret underground passage into other sea gods' palaces?"

The goddess of the sea was stomping around the room at the top of the lighthouse, where the fire would have been lit. Kali could see the tower shaking as she raged. Obatala's soothing voice kept getting louder and louder.

"Boy," Gus said, "I would not want to be Zeus when they can finally leave Africa and track him down." He was sitting on the green marble floor, leaning against Diana's legs as she perched on something that looked like a pirate's chest. This room was a lot like the one they had come through when they first got to Africa, vast and hotel lobby-ish, except that it didn't have a pile of sand at one end or a big honking ship in the middle. Instead it had a lighthouse, plus a few coffins, and the walls were lined with tall blooming orchids.

Olokun had interesting taste.

"I don't know why they can't just leave Africa now," Tigre said. "If the other gods broke their word . . . "

"I think they still can't break their end of the bargain," Kali said. "Especially not if they want justice later."

Something flew off the top of the lighthouse and Tigre dodged out of the way before it hit the ground. It was an old Roman helmet, clanging loudly as it spun across the floor.

"Are you sure we shouldn't have waited for Quetzie?" Tigre asked, watching it spin.

"Now, how would a giant bird feel about being stuck under the ocean?" Kali asked. "Obatala sent a messenger to bring her back. Don't worry, she'll be waiting when we return with Poseidon's trident."

"*If* we return," Tigre said.

"Catequil," Kali said sharply. "Don't start that again."

"Catequil," Diana said with relish. "It's such a cool name. Catequil, Catequil, Catequil."

A lizard darted into the room, picked up the Roman helmet, placed it neatly in a pile of other bits of armor, bowed politely to them, and darted out again.

Diana gave Kali a sideways look, like she wasn't sure

she'd really seen that. Kali lifted her hands palms up. *I have no idea.*

Squish squish squish. Olokun slithered down the steps of the lighthouse on her scaly, sluglike legs and stormed over to them. Her pale green hair was going mad around her dark green face, as if it might fly off and kill Zeus all by itself. Obatala followed her, looking tired, with Oya bouncing behind him.

"All right!" Olokun huffed. "I'll show you the way to that traitor Poseidon's palace. They won't be watching for you there. Their eyes will be on the coastlines of Africa. But when you're done with his trident, I want it for my collection." Her hair stood straight up. "That should serve him right for lying to me."

She sailed off around the tower.

"Good luck," Obatala said. "If you succeed, I doubt we'll see you again—once you have the trident, you'll need to hurry to the mirror before they can stop you."

"We'll see whoever wins the power in the end, though!" Oya said. "You know, when we're all gods again." She hugged Tigre, who blushed cutely. Kali heard her whisper, "I hope it's you, Catequil," in his ear.

Kali and the others hurried after Olokun; her underground palace seemed to stretch for miles. Kali wouldn't have been surprised to find that it went all the way around Africa. Tigre, Gus, and Diana were right behind her as they followed Olokun through an elaborate labyrinth of stone walls and columns and statues. Kali was pretty sure they passed a room full of giant heads from Easter Island.

Finally Olokun stopped in front of a wall mosaic. Two lizards ran out of a nearby doorway and stood on their hind legs beside her, looking attentive and helpful.

The mosaic was made of glass tiles in shades of blue and white. Olokun snapped two of the tiles free and handed them to the lizards, who each took one between their small front feet. Then she murmured something to the wall and slid one of the mosaic tiles still on the wall sideways into one of the empty spaces.

All the tiles began to shift, sliding two by two around and around, *like one of those puzzles where you have to put the picture back together by sliding them back in order,* Kali thought. Kali's little sister Beth had had something like that, a happy face with one empty corner, but she'd mixed it up so badly that no one could put it right, and Beth had cried about it for hours.

Slowly a scene took shape on the wall—the opening of a tunnel, lined with sleek glass tiles, with a stream of water running along the bottom.

"There's one of the ways into Poseidon's palace," Olokun said. "It's a tunnel that runs through it, bringing freshwater in and out. Calls himself king of the sea, and he can't even be bothered to purify his own freshwater—he steals it from the land instead."

"Where is that?" Diana asked.

"Deep under the Mediterranean, of course," Olokun said. "But when the picture is finished, you'll be able to step right through and be there. How else do you think I monitor my oceans around the world?"

The lizards nodded vigorously.

"I wonder where he keeps his trident," Kali said.

Olokun snorted. "Probably under his pillow."

"Then what do we do?" Tigre asked. He jumped as another lizard ran into the room, skittering over his foot and stopping next to Olokun with a bow.

"Whatever you want," Olokun said. "But your best bet is to use your stolen ship to make a run for Mexico." She rubbed her hands together. "I hope you destroy all their plans. I hope the gods are humiliated in defeat."

"What about Quetzie?" Tigre asked again.

Kali wondered if there was a single human he cared about as much as he cared about that bird. "Could you ask Obatala to tell Tigre's bird friend to meet us at Poseidon's palace?" she asked.

Olokun looked down at the third lizard, who flicked its tail back and forth, nodded, and raced back out of the room.

There was a clicking sound from the wall, as if the mosaic had finally snapped into place. Olokun took one of the missing tiles back from a lizard. "Are you ready?" she asked.

Kali glanced at the others. They were all nodding, although Diana looked a bit dizzy. "Yup," Kali said.

Olokun snapped the tile into place and picked up the other one. "Bah. I wish I could go with you. If you accidentally skewer Poseidon with his own trident as you go through, I won't mind." She tapped the last tile into place and stepped back.

The mosaic made a bubbling sound and the tiles seemed to melt together. Kali stepped forward and stuck her hand into the mosaic. The air on the other side felt cool and breezy. Taking a deep breath, she stepped into it with a splash.

The tunnel looked the same in real life as it did in the picture, but it was a little darker and smaller than she had expected. She could touch the walls on either side with her arms only half-extended, and the ceiling of the tunnel was right above her head. She looked back and couldn't see anything but more tunnel—no treasure room in Olokun's palace, no lizard staff, no other avatars. Then Tigre popped out of the air, followed by Diana and Gus holding hands.

"Wow," Tigre said, and Kali put a finger to her lips to signal for quiet. She pointed, and together the four of them crept along the tunnel, tiptoeing in the shallow stream.

Ahead of them, light was shining through a hole low in the wall, reflecting off the glass tiles. Part of the stream ran through the grate into the room below. Kali crouched to peer through the small holes and saw a huge pink and gold tiled bathroom. The stream ran in a happy waterfall down from the grate, splashing into basins set at intervals in the wall below it. Kali could see that there were two other waterfalls coming from this same tunnel farther along the wall, and there were others on the wall opposite as well. A large bath took up one of the side walls, big enough for several people to sit in it at once, and smaller, square baths were set along the last wall. Three nymphs in long sea-foam dresses were flinging pink flower petals into one of the baths, which was full and steaming with hot water.

"Nereids," Diana whispered, pointing to them. "Like

naiads, but they live in the sea instead of in freshwater."

"Maybe they're making a bath for Poseidon," Gus suggested.

"Ew," Diana said. "That is something I do *not* want to see."

"Shhh," Tigre said, and it was so unexpected for him to tell them what to do that they all went quiet.

"It's been almost five years," giggled one of the Nereids. "Amphitrite is *so* mad! I have no idea what they're fighting about!"

"He probably doesn't either. Can you imagine not talking to your husband for all that time?" another one said. "I don't think he even noticed for the first year!"

"Well, he's hardly ever here," the third one pointed out. "He was really busy with the Polynesian thing when it started, remember?"

"Maybe *that's* why she's mad," the first one said. "Didn't they go to Bora-Bora for one of their honeymoons?"

"Oh wow, you're totally right!" squealed the second. "She loved it there!"

"But he didn't really destroy Bora-Bora," the third one said. "Didn't he tell her it's coming back?"

"Yeah, but I bet he didn't ask her what she thought first. He never listens to her! He's always like, 'I'm, like, this majorly important god of the sea, and you're just a nymph who was lucky enough to marry me.'"

"Harrumph," said the second Nereid. "If it were me, I'd've stopped talking to him a lot longer than five years ago!"

"I know!" said the first one. "He is so not cute enough for her to put up with this! Plus he gives her terrible presents. Did you see that pearl necklace he left on her mirror? It's like he pulled the pearls right out of our own garden. He didn't even make sure they all matched."

"He was so stompy about the avatars disappearing," the third Nereid giggled. "Amphitrite hasn't been that pleased in ages. He was all 'Wretched mortals! Ruining everything!' and she was just smiling and smiling. It was too funny!"

"Oops, I think that's enough petals!" said the first Nereid, laughing. The entire surface of the bathwater was covered in pink flowers. "Let's go tell her it's ready." They fluttered out of the room, still chattering.

Kali pointed to a set of holes farther along the tunnel. Tigre led the way as they padded softly over to them and crouched again. These grates looked onto a bedroom decorated with dolphin mosaics. Pale blue curtains hung around the bed and a matching carpet that looked like it might have been woven of blue seaweed covered the floor. The waterfalls rustled down the wall into silver-lined basins and then vanished through a grate in the floor.

A woman was sitting at a small table, staring at herself blankly in a mirror. Something about her posture made Kali think she might be royalty. Her light blond hair was slightly greenish, like Kali's sister Jo-Jo's hair sometimes got after she'd been swimming in chlorinated pools all summer. It was pinned up in small nets that looked like miniature fishing nets. Her robes were long and white and draping.

The woman leaned toward her reflection and pulled at the skin around her eyes, smoothing away nonexistent wrinkles. She didn't look a day over twenty-five, but she was staring at herself like she saw an eighty-year-old instead.

A door slammed in the wall behind her. She neither flinched nor turned around. Kali poked Tigre, who happened to be beside her, as Poseidon stormed into the room. He was clutching his trident in one hand, and his long beard was flouncing angrily.

"Still no sign of them!" he grumbled. "What are they *doing* in there? Do you think the African gods have eaten them?" he asked hopefully.

Poseidon's wife picked up a tiny pot of white goop and began dotting it around her temples, smoothing it into her skin.

"Well, we're lying in wait for them when they come out," he said, as if he hadn't noticed he was being ignored. "I don't know where else they think they can go. Did I tell you the strangest thing? The Sumerian avatar seems to be dead. As far as we know, she just went into a coma and died. Isn't that peculiar?"

Kali felt Diana flinch.

"And, of course, the Egyptian is stuck as a stag now. I don't know what our girl did, but it's not coming off, that's for sure. So the only one we can find is Thor, and all he wants to do is carry that odd little moon-headed child around on his shoulders, showing her the sights of New York. What is *wrong* with these avatars? I wouldn't be this wobbly if someone turned *me* into a human." He stamped his trident on the floor.

Amphitrite frowned a little bit at her reflection. She pulled a jewelry box toward her and began picking through it, taking out pearl brooches, pearl earrings, pearl bracelets, and arranging them carefully on the table in front of her.

Poseidon opened his mouth to speak again, but a light tap on the door interrupted him. He thumped over and threw it open.

The three Nereids from the bathroom were standing there. They all goggled at Poseidon and tried to peek around him at Amphitrite.

"Um, um, um," one of them squeaked. "Miss, your bath is ready."

"Full of petals, just like you like it," said another.

"A bath!" Poseidon boomed. "That sounds like a perfect idea."

He had his back to Amphitrite, facing the Nereids, so he didn't see her turn slowly to give him an icy look.

"I think I'll take a bath," Poseidon said. "Maybe it'll calm my nerves. Those blasted avatars have me so on edge. You say it's already poured? And heated?"

"Well—well," stammered one of the nymphs, "it's for—the queen, she asked for—"

"That's all right, Clio," Amphitrite said. Her voice sounded like stingrays drifting across the bottom of the ocean. "Let my husband have it."

"Such a good idea," Poseidon said, starting out the door. The nymphs crowded out of the way.

"Poseidon," Amphitrite said, "perhaps you should leave

your trident here. You know how it gets rusty when you take it in the bath with you."

The sea god didn't even seem surprised that his wife was suddenly talking to him again, although the Nereids looked as if their eyes were about to pop out of their heads. "True," he said, shaking the trident a little. "It's awfully stupid. You'd think a magical indestructible trident that has traveled through all the world's oceans could take a little heated bathwater. Ah, well. Thanks for watching it for me, Amphitrite."

He leaned it against the wall by the door and went out. Kali nudged Tigre again. It was right there! The nymphs stared at Amphitrite, mouths agape.

"Shoo," Amphitrite said, standing and walking to the door. "Let me know when he's coming back." She shut the door in their faces, picked up the trident, and paced back to her dressing table. For a moment she stared at her reflection, and then down at the pearls spread across the tabletop.

She lifted the trident and smashed it into the mirror. Glass flew in all directions, some of it leaving flecks of blood on her white arms. Then she smashed all of the pearls, piece by piece, until her dressing table was a splintered wreck on the floor, covered in a shimmering iridescent pearl dust.

Wow, Kali thought. *Someone is really mad about something.*

Amphitrite stepped back, taking a deep breath. Then she turned and looked straight up at the grate.

"Welcome, avatars," she said, hefting the trident in her hands. "Is this what you're looking for?"

• • ● • •

Tigre didn't know what to do. Should they pretend they weren't there? Try to run off down the tunnel? Jump down and muffle the queen so she wouldn't give them away?

Diana tugged on the grate, then turned to look at Kali, who leaned forward and yanked it free, leaving a crumbling mess of rock around the hole where it had been. Diana wriggled through the hole and dropped down to the blue carpet below.

"Hi," she said to Amphitrite. "I'm Diana."

"I know," Amphitrite said, sounding amused.

"How long did you know we were there?" Kali asked, swinging herself down beside Diana. Tigre and Gus exchanged looks and followed them. The seaweed rug was springy under Tigre's feet as he landed. Up close, Amphitrite was taller than he expected, and pale and cold like polished marble.

"I heard you splashing along a while ago," the queen said. "I'm sure I'm the only one who noticed, though. I do a lot more listening than most people in this palace." She spun the trident in her hands.

"You know why we're here?" Gus asked.

"My husband's been going on and on about an indestructible mirror hidden in a cave," Amphitrite said. "Even he isn't sure that this will work on it." She stopped spinning the trident, held it thoughtfully in front of her for a moment, and then handed it to Diana.

"Really?" Diana said, taking it in both hands. She staggered a little, as if it was heavier than she'd anticipated. "You'll let us have it?"

"Perhaps if Poseidon gets taken down a peg, he might notice there are other people living in this palace," Amphitrite said frostily. "And without his trident, he won't be sinking any more islands."

"But—" Diana started to say, and Kali poked her in the arm.

"Don't argue with the lady," Kali said. "Let's take it and go, quickly."

"He takes endlessly long baths," Amphitrite said, "but it'll take you a while to get out of here, so yes, you should go." She pointed to another door in a side wall. "That passage will lead you to the front gates."

"Thanks, Amphitrite," Diana said. The queen lifted one of Diana's red curls for a moment, turning it like she hadn't seen anything so bright in a long time.

"Perhaps I'll see you again when you're leader of the gods," the nymph said.

"Oh," Diana said with confusion, looking at the others. "That's not—I mean, I'm not going to—"

"Come on," Kali said from the doorway. "Thanks again, your highness." They could hear Amphitrite laughing as they stepped into the hall and shut the door behind them.

The passageway was long and white with elaborate coral outcroppings running along the ceiling. At first Tigre thought there were patterns of jewels set into the walls, but as they hurried along the hall he realized it was lined with aquariums full of dazzling fish. Their sunflower yellow and orange-and-white-striped and dark, iridescent purple-black shapes darted between castles of coral, mouths opening and closing, big bubble eyes staring blankly at the avatars as they ran past. More passages and doors led off in several directions, but they stayed in the main hallway as it began to slope upward.

On the other side of the aquariums, Tigre thought he saw more nymphs in their long, shimmering dresses, gossiping on fluffy green couches or chasing snapping crabs around intricate rock gardens. None of them looked up or seemed to notice the avatars running by.

Diana stumbled, holding her side with one hand, the trident hanging heavily from the other. Tigre stopped to wait for her as Gus caught up from the rear.

"Are you okay?" Tigre said. "Do you want someone else to carry it for a while?"

"Sure, thanks," Diana said, handing it over to him casually, as if it were just a pencil and not the most powerful weapon in the pantheons. "It's a bit heavy."

She wasn't exaggerating. The trident was a foot taller than Tigre and made of solid, goldish-green metal, and it felt like it weighed as much as he did. The three prongs were wickedly sharp at the end, the center prong sticking out straight while the other two curved slightly to the right and left. A wave-shaped half circle of green gems was set in the handle on either side where the prongs split into three.

Tigre hefted it in both hands, wishing again that he had a little god strength to help him out. He nodded at Diana, trying to look like it was no problem. She smiled gratefully, Gus put his arm around her, and they all started running again.

Kali was waiting for them at the end of the passage, which opened into an enormous front entrance that had no less than seven sweeping marble staircases and twelve balconies overlooking it. They had come out at the top of one of the staircases, and Kali was leaning over the nearest balcony, looking down. The ceiling here was so far above them that Tigre could only see the shadowy flicker of shapes moving high above. He guessed that it was glass, and that he was looking out at the ocean from the very bottom of it.

A set of tall brass gates stood at the end of the room closest to them, reaching from the floor all the way to that ceiling, impossibly high above. The gates were close enough to the balcony for the avatars to reach out and touch them. Beyond them Tigre could see a towering wall of water that teemed with sea creatures. He wasn't sure why the water didn't flow through the holes and curlicues in the gates, but he guessed it was an enchantment of some kind.

The gates were guarded down below by two glossy brown creatures with the heads and front legs of horses, but long fishlike tails swishing along behind them. They trotted back and forth busily in front of the gates, their ears pricked for sounds of intruders. One of them snapped his teeth at a tiny shark that swam too close, and it sped away, swishing its fins indignantly. But their attention seemed to be focused outward; they didn't notice the avatars above them.

"I don't want to try opening those gates," Gus whispered, crouching below the wall of the balcony. "We could drown the whole palace." Tigre crouched beside him, resting the trident on his knees.

"And more important, us," Kali agreed. "Besides, if we swim out into the ocean down here, we'll get that horrible water pressure sickness thingie, won't we?"

"Maybe," Gus said. "I don't know how far down we are."

"Far enough that we won't be able to hold our breaths long enough to get to the surface," Diana said. "But maybe we could from up there?" She pointed up at the ceiling.

"How would we get up there?" Tigre asked. He glanced up. The stairs beside them spiraled up a few more stories, stopping at balconies along the way, but they only reached halfway up the long wall.

"We climb the gate," Kali said. "Let's try it."

They ran up the stairs, around and around, their footsteps pattering lightly against the marble. Tigre scraped his hand on the rough coral banister and flinched. His arms were aching from carrying the trident, and he didn't dare look down to see how high they were.

The staircase ended at another balcony and another hall stretched down into the palace. Kali glanced over the railing, but Tigre kept his eyes fixed on the gate an arm's length away. How could he possibly do this? How could he climb and carry the trident at the same time? Perhaps he should give it to Kali; she was the strongest of all of them. But she couldn't swim, and once they got out into the water she'd be in the most trouble.

"Are you going to be all right?" Diana asked him, as if

she'd read his mind. "You'll need both hands to climb."

"Maybe you can make a sling with your shirt," Gus suggested. "Tie it around the trident and then around your chest. Here." Tigre's shirt was off before he could stop them, and Diana and Gus began twisting and knotting it, arguing over how to make it hold. He held the trident in front of his chest, feeling a little silly.

Kali leaned out and grabbed one of the metal curlicues that adorned the gate. "I'll go on ahead and look for a way out," she said. The brass creaked a little as she swung off the balcony, hooking her feet lightly into the holes in the gate. She reached up for another handhold and started to climb, cautiously at first, and then faster as she figured out the pattern of the gate. Tigre watched her long dark hair sway as she pulled herself up.

"My arms are never going to recover from this," Gus said. "Next time we save the world, let's have less climbing."

"And stairs," Tigre agreed. "Fewer stairs."

Gus tied the shirt firmly around the trident and looped it over Tigre's head and arm so the trident rested against his back. "How does that feel?" Gus tugged on the fabric, testing the knots.

"Okay," Tigre said. "I think it'll hold."

A piercingly loud whinny sounded from the hall below them, and they all jumped.

"Uh-oh," Diana said.

The horse guards had spotted Kali climbing the gate. They both screamed, and Tigre heard the pounding of hooves converging on the entrance. He glanced down the hall and saw something slithering rapidly toward them, teeth gleaming in the watery reflections. He thought *crocodile* and then he was on the gate, dragging himself up hand by hand with Gus and Diana clambering ahead.

Soon Tigre was gasping for breath. The trident seemed to be getting heavier, as if it was physically trying to pull him off the gate. *I'm going to do this. I'm going to prove that I should be here.*

"There's a gap at the top," Kali called. "Diana and Gus already went through. Come on, Catequil. You can make it."

The sharp metal dug into his hands, and sweat dripped down his forehead into his eyes. He forced himself up another foot, and then another.

And then he felt Kali's hand on his wrist, supporting him as he threw himself up the last few inches. She was straddling the top of the gate, lying on her stomach with her head turned toward Tigre. There was a small gap here between the top of the gate and a solid block of glass that stretched overhead. On the other side of the glass, Tigre could see fish darting through the water and the bright orb of the sun far above them.

"Careful," Kali said. "Once you squeeze through here, you'll be in the water. See?" She brought her other hand around and he saw that it was dripping wet. He also saw that she looked uncharacteristically nervous.

"When we get back to our real lives," he said, "I should teach you how to swim."

She smiled. "I'll hold you to that," she said. "Although for the record, I still think swimming is stupid."

Tigre hauled himself onto the top of the gate, feeling his fingers sink through something that felt like clay before they broke through into water on the other side. He slipped his legs over, trying not to imagine sharks sneaking up on them. Maybe even futuristic evolved sharks, like Quetzie was a futuristic evolved quetzal. *Stop thinking about Quetzie-sized sharks.*

"Okay," he said. "If I can make it, you can."

"Thinking positive now?" Kali teased. "What have you done with Tigre?"

He took a deep breath and pushed himself over into the ocean. Water rushed up his nose and into his eyes, blinding him. He flailed for a moment, trying to remember which way was up, and then started paddling frantically toward the light. The trident felt like an anchor strapped to his back. His lungs were bursting. His arms and legs were weak from climbing, and as much as he kicked and beat the water, it seemed like he was drifting down faster than he was swimming up.

Something moved above him—two shapes, diving straight at him. *Sharks!* He jerked back in terror, but then one of them held out his hand, and Tigre realized that it was Gus and Diana. He held out his arm and Gus grabbed it in a fierce grip, beating his feet to drag them both up to the light. Beside him, Diana was swimming with Kali, their hair flaring out behind them in the clear water as their legs scissored back and forth.

A cheerful Mediterranean sun beat down on their heads as they all bobbed to the surface, gasping for air. Kali was cursing and thrashing about, trying to figure out how to stay afloat. There was no sign of land in any direction; just an endless sea of bobbing blue-green ocean. And as soon as Poseidon figured out what had happened, he'd be roaring up behind them in his chariot. And he'd be *angry*.

"The ship," Tigre sputtered, his arms almost too exhausted to fight the weight of the trident. "Kali—"

Gus swam over to Kali and tugged on her belt. She swatted him away furiously and fumbled with the *Skidbladnir* pouch. Waves kept swamping over her head, but finally she pulled out the tiny square of magic Viking ship. She set it in the water in front of them and Diana reached over to help unfold the sides.

"Hurry," Gus urged.

"*You* can convince it to unfold faster if you—" Salt water splashed in Kali's mouth and she spit it out, glaring daggers at Gus as if it was his fault she'd been interrupted.

Helloooooooooooooooooooooooooooooooooooooooooo!

Tigre felt his heart leap. He looked up at the sky, where the most beautiful bird he'd ever met was swooping back and forth, her tail swirling majestically behind her.

"Quetzie!" he yelled joyfully.

"Hooray!" Diana shouted.

I missed youuuuuuuuuuuuuuu, tiger-boy!

I missed you, too, he thought back to her.

The neoquetzal spiraled down to land in the water with an almighty splash. She paddled over to Tigre and offered her wing so he could hold on to the feathers.

Ooooof, she said. *Youuu've gained some weight!*

He pointed to the trident slung across his back and she

ooooooooooohed admiringly. *Pretty,* she said. *Sparkly. Not as pretty as me, thooough.*

"That's true," he said with a grin, and she flicked her tail feathers, beaming.

I'm sooorry I lost you for a while. I went on ahead to Africa and fooound this beauuuuuutiful place full of avooocados. I looooove avocados! Sooo I'm afraid I got a bit distracted. She looked remorseful.

"It's okay," Tigre said. "I'm glad you're here now."

The main body of the ship was completely unfolded, and the masts were beginning to pop up. The rope ladder unfurled from the railing and the end splashed down beside them.

"That's lucky," Gus said. "I thought maybe it'd be rolled up on deck again."

"I think it stays as you left it," Kali said, hooking her arms around the rungs. "So, no ramp. Ever again. That'll be splinters at the bottom of New York Harbor forever."

"Will you quit it with the ramp?" Gus said, but Kali was grinning. She looked a lot more cheerful now that she had something to hold on to.

"Come on," she said, starting to climb the ladder. "Just a little more climbing, and then we can get dry and sleep and eat some, like, reindeer meat or whatever it is while the ship sails us to Mexico."

Oooooooooooooooh, Quetzie said. *Mexico! Pretty! Fuuull of bats!*

"Bats?" Gus said. "Really? Bats? Um. Really?"

"Start climbing, 'fraidy cat," Diana said teasingly, shoving him at the ladder.

Tigre put his arms as far around Quetzie's neck as he could, hugging her. Now things would get better. Now the gods could chase them as much as they liked.

The stooorms will come again, Catequil, Quetzie said as Diana and Gus climbed the ladder. *But I hear youuu might have a new trick to stop them?* She clacked her beak hopefully.

"I don't think my miniature storms will do anything," Tigre said. She was right, though. He could feel clouds gathering at the horizons like an itch below his skin.

Try it, she said, nudging him. *I want to see. I bet it'll help.*

"Really?" Tigre said. "Okay, if you think so."

Kicking with his legs to stay afloat, Tigre scooped a handful of water up and blew on it. The tiny cyclone appeared in the air, but instead of disappearing, this time it stayed in place, drawing water up from the ocean. Experimentally, Tigre gave it a little shove, and it whirled off to the west, where the sun was setting in a blaze of orange.

"Huh," he said.

Mooore! Quetzie demanded eagerly. *Moooooore!*

Tigre did it again, making a hurricane this time, and nudged it off to the south. Then he made two more thunderstorms and sent them north and east. He wasn't sure if it was his imagination, but they seemed to be getting bigger as they sailed into the distance.

Coooooool, Quetzie said. *That should keep them busy for a while!*

Tigre hauled himself onto the rope ladder, his fingers tingling as if he'd just plunged them in ice and then run them through a flame. *Did I really do that?* he wondered, feeling exhausted and triumphant at the same time.

Perhaps I'm really a god after all.

The coast of Mexico was a wild mass of jungle. Gus had no idea how they were supposed to beach the ship, let alone make it any farther into the interior, but Kali said she'd given *Skidbladnir* more specific directions this time, and she was convinced that it would take them straight to the Cave of Illusions—or at least, to somewhere where they could get to the Cave of Illusions.

This time the journey had been much less nausea-inducing. Tigre had sent more storms off in all directions. As Quetzie described it, from above it looked like a ring of dark clouds around the sunny spot where they were sailing, and the storms were so fierce that even the thunder gods were having trouble battling their way through.

One of them is standing on a cloud, belloowing, "I'M *THE GOD OF STORMS! I BRING THE THUNDER! I BRING THE LIGHTNING! STOOOP RAINING ON ME!"* Quetzie reported, landing on the top of the tallest mast. Diana laughed, and Tigre looked bashfully pleased.

Gus had been having nightmares since the escape from Poseidon's palace, but he tried not to let Diana know about them. He'd had to use Oro's strength again for the swim out, especially when he went back to help Tigre. Oro, being a Polynesian god, was a powerful swimmer; Gus wasn't sure he'd have gotten Tigre and the trident to the surface without the god's help. But now Oro seemed to be simmering right below the top layer of his skin, burning along the ridges of Gus's tattoos. Every time he dreamed about running through forests and killing people with sharp whalebone spears and strange, blood-stained greenstone weapons.

He sat down beside Diana, who had rigged a bearskin tent on the deck so she could sit outside but still stay in the shade. She stuck one of her pale hands into the late afternoon sunshine for a moment.

"I wonder if my brother can see us," she said. "Or if he knows what we're about to do. He won't be happy that I want to return to my human life. He's afraid of losing me." She turned her hand, then pulled it back into the shade and leaned on Gus's shoulder. "I guess I'll miss him, too. I wonder what'll happen when we break the mirror. Will we be stuck in Mexico? That'll be weird. 'International pop star emerges from cave in Mexico, covered in bat guano, after mysteriously vanishing for three weeks.' The media's going to go nuts. 'Strangest breakdown ever! What drugs is she on? Who's the mystery guy she ran off with?' Hope you're ready to be followed around by tabloid photographers all the time." She sighed, and he squeezed her shoulder.

"Yeah," he said, "that'll be much worse than being chased by homicidal gods and giant glass dinosaurs."

She laughed.

"Let's worry about it later," he said. "We have an indestructible mirror to smash first."

"True," she said. None of them had brought up what Eshu had said about consequences and power—the idea that one of them had to stay behind and become immortal, while the rest of them went back to their lives. Gus didn't think any of them wanted to do that. He certainly didn't. Knowing that Andrew was still alive, just on the other side of this illusion, made him even more determined to get home. He wanted to sit on their couch and watch TV and eat pizza for a month.

"Uh-oh," Diana said, sitting up straight. "Serious face this way comes."

Kali was crossing the deck toward them with Tigre behind her. She looked stubborn; he looked disgruntled.

Kali stopped in front of them, crossing her arms.

"Would you please tell this boy that his giant bird is not coming into the Cave of Illusions with us?" she said.

"Why not?" Tigre said mutinously. "Maybe she can help us."

"How?" Kali said. "She can't fly in there. And you might have noticed she's not exactly inconspicuous. How are we supposed to sneak up on them and smash the mirror with *an enormous bird* hopping along behind us?"

"They'll know we're coming anyway," Tigre pointed out. "Just because they can't get to us right now doesn't mean they haven't figured out where we're going."

"Well, that's cheerful," Diana said.

"Besides," Kali went on, "we need Quetzie to go back to New York and get Thor."

"Thor?" Gus and Tigre said simultaneously.

"He should know about this," Kali said. "He might want to come be a part of it. Or he might want to get back to Norway or wherever so that when the illusion shatters, he isn't stranded in New York." Gus pictured that—poor hapless Thor, wandering around with Miracle on his shoulders, only to have her suddenly vanish and hordes of grouchy New Yorkers appear all around him instead. If he wasn't warned that the real world was coming back, he might get hit by a subway train or thrown in a mental institution or something.

"She's right, Tigre," Gus said. "Sorry."

"But what if Quetzie doesn't get back in time. . . . " Tigre's voice trailed off as he looked up at the neoquetzal's red and green feathers, shining in the sunlight.

Nobody answered him. Gus could guess what he was feeling. *In time to say good-bye.* Quetzie was part of the illusion, even if she didn't know it. In the real world, there were no giant talking quetzals. When they shattered the mirror, Quetzie would disappear along with the crystal hunters, the wall around Africa, the rubble in Los Angeles, the giant nest on top of the Empire State Building, Aleph and Bet from the museum, and Miracle. All the gods they had met would disappear back to their immortal realms—no more Apollo or Oya or Shiva to talk to. Manifesting in a world full of humans, according to Oya, was difficult and power-consuming. Of course, that also meant no more Tlaloc or Isis or Zeus, which helped.

Tigre rubbed his eyes, turning his head away from them, and walked to the back of the boat as Quetzie landed on the railing, making the ship rock.

"Poor Tigre," Diana said.

"Maybe she'll be born in the real world as a regular bird," Gus said. "And Aleph and Bet and Miracle will be normal kids."

"I'm not sure Quetzie would like being a regular bird," Diana said.

"Hey," Kali said, shading her eyes, "I think we're coming up to something."

Gus and Diana scrambled up to join her at the railing. *Skidbladnir* had been scudding lightly along the coast, but now it was steering toward an inlet—a missing slice of land where cliffs rose up on either side of a long, winding finger of the sea that stretched inland.

Diana took Gus's hand as the ship sailed between the tall rocks at the entrance. A few of them were oddly shaped and predatory-looking, as if they had once been jaguars crouching in the sea, but the waves had worn them down.

It was dark in the inlet, the cliffs on either side casting heavy shadows over the ship. Gus glanced up at the tendril of blue sky they could see far above them. The ship rocked again, and they all turned around as Quetzie lifted off from the stern. She whirled her long tail feathers at them as she sailed up into the sky.

Tooodle-oooooo! she called. *Gooood luck! I'll be back sooooooooooon!*

They all waved until she vanished into the clouds. Tigre joined them at the railing, blinking hard.

"I tried to explain all this to her," he said, "but I don't think she believed me. She said I'm being silly and of course she's real. And that she'll see me again once we've saved the world." He sighed, and Diana touched his shoulder sympathetically.

The ship navigated slowly around a bend in the river,

and Gus saw sunlight shining on water ahead of them. The inlet ended in a small lake surrounded by tree-covered slopes. Gus spotted several monkeys swinging through the branches, gaping at the Viking ship as it swung around and stopped not far from shore.

"There," Kali said, pointing. A dark stone opening was set in the hillside near the lake. Gus had the creepy feeling that it was waiting for them—that once they stepped inside, it would snap shut and swallow them whole.

Diana looked dubiously at the cave. "Are we going in there now? Even though it's getting dark?"

"I think it's going to be dark in there no matter when we go in," Kali said. "And the longer we wait, the more likely it is other gods will show up to try to stop us."

"I agree," Tigre said, slinging the trident onto his back again, this time with a leather strap that looked a bit stronger than his T-shirt. "My storms won't keep them away for long."

Diana's hand tightened around Gus's. "Okay. Let's go," she said resolutely. With a snapping sound, the sails started rolling up, as if the ship agreed too.

Kali gave them each a torch, a coil of rope, and a pickax, then climbed down the ladder first and waited as they each came down and splashed to shore. Mosquitoes descended upon Gus instantly and he slapped at them, feeling the sting in his tattoos.

The ship made a little sound like paper being flicked as the last few corners folded up. Kali tucked it back into the pouch and waded over to them. The light was starting to fade quickly, especially under the trees. She touched each of their torches, and the ends burst into flames.

"That should last," she said.

"Neat," Diana said, turning her torch from side to side.

None of them spoke as they crept up the slope to the cave. A stream ran down from the mouth of the cave to the lake, and as they got closer they saw that inside the cave it became a small river, about as wide across as Gus could stretch his arms, spilling over sand-colored rocks and splashing the ledge on either side.

Kali went first, lifting her torch as she walked carefully over the wet rocks beside the river. Tigre followed her, one hand on the handle of the trident, ducking to avoid the stalactites that jutted out of the roof. Diana went next, and Gus stayed right behind her.

It got darker and darker, even with their torches raised, and the path got steeper as they climbed. After a while Gus was nearly on his hands and knees, scrambling over rock piles as the roof pressed down above him. The river gurgled nearby, but he couldn't see it anymore. Several times he thought he felt leathery wings brush against his face, making him jump, but he never saw anything except their own shadows in the light cast by the flames.

"Ew," Diana whispered as something crunched under her sneaker. "Look out, Gus, there are serious creepy crawlies in here."

He held the fire closer to the floor and saw a pair of cockroaches run under a rock. Farther up the wall, gigantic prehistoric-looking insects with far too many legs scuttled away from the light.

It was cold in the cave, much colder than outside, and

so damp that water soaked through his palms and the knees of his jeans, making him feel like he had never been in the sun in his life.

At the top of a jumbled pile of rocks, the path changed. Suddenly the ground dropped away on one side, leaving them edging along a narrow ledge, their backs pressed to the damp rock wall behind them. Gus did not want to think about the things he might be touching as he slid along, trying not to jump each time he felt tiny feelers brush his arms.

The ledge turned a corner up ahead. Kali went around it, and then Tigre, and then suddenly it seemed darker, as if Kali's and Tigre's torches had been snuffed out.

"Kali?" Diana whispered. "Tigre?" There was no answer. She looked back at Gus, and he shrugged. Maybe the acoustics were weird and they couldn't hear her.

Diana held her torch out and peeked quickly around the corner. "Oh no, they don't," she whispered, flattening her back to the wall again. She reached out and took Gus's hand in a firm grip. "They've disappeared," she said. "Some kind of gods thing. But I'm not letting anyone split up you and me again."

Gus felt warm despite the chill of the cave. He nodded.

Hands clasped, they slid around the corner of the ledge . . . into Gus's old living room.

A FEW WEEKS AGO . . .

With a roar, the god yanked a tree out of the ground and snapped it over his knee. He flung one half out to sea, where it landed with a tremendous splash, and then he began smashing the rest of the trees around him with the other half.

It's not really fair on the forest, but at least he isn't killing the messenger, *thought the messenger.*

"How long have they been planning this?" Oro shouted as bits of wood and bark flew in all directions. "How dare they? HOW DARE THEY?"

"Ouch," said a new god, emerging from the forest. He grabbed the broken tree from Oro and held it to his chest protectively. "Is that really necessary?"

"We should kill them all," Oro said. "We should do it now, before they can see us coming."

Tane, god of the forest, looked at him with pity in his eyes. "And how would we do that, Oro? We have nowhere near the power of Zeus, or Osirus, or Odin. Not forgetting that they are gods, and cannot really die."

"They can get tied up, though," Oro growled. His tattoos writhing across his skin. "We could lash them to volcanoes and watch lava pour over them as they scream in agony."

"Good grief," Tane said. He turned as another god hauled himself out of the sea onto the rocks. "Tangaroa, are you hearing this?"

Tangaroa shook salt water out of his ears and pushed back his wet hair. "I agree with Oro. We should do something."

"Something feasible, though," Tane said. "And something that doesn't involve violence to trees, please."

"When is it supposed to happen?" Tangaroa asked.

Oro pointed to the messenger, seated cross-legged on the rocks. "He says it's only a few days away. They've been planning this for years, and never once mentioned it to us. How dare they treat us like inferior gods? They're going to get rid of us, he says. They're planning to destroy our home and everyone who even remembers us. I'm going to KILL THEM! I'm going to DROWN THEM IN THEIR OWN BLOOD!"

"Calm down, Oro," Tane said. "There must be something we can do. Perhaps if we talk to Odin, he'd let us join in."

"It's too late," Oro shouted. "Their avatars have been alive for years!"

"Perhaps it's not too late," said the messenger.

They all turned to stare at him. "You have a suggestion, clever Maui?" said Tangaroa.

Maui smiled. "There's a way in. We just have to steal a human body and throw a god into it. If he's touching a true avatar when the shift happens, he'll be dragged along."

"If?" Tane said. "That sounds unlikely, to say the least."

"Trust me," Maui said, his smile growing wider. "I can set it up."

"But which god?" Tangaroa said. "Not you, Maui. The world couldn't survive you having that much power, if you did win."

Maui looked briefly displeased as the other two gods nodded.

"I will go!" Oro declared. "I would love to do some killing."

"Of course you would," Maui said, rubbing his palms together. "I will find us a pawn and put him in place. You be ready."

"Shoved into a human," Oro murmured, flexing his powerful arms so the tattoos rippled. "It will be small in there, won't it? Cramped. Try to find me a big one."

Maui grinned, and Tane had the strong feeling that he'd be finding Oro quite a small person to be shoved into.

"It should be someone with courage and imagination," Tangaroa said. "The kind of human who won't be driven mad by a god suddenly appearing in his head. One who might even understand it. There are some like that out there."

"Choose someone with a kind soul," Tane said. "One that will balance out Oro's violence."

"As if he'll have any say," Oro snorted.

"He will at first," Maui said. "You'll have to struggle to be heard. Human souls are tenacious, and you won't have time to adjust to each other before the shift happens. You'll have to work with him for a while."

"But I'll take over eventually," Oro said. "Right?"

"If you try hard enough," Maui said. "But one thing, Oro. This is only temporary. You have to squash the human soul, and you have to win the battles; that is the only way you'll keep the

power. If the human soul pushes you back, or if another avatar wins, you'll snap back to your god self, the vessel will be entirely human again, and you'll be no more powerful than you ever were."

"I won't die?" Oro said, sounding surprised.

"The rules are a little different here," Maui said. "You weren't born in this form—it's more like possession than being a true avatar. Which means you can be thrown out, so hang on as hard as you can."

Oro's eyes glinted dangerously. "I will," he promised. "Believe me . . . I will."

Cave of Illusions

Kali recognized the smell first. It was the smell of illness and chemicals and death, although not the kind of death she liked—not the ripping, tearing, burning, sudden kind of death. This was the lingering kind, the long, guilty kind.

Her torch went out. She reached to touch the end, to light the flame again, and realized she wasn't holding a torch anymore. The ground below her wasn't rocky or uneven, but flat, and there was no longer a drop to her left.

Also, she was alone. Tigre, Diana, and Gus had disappeared. She felt around in the dark until her hand touched something smooth and cool. A door handle. She turned it, and walked out into a hospital room.

The fluorescent lights flickered, sucking the life out of the faces that turned toward her. In the bed, her stepfather, Bill, smiled weakly.

"Hey, kiddo," he said. "Your mom and I were just talking about you."

Kali's mother, Ellen, kissed his hand, her blond hair limp around her face. She looked even more tired than he did. But her eyes were cold as she glanced up at Kali.

"Your mom," Bill went on, "has this silly notion."

Kali's heart was pounding. Bill was dead. Bill had died over a year ago. She knew this couldn't be real, but the smell of the hospital was exactly as she remembered, bringing back the horror and the guilt she'd pushed to the back of her mind.

"She seems to think you hate me," Bill said, patting Ellen's hand. "She thinks perhaps you made me sick."

"She never said that," Kali said. "She might have thought it. But she'd never say it."

"I'm telling her she's wrong," Bill said tranquilly. "You're my pal, my strange little girl. We watch the Discovery Channel together."

Kali nodded. "I don't know," she said, and caught her breath. "I mean, I wouldn't. Not on purpose. But what if . . . without meaning to . . . I don't know."

"I do," said a new voice.

Kali froze.

There was another man in the room.

She was sure he hadn't been there a moment earlier. When she'd walked in, there were only Bill and her mother. And yet now there he was, standing in the corner beyond Ellen with his arms folded. Watching Kali with laughing eyes.

He looked like her. Dark hair, honey-colored skin, narrow shoulders, even the same way of leaning forward a little, like he was ready to dance or fight or kill or run at a moment's notice. He looked nothing like the ruddy, barrel-chested, blond policeman lying in the bed. Kali's hand flew to the bone pendant she always wore around her neck—the one he had left behind when he left her mother, with her name carved in it.

Ellen looked back at him with a puzzled expression. "I can't remember your name. Wasn't I in love with you once?"

"Well," said the newcomer, "you thought you were."

Kali's anger flared. "You're a god, aren't you?" she said. "What did you do to my mom? Did you use magic on her?"

"You should be grateful," the stranger said. "Otherwise you might have been born in a different human. You certainly wouldn't have been as strong as you are, if I hadn't fathered you, given you your name, and then left."

"You messed with her life," Kali said. "Having me ruined everything for her. I even ruined this." She pointed at Bill. "The one guy she really loved, no sorcery required. Maybe you're not as hot as you think you are."

Bill chuckled.

The dark-haired man gazed at the bed, at the tangles of wires and tubes. "This doesn't exactly look like your style, Kali."

"I didn't think so either, at first," she snapped. "But who knows what I could do? Maybe I did it without meaning to. And after all, he is dead. Same result."

"Ah, that's a bit harsh," Bill interjected.

"No," said Kali's father, shaking his head. "I know you, Kali. You're my daughter. You are a killer, yes. A violent, twisted death-dealer. But if you wanted him dead, you would have made his car explode. Not this slow, boring, dripping away of life."

Kali met her mom's eyes, which looked surprised now instead of wary. Was it true?

"Sometimes bad things just happen, sweetheart," Bill said.

"Really?" Kali said. She felt a tight knot in her chest easing.

The strange man nodded. "Sometimes I even have nothing to do with them," he said with a grin. "And sometimes I do. I loved the accidents you caused as a child—the death, the destruction that made you doubt yourself. I guessed that making you this strong would lead to that. How could a mere four-year-old control her temper tantrums?"

"Who are you?" Kali said. "You're not from my pantheon. I don't know you."

"I've been here a long, long time," he said, his voice low and dark. "Do you want the power, Kali? Are you tempted to be the victorious avatar?"

"No. I have to go back," Kali said slowly. "I have to take care of my mom. I want to see my sisters grow up. This time I'm going to be normal. I'm going to take care of them." She took Bill's other hand and squeezed it. "That's what I want. I'm going back to look after them." Bill squeezed back, smiling proudly at her.

"Are you sure you can resist?" her dark-eyed father whispered. "When you're standing at the mirror, and the power comes pouring out—are you truly strong enough to turn away from it, my daughter of the bloodstained hands?"

"That's not all I am," Kali said. "Tigre told me. I'm more than that."

He narrowed his eyes thoughtfully. "So I hear. All right, let's talk to the other side of you. What if I offered you a gift to stay mortal? What if I offered you another sister—my daughter of the moonlit eyes?"

"How could you offer me a person?" Kali asked.

"I created her in this world, didn't I?" he said. "She was my great power source—the people I had her sacrifice for me . . . the power she poured into my veins . . . the dark nightmares I sent her in her dark, underground life . . . "

Kali inhaled sharply. "Miracle."

The man licked his lips. "Willing human sacrifice—the most delicious. But it doesn't have to be like that. She could have a normal life, be an ordinary girl in your regular world. All you have to do is turn down the power and stay mortal, and I will send her to you."

"That's it?" Kali said. "You're not going to try to trick me out of the power? You're going to bargain with me instead?"

He smiled. "You're too clever for the usual tricks, I think. Perhaps you get that from me. No, this is an honest deal. Don't take the power—which you don't want anyway—and in exchange I'll give you Miracle in a world where she can have a much happier life. What do you think, daughter? Will your nurturing, altruistic aspects triumph over your violence and ambition?"

Bill squeezed her hand again like he was trying to

tell her something, but she couldn't tell what from his expression.

"Think about it," Kali's father said. "I think you'll make the right choice."

He blinked and then vanished. The hospital room began to fade out like someone was dimming the lights. Bill's kind eyes were disappearing for the last time.

"I think you'll make the right choice, too," Bill said, and then he was gone, and so were Kali's mother and the fluorescent lights and everything else. Kali was back in the cave. A lit torch was lying on the floor, guttering in a low breeze.

Prove it, a voice whispered. *Prove that you're more than a goddess of destruction. Show us that other side of you, Kali.*

Diana could tell from his reaction that Gus knew where they were. He looked completely freaked out, although as far as she could tell, it was an ordinary living room in a nice, suburban house. There was a couch, a TV, a stereo, tall windows with long curtains, a piano with a couple of photographs in silver frames arranged on top of it. By the front door were two pairs of discarded work boots, identical except that one pair was a few sizes bigger and had a dent in the left toe.

Music was playing. To her surprise, it was one of her own early albums. She crossed to the stereo and picked up the CD case. "That's so weird," she said. Her gaze went to the photos on the piano. One was of two little boys with reddish-brown hair, dressed in *Star Wars* Halloween costumes. The other was a family shot, two brothers with two smiling parents, and she'd seen it before, tucked into the corner of a mirror in an apartment in Los Angeles.

She turned around quickly. Gus was holding his elbows and staring at the floor, as if everything might fall out if he didn't hold it in.

"Oh my God, Gus," Diana said, hurrying over to him. She put her arms around him and pulled him close to her. "This is your house."

He sank to the floor and she knelt with him, rubbing his arms. The carved tattoos felt odd and rough under her fingers.

"It's the night they died," he said softly.

"How can you tell?" Diana asked, knowing who he meant.

He glanced at the stereo. "It was the first night I had that CD. And I was reading that *TV Guide* before I went out." He pointed at the magazine on the coffee table.

"It's just an illusion," Diana said, taking his hands in hers. "We're in the Cave of Illusions, remember? We should have expected this. At least we're together, right?"

Gus nodded.

"The gods are just trying to mess with your head," Diana said. She touched his face. "Don't let them get to you. They'll get bored and it'll go away. They're only trying to scare you off."

"Well . . . not exactly, love," said a new voice. "But you're half-right, I'll give you that."

Maui was sitting on the top of the couch, his bare feet resting on the sofa cushions. He looked relaxed and happy, his tousled hair loose around his face.

"Oh, wow, hey," Diana said, surprised and wishing she didn't feel so pleased to see him. "Gus, this is Maui. He's from your pantheon, actually."

Gus squinted at him, bewildered. "I thought all the Polynesian gods were wiped out," he said. "I mean, I guess not really, but I thought at least they couldn't get into the illusion."

"I'm a bit of an exception," Maui said, laughing. "To pretty much everything."

"Hey, look," Diana said, waggling her fingers at him. "I'm alive! Isn't that exciting?"

"No thanks to me," Maui said with a grin.

"You saved me from the big snake," Diana pointed out. "And the wolf thing."

"Yeah, but I sent them after you too," Maui said. "It was a whole get-you-to-trust-me plan." He sighed and flung his hands in the air. "Totally worked, and yet you still wouldn't listen to me about skipping the African underworld and going straight to Hades. Wouldn't have pegged you for being so stubborn, I must admit."

Diana's smile fell. "What are you talking about? You were just helping me find Hades."

"Hades?" Gus echoed. "Diana, if you'd reached Hades, you would have been stuck there forever. You would really have died, completely."

Diana was shocked. "And you knew that? You were trying to kill me?" she said to Maui. This information didn't seem to match the cheerful look on his face.

"Well, of course," Maui said with a shrug. "Can't blame a bloke for trying, right?"

"Um, yeah, I can!" Diana cried.

"I just wanted my guy here to win," Maui said, indicating Gus. "You get it, right, Di? If you'd died, that war god inside him would have gone off his nut. He'd be all powerful and big and angry and then he'd win this thing, hands down. It's only because Mr. Restrained here keeps holding Oro back that they haven't won yet."

"I don't want to win," Gus protested. "I'm the wrong person for this. It's an accident I'm here."

"Pssht," Maui said, waving his hand. "There's no such thing as accidents in mythology, my friend. You were more like—what's the phrase you like—the chosen one." He hopped off the couch and picked up the photo of Gus's parents, shoving back his hair. "You seemed like the right choice. Lots of good qualities, easy to manipulate, even a bit of Australian blood in you, way back." He tapped Gus's dad's face. "Must say I'm a bit disappointed, though. I figured you for an angrier guy, especially after this happened." He tapped the glass a little harder, and it cracked, leaving jagged splintery lines across Gus's mom and dad.

Diana was getting a bad feeling about this. Gus was breathing faster, and she saw his hands close into fists.

"But the earthquake," she said. "The scene at the theater, when the change happened—it was an accident we were standing next to each other, an accident that we grabbed each other at the right time. You couldn't have planned that."

"Oh, really?" said Maui. Suddenly the cute Samoan-looking boy was gone, replaced by a burly, bald man with coyote tattoos on his arms. He grinned at Gus. "Remember me?"

Gus started. Diana had a vague memory of seeing the bald man backstage. He'd sent Gus to stand next to Diana and watch a piece of scenery as he lowered it from the ceiling. One that had nearly fallen on her . . . throwing her into Gus, right when the change happened.

The man's face blurred, and then Maui was standing there again. He grinned charmingly. "Impressed?"

"But—" Gus said, then stopped and pressed his hands to his face for a moment. When he dropped them, Diana felt a stab of fear. She'd seen that look in his eyes a couple of times, when Oro was taking over. "Tell me you had nothing to do with *this*," Gus said, and Diana knew what he meant. "Tell me you found me afterward."

Maui chuckled. "Oro thinks so. He thinks I only found out about the contest a few days beforehand. But I am much, much cleverer than that." He set the photo back down on the piano, spinning it on its face. "Of course I did this. An old man on an icy road? One who mysteriously disappears afterward? Sounds like a great trick to me. I had to get you into place, after all." He looked right at Gus. "Like I said. There are no accidents in mythology. Not even car accidents."

With a cry of fury, Gus launched himself across the room at Maui.

"Gus!" Diana yelled.

Gus's fist slammed into Maui's nose with a crunch. Maui staggered back against the piano, blood spattering the white keys. But before Gus could hit him again,

Maui's foot shot up and twisted around his legs, knocking Gus to the floor. Maui kicked him viciously in the side. Gus grabbed his ankles and yanked him over, rolling to pin him down and punch him in the face again. Maui's head cracked ominously against the piano leg, but he kept struggling. Blood was streaked across the beige carpet.

"Gus!" Diana cried in horror. Faint green lines were appearing on Gus's face: whorls on both cheeks, jagged bolts across the forehead. It was like another face was coming out through Gus's—a dark, tattooed, furious face.

She jumped over the coffee table and grabbed Gus's arm as he raised it to punch Maui again. "Stop it!" she shouted. "Don't let him win! This is what he wants!"

"I must. Kill him," said a voice from Gus's mouth that didn't sound anything like Gus.

"No," Diana said, shoving him away from Maui with all her strength. She stood between them. "Gus, you can't kill him. You can't give in to Oro. Remember what he said—he wanted me dead so Oro would take over."

"That could still be arranged," said Maui's voice behind her as a sharp edge pressed into the side of her neck. She stood still, feeling her veins throbbing against the greenstone knife, as he put his other arm around her shoulders and pinned her to him. He was built like Gus, with strong upper arms, and his T-shirt was too soft and friendly to belong to a killer.

"Let her go," Gus growled, and this time his voice was somewhere between Gus's and Oro's.

"He's not going to kill me," Diana said. "You've lost, Maui. Go away and leave us alone." *Impressive lack of tremble in the voice. No idea how I managed that. There's no reason he wouldn't kill me. He's not bound by any of the rules. Don't let on that I know that. Don't let Gus see that I'm scared.*

"Why aren't *you* more angry, little goddess?" Maui murmured in her ear. "The gods messed with your life too. Shoving Venus in there against either of your wishes. Splitting your soul in two. Diluting both halves."

Diana realized that she hadn't thought about the two halves of herself in a long time—not since dying. She didn't feel like there were two sides of her anymore. She felt like there were a lot more, and that that was probably a pretty normal, human way to feel.

"It didn't dilute them," she said. "It made them both stronger. I'm not two goddesses anymore. I'm just me. Like you are just Gus, Gus. And that's all I want you to be. You don't need Oro. I love you, Gus, just Gus, only Gus."

The war fire in his eyes was dying down. "He killed my parents," Gus said.

"And brought us together," Diana pointed out, "so that we can save the world. Don't let him get what he wants." She hissed in a breath as Maui poked her harder with the knife.

The green lines faded back into Gus's face, and he unclenched his fists, trembling with the effort.

"Blistering fishhooks," Maui muttered. "You're both so bloody aggravating. I thought mortals had gotten easier to play with since my time."

"Nope," Diana said, wincing at the tingling line of pain where the knife's point scratched her. Maui twisted it a little, tapping her shoulder thoughtfully with his other hand.

"Well," he said, "I guess I'll let you live. It'll make the end more interesting, since I can see neither of you want the big bad power anyway."

"That's true," Gus said. Diana didn't answer. Either of them might hear the tremor of doubt in her voice. After all, being all-powerful . . . she could do a lot of good that way. It would make Apollo happy to have her back. There was nothing in her regular life to return to, just more of her mother's micromanaging and cameras flashing and melodramatic stories in the papers every time she gained or lost a couple of pounds. Now that it was within reach, she was remembering what it was all like. But she hadn't told Gus any of this yet.

Maui thrust her away from him so she tripped on the rug and fell into Gus's arms. He wrapped them around her, and she noticed that the ridges of his tattoos were not as deep as they had been a few moments ago.

"Too bad," Maui said, his charming smile returning. "We could all have been great friends, once upon a time."

Then he vanished, and the living room faded into darkness around them.

Tigre didn't know how Kali had gotten so far ahead of him. She had been right in front of him when he came around the corner, but now her torch was flickering all the way on the other side of the big cavern. He jumped quickly down to the sandy floor and ran across, holding his torch high. The trident thumped heavily and a little painfully against his back.

Out of breath, he caught up to the girl holding the torch as she stopped in front of a black, swiftly moving river.

"Kali, good grief," he panted, and then in the flickering firelight he realized that the girl's hair was blond. *Diana?* Before he could check behind him, the girl turned around, and he nearly toppled over.

"Tigre?" Vicky said disbelievingly. "What in Sam Hill are you doing here?"

Tigre felt his voice seize up, as it usually did around his ex-girlfriend. "V-Vicky? W—wh—"

"Stop stammering," she snapped. "How did you get here?"

"I'm—well, it's a long story," he said. "Um, there was this bird, and everyone disappeared, and I was in the jungle, but then I went to New York—"

"Okay, okay, enough," she said. "I don't have time to deal with you right now. I'm a little busy saving the world." She switched her torch from one hand to the other with the same smug expression she'd had when she won their school spelling bee.

"*You're* saving the world?" he echoed. His brain was still catching up to the rest of him; his heart was pounding and his knees felt wobbly.

"Yeah, I am, catch up," she said, snapping her fingers. "My friends will be here any minute. It's crazy, Tigre. It turns out I'm, like, this ancient Celtic goddess! You wouldn't have heard of her because you never pay attention to school or to me or to anything but those stupid dogs at my dad's office. But this totally explains a lot, don't you think? Like how pretty I am. I kind of always thought I was different from everyone else. Well, not different like *you*, not, like, creepy-weird-different with a thing for animals. More like special-different. And I was right! I have these crazy powers and I met these other guys who have powers too, and we're here to break this mirror and save the world and stuff." She popped her gum. "It's going to be awesome."

Tigre's head was aching. Could there be another group of avatars? And *Vicky* was one of them? "But that's what happened to *me*," he said weakly. "I'm an Incan weather god."

Vicky stared at him for a minute with her mouth open, the hard little wad of green gum stuck to her back teeth. Then she threw back her head and started laughing.

"Tigre, that's *hilarious*!" she cried. "You, a god? Seriously?" She clutched her stomach, tears of laughter streaming down her face. "Oh wow, like, seriously, the *last* person on Earth that I'd *ever* choose to be a god would be you. I mean, no offense, sweetie, but you totally suck at everything."

Tigre flinched. "That's not true," he said, but it came out more petulant than confident.

"What would you even do with all the power in the world?" Vicky asked. "Heal sick puppies? 'Cause I'm going to make world peace, and then I'm going to build spaceships to Mars, and then I'm going to make peas and broccoli taste like chocolate." She folded her arms.

"Come on, Tigre, when have you ever done anything without being told? When I broke up with you the first time, you were like, okay, and then when I wanted to get back together, you were like, okay, and then when I broke up with you *again*, you were like, whatever." She smacked him in the forehead and he staggered back a step. "Who would ever put you in charge of anything, let alone the whole world?"

Tigre felt like an idiot. He felt like he had every day in high school, too big for the space he was in, awkward and fumbling and always saying the wrong thing or, usually, saying nothing at all, which often turned out to be wrong, too. He rubbed his head and turned to go. Wherever Kali had disappeared to, she didn't need him around ruining things.

"Whoa, hey, Tigre," Vicky said. "Is that Poseidon's trident?"

"Yeah," he said, remembering. He reached back and touched the smooth metal of the handle.

"Dude, that'd be so useful," she said. "We've got this hammer, but I don't think it's going to work. Can we borrow that? I mean, you're not using it, right? And we can use it to save the world."

He turned around slowly. Vicky was holding out her hand for the trident. Her blond hair shone in the firelight, and the sound of her gum chewing echoed in the cave.

"Oh," Tigre said. "I get it." He stood up straighter, feeling a rush of relief and self-confidence. "You're not Vicky."

She chewed for a minute, staring at him.

"Damn," she said in a male voice. The blond hair flickered, turning bright red, and a crooked, pale, handsome man with a cunning face appeared in her place. There were a couple of shiny red scars around his eyes, but they seemed to be fading as Tigre looked at them.

"I had a feeling asking for the trident would be pushing it," he said with a sly smile.

"Who are you?" Tigre asked.

The man bowed stiffly, as if his joints hurt. "My name is Loki."

Tigre tugged the trident around to point it at him. "What do you want from me? What did you do with my friends?"

"That won't do anything," Loki said, moving the tip of the trident aside with two fingers. "I'm only vaguely here. Not enough to hurt. Really I'm still tied to a rock with venom dripping on my face." He pointed to the scars. "But I wanted to appear to you personally. You've been great fun to watch. Absolutely one of my favorite characters. All that moaning and worrying over one little murder. I'm quite pleased."

Tigre's hands tightened on the trident. "You're talking about the old man."

"Obviously," Loki said. "Yes, of course you didn't kill him. I did. Or at least, my son did. He's a wolf, you know—the one who isn't a giant serpent. He's tied up too, but his shadow escapes now and then, and he has these wonderful big claws." Loki held up his hands and sharp claws shot from his fingertips. "Yum. Lots of blood.

I thought that might confuse you, and my goodness, did it ever. Also, I stole your dreams. You can have them back, not that they'll do you any good after you go back to being mortal. I guess you'll foresee a lot of sitting on the couch watching sports. Maybe a few arguments with your parents about how you can't find a job. Probably a lot more nightmares." He closed his hands and opened them again; the claws had disappeared.

"But you know as well as I do that you'd be useless as leader of the gods. More power won't help. It's not that you're powerless. You're just—incompetent." Loki shrugged. "You've accepted that before; no need to fight it now."

"I don't want to be leader of the gods," Tigre said. "I think it should be Kali."

"All right," Loki said genially. "We'll see what we can do about that." He cupped one hand around his ear, and Tigre heard shouting in the distance. "Oh dear. It sounds like it might be too late already. I think your friends are at the mirror. The Illusion-Binders will crush them easily without the trident." He shrugged. "Well, better luck in the next cycle, right? Isn't that what your gods say?"

But Tigre was already running up the river toward the noise, toward the glowing cave at the top of the rocky slope.

Loki chuckled, shaking his head, and disappeared.

Kali found Diana and Gus looking lost in a field of stalagmites.

"Cave of Illusions," Diana said ruefully. "Not my favorite place."

"What did you see?" Gus asked Kali.

"It doesn't matter," Kali said. "What matters is finding the mirror, and I *think* that might be a clue over there." She pointed at a cave farther up the river. A ridiculously bright radioactive green glow was shining out of it. "You know, just a hunch."

"Where's Tigre?" Diana asked.

"I was hoping he'd be with you," Kali said.

"We can't go in there without the trident," Gus said, looking worried.

"He'll catch up with us," Kali said. "I have faith in him." *Wow . . . I really mean that.*

She led the way to the cave, scrambling over the wet stones with the other two close behind her. At the entrance Kali peeked in, took a deep breath, and stepped inside.

"Here's a tip," she said. "Next time you want to hide your super-secret creepy cave to do your dark magic in, maybe try not lighting it up like a Christmas candle."

The six gods in the cave glared at her. Overhead, millions of glowworms were crawling over each other, their tails giving the cavern an eerie blue-green glow. Long glimmering strands hung down from the ceiling like curtains of wet glass beads, reflecting the light.

On the floor in the center of the room was a circle of obsidian glass so dark the light around it seemed to fall into it. Trails of smoke rose from it like the ghosts of ancient fires, slinking to the roof of the cave and wrapping themselves around the glowworm strands. It looked like raindrops glittering through fog, reminding Kali of cold winter mornings on New York buses as she rode back and forth to school, huddled in her coat.

The gods were arranged evenly around the circle, holding their hands out over the smoking mirror. Kali stepped closer, feeling a pulsing heat in the rocks below her feet. Diana and Gus stayed back, holding hands again. In the mirror she could see the whole world, not as continents and oceans but as a million images flicking past in the darkness, a million tiny screens overlapping each other across the surface of the mirror.

Teeth flashed and a winged jaguar screamed. A crystal pterodactyl launched itself off the Eiffel Tower, its electric veins pulsing with purple energy. An old woman huddled in an empty farmhouse, alone and scared, whispering to a clacking set of wooden beads. An emerald green bird spiraled up from an icy city beside a fjord as a redheaded former god waved good-bye, his hand on the shoulder of a tiny bald girl.

A bright heat beside her made Kali turn. The closest god had skin the color of vine-ripened tomatoes, and when he smiled at her she could see his seven tongues flickering with fire.

"Agni," she said. The Indian god of fire. They had a lot in common. "I'm here to destroy this."

He kept his hands over the mirror, but he nodded. "I have immortality ready for you."

"Not for me," Kali said. "I'm going home." *With or without Dad's bribe.*

Agni turned his hands, transfixed by the fire reflecting in the dark glass. "Shiva will be devastated."

Kali felt an ache in her chest at the thought of losing

the partner she'd loved for thousands of years. Before she could speak, a shout came from the god across the circle.

"You won't be destroying anything!" His voice had jaguars prowling in it, and his eyes were small, dark mirrors like the big one on the floor between them, sucking in her reflection and devouring it. The god's head was a black skull with bands of yellow and turquoise running across it. He closed his hands around two tendrils of smoke and they collapsed; somewhere in the mirror, a human voice screamed in pain.

Beside him, a striking yellow-skinned woman with a lion's nose and ears nodded, flexing the long, hooked claws on the ends of her furry fingers. "But you can fight to the death here, if you want," she purred loudly. "We would love to watch."

"Sorry. Nobody's going to die today," Kali said.

"It's the only way to end the illusion," said another god, this one with two faces like Mawu-Lisa, but both male—one looking forward and one back. "Once one of you wins, we'll let it go. Otherwise, what are you going to do? Break the smoking mirror? With what?"

"With this."

I knew it. Standing in the mouth of the cave, brandishing Poseidon's trident with wobbly arms, was Tigre. Diana and Gus threw their arms around him, nearly knocking him over.

"Um, guys, I'm trying to make a dramatic entrance here," he joked.

"Took you long enough," Kali said, punching him in the shoulder.

"I know who's been messing with us," Tigre said intently. "The god who's been following us around and rearranging our lives."

"We saw him too," Diana said. "It's Maui, from the Polynesian gods."

Tigre gave her a puzzled glance. "No, it's a Norse god called Loki."

"This was definitely Maui," Gus said.

"It's both of them," Kali said. She'd started to figure this out in Africa, and now it was all fitting together. "And Eshu and Legba and Anansi, and all the tricksters in all the myths in all the world. They're all one god—a shapeshifter who can be everywhere at once, moving across the pantheons. Like Eshu said, he's one of the most powerful gods in the world, because he can be any trickster in any pantheon whenever he likes."

"Why, thank you," said a smooth voice. Kali's father was standing between them and the mirror, his yellow eyes gleaming. Kali saw Tigre glance back and forth between her and him; he probably saw the family resemblance.

"I know who you are now," she said. "In this form, I mean. You're Coyote."

He grinned wolfishly. "Clever girl." The gods around the mirror looked shocked and outraged—and a little afraid, if Kali read their faces correctly. Coyote winked at them. "Didn't expect to see me again, did you? Thought you could exclude us and take our land and lord it over us for the rest of eternity."

"Why did you do this?" Diana asked. "Why mess with the gods' plans?"

"We had many reasons," Coyote said. His face shifted as he spoke.

"Revenge," said Loki.

"Revenge," said Eshu.

"Revenge," said Maui.

The features blurred back into Coyote's face. He looked thoughtful for a moment. "All right," he said, "maybe just the one reason."

"And because he likes chaos, and trouble, and power," Kali said. "In all his forms."

Shapes were appearing behind Coyote, filling the cave around the mirror. Kali saw Apollo wringing his hands; Odin glowering darkly; Tlaloc with his mouth opening and closing in shock. Zeus was almost pulling out his beard, looking flustered and horrified, and Poseidon stood fuming beside him. Isis and Hera, side by side, were wearing identical *I told you so* expressions. The judges were there too: Athena with her owl and wise gray eyes, Maat with her scowl, Ganesh waving his trunk, Shamash and his golden disk, still inscrutable. Even the faint outline of Inti managed to make a wavering appearance.

And there was Shiva, watching Kali, his eyes finding hers before he'd even fully manifested. She blew him a kiss and he smiled.

"You can't do this," Zeus sputtered at them, clearly trying to pretend that Coyote wasn't there. "Someone has to win. That's how the game works."

"You can't just release all this power," Odin agreed, "or the universe will collapse. If you must break Tezcatlipoca's mirror, one of you has to step forward and take the power."

"Hey," snarled the Aztec god with mirror eyes. "Who said anything about breaking my mirror? I didn't agree to that."

"It should be you," Tigre said to Kali. "You're the strongest and the bravest."

Zeus moaned. "Now we're going to *talk* about it? You're going to *agree* on a winner instead of fighting for it?"

"Thanks, Tigre," Kali said, ignoring Zeus, "but no way. The universe doesn't need a violent psychopath like me in charge. It should be Diana. She beat two of the other avatars, and she's still a good person. I think she'd use the power well. I should go back and look after my family." Kali avoided Shiva's eyes. She didn't want to see the look on his face right now.

Diana's expression was torn. "But—" She glanced down at her hand in Gus's.

"I agree," Gus said. Zeus brightened.

"Gus!" Diana cried. He turned her toward him, looking into her eyes.

"They're right about you," he said. "You would make the best leader of the gods."

"But what about us?" she asked.

"I don't want you to die," he said. "I don't want you to die ever again. I know it means we can't be together, but as long as I know you're out there, and you're going to live forever, then I can handle it. I can handle it better than ever watching you die again."

Diana bit her lip.

"Sounds good to me," Zeus said jovially. "An excellent plan."

"Kali," Shiva pleaded, but she kept her eyes on Diana.

"Tigre," Diana said, "throw the trident."

Tigre hefted the weapon in both hands and Coyote stood aside, smirking.

"No!" Tezcatlipoca yelled. He crouched and sprang, leaping over the mirror to stand in front of them. His eyes flashed in the blue light and his lipless mouth grinned hideously. "If you won't kill each other, allow me to help." He leaped forward, fast as a jungle cat, long claws reaching for Diana's face.

Kali was there before he landed, smashing her elbow into his face with the sound of a thousand tiny mirrors shattering. Gus pulled Diana back as Kali threw the god to the floor and he sank his claws into her arms, leaving long bloody gouges and yanking her down with him. She let out a yell of pain.

"No, no!" one of the judges shouted. "This is most improper! Only avatars can fight other avatars!"

Kali tried to drive Tezcatlipoca's head into the floor, but he was too strong. She lashed out with her boots, trying to kick him, but he was hard as bone all over. Desperately she twisted in his grip, looking for a weapon, and then she saw Tigre run past with the trident held high.

"NO!" bellowed Tezcatlipoca as the trident's prongs hit the surface of the shimmering world.

A fearsome gong sound shook the cave, and the dark glass shattered into millions of pieces. The pieces flew up and away, vanishing along the cave passages and through the holes in the rock walls. Left behind, floating in the air, was a small whirlwind like the ones Tigre had learned to make, except that this one had a soft amber glow.

Tezcatlipoca let go of Kali and fell back to the floor. His dark glass eyes were alive but empty. He didn't move as she climbed to her feet and stepped back, her injuries aching painfully.

Greedily, several gods stepped forward as if entranced, their arms outstretched toward the whirlwind, but the judges blocked the way.

"Shall we tell the judges the bad news?" Coyote said, sliding up behind her. "That none of you want the power? Too dangerous, too unsure of yourselves, too attached to your little people and your little world—too human, really, is what all of you are."

"Maybe that's not so bad," Gus said. "Maybe that'll help us remember what gods were created for in the first place. Maybe instead of just demanding worship, we'll do something to earn it." He squeezed Diana's hand. "Well, Diana will."

"No," she said, shaking her head. "I'm staying here with you."

"Fabulous," Coyote purred.

"But . . ." Gus said. "But what'll happen to Diana and Venus when you—when you—"

"What happens to anyone when they die?" Diana asked him. "We don't know, do we? I mean, okay, I saw a bunch of underworlds, but that's not where we'll be, you and me. I think we'll find out when it happens." She took his hand. "Just like regular people."

"I guess that just leaves me," the Trickster said. His features shifted, and the hungry, scarred face of Loki peered out. "Since none of you seem to want it . . . " He reached toward the amber whirlwind, his eyes shining. Kali saw several Norse gods across the cave clutch each other in terror.

"Wait. I do," Tigre said, blocking the Trickster's way with the trident. "I want it."

"Really," the Trickster said contemptuously. "A nobody like you."

"I won't be a nobody after this," Tigre said with a grin. "I'm choosing my own fate." He threw a significant look at the faint Aztec gods wavering in the glowworms' light, and then he turned to Kali and held out his hand.

"Come with me," he said.

"What about Miracle?" the Trickster snarled at her. "What about your oh-so-angelic side?"

She looked at him, and then at Tigre, and then across the cave at Shiva, who had his hands pressed to his chest like his heart was collapsing.

"You know," Kali said, "if I were the supreme goddess of the universe, I could do as much good as I wanted to. I could bring Miracle to the world myself. And I could send *you* back to the myths where you belong."

She took Tigre's hand.

"I don't think so," the Trickster growled. "Not after all of this."

He lunged for the whirlwind. Kali spun and kicked him in the stomach, sending him flying back into the wall. Diana and Gus grabbed his arms.

"Quick!" Gus called. "He's shifting!"

Kali could see Coyote's nose getting longer, sharp teeth appearing, fur sprouting along his skin. Tigre seized her hand.

"Ready to be gods?" he asked.

"Boy, am I," she said, and as they touched the whirlwind together, she could hear the whisper of his thoughts inside her head.

What are we going to do with all this power? I have a few ideas. . . .

Sunday, January 27, 2013
A cabin in the woods of northern Washington State, 11:05 a.m.

John Fletcher was halfway under his truck, trying to fix the rattling noise it had been making all week. He reached for a wrench, feeling around on the ground, and someone put it in his hand.

Startled, he hooked his fingers on the edge of the vehicle and rolled himself out. It was rare to get visitors all the way up here. If one of those reporters had managed to hunt him down, he was going to beat him with a shovel.

He blinked in the bright sunlight.

"Hey, Dad," Diana said, crouching beside him. "Surprised?"

He stared at her for a long moment as if she were a ghost, and then stood up and grabbed her in a bear hug. Diana squealed as he lifted her off the ground and spun her in a circle. She'd forgotten how big he was.

"I thought you were dead," he said in a ragged voice, setting her down again. His face was streaked with tears and car oil.

"So did a lot of people, including me," she said. "But I'm back and—if you're okay with it—I was kind of hoping I could come live with you."

He rubbed his eyes with one hand, his huge smile giving her the answer. "I don't want to be a star anymore," Diana said. "I want Venus to stay disappeared. I want to be normal, and I want to be with you."

Her dad picked her up again, his shoulders shaking. "I can't believe I'm getting you back and *really* getting you back all at once," he said. "This—I dreamed about this, but I never thought it would happen."

"Before you say yes," Diana said, laughing as he squeezed her. "There's a few people I want you to meet."

He put her down and noticed the boys standing behind her for the first time. "Hey," he said, "you're the kid who disappeared with her."

"This is Gus," Diana said. "My boyfriend." That felt very odd to say, but "the guy who saved me from the underworld and gave me a reason to stick around in the real world" seemed a little complicated to explain right now. "And this is his brother, Andrew. He'll be going back to Los Angeles for a while so he can marry this girl Ella."

"Well, I thought I'd start by asking her out," Andrew said, blushing. "Since this guy tells me I'll be happy I did." He tousled his brother's hair.

"Nice to meet you, sir," Gus said, shaking her father's hand. Diana was glad she didn't have to explain his full-body tattoo, since it had vanished along with Kali and Tigre. She was also happy that Gus was wearing glasses again. In her opinion, he was even cuter that way.

"Where have you guys been?" her dad asked.

"It's a really, really long story," Diana said. "And I'll be pretty surprised if you believe any of it."

"I believe it," Andrew offered.

"You would," Gus joked and ducked as his brother reached for his hair again.

"Well, it's a big cabin, and you can all stay as long as you want," Mr. Fletcher said. "I'd love some company after all this time."

"Um," Diana said. "This isn't quite everyone. . . ."

MONDAY, JANUARY 28, 2013
BROOKLYN, NEW YORK, 4 P.M.

Ellen Nichols turned the letter over a few times, and then tore it open with shaking hands.

> *Dear Mrs. Nichols,*
>
> *You don't know me, but I'm a friend of Kali's. She's sorry she couldn't come back to tell you this herself, but she wanted me to tell you what happened—most important, that she didn't run away. She didn't want to leave you and the girls. She loves you very much, but she has to do something important. You might have guessed it has something to do with her powers. She's taking care of the world*

now, so I told her I'd take care of you and her sisters. I'm enclosing four plane tickets—I can tell you everything when you get here—

"Mommy?" Beth said, tugging on her mother's sleeve. "Mommy, why are you crying?"

"Is it Kali?" Jo-Jo asked perceptively. "Mommy, is she coming home?"

Ellen pulled her daughters close. "No, Kali can't come home, sweetie. But she's okay. We're going to be all right."

SOMEWHERE, SOMEWHEN, EVERYWHERE, ALWAYS . . .

"This is completely ridiculous," Kali pointed out. "It's not even really water."

"Would you rather I threw you in an ocean?" Tigre asked. "I promised to teach you to swim."

"Okay, but this is more like flying," she said. "I mean, we're in the clouds. This I can do. It's water up my nose that throws me off."

"I could put *some water up your nose," Tigre threatened.*

Shiva laughed. "You're both ridiculous," he said. "You'll have all your immortal memories back soon, and then you'll know how to swim perfectly well."

Kali rolled over on her back, scooping bits of cloud onto her stomach. "I don't remember swimming. I remember getting really gigantic and stomping around making tidal waves."

"Yeah," Shiva agreed, "that sounds like you."

"Don't you make fun of me," Kali said. "Remember—you're on your best behavior for the next century. Or else."

"I know, I know," he said, smiling and raising his hands in surrender.

"So what should we do now that we're in charge of the world?" Kali asked Tigre. "Wait, let me guess—you want to save polar bears and elephants and pandas and Panamanian golden frogs." He grinned. "Yeah, I'm on to you, mister," Kali said. "I saw the first thing you did when you became all-powerful."

Tigre sat up and peeked over the cloud bank. His god memories were coming back, and he felt stronger all the time. Loki hadn't scared him off—if anything, he'd convinced him that Tigre might be important enough to handle the power, since the Trickster had bothered to try and stop him. And the dreams had returned, as promised. For instance, Tigre knew that Kali's mom and Diana's dad were going to live happily ever after, as were Diana and Gus. He knew that a certain small, round, African goddess would be visiting him soon. He knew that the strange golden stag that was now living in Central Park would never be caught, and that stories about it would fly around New York for the next century. He knew that a guy in Sweden named Thor was about to have a new baby sister, and that he would insist on naming her Miracle. He knew that there were some things worth using your power on.

I'm immooooooortal! *Quetzie sang, dancing across the clouds, her shining feathers spinning out behind her.* I'm the messenger of the gods! I'm going to be beauuuutiful forever!

Tigre smiled. So this is how it begins.